MOURNING BECOMES CASSANDRA

CHRISTINA DUDLEY

Bellevue, Washington

Mourning Becomes Cassandra

VITA

Published by Bellavita Press
Bellevue, Washington 98004
www.bellavitapress.com

Printed and bound in the United States of America

LCCN 2009903400

ISBN 978-0-615-28977-9

To my husband Scott.
You inspired the very best parts of this book
and, along with our children,
suffered neglect while it was written.

• • •

ACKNOWLEDGMENTS

Many thanks to my initial group of devoted readers, who generously and enthusiastically provided feedback, helpful suggestions, and encouragement. They paid me the ultimate compliment of wanting to read on and not requiring any hounding. The story is better for their input.

In particular, thank you to Lucia Kim, who lifted my spirits with her eagerness and whose readerly experience brought me the "Christian fiction" perspective; Coco Fulton, who made sure no one in the book got pious and who, by reading the last several chapters in one day, let me witness a mini-miracle; Carrie Nordberg, who lent me her sharp editorial eye, besides Cass's lovely voice and uncharged cell phone; my sister Cindy Spann, who suffered through the religious stuff and helped me out with Kyle; and Christine Corneille, who graciously let me improvise off elements from her life and even let me steal a joke or two. My divot became more of a crater, wouldn't you say?

Thank you to Jorie Gulbranson for hooking me up with Terri Kraus. Terri, I cannot thank you enough for reading through my book out of the goodness of your heart and bringing your published expertise to bear. You have a wonderful sense for the timing and movement of a scene. I owe you a gelato.

Finally, my family showed great forbearance through this whole process. The house got messier, I got more absent-minded, a school bus or two got missed, a few thousand dollars evaporated...Thank you for putting up with me. You are a blessing.

CHAPTER ONE:

Blindsided

When your parents name you something like Cassandra, you would expect to see things coming, but the year I turned 31 caught me completely unaware.

At an age when most of my acquaintance—including me—had joined the ranks of the happily-paired-off and reproducing, I was called to leave that hallowed group and rejoin the Third Wheels of the world.

On the longest day of the year, one failed heart led to my husband driving off the road and flipping into a ditch, taking our toddler daughter with him, while I obliviously sweated through a Hot Yoga class downtown.

I'd tell you about the weeks that followed, except the memories have the grainy quality of old home movies. There was plenty of weeping, some hysterical, mostly me, amplified by my in-laws. Church friends trooping through the house bearing hot meals that I think I occasionally sampled. Garbage bags full of paper plates and plastic ware. A service where I got stuck in a receiving line, shaking hands with people I recognized and didn't recognize, like Facebook friending come to life.

Who was that guy? Did he go to college with Troy, or did he come from my own junior high algebra class? What the heck is she crying about? Did she have a thing for Troy? Am I even at the right service?

And finally one of those Moments in Life Which No One Ever Tells You About: me alone in the empty house after everyone is all gone and the funeral-baked meats are history and even the cards have stopped coming. Me and a closet full of Troy's clothes and the garage bins stuffed with hand-me-downs that Min didn't live to grow into.

• • •

Fast forward a year. Really, this isn't difficult to do because I remember almost nothing about that first year. Maybe because I spent most of it in bed. Friends and family came around frequently, forcing me to get up once in a while, but the instant they were gone—boom!— back in I'd go.

I'm embarrassed to say that, an entire year later, not much had changed: the house looked exactly the same, complete with Troy's and Min's things still unpurged. Exactly the same, except for the months of bills and correspondence piled up on the dining table, unopened, and the dumpster that had just been dropped off in the driveway. Mom called to tell me, gently as ever, that now that I'd passed the one-year mark, it was time to get on with it.

"'It' what?" I asked. "Get on with what?"

"Your life, sweetheart," she answered calmly. "I've ordered you a dumpster so you can clean out. Do you want Dad and me to come up and help you?"

"No, no, I can do it."

"And you may want to call Raquel and let her know you're cleaning out, Cass." Raquel was my mother-in-law. I supposed I would have to, but given Raquel's pack-rat tendencies, I didn't see me picking up the phone until the dumpster was long gone.

For a few days I had been steeling myself for this, the Grand Purge, the Beginning of the Second Half of My Life, but now that the dumpster sat out front it all seemed too much. Really, it had only been a year—did Mom really think I was up to this?

Several hours later, I was still sitting on my bed, nothing accomplished, holding the flame-thrower of a lighter Troy would use to start fires in the fireplace—pressing down the safety with my thumb and pulling and releasing the trigger. Because wouldn't it actually be easier to burn down the house than to sort through it? Easier emotionally, I mean. Trade in the slow torture and hours of crying by myself for the distraction of an insurance hassle.

I pulled on the lighter trigger again and admired the burst of flame shooting out like a dragon's breath. But what if the hassle wasn't distracting enough, since I would have to confess to setting the fire myself? That meant even at best I wouldn't get any insurance money, and at worst I think I'd get jail time.

I pulled the trigger back again: pull on … release off … Then again, what a relief to torch those Penney's buy-one-get-one curtains that came with the place. They were some textured, artificial material that would probably burn blue and toxic.

The last thing I needed, at any rate, was more insurance money coming my way. I was already at a loss what to do with Troy's life insurance payout. Some mornings I thought I would give it all to the church or one of our charities; other mornings I thought I'd buy a one-way ticket to Antarctica or real estate on a snowy Himalayan peak, where I could live hermit-like; then again, I might need that money to fund my total re-education, if I decided to start over and become something completely other: an astronaut or a glaciologist or a game warden. I flicked the lighter again. The only thing I knew for sure was that, whatever I did, it wouldn't require this two-bedroom, two-bath house.

The phone rang. On the fifth ring I checked the caller ID: Joanie. Anyone else and I might have let the machine get it, while I went back to my pyro fantasies, but Joanie had always been missing the sympathy-and-tact chip, so I didn't mind talking to her. I could trust her not to ask in a low, hushed, deathbed voice, "How are you, *really*?" Those voices and questions always triggered tears, followed by a bad headache.

"Hey, Joanie."

"Hey, there you are—are you busy? Got a minute? I wanted to spring a good idea on you."

Joanie had her good ideas about every half hour, 99% of which never came to anything, but I felt a little curiosity flicker. "Is this about the dessert place you want to open? Or the bed-and-brunch, so you don't have to get up too early to cook?"

"No, no." I pictured her waving these off. "My brother Daniel— the lawyer one—he's thinking of buying this giant house as an investment. It's even got one of those mother-in-law guesthouses that's bigger than most people's normal houses. I was thinking he could live in the mother-in-law, and me and you and Phyl could live in the main house and—"

"Phil who? Is this someone you're dating?"

"No, no," she said again impatiently, "Phyllida Levert Phyl. Phyl-with-a-y Phyl. Anyhow, if we did Daniel's cooking and cleaning, he'd give us reduced rent."

I felt a little laugh in my throat. Rusty, but it was there. "Isn't this the brother who sleeps with a different supermodel every couple weeks? What makes you think he'd want housekeeping staff around?"

"Because every man wants women around to do all the work. Especially Daniel! He just doesn't want to have to marry someone to get the free labor. And since he'd be living in the in-law, he wouldn't even have to be with us. He could just grab his dinner and go back to his place. We could even cook enough for whoever he's sleeping with. I figure if we rotate the cooking and cleaning it's no big deal. It's a win-win. Come on, Cass—don't you want out of that house? I would. It's gotten creepy, like your own personal ancient history museum. Just pack a suitcase and set fire to the rest."

The lighter fell out of my hand. "How did you...?"

I recovered hastily. "Where's the house, and did you run this idea past him?"

"It's in Clyde Hill, just a quick bus ride from downtown. You'd hardly even need a car. And yes, I did run the idea past him. What does he have to lose? He already pays to have meals delivered to his condo and to have someone clean for him. This way he'd get permanent benefits, plus some rental income from us."

"But what did he say?"

"He said it sounded okay by him, as long as we agreed that if he hated us, he could kick us out. But we'd be ideal! We're quiet, clean, good cooks. Most of our friends are churchy types. And I told him you guys already knew he hated church and church people, and that we would promise not to try to convert him. We could put that in the lease!"

Since God and I weren't exactly on speaking terms at the moment, this would be no problem. Not that I'd ever been much of a sandwich-board-wearing Bible thumper anyhow, but right now I wasn't in the mood to talk faith at all. In fact, my moods no longer ranged far afield. Depression, loneliness, anger, depression, loneliness, anger. I hoped my voice didn't sound too pathetic: "But Joanie, do you and Phyl really want to be hanging out with a depressed, lonely widow?"

Joanie snorted. "NO! I don't want to hang out with a depressed, lonely widow! That's why I want you to live with us—I've given you a year to be a depressed, lonely widow, and you're not snapping out of it. You need community. I can see you already have potential to become some kind of crazy cat lady if I don't intervene."

Her lack of sensitivity made me think she was sincere. "What would he want for rent?"

My eyes flicked to the closet. Maybe I could just sell the house as-is: complete with man's wardrobe, size Medium, baby toys, overflowing file cabinets.

"Almost nothing. Under market. You'd get your own room and bathroom, and so would Phyl, and so would I."

An unfamiliar thrum of excitement started in my stomach. This might be one of the 1% of Joanie's ideas that actually flew. "Did you talk to Phyl? What did she say?"

"Well, you know Phyl. She's been wondering what to do since her roommate got married. This way she doesn't have to find a new one. Plus she can indulge her fantasies for my brother. You know, where she converts him from a self-absorbed sexaholic into a thoughtful, one-woman Friend of Jesus."

The rusty laugh made it out of me this time. "But the lease! The 'no-conversion' clause! I don't want her wrecking this for us. Besides, it'll be fun to observe Daniel and his mating habits. We'll be like the Jane Goodalls of Clyde Hill."

I pictured Joanie clapping her hands together because she dropped the phone. Contact with some hard surface speed-dialed someone, and then her voice came back, excited. "So you're in? I knew this was a good idea. One of my really good ones. You're starting fresh, baby! It's gonna be like *Sex and the City*."

"Or *Celibacy in the Suburbs*, more like."

"Yeah, yeah. I meant Daniel would be having all the sex. Okay, so did you shower yet?"

It was three o'clock. I smoothed my sweat pants guiltily. Sometimes it was like Joanie had some kind of spy cam on me. She didn't wait for me to answer. "Well, take one now because I'll be there in twenty minutes to take you to see the house."

. . .

Six weeks later, my house was on the market, and I was pulling up to the new one in a borrowed pick-up truck loaded with the few things I hadn't purged. All the big items—my bed and desk and other pieces of furniture—were already here, thanks to some friends' husbands' help, so I had mainly the dregs. My past life was in my battered suitcase. I'd reduced it to a wedding album, Min's baby book, ten CDs of pictures, and some college letters from Troy, but my wedding ring escaped the purge—I was still wearing it.

Clyde Hill was the former tiny town, now swallowed-up suburb, just north of downtown. Houses tended to be huge and Craftsman-y, and Daniel's fit the mold completely: *café-au-lait* in color, with darker trim and a brick-red front door, four bedrooms, 3-½ baths, a big remodeled kitchen, three-car garage, partial view of the lake and the Olympics. Since few people in the Northwest troubled themselves with a pool, the former owners put in the 2-bed, 1-½ bath in-law apartment just off the vast deck. Japanese maples and an ornamental cherry tree studded the front, and I could see a couple native evergreens rising up behind the house. Phyl's green thumb had already made changes from the first time I visited the house: small planter boxes and hanging baskets had appeared, stuffed with flowers, punctuating the wraparound porch.

Somehow moving in with Joanie and Phyl and, I suppose, with Daniel, didn't feel as pitiful as finding some sweet old retired lady from the church to live with me. I'd known Joanie for several years. She and her then-fiancé had signed up for the New Marriage class at church with Troy and me, and though Joanie and Keith broke up shortly after, she and I became fast friends, a relationship that survived my marriage and Min coming along. Joanie had been in and out of two more engagements in the meantime, ending the latest six months ago. In her own way I suppose she was as commitment-phobic as her brother. He certainly couldn't be more attractive than she was, with her long red-gold hair and intense blue eyes. Whenever one fiancé got the boot, another one appeared soon after to take his place.

Joanie always jokingly described herself as "the only white sheep in a family of black sheep," the good girl who joined a church youth group in high school, to her atheist family's horror. If that weren't bad enough, Joanie also pledged a sorority in college and majored in business. When she quit her marketing job to work in our church worship department, that surely must have been the last straw. Joanie's artistic, vegan, Portland mom was deeply embarrassed by her, and her brother hardly less so. Presumably Joanie's father would have cringed as well, but no one had heard from him since he walked out a couple decades ago to reinvent himself somewhere in South America.

Phyl (or Phyllida, as only her mother called her) was a newer friend, by way of Joanie and the everlasting church singles events they haunted. Phyl was divorced. Her husband had been of the lyin' cheatin' variety, and he quickly traded her in for a newer model, but Phyl nevertheless continued to have a soft spot in her heart for the worst kind of men. She combined religious zeal with bad character judgment, so that her relationships usually involved much fervent prayer that the man she was attracted to would be magically transformed into the kind of man she *ought* to be attracted to. If there was any flaw in our new living plan, it was that Phyl would certainly fall for Daniel, make everything horribly awkward and lead to us all getting kicked out. Joanie and I hoped that, between us, we could corral her.

Of Daniel, I knew only what Joanie told me. He had drunk and slept his way through high school and taken his SATs stoned, like a good black sheep, but he was smart enough to pull off good grades all through college. His mother suspected blossoming bourgeois ambition when Daniel went to law school and into practice, but his continued allergic reaction to marriage, family, commitment, and religion allayed her fears. In fact, he had reached the advanced age of 34 without managing a relationship that lasted even a month and without (to Joanie's knowledge) spending a thought or a penny on anyone besides himself. Fortunately for us, despite thinking his sister a hopeless religious nut who was sure to have homely, goody-goody friends, Daniel professed himself willing enough to take us on when it offered him such material advantages.

• • •

The second the old pick-up sputtered to a halt, Joanie burst out the front door. "There you are! Come on! Throw your stuff in your room because Chaff is going on a day hike today, and you've got to come."

"Chaff" was our secret joke name for the big singles group at church. It was really "YAF" for "Young Adults Fellowship," but everyone there was pushing thirty, and in a church of happy families, singles always have the red-headed stepchild thing going on.

I eyed her irritably. "Joanie, don't start. I'm not going to any singles event."

"Then why are you dressed up for the first time in over a year?" she demanded.

I was, in fact. A new stage in life called for more than sweatpants, I felt, and I had donned one of my few skirts and cutesy pairs of shoes for the occasion.

I shrugged. "Felt like it. But I'm going to finish moving in and then go back and clean up some more." Shoving a box into her hands, I grabbed my suitcase. "Help me out."

"Cass, don't be like that. You're unemployed. You can do that kind of stuff any time."

"Yes, but I plan on doing it today."

My room was at the top of the stairs, facing out on the driveway. Sunlight streamed in the angled bay window and skylight, and I felt that thrum of excitement again. I no longer was a home-owner. In fact I was now, at 32, a glorified housekeeper renting a room—but at least it was a gorgeous room in a more beautiful house than I could ever have hoped to own.

Joanie threw the box I'd given her carelessly on the bed, and I watched my toiletries and underwear spill out. "But, Cass, when you say 'no,' do you mean 'no' to a hiking trip or 'no, don't ask me to go to Chaff events'?"

"Yes and yes. Yes, I mean no hiking trip, and yes, don't ask me to go to Chaff events. For Pete's sake, Troy only died a year ago. His ashes have barely cooled." I led her back downstairs to pick up another load.

"A year!" Joanie huffed. "You should see some of those guys whose wives die! They're back at it so fast I wanna tell them to stuff their next wedding invitations in with the memorial thank-yous—save a stamp. Why don't women do that?"

"Joanie," I said through gritted teeth. "I love you, but you're being hideously insensitive." That brought her up short. It was impossible to be angry with Joanie long because she meant well.

Giving me a repentant squeeze she said, "Oh, never mind me. I'll leave you alone today. Phyl and I will go. There's a super cute new guy who showed up at Chaff last week, and he's not even fifty or twice divorced, so Phyl and I are going to try and beat off the seventy other ladies. We don't need your competition."

I didn't even dignify that with an eye roll. "So if you and Phyl are gone all day, am I on for cooking Daniel some dinner tonight?"

"Done. It's already in the fridge, and enough for you, too. I made out a schedule and chore list and put it on the message board. Take a look and let me know what you think. He and his latest 'house guest' are on the back deck canoodling, I think—you want to come meet him?"

"With such a description, how could I resist?" I asked. "What about Phyl? Did she already make her introductions?"

"Oh, you better believe it! When she saw him, she went all breathless and melting. Good thing Daniel goes more for your breasts-of-steel type, or we'd be in trouble. You've got to see the gal with him now—classic Daniel."

When we finished unloading the pick-up, we discovered this seventh wonder in the kitchen. Joanie had nailed it: even doing something as mundane as refilling coffee mugs, Daniel's latest was indeed a sight to behold—all glossy blonde hair, mile-long legs, teensy tank top, and bouncing bosom. Awkwardly I held out my hand to this vision. "Hi, I'm Cass, one of Daniel's housemates."

After giving me a quick look-over and finding nothing threatening, Miss America shook my hand and said, "Nice to meet you. I'm Missy."

Seriously? Joanie grimaced at me and rolled her eyes behind Missy's back as we followed her outside.

"Daniel," Missy purred, dropping onto the chaise longue, "I've got your refill for you."

Only when he lowered his newspaper and I saw his face did I realize I wasn't seeing Daniel for the first time.

Troy and I had a favorite Italian restaurant downtown, and after I weaned Min and we started going out occasionally again, we often went there. One of our favorite date activities was watching other people and fictionalizing what we saw; it was our own improvised version of reality television.

Meeting Daniel we called the Close Encounters Incident. It must have come shortly before Troy died, one of those days near the solstice. In western Washington you can never count on beautiful weather until after the 4th of July, but this was one of those surprise June evenings, warm and mellow and bright out. Restaurants scrubbed down their patio tables and set them outside cheek-by-jowl because absolutely no one wanted to be indoors, and Fabiano's was no exception. Troy and I had spent most of the meal making up a story for the nearby three-generations table, grandfather, father and son, but the lone woman in the corner caught my eye more than once. She kept checking her make-up in a small mirror and adjusting her bra, not that it needed much adjusting, unless she were trying vainly to keep herself poised just at the point before she spilled out. She was beautiful, to say the least—so whence the insecurity?

My answer came the next moment, when someone brushed past our table, bumping it. My glass of Shiraz rocked alarmingly, but, having a small toddler at home, my reaction times were nothing short of miraculous, and my hand closed on its bowl to steady it just an instant before another hand closed over mine. Startled, I looked up into a pair of very, very blue eyes. "Excuse me," he murmured. "I see you have your wits about you."

Whatever my physical instincts, my mental sharpness deserted me at that point, and I'm afraid I just gaped at him with my mouth open, feeling a warm blush overspread my cheeks.

He was easily the handsomest man I'd ever seen off a movie screen: tall, well-built, thick golden-blond hair, classical features.

Taking in my awestruck expression, his mouth twisted in amusement. Slowly I became aware that his hand was still covering mine. It was warm. I dropped my eyes to it in confusion, just as he released his grip, and I felt Troy kick me under the table. The spell broken, he moved on to sit with the spilling-out beauty, and then I noticed Troy was laughing silently into his napkin—not just laughing, *dying* laughing, wiping-away-tears laughing.

I scowled at him. "What? It's not as if you weren't glued on that guy's date after I pointed her out to you!"

When he regained some measure of control, Troy gave me a mock-innocent shrug. "All in a spirit of scientific inquiry, Cass. Her breasts defy gravity, you've gotta admit. But you should have seen the look on your face—you're still blushing."

My hands flew to my cheeks. Blushing was my bane, always giving away more than I wanted. "I should have a few words with that guy for the way he was looking at you," my husband chuckled, "but you do look pretty, so maybe he couldn't help it. We'll have to forgive each other: Tier One people are just too beautiful to be ignored."

Troy had a theory about the world: if you pictured all the people in it, they fell into one of three tiers, rather like the food pyramid. Tier One: the very tiny tip of the pyramid, was made up of the world's most unnaturally beautiful and enviable people, like retouched movie stars and models and the couple at the next table. Tier Two: this made up most of the pyramid, being huge and spanning sub-tiers ranging from quite-attractive all the way down to not-repellent. And Tier Three held the unfortunate of the world: people prevented from being found attractive by one or more overwhelming flaws, sometimes beyond their control. Lepers, was the example Troy always gave. Or inseparable conjoined twins. Think Chang and Eng.

Pointedly, I turned my chair away from the beautiful couple. "Well, hon, we'll just have to comfort ourselves with your well-known corollary: Tier One stays small because members of it have a difficult time finding suitable mates. Now are you going to finish that tiramisù, or am I?"

Now here, a year and a lifetime later, was the mysterious stranger from the restaurant, every bit as handsome as I remembered, and we would be housemates, of all things. But this rather absurd fact hardly registered because I was frozen by a momentary vision of Troy laughing at me that night. How many jokes had we shared in our fourteen years of knowing each other? If he had any kind of consciousness now, was he laughing again, to see me having another Close Encounter? I felt the familiar tightening in my throat and burning behind my eyes: don't cry don't cry don't cry.

Through a rushing sound in my ears I heard Joanie introduce me, as Daniel's gaze flickered over me without recognition. A relief, given how I didn't think I could speak. One comment like, "Wait, didn't I see you at Fabiano's with your husband?" would have finished me. For once I was glad to be the kind of girl that men don't notice unless they trip over me or, alternatively, co-edit the Yearbook with me, as Troy had in high school.

I'm pretty standard: average height, average weight, brown hair and eyes, reasonably attractive, and it took Troy half the year to figure out we were more than friends and that he actually preferred me to his girlfriend. But he loved me ever afterward, even when I had various misgivings and misplaced affections.

My husband.

Daniel muttered something that sounded like, "Nice to meet you, Cathy. Welcome."

And, without the heart even to correct him, I nodded and the deal was sealed.

CHAPTER TWO:

Laying Low

"Here, dear. Dear?"

The elderly woman next to me pulled gently on my sleeve. In her other hand was the offering plate, which she was apparently trying to pass along the row. Apologetically, I smiled at her and handed the basket to the usher; I had been deep in an argument with God.

Although I felt like the estranged, drag-of-a-great-aunt who shows up at the holiday dinner just to put a damper on things, I still attended church. Even that first year when I could barely get out of bed I came. Unwilling, alienated, completely absent in spirit, I came. Why, I couldn't exactly say. Maybe because I'd gone all my life. Maybe because I didn't have anything else to do. Maybe because I was afraid if I let this go as well, there would be nothing left to me; I would disintegrate—float away on the wind.

Back in the days before my life went down the toilet we'd always gone to the 9:30 a.m. service. It was the big family one—loud band, all our friends, the nursery and Sunday school jam-packed. We assumed 8:00 was for the blue hairs, the "frozen chosen" Troy jokingly called them—all the grandmas and grandpas who got up at 4:30 and wondered why the church didn't have a 6:00 a.m. service.

In the past year Joanie and Phyl tried several times to get me to join them at the Sunday evening service, the *de facto* singles and college gathering, but post-death-and-destruction I went to the 8:00 a.m., preferring to sit among strangers who wouldn't ask any questions. It turned out Troy and I were wrong: grandparent-types made up only one contingent of those around me; there were also harassed-looking young parents whose kids woke at the crack of dawn, active types who wanted to get church out of the way before a day hike, and morning persons of all generations.

The early service had several fringe benefits, moreover. For one, it was a piece of cake to get a seat. This morning when I slid into the very last balcony pew, the little old lady there smiled at me benignly and without recognition. Probably a widow, too. Two peas in a pod, that was us. For another, since Troy and I never attended the traditional service, there was nothing to remind me of him. Hymns with a choir and an organ actually carried me back to my study-abroad quarter at Oxford, where I attended a little church close to Magdalen College. After a brief, intense crush on my brilliant tutor with the lame orthodonture, I had returned, tail between my legs, begging Troy to take me back.

I only knew one of the hymns this morning, which was fine, since I didn't feel like singing. Or listening to a sermon or praying or talking, for that matter. It was the last weekend of the summer vacation, so a guest speaker was filling in for the senior pastor. During the sermon my mind wandered frequently, but the general topic was the joy of service. The joy of getting outside oneself. Well, if there was ever a place I'd love to be right now, it was outside myself. But what would I do? No more volunteering in the nursery, like I used to. Besides the germs and diapers, I didn't want to see any little children who would remind me of Min. And I'm sure all my friends picking up and dropping off kids would rather just "get 'er done" without having to see me moping about the place.

For a few minutes, to avoid deep thought, I pictured decorating my new room. I could paint the walls a dark buff. Re-cover the cushion in the window seat for a reading area. Hang that chickadee painting some friends gave me by the book case. Then I planned my first few dinners. Was vegetarian cooking out? Did everyone eat fish or beef? I had forgotten to ask. Then I thought of Great American Novels still waiting to be written. The sermon was still going.

Defeated, I screwed my eyelids shut. It was almost embarrassing to try to talk to God, since I hadn't been praying for months. Who wanted to talk to someone you were mad at? Especially if He wouldn't answer, and nothing could be resolved?

Arguing with the Almighty was also a fairly new experience for me, dating only from when he let Troy and Min die. Was it too much to ask, that He could have let Troy's heart fail when he was sitting on the couch at home, with me right next to him to call 9-1-1? Or was it too much to ask that He could have spared Min? Min had spent 90% of her time with me, for Pete's sake, and one of the few times she's alone with her dad, they have to be in a car, and his heart has to give out suddenly? Troy's death I could almost get my mind around—a bad heart is a bad heart, and since he was only 31 we hadn't known about it. But what was the deal with Min? What part of His Wonderful Plan for My Life did it screw up to leave her on earth?

I learned in the church's Grief Recovery class what I already knew intellectually: that it was okay to be angry at God. But it still made me uncomfortable. Maybe my faith had tended too much to the what-a-friend-we-have-in-Jesus side, only to discover that that friend was not averse to letting circumstances stab me in the back. It felt like having the faithful family guard dog, who rescued you from house fires in the past, turn on you and maul you. Bad analogy, I know, to compare God with a dog. Sit, Lord. Stay. Lie Down. Turn water into wine. Fix my every problem. And heaven knows no one has ever gotten God to heel. On the other hand, like an unruly pet, faith could be euthanized when it didn't meet expectations.

The atheists and agnostics in my life were trying hard to bite their tongues, but I could read their thoughts: *Cass, doesn't this prove it's all random, or that, if there is a God, He's a jerk? Religion's great if you find it comforting, but in your case, shouldn't you get off your knees and stop worshiping this figment of your imagination?* And on bad days I thought they were probably right, but on other days, most other days, I figured God is God, and He can do whatever He pleases. While I certainly wish He would have asked for my input in this situation, I was willing to believe there were more things going on in heaven and earth than were dreamt of in my philosophy.

The speaker was talking about some time he made some big *faux pas* at the homeless shelter, and the people around me chuckled appreciatively. So fine—God was God, and Troy and Min were gone, for whatever reasons. Now what? What on earth was I supposed to do with my life? And was there any way I could get through the rest of it under the radar?

I had woken up that morning with a faint headache after dreaming about Min: her first birthday, and the terrific face she made when she first tasted frosting. Hey, Minnie was my first baby, so like millions of other first-time moms I was something of a nutrition Nazi. One of my food rules was that we weren't going to give her any sugary sweets for the first year, to see if it could prevent her from developing a sweet tooth. In my zeal, I considered a sweet tooth the gateway condition to childhood obesity and early-onset diabetes. But my experiment didn't work. After that first puzzled taste, Min licked every speck of frosting off her cupcake and begged for more. Like mythologists of old, I learned that once desire was out of the box, there was no stuffing it back in. Min spent the remaining months of her short life being an absolute sugar fanatic, willing to do anything for M&Ms or a cookie, and I worriedly imagined her first high school boyfriend getting whatever he wanted from her for a couple Oreos.

Once Min tasted sugar, there was no pretending she was going to be content thereafter with only sour, salty, bitter, and umami. Could I? *If I lay low, God—keep my head down and behave myself—will you let me be? I leave you alone—ask for nothing—and you leave me alone?*

I wouldn't say the heavens opened and angels ascended and descended, but the speaker sat down at last, and a teenage girl stood up to speak, recapturing my attention.

She was average height and maybe sixteen, with lank brown hair and conservative clothing that she looked rather uncomfortable in. She cleared her throat a couple times and glanced nervously to someone seated off to the side.

"Hi, I'm Ellie," she read from her cards. "I came to Camden School last spring after being kicked out of my old high school for doing drugs. Camden School is an alternative school for students like me who haven't been succeeding in the regular public school system. I'd been doing drugs since middle school and gotten in lots of trouble and didn't know how to change my life. At Camden School I meet with a substance abuse counselor and get lots of one-on-one attention from my teachers. They really care about me here, and I have been sober for four months. I really missed school this summer and seeing my friends and teachers, and I can't wait to start again next week. I am also excited about getting a mentor this year. A mentor is an adult who can hang out with me regularly and do occasional activities with other students and mentors. This church is one of the big financial supporters of our school, and I want to say thank you for helping people like me. We also depend on many volunteers at our school to help with fundraising and special events and tutoring and mentoring. If you would like to help in any of these areas, please see the information in the bulletin. Thank you."

Ellie delivered this entire speech on three breaths, tops, and when she sat down there was a wave of encouraging applause. Feeling a burning sensation in my chest, I scrabbled with the bulletin to look at the blurb on Camden School. As if they were a message for me, the letters seemed to jump from the page, like the red-letter sayings of Jesus in my mother-in-law's King James.

But how could it be? My life was in shambles, and I didn't know the first thing about teenagers or drug addiction. On the other hand, surely I could hang out with a teenager and encourage her to stay on the wagon and in school? But what would any teenager want with some pathetic woman who had lost everything and had no idea how to start from scratch? Didn't they want hope, instead of, "Work hard and play it straight, and one day your life, too, might go up in flames"?

Discouraged, I wadded up the bulletin and threw it on the floor, only to glimpse the raised eyebrow of the woman next to me. Clearly she wasn't excited about me littering in the Sanctuary. Too long used to behaving myself, I picked the bulletin back up and stuffed it in my purse. *Fine, God, I'll keep it. But if you really have the crazy idea I should mentor someone, you're going to have to make it a little clearer.*

When the service let out, I darted out the front doors. It would mean a longer walk, but it would also mean avoiding most people I knew. Our church had torn down its 50s-style A-frame recently and rebuilt as big a building as the city would allow—modern, with huge windows of greenish Northwest glass and a modest cross on top, so as not to frighten people like Daniel, who wanted to vomit when they thought of church. For the entire sixteen months it took to rebuild, we met in the Bellevue High School gym, where the sight of the basketball hoops and the smell of Cafeteria Lunches Past gave former alums like me similar urges to vomit when they thought of church. Already we were bursting at the seams again, causing longtime members to complain that they didn't recognize anyone, but there's nothing like a mega-church if your goal is to avoid people. You have only to change services to cut yourself adrift.

Sure enough, besides throwing one wave across the parking lot to Dave and Sandy Lucker, I escaped unnoticed.

. . .

Phyl and Joanie were having a comfortable coze in the kitchen when I got home, Joanie still in sweats. Helping myself to coffee, I plunked down next to Phyl.

"How was church?" Joanie asked. "I can't believe you go to the early service! Do they have to remove half the pews to fit all the walkers and wheelchairs?"

I blew on my coffee and reached for the half-and-half. "It wasn't so bad. Just about everyone was ambulatory. I knew one of the hymns."

"Who preached?" Phyl asked in her gentle voice.

"Some guy from Idaho. It was about service."

"Yuck and yuck!" yelled Joanie. "Maybe I won't go tonight. Who needs more guilt? I still haven't recovered from the time Chaff went to hand out sandwiches to the homeless, and I got Mr. Complainer who didn't like turkey. Who knew homeless people were so picky?"

"I had a nice conversation that time," Phyl objected. "I met this lady with such a sad story, and I kept thinking, 'This could be me.'"

Joanie rolled her eyes. "Well, next time I'll hit up the ladies. I'm sure Jesus would have told my guy to just choke down the damned sandwich and be grateful."

Phyl frowned. Before they could really get into it, I interjected hastily, "Speaking of Chaff, how was the hike yesterday? Was the cute new guy there?"

Joanie took the bait. "YES! Only, it turns out James is a mere 27, so a lot of us circling sharks had to quit chomping at his cage—"

"Joanie, I wish you wouldn't talk like that," Phyl protested. "How can anyone at YAF try to get to know anyone, if you're always going to make it sound so predatory?"

"But the good news is," Joanie went on blithely, "James brought this friend—older friend—his old Sigma Nu big brother, I think—who is just as cute and just as cool, though unemployed."

"He already asked Joanie out, of course," sighed Phyl.

"He's unemployed?" I asked skeptically. "Is he going to take you to the soup kitchen?"

Joanie shrugged. "We may have to scrounge for sandwiches the homeless people reject, but at least he's cute. And I said Roy was unemployed, not unemployable. Big difference."

"So when is this date happening?" I asked.

"Coffee after church tonight," Joanie replied. "Which means I guess I have to go so I can talk about it with him."

"Who got James, then?" I asked.

"I think at least three women asked him out," Phyl answered. "And I'm pretty sure he took Brooke Capshaw up on it."

"He had to," Joanie said ruthlessly. "She's short. He's short."

"Shorter than you, Joanie," I said. "Not everyone is almost six feet tall."

"Yeah, but I'd put him at max 5′8″."

"He's tall enough for you, Phyl," I broke in again. "And you're younger than Joanie and me—"

"Hey, don't lump us together," Joanie protested. "You're 32 and I'm only 29."

"Yes," I agreed, "and Phyl is only, what, 28?"

Phyl fidgeted and dumped more sugar in her empty coffee cup. "Uh huh, but I don't think James is my type. I mean, he seems very nice and all, but a little tame."

Even as she spoke her eyes were drawn out the bay window, and I followed her gaze. From my seat I could just see half of Daniel's back. He was in what must be his favorite spot, lounging on the deck reading the newspaper.

Joanie and I exchanged looks of dismay.

"Well…" Joanie drawled, "I'm sure you'll find someone less tame and more unsuitable to like, Phyl. In any case, since Roy is unemployed and I think I'll want to see him more than he can afford, I have a brand-new idea for our brand-new household."

Now Phyl and I exchanged amused glances.

"What now?" I asked. "Cough it up."

To our surprise, Joanie leaned over and banged on the window pane. "Daniel! Could you come in a second? I want to run something by you."

I could see Phyl hold her breath as we waited for him. After some moments he came in the back door and threw his folded newspaper on the counter, running his hands through his tousled blond hair and nodding briefly at me. "What, Joanie?"

She slung an arm around him and cuddled. Joanie has always been very demonstrative physically, something I think her many fiancés enjoyed. Nor did her brother seem to mind, and he put his arm on her shoulders. They really were amazingly good-looking together. "Okay, Daniel," she said, "I've got this great idea for our house that can involve you or not involve you, but I'd love for it to involve you."

"Oh, for Chrissake, Joanie. Are you planning some kind of tent revival in the backyard? The answer is no."

"No, stupid. It doesn't even necessarily involve church—"

"'Necessarily'?" he echoed warily. "I thought that's all you girls did. Speaking of which, why are you all sitting around, instead of getting your butts to church on a Sunday morning?"

"Phyl and I will go later," Joanie explained impatiently. "And Cass has already been."

Daniel glanced at the clock and whistled. "I guess the grass won't grow under your feet."

Over me, more like, I thought.

He dropped a wink at me. "And didn't you say your name was Cathy?"

"Cass. It's Cass—short for Cassandra," I replied, a little flustered by the wink.

"I was just thinking," Joanie began again, thumping on Daniel's chest to get his attention, "wouldn't it be cool if, once a week—say Thursdays, since that's one of my days to cook—we had some kind of standing open house here. We could each invite one or two guests for dinner, with advance notice, of course. It'd be the one night of the week when we all tried to be home together to eat and hang out. It could be pot-luck, but you and your guests could be freeloaders, if you want."

"Whoa, whoa, whoa." He backed out of her encircling arm. "No way am I hosting the weekly church picnic, and what makes you think I want to hang out with you and your friends—no offense—" He grimaced in the direction of Phyl and me.

"None taken," whispered Phyl.

"I'm not talking about a church picnic," Joanie retorted, her voice getting that little annoyed edge I recognized. "I'm talking about having one night a week for friends and family and community, and showing a little hospitality! I wouldn't even necessarily invite a church person, and neither would Phyl or Cass—"

"This is Joanie's idea," Phyl breathed.

Joanie shot her a scathing look but plowed on. "And you and your friends or girlfriends or co-workers wouldn't even need to come, but I wish you would. Come on, Daniel, it'll be fun! Just say we can host it and try to come. If you hate it you can just get a plate of food and go hide at your place."

He threw up his hands in surrender and gave her a loud kiss on the cheek. "Fine. We'll try it once. One or two guests each, max. This is going to be a crazy week at work, so what time do I have to be here?"

Squealing, she hugged him. "Say 6:30 for drinks and hors d'oeuvres, and we'll eat at 7:00. And let me know if Missy or someone else is coming. I wish we could send an evite, but I don't want to until we've thought of a name for the house."

He extricated himself again and waved vaguely at us. "Why does a house need a name? You girls deal with that. I've got to go in to the office."

And he was out the back door before Phyl could ask, "He has to work on Sunday?"

Joanie plopped herself back down triumphantly. "That was easier than I thought."

I frowned at her. "Shouldn't we have made sure things were going smoothly before trying to push him around?"

"You call that pushing him around? You don't know Daniel. He didn't care about it. If he did and he felt strongly, there wouldn't have been a thing I could do or say to budge him. Just like if there was something he set his mind on, nothing could stop him from getting it. We'll see if he even shows up."

"I think he will," I said slowly, "If only to make sure we aren't baptizing people in the birdbath."

"You're going to invite Roy," Phyl said, "And Daniel will probably have that gorgeous Missy, but who do you think Cass and I should invite?"

"Oh, for crying out loud," Joanie complained, "it's not a quadruple date. Ask anyone you want! Anyone you'd like to have for dinner. Or no one at all. It's just meant to give us a consistent time and a space for entertaining and being together without having to clear things with Daniel. Now help me think of a name for our house."

CHAPTER THREE:

A Failure to Communicate

Our first official dinner together would prove typical: Daniel was still at work, and Phyl and Joanie had to bolt and run to make the 7:00 church service. By 6:55 I had the house to myself and was doing the dishes in peace, having made Daniel a plate of Phyl's chicken casserole and put it in the microwave with a note.

Dinner conversation had centered on the house-naming. Phyl tended toward the literary, but Joanie and I vetoed Pemberley, Elsinore, Innisfree, and their ilk as too pretentious. She in turn disliked the ironic names, absolutely no Hovel or Anthill or Woodshed.

"It's a beautiful house," Phyl protested softly. "It should have a beautiful name. What would Daniel think if we named his beautiful house 'the Woodshed'? It's cliché, but you know what they say—a man's home is his castle."

"The Castle!" Joanie hollered, thumping the table. "Not that I think Daniel would give a rat's ass what we call it."

"No, even better," I laughed. "How about the Palace? That way this could be the Palace kitchen, like that restaurant in Seattle. And

Daniel's little in-law could be the Woodshed."

Phyl shook her head. "No Woodshed."

"The Lean-To!" Joanie said eagerly. "Like in *Little House on the Prairie*. You wanted literature, Phyl." She raised her glass of iced tea. "I propose a toast to the Palace and the Lean-To!"

Phyl looked like she might draw out the argument, but since I raised my glass she gave in and toasted with us.

I was just wiping down the stainless-steel sink when I heard the front door open. Daniel. At least he was alone, since I forgot to make Missy a plate. Somehow the thought of being home alone with him made me a little nervous, not just because I'd always felt intimidated by the Head Cheerleaders and High School Football Captains of the world, but because talking to any man post-widowhood seemed fraught with difficulty.

He poked his head in the kitchen. "Where's Joanie?"

"Church."

Daniel made a scoffing sound. "How could I have forgotten?" Everywhere I chose to stand seemed to be in his way, and I tried not to leap like a startled deer when he backed me up against the counter so he could reach for a wineglass. The glint in his eye made me suspect he enjoyed my discomfiture. "Smells good. What did... Felicia... make for dinner?"

"Close. Her name is Phyllida, but we call her Phyl. If it helps you remember, her name means 'greenery' or something, and she's a total enviro-freak. Tonight she made a politically-correct chicken casserole." I pointed to the microwave, trying to stand my ground and not step back from him.

His very blue eyes met mine sharply. "Look... Cass... sorry about the name problem. I'm not very good with them."

"It's okay," I replied, moving away from him on the pretense of hanging up the dishcloth. "I meant sincerely that you were close when you guessed Felicia. Just like you were close when you guessed 'Cathy' for me. I'm terrible at names, so I'm impressed you actually get in the ballpark."

He grinned then and went to punch the buttons on the micro-wave.

Having finished cleaning, I debated whether or not he would want to make conversation while he ate and decided probably not. But it was weird to share a house with another person and not make any attempt to get to know him. Well, he could always take refuge in the Lean-To if I got too annoying.

"Joanie says you're a lawyer," I began. "What kind of lawyer?"

He stuffed a giant bite of casserole in his mouth and had to chew for a minute, looking measuringly at me all the while. Maybe most women who addressed him uninvited were hitting on him. Ugh. I was pretty sure I'd kept my tone businesslike.

He reached for the pepper mill, and I thought of Esther appearing before Ahasuerus without first being summoned. Would Daniel hand me the mill, like the royal scepter, and bid me speak, or would he behead me? Instead, he gave a few grinds and replaced it.

"Intellectual property," he answered at last. "Trade secrets, that sort of thing."

"Do you mean inventions?"

"Sort of and sometimes. Companies develop anything—new technologies, inventions, even software programs or architectures—and they need legal protection for these things to keep their competitive advantage. If another company steals these things or benefits from them, they should have to pay for it, just like you would have to pay if you were a musician and wanted to record a cover of someone else's song."

"So if I invented something and wanted to get it patented and protected, I could go to you?"

His mouth twisted in amusement. "Are you speaking hypothetically? What kind of invention?"

I pulled one of the barstools closer to the table and sat down. "Oh, I've thought of all kinds of things. What about contact lenses that darkened in sunlight, like those glasses which turn into sunglasses automatically?"

No response. He kept eating, so I tried again. "And then I thought of a chair, like a disc on a stiff bungee cord, that you could suspend from the ceiling and sit on, so that when you were holding a baby, the baby would think you were still standing, but you would know you were sitting."

"What?" he looked mystified. "What would be the point of that?"

I forgot babies were completely unknown quantities to him. "Because when babies are fussy, they like you to hold them while you walk around or bounce up and down, and that gets exhausting for the parent after a while."

He shrugged, losing interest. "Well, we don't really handle personal inventions."

Now he tells me.

There was a pause, while I waited for him to take a turn asking me something, but he seemed content to eat in silence. I hid a smile. I had forgotten how, when Joanie got frustrated with him, she would say, "Daniel is complete in himself—or is that completely into himself?"

Once more into the breach. "Do you have to work a lot of weekends?" I asked.

"Depends on the caseload. One of the partners is on family leave now, so some of us are taking up the slack." His grin came and went again. "Maybe Josh might be interested in your disc bouncy chair now."

"Well, it's my idea, so he'd have to pay big time for it," I cracked. His expression didn't change. For the love of Mike, did he think I was serious?

"And you know," Daniel continued, as if I hadn't spoken, "It'll never sell unless you can think of a catchier name for it."

Stung, I retorted, "'Disc bouncy chair' was your name for it, not mine! Of course I know it needs a better name. I was just giving you one of my hypothetical inventions." This time I definitely saw his mouth twitch and suddenly realized he was only yanking my chain, and I had thought *he* was serious.

More silence. No wonder he slept with so many women—otherwise he might have to talk to them! He was just about done with his plate. "If you want seconds, there's more in the fridge," I offered.

While he loaded up again I made a final attempt. "Okay, if you don't do personal inventions, what's an example of something your firm would handle?"

Daniel turned slowly from the microwave. "A little of this, a little of that. They're trade secrets, remember? I could tell you, but this would be your last night on earth."

This time I did laugh. "Fine then, keep your precious secrets. I'm off to go hack into your computer." I'd done my conversational duty for one night. Time to check my email.

• • •

Raquel, my mother-in-law (ex-mother-in-law? former mother-in-law?), had sent me three messages. We found it easier to email than to talk on the phone, since one or the other of us would start crying and set the other one off. Sighing, I clicked open the first.

Hello, Cass.

I thought about calling but knew you would be busy
with moving into your new place. We are so happy
for you making a new start. Please let us know if you
need anything. You will always be family to us. In fact,
if you don't feel like going as far as your family's this
Thanksgiving, we would love you to join us. Max has been
repainting the cabin.

Raquel

Ugh! Sitting around the Thanksgiving table with Max and Raquel
and Troy's brothers' families sounded truly horrible. I loved them,
but they were big drinkers, and it was sure to end in everyone throwing back even more than usual and ending up weepy and interrupt-
ing each other to propose maudlin toasts to Troy. Kind of like how
we spent the week of the memorial. And the last few Ewan family
gatherings. And once Raquel was really lit, she'd be sure to drag out
the hand-embroidered dresses from Troy's little sister, who also died
young, and tell me how she had been saving these for Min to grow
into. No way. I would rather spend Thanksgiving at the local Denny's
than torture myself like that.

Feeling dread, I clicked on the next one.

Hello, Cass.

Max was up in the attic today and found a box of Troy's
swim trophies and ribbons. We would like to keep
several, of course, but would you like some?

Raquel.

I groaned and laid my head on the desk. When I had cleared out
the old house, Raquel came by two consecutive days to cart away
U-Hauls full of Troy's and Min's things, all the time giving me reproachful looks that I would even consider parting with the stuff. I

think she expected me to set up some kind of shrine with the relics and was deeply wounded by what she took for my callous, let-the-dead-bury-the-dead attitude.

Numero tres:

> Hello, Cass.
>
> Little Minnie would have been 30 months next week. They are going to redo the playground at the park I used to take her to, so I thought it would be lovely if we bought a few of the bricks to put her name on it. And Max thought we should sponsor a drinking fountain with Troy's name as well. We don't expect you to contribute, of course. We just wanted you to know it would be there.
>
> Raquel

Okay, she won. I was crying, but at the same time angry with her for dragging me down with her. A year had gone by. Why couldn't she just let me enjoy a few months of denial? We'd been doing grief her way this whole time. Other than Mom ordering up the dumpster, my own parents were giving me space, not talking about it and trying to offer distractions: did I want to join them and their friends on their Caribbean cruise? Did I want to move closer to home? Why didn't I get a subscription to the theater?

I supposed I wasn't being fair. Raquel and I were in a tug-of-war over how to grieve. For her it meant endless do-you-remembers and treasuring every tangible thing you could associate with them. When I did too much of this with her or with anyone, I felt like I was drowning. I couldn't breathe. I was being swallowed alive. Any death you could think of where air was an issue. I guess I was my parents' child—I just wanted to shelve it for a while. Not that I wanted to join my parents and their retired friends on a Caribbean cruise, but I did want a break from memory. The theater ticket idea was tempting, to tell the truth. Why else would I be avoiding my married-with-children friends and crashing with a bunch of singles, except to pretend that maybe none of that awfulness ever happened? Wearing my wedding ring was my one concession. I didn't really want to be single, either, and have to deal with issues of singleness. With my ring I could also pretend singleness didn't exist.

Taking a deep breath, I wrote her a quick response:

> Hi, Raquel.
> The move went fine, and I am settling in. Thank you for the invitation, but I think my new housemates and I are planning a Thanksgiving shebang [total falsehood which I would have to rectify]. Please keep Troy's swim trophies. I can see them there.
> The playground memorials are a beautiful idea. I like to think of children playing around Min's bricks and drinking from Troy's fountain.
> Hope you both are well. The cabin will look great when Max is done repainting.
> Love, Cass.

If I was going to stay in denial, I needed to get busy.

Just then I heard my phone chirp in my purse. Troy must be rolling in his figurative grave to think I decided to go without a landline at the Palace because my cell phone historically spent more time dead than charged. Digging it out of my purse, the crumpled morning's bulletin came with it. "Calling All Mentors!" shouted the little headline for Camden School when I smoothed it out on my desk.

Nice try, I told God. *You'll have to do better than that.*

· · ·

Sometime around 10:00, when I was tucked up in bed re-reading *David Copperfield*, Joanie poked her head in. Seeing me awake she slipped in, shutting the door behind her, and did a running leap onto my bed.

"Grief, Joanie! Watch out for my legs!" I complained.

Unrepentantly she flopped over on her stomach right next to me and propped her head up on her hands. "Ask me how it was, Cass. I love living with you and having you right here. I don't even have to pick up the phone."

"How was it, Joanie?" I asked obediently. "I assume you mean coffee and not church."

"Yes, I mean coffee!" she said exultantly. "Roy is so great! He may be unemployed but he's gorgeous, plus he's fun to talk to and has lots of interests and asked me about me. And he totally wants to come to our first open house on Thursday."

"No big surprise there. Do you think the cute short friend will come too?"

She sat up suddenly and looked hard at me. "We didn't even talk about him, and I didn't think to ask, since Phyl wasn't interested. Are *you* interested? I'll ask for you. You're so short I'm sure he's taller than you."

I shook my head, horrified. "No no no! I didn't mean that. I don't want him either. Let Brooke Capshaw have him." She was getting that speculative look in her eye, so to change the subject I demanded, "Did Roy ask you to marry him yet? And did you say Yes and Yes and then No, never mind?"

She mock-scowled at me. "What a grump. Aren't you even going to ask me how he made it to his age without being gay or divorced?"

"I assumed he was both."

"Oh, ha ha," Joanie said sarcastically. "No, really, Cass, he's been overseas for the past four years teaching English in Cambodia for World Vision. Isn't that the coolest?"

I pretended to consider, just to tease her. "Fairly cool...but just because he's an idealist doesn't make him a monk. He probably had a *Madame Butterfly*/*Miss Saigon* thing going on."

"What are you talking about, Cass? You mean he was an opera fan?"

"No, goof," I laughed. "What's wrong with being an opera fan? I meant he might have had a love affair with someone in Cambodia and left a souvenir or two behind. Did he ask you how you feel about kids? Or being a stepmom?"

She whipped one of my pillows out from behind me and walloped me with it. "So cynical today. I was going to give you the play-by-play of our conversation, but I guess I'll save my raptures for Phyl, then."

I gave her an apologetic squeeze. "I'm just giving you a hard time. I want the play-by-play. It'll take my mind off my mother-in-law's weeping and gnashing of teeth."

"Oh, *no*. Have you heard from her again?"

"What do you mean 'again'? I still hear from her practically every day. We're quite the e-mourners," I explained. "So I did that, and when Daniel came home I tried to have a basic getting-to-know-you conversation. He was very evasive and non-curious. I can't say it was a success."

"Poor you," she crooned. "And here you are taking refuge in some thick, boring book. Let me share my much more exciting evening with you..."

In her own way Joanie could give Dickens a run for his money in the details department. By the time she got around to Roy dropping her off and squeezing her hand significantly it was past 11:00. I kicked her out and, despite all, fell asleep almost right after putting out the light.

CHAPTER FOUR:

Open House

Late Thursday found Joanie, Phyl, and me in the Palace kitchen, preparing for our first open house. Joanie had chosen a Mexican theme and planned more food than five or six people could eat, but if Daniel showed up we wanted him to find it worthwhile.

Perched on a barstool, I diced tomatoes for the Spanish rice, while Phyl arranged the last of the summer flowers in bud vases. "Do you think Daniel invited Missy?" she asked, frowning over some limp helenium culled from the yard.

"Doubtful," said Joanie, smoothing sour cream over the seven-layer dip. "With just the few of us, it would be like inviting her to a family wedding. Sends the wrong message."

Laughing, I dumped the tomatoes and chicken broth in the rice cooker. "Yes, God forbid he send the message that Missy actually means something to him. Phyl, you better get going with the margaritas—it's almost 6:30." You wouldn't guess it, to look at Phyl, but bartending was one of her chief gifts. Another was recycling; even in a place where large segments of the population could sort plastics by touch, Phyl qualified as a total green freak and had even turned it into a career, working for the City's Environmental Services. She was the reason there was not a paper plate or piece of plastic ware to be found in the Palace.

The words were scarcely out of my mouth when the doorbell rang. Dancing to answer it, Joanie returned pulling Roy by the hand and waving his bouquet of chrysanthemums. Roy lived up to expectations, being over six feet tall and lean, with hair as red-gold as Joanie's and the worshipful expression shared by her previous three fiancés. As soon as the friendly introductions were over, he pulled a barstool closer to where she was cooking and parked himself there.

"I bet six months till he proposes," Phyl whispered, as if Roy could possibly hear her over the blender crushing ice.

I snorted. "After four years in Cambodia? I'm betting eight weeks." To give them some privacy, Phyl let me help her rim the glasses with lime and salt, though I could see her bite her lip when she saw my inexpert results.

The doorbell rang again, and we looked at each other, puzzled. We weren't expecting anyone else, and Daniel wouldn't ring the doorbell. To my surprise, it was Missy, stunning in a black halter top and jeans. Did this mean that, Joanie's opinion notwithstanding, Daniel didn't mind sending her the wrong message? Or that he did, in fact, want to make her feel significant?

Missy grimaced when I opened the door and tried to peer around me. "Hey, there, Cathy. Daniel said to come by for dinner tonight. I brought some libations." Before I could do more than take the Chardonnay bottle and usher her into the kitchen, the bell rang again. Who on earth…?

The porch was crowded with people this time—had Daniel invited his entire office? Panicked, I thought of the fajitas-for-eight cooking in the kitchen and mentally rifled through the pantry for more we could throw together, until I noticed that some of the crowd were toting grocery bags, and there were coolers and offerings being unloaded from various trunks. Phyl was going to have a cow when she saw all the clamshell containers. And what would everyone eat off of? Cars lined both sides of our street for several houses in each direction. Names and faces and contexts soon blurred together; the hall closet wouldn't close on all the jackets and purses; and potluck offerings soon hid all those acres of granite counter.

One last ring of the doorbell.

"Wyatt Collins," said a stocky, balding man, when, zombie-like, I opened the door once more. "Law school buddy of Danny's. And this is my wife Delia. Saw Danny right behind us, but I don't think he can get up the driveway to the garage." Well, if he couldn't it was his own fault.

Over Wyatt Collins's shoulder I could see the master of the house unfolding from the low seat of his vintage Corvette, relaxed and empty-handed. Scrunching aside to let the Collins' in, I stared insistently at Daniel to catch his eye.

"What happened to 'two guests, max'?" I hissed, when he was close enough to hear me. "Did you wake up thinking you were The Great Gatsby?"

He raised one eyebrow and pushed me gently inside so he could shut the door. "I couldn't let you religious wackos outnumber me."

• • •

Our carefully-planned Mexican dinner became a global mishmash: baked beans next to hummus next to *siu mai*, smoked salmon jockeying for counter space with California rolls and fruit salad, but at least everyone got enough to eat. To this day I don't know how many people we had total or who everyone was or how they knew Daniel.

He never afterward invited so many, and indeed most of them never showed up again, as far as I recall. I suspect he was just making his point: this was his house, both Palace and Lean-To, to use as he saw fit, and we were on a loose leash but a leash all the same.

Thankfully, the evening was so mild that, rather than confining themselves to the kitchen, people spilled out on to the deck. Such a crowd relieved me of the need for mingling, especially since they knew each other better than I did, and I was free to eat and people-watch. I amused myself by trying to guess which of them were lawyers—the ones drinking the most? The ones talking the most? One of the biggest drinkers and loudest talkers had attached himself to Phyl; he was apparently a longtime buddy of Daniel's, good-looking enough, but we both saw the tan line on his ring finger, and she had to keep glomming on to different groups to escape him. Joanie also had her fans, but none of them managed to shake Roy. There seemed to be an understanding among the men present that Missy was off-limits because of Daniel, even though Daniel himself didn't seem to pay her much attention. She would gravitate toward him, listen in on his conversations, volunteer comments herself, but the second she laid a hand on him, faint tension would appear around his mouth, and he would find some pretense to move out of reach. Missy and I weren't the only ones to notice his growing disenchantment; a striking brunette hovered nearby, flirting more boldly with each beer she downed. The heir-apparent, perhaps?

At one point I found myself sharing the chaise longue with Delia, Wyatt's shy, self-effacing wife, and Julie the Droopy Paralegal. I wasn't clear on the causes of Julie's droopiness; she muttered something about having just broken up with her boyfriend, who may or may not have been present. Wyatt and Roy had discovered a mutual interest in wildlife photography and gotten pretty absorbed in comparing notes. Joanie was hanging on Daniel, much to Missy's ill-concealed chagrin and the brunette's confusion.

"How did you and Wyatt meet?" I asked Delia politely. Droopy Julie gave a dramatic sigh, which Delia and I ignored.

Delia smiled and ducked her chin a little. "In the library at the law school. I was a senior on work-study there fall quarter, and he kept coming by to ask me questions and trying to check out reference books that couldn't leave the library."

"He seems like a nice guy. Was he into the wildlife photography back then?"

Delia laughed. "No, back then, he was just into the wild life, period. Especially because he hung out a lot with Daniel. I don't know how they graduated."

"The more I hear about Daniel, the more I wonder that, too. He's sure into the wine, women and song."

"No kidding," Droopy Julie interjected. Had she preceded Missy at some point? She was rather plain, by Daniel's standards, but maybe I wasn't making allowances for her current droopy state.

We all gazed thoughtfully at poor Missy, who was pouting gloriously into her glass of Chardonnay.

"Wyatt wasn't so into the women," Delia said presently, "but he was all for the wine and song. Daniel's promised him we're going to play some Rock Band tonight."

"All of us? What do you play? Joanie has a great voice, so she does vocals."

She smiled timidly. "I'm actually pretty good on drums. Wyatt sticks to the bass because it's the least to keep track of, and Daniel does guitar. Do you play?"

"Only a few times with my husband's brothers. Of course they stuck me on vocals, but I couldn't say I was any good at it. I could muddle through the few songs I'd heard before."

"Your husband's brothers?" Delia looked puzzled. "Are you

divorced?" Droopy Julie perked up a little, to think I might also have a broken heart.

I sighed inwardly, kicking myself for my slip. I absolutely *hated* always dragging around my tragedy like a ball and chain. A real conversation killer. "I'm widowed, actually, but it's okay…" I babbled, holding up a hand to wave away her sudden gasp and crestfallen look. "Here, can I take your plate?"

As I fled, I overheard Droopy Julie murmur, "God, how awkward! She doesn't look old enough to be a widow—I wonder what he died of."

I ducked back inside, feeling that familiar lump rising in my throat and hating it. The kitchen looked like a take-out container graveyard. Painstakingly, I scraped food scraps into the yard waste bin and started rinsing the dishes, so I would have time to get my emotions back under control. Maybe I should have a signboard printed up: *Cass Ewan. I have been recently widowed and lost a child, and I do not want to talk about it. Thank you for your donations!* Hearing the door open, I quickly dashed my sleeve across my eyes.

It was Missy, still looking unhappy—or like Miss America unhappy. Miss America after she's posed for inappropriate pictures and has to relinquish her crown to the runner-up.

"Would you like anything else?" I asked huskily and then cleared my throat.

She didn't appear to be listening, but she came toward me languidly. "You're Cass, right?"

"Right."

"I heard your roommate just now telling someone else that you were a widow." Crap! Maybe I should just get on the Palace's fancy intercom system with a Public Service Announcement. The dishes rang and clanked as I loaded them with unnecessary force.

"So you lost your husband."

Hence the term 'widow,' I thought sarcastically. And I've lost a child, too, but who's counting? "Yes," I said warily.

"That's so sad."

Tell me about it. I took a deep breath to steady myself. For Pete's sake, Cass, she's only trying to express sympathy, and you treat her like she's somehow responsible!

She laid her plate on the counter. "At least… at least you've had a husband. I don't know if I'll ever get married, at this rate. All my friends are getting married."

I almost laughed with relief. Self-absorption has its benefits, and I pounced on this opportunity to change the subject. "Of course you will, Missy. You're absolutely beautiful and—and—friendly. I'm not sure guys like Daniel are going to be your ticket out of singleness, however."

Missy flipped her long hair back impatiently. "He's hard to read. He seems to like me sometimes. I thought we had a great time last weekend, and then he didn't even call me until today. And he went and invited those other friends, and his sister keeps hanging around his neck, and he doesn't even seem to be trying to be with me." She glared at me as if challenging me to deny any of this.

"Like I said, he may not be marriage material. He's just to… have fun with…" I petered out awkwardly.

Her eyes flashed. "And he is fun, that way. I just thought it meant something more to him. I mean, last weekend—"

Before she could give me the gory details, the door opened again: Joanie and Roy, carrying stacks of dishes, followed by Phyl with her pile of Portmeirion. Having no paper plates is fine for a small dinner party, but tonight's surprise turnout had taxed even the china resources of our combined households. As it was, a few of the guests were eating off Phyl's Christmas plates because my stoneware was boxed in the attic.

It must have struck Missy that, with Joanie inside, Daniel was now wide open to the brunette's advances; hurriedly she sloshed herself another glass of Chardonnay and went back outside.

"Your brother knows some interesting people," Roy began conversationally. He was drying dishes for Joanie. "Had you met any of them before?"

"Some. The Collins'. Missy, of course. That guy Tom who was trying to hit on Phyl."

"I think he's married," said Phyl. She was carefully wrapping up leftovers and rinsing the clamshell containers.

"He is," said Joanie succinctly. "But always on the prowl—kind of like your dear ex."

• • •

By the time dinner and the dishes wrapped up, it was already nine o'clock, and a significant portion of people took their leave. Rock Band was up next on the agenda, but with so many people wanting to play, everyone would spend a fair amount of time rotated out. Phyl and I seemed to be the only ones not interested, so we decided on a game of Scrabble. Dashing upstairs for my board, I came upon a couple making out on my bed, still clothed, thank heavens. Mortifying. Grabbing the game box, I made apologetic sounds, while they scrambled up and out, never to be seen again.

Joanie was getting things underway when I got back downstairs. Not for nothing did she work in the church worship department; with her voice and talent for mimicry, she distracted Roy constantly from his own screen prompts.

After opening up the next set of songs, Joanie handed off to Missy and came to check out the Scrabble progress, but Missy's performance made concentration difficult. She was making up for her weaker voice quite effectively by adding plenty of hip gyrations and general booty shaking.

"If I tried that, it would be pure comedy," I observed, as Missy cavorted about, getting in Daniel's face.

"Oh, yeah, you gotta have at least D cups to pull off that move," agreed Joanie.

"Don't you think you could get away with it with only C cups?" I asked. "It's all about distance and perspective. See, if you got right up in someone's face like that, D cups become superfluous."

"Hell, at that distance, A cups would do you!" Joanie hooted.

Phyl eyed our snickering with soft reproach. "Stop it, you two. It's catty."

"I'm marveling at her skill," I sputtered mock-defensively, "Anthropologically speaking, that girl will get to pass on her genes. She's sure got Daniel's attention now." He was leaning over to kiss her, the most notice Missy had gotten from him all evening.

"She is pretty," Phyl sighed. "Usually everyone's avatar looks way better than they do, but I think she wins hands-down." She lay down her four-tile overlap, blocking my way to the triple-word score.

"Darn you, Phyl!" I groused. "I had a million-pointer to put there. Yeah, most people's avatars look way better because most people are solid Tier Two."

"Tier Two?" asked Phyl.

I nodded, explaining Troy's theory. "And Daniel and Missy are definitely Tier One—as is Joanie, for that matter. I'd put you at High Tier Two and me at solid Middle Tier Two. In fact I don't think there are any Tier Three people here tonight, since most people make it into Tier Two. Tier Three people have to have some overwhelming flaw, like limbs eaten away by MRSA."

"Or like the guy at the billiards place who tried to hit on me but didn't have any arms," put in Joanie.

"What was he doing at a billiards place, then?" I laughed. "He should have played to his strengths and done soccer."

"Or hurdles."

"Or hackysack."

"Or limbo."

"Or luge."

We were rolling around cackling by now, and even Phyl's disapproving mouth was twitching. "If you two are this way on one margarita, we might need to make these open houses dry."

Sometime later, Daniel and Missy were rotated out. Daniel came over to check out our game board, and I could almost hear Missy's irritated huff. She began running her fingers up and down his back, without measurable results.

"Who put down 'bastard'?" he asked.

"Cass, of course!" said Phyl, deprecatingly. "Ordinarily I try to keep it clean. She could have played off my 'd' and made 'dastard,' but she couldn't resist. "

"That would've opened a triple-letter for you," I defended. "And 'bastard' being a totally legitimate word, so to speak, there was no reason to pass up a bingo opportunity."

"What's a bingo?" asked Daniel.

"When you play all seven letters in one turn," I explained. "You get fifty bonus points. That little 'bastard' is the whole reason I'm trouncing Phyl."

"You should play with us some time," Phyl coaxed. "And you too, of course, Missy," she added belatedly. "We always try to get Joanie to play, but she says she can't spell."

Missy shrugged noncommittally, but Daniel said, "I'd like to. I think I know at least as many bad words as Cass."

He actually winked at me when he said this, which goaded me into replying, "Oh I'm sure you could teach us all something about bastards." Expecting him to be affronted, his quick grin surprised me.

Phyl looked ready to melt under the charm onslaught, so I kicked her under the table to get the goofy puppy look off her face. "Let's go, Levert. I have a great word to play if you don't mess it up." Having Daniel watching seemed to addle her brains, and she kept shuffling her tiles around nervously until he and Missy wandered away.

"Honestly, Phyl, what are you thinking?" I demanded.

"Nothing! I'm not thinking anything. He's just so handsome! Tier Two people can *look* at Tier One people, can't they?"

"Phyl, it's not just his looks," I tried to reason with her. "It's his whole approach to life, his goals, his beliefs. Daniel is almost a different species. If you tried to mate, you'd probably have sterile offspring. Like mules. Cross a donkey and a horse, and you get a mule."

"And I suppose I'm the donkey?" Phyl complained.

"If you fall for someone like Daniel," I warned, "I think the biblical word would be 'ass.'"

• • •

It was 10:30 before the Collins' and Roy took their leave. Missy was practically wilted with lack of attention, but she revived when Daniel leaned to murmur in her ear and they headed off to the Lean-To.

Talking over the open house was almost as fun as the thing itself, and we all agreed that, apart from Missy, everyone had enjoyed themselves. "And she should be cheering up right about now," Joanie yawned. "Besides, I don't think she'll be around for more than one more open house. I should have warned her that the less she fawns on him, the longer he'll like her."

"But you fawn on him all the time," Phyl pointed out. She was laying on the sofa with her eyes shut.

"That's me," said Joanie simply. She was scrunched up in the armchair, leaning her head against me as I draped on the arm. "I'm touchy-feely."

"And he can't suspect you of wanting to marry him," I added. "Poor Missy. At least by dating Daniel she might get fed up with men who don't treat her well." Phyl looked as if she might say something, but catching my eye, she shut her mouth firmly again.

CHAPTER FIVE:

Meeting Kyle

Over the next couple weeks I found myself settling into a cautious new happiness. The grief was there, to be sure, but shut up tight and put high on a shelf to worry about later. How could I not be distracted and excited, to wake up in an unfamiliar place with sunlight streaming in and the smell of coffee brewing downstairs? I couldn't shower and get ready fast enough to join Joanie and Phyl in the kitchen for quality time before they headed off to work.

We quickly learned each other's habits. Phyl was a hot breakfast gal and never sat down with less than two eggs scrambled, toast, and juice. Joanie would eye this feast askance, unable to stomach more than coffee and some bready item before ten o'clock. For me it was always cold cereal and Earl Grey tea, and Daniel would usually dash in, fill his commuter mug with coffee and, often as not, steal Joanie's dry toast on his way out.

"You big loser," Joanie yelled after him, one morning. "We cook you dinner, not breakfast!"

By eight o'clock the house was mine. I wasted a lot of time in the beginning, reading the paper or dinking on the piano or figuring out good neighborhood walks, but I had already wasted the past year of my life lying in bed, and now I had responsibilities to my housemates, besides. New house, new start. Soon I divided my day into blocks of duty and reward. Start with housekeeping responsibilities, then read the paper. Exercise before settling down to a few hours' work.

As for the whole mentoring thing, I pushed it to the back of my mind and defiantly recycled the bulletin.

Cooking days were a delight. I'd always loved to cook, but after Min came along, lack of time and energy had reduced me to seven tried-and-true quick meals. If-it's-Tuesday-it-must-be-taco-salad kind of thing. Now I could spend all the time I liked, and my first Palace offerings were rather elaborate: chicken breasts stuffed with apples and gouda, pork tostadas with homemade chutney. Phyl and Joanie were effusive in their praise, but Daniel, who came home any time between 6:30 and 8:00, would raise a skeptical eyebrow as he watched these creations rotate in the microwave. Apparently if everything I cooked him was going to be reheated, I would have to choose more microwave-friendly creations. Phyl's casseroles and Joanie's stir-fries didn't turn to cardboard jerky when nuked, after all, and I didn't want to be the cook whose meals his lordship dreaded.

When my household responsibilities were under control, I turned to my Brilliant Career. Before Min was born, I did some freelance work writing grant proposals and helping with fundraising, but the thought of tapping those connections now made me feel slightly nauseous, since I had last seen them, solicitous and awkward, at Troy's and Min's memorial. Ugh. Besides, I might as well take advantage of this moment in life when I wasn't cash-strapped and try my hand at something completely different.

For lack of a better idea, I decided to experiment with some creative writing. But what to write? After more hemming and hawing,

I settled on trying a movie novelization as a warm-up. That way I wouldn't be bothered with generating a plot and could just focus on getting a story on paper. I figured if I tried one of the *Star Wars* movies I could compare my results with an existing novelization, but this turned out to be more complicated than I thought, because I was no expert in all the myriad star ships and fighters and destroyers and droids and whatnot.

One afternoon found me trolling the nerdy section of the library, searching for *Star Wars* picture books. Having found a couple likely candidates which I tucked under my arm, I was just adding a volume of detailed spaceship cross-sections when I felt a middle book squidge out and tumble to the floor, hitting me squarely on the toe with its corner. "Franklin D. Roosevelt," I hissed, hopping on my uninjured foot.

When I reached for my fallen book, I heard a derisive snort. Startled, I looked up to see a tall, lanky teenager with pale blue eyes and longish brown hair, combed forward. He was wearing the standard Northwest uniform of frayed jeans, layers of t-shirts and flip-flops, and he was grimacing at the title in my hand.

"What?" I asked warily.

He shrugged without meeting my eyes.

"You don't like this book?" I persisted. "I don't super know what I'm looking for, so advice is welcome." When he didn't answer, I tucked it back under my arm, only to see him raise his eyebrows in a don't-say-I-didn't-warn-you fashion. "Wha-a-a-t?" I demanded. "If you want to say something, say it—unless you're mute or something."

"No way do you want that one," he declared at last in a raspy voice. "The guy can't write for crap, and he even gets some of the basic facts wrong. Can't tell a podracer from Padmé's ass."

"Oh!" Surprised at my success, I replaced the offending volume on the shelf. "What do you think of this one?" Indicating the cross-section book.

Another snort. "I met the guys who did that one at a book-signing. They were cool—well, one of them was a total loser—but he was all pissed because he didn't like his latté. He kept saying stuff like, 'What, they don't do foam in Washington?' Like he was some kind of sorry-ass coffee expert when he wasn't doing *Star Wars* books."

I blinked at him. "So... but you think this cross-section book is okay? Accurate, I mean?"

He shrugged. "Yeah. I mean *he* sucked, but he knows his shit. Why do you wanna know? You don't look like the typical person I see in this aisle."

"Because I'm not a guy?"

"For one. You work here?"

"You mean, am I a librarian?" I screech-whispered. Grief, I could handle his sailor's mouth and criticism of my book choices, but no way would I put up with being mistaken for a librarian.

He looked puzzled by my irritation. "Yeah, are you a librarian? What do you want with these books?"

"I'm trying to write a book," I grumped. "But I didn't know there was so much stuff I would have to learn. If you're such a big expert, maybe you could help me pick out the good books."

He shrugged again and began running his finger down the row. "Decent. Total bullshit. B.S. Decent. This one's good—hardcore nerd porn."

I followed behind him, hastily pulling out the "decent" and "nerd porn" ones. "Thank you." I hesitated, then hitched the books to one arm so I could hold out my hand. "It's nice to meet you. I'm Cass."

He stared at my outstretched hand. "Huh. Okay, I'm Kyle." He put his hand limply in mine for a split second and then pulled it back and stuffed it in his pocket. "What kind of book are you writing? Are you trying to make up one of those back stories that the movies don't cover? '*Still More Legends of Tatooine*' and crap like that?"

"No," I admitted slowly. "I've never done any fiction writing before, so I'm just trying to write a novel version of one of the movies. A novelization. For practice. How about you? What do you do besides read *Star Wars* books?"

Kyle started fiddling with one of the sub-par books, tapping it up and down on the shelf. "Nothing. Well, school started last week, but I'm thinking I'll just go sometimes."

Sometimes was right. Here it was Tuesday, and he was at the library. "Which school do you go to?"

More book fiddling. Then, reluctantly, "Camden School."

"Camden School!" I screech-whispered for the second time, feeling my heart rate accelerate. Guiltily I remembered the discarded bulletin. I said God would have to be pretty clear if he wanted something out of me—did this count? "I've heard good things about it," I ventured.

Still avoiding my eyes, Kyle muttered, "I just started there, but I already hate it because it's a bunch of druggies and the classes are stupid."

"Well, if you're not a druggie, why are you there, then?" I asked, rather deflated.

"Kicked out of Bellevue High for vandalism and other stuff. Stupid administrators want to charge me with a felony, but the lawyer's getting the prosecutor to divert the case."

"Oh," I said lamely, having had no idea that normal kid vandalism or mysterious "other stuff" could even be a felony, nor any clue how the juvenile justice system worked. Maybe this was a sign that mentoring would indeed be out of my league. Then, to my surprise, I heard myself say, "Well, do you want to walk over there now with me? You could help me more with the *Star Wars* stuff."

Kyle shrugged again but submitted to his fate. The Camden School was housed in a former church just in back of our church, about a fifteen-minute walk from the library. In an unexpected act of chivalry, he grabbed the picture books from me and carried them without a word.

"Do you have a mentor?" I asked, as we huffed up the hill. His strides were so much longer than mine that I was trying not to compromise my dignity by breaking into a trot.

He shook his head.

"Do you want to get one?" I persisted.

"I don't know. What would I do with some old person?"

I decided to overlook this. "Well, it could also be a young person. I—I was thinking of volunteering. I think you would hang out, I guess. I might ask about it today, and I could let you know."

"I wouldn't want a girl mentor."

Really, he was impossible. "I'm not trying to be your mentor, Kyle! Guys get guy mentors, I'm pretty sure."

Kyle mulled this over. "I guess it would be all right. As long as he wasn't like my dad. That would suck big time."

I figured it would be too nosy at this point to pursue that subject—not that Kyle seemed particularly hung up on the social niceties—so I stuck with *Star Wars* questions until we reached the school. He handed me back my books and, staring at the sidewalk, said abruptly, "If you want me to read your book and make sure it's okay, I could do that."

He was such an odd mixture of alien teenage boy and gallant knight that I couldn't read him, but I felt touched nonetheless. "It's a deal! I wouldn't want it to be crap, after all." He scribbled his email address on my library receipt and then darted inside without even looking at me or saying good-bye.

Hesitating with my hand on the door, I had another brief, one-sided argument with God. *Okay, already, you got me here. And Kyle seemed like a good kid. If you insist, I'll just go inside and ask about it, but no promises! What do I know about drugs or vandalism or connecting with teenagers?* Taking a deep breath, I went inside.

I found myself in a small, neat reception area, reminiscent of a 1970s dentist's office. "Hello!" a young woman greeted me from behind her desk. "Are you here for the mentors' meeting?"

"What?" I gasped.

"The mentors' meeting," she repeated, taking in my amazed expression. "The meeting to learn about becoming a mentor. It starts in the Director's office in about five minutes. Or maybe you have a child you want to enroll here..?" Given that I was only 32, that meant she either thought I looked like 42 or that teen pregnancy was nothing new in the population they targeted. I was going to go with that.

As for the mentors' meeting, there it was, I suppose. My sign. I guess I was going to become a mentor. Maybe God found it easier to produce a *deux ex machina* than to tackle the heavier stuff. I managed to nod, and, after regarding me curiously another moment, the admin pointed to the hallway. "First door on the right."

Feeling her eyes on my back and wishing I'd dressed up a little, I forced myself to walk down the hallway. All the doors on either side were closed, and behind them I could hear the hum of voices. In the Director's office a few other people were already waiting, most of whom I'm sure Kyle would classify as old, though there was one man about my age. I wondered randomly if they also had been tricked by God into being there. When their heads turned to look at me, I pinned on a general smile and took an empty chair.

"Won't this be exciting?" the lady next to me asked. A willing victim, then. She looked to be in her seventies, with neatly waved white hair and hazel eyes, and she sported a bright quilted jacket with appliqués that I didn't think would go over so well with teenage girls. "I've never done anything like this, but I heard that student speak in church and thought I might give it a try."

I felt rather embarrassed to think I'd been putting up such a fight when someone twice my age was being more adventurous. "I was on the fence," I admitted, "but I ran into one of the students just now at the library, and he seemed like a good guy. We walked back up here together," I added, leaving out the vandalism and cussing parts.

"At the library?" huffed one of the older men. "Well, I guess if you're cutting class, that's not such a bad place to be."

I smiled benignly. "I ran into him in the science fiction section. He knew a lot about *Star Wars* but didn't seem to know much about the mentor program."

"He knew a lot about *Star Wars*?" The younger man spoke up, leaning forward. Looking directly at him for the first time I realized he was very attractive. He was of middling build—Joanie would certainly call him "short"—with a pleasant face, gray eyes and curling brown hair. His looks didn't knock the wind out of you, like Daniel's tended to if you weren't prepared, but there was something about his overall demeanor: the way he held himself alert and attentive, the smile in his eyes, the way of looking at you as if you were either very important or very interesting or both. I imagine the word I was looking for was "charming."

I was thankful for my wedding ring, which I twisted self-consciously. At least I could converse with him without him thinking I had anything in mind. Or not. Maybe only women looked for wedding rings. He didn't have one, for example. "Yes," I answered. "He'd read a lot of the books about the movies and had even met some of the authors, so he had very definite recommendations to give me. I didn't dare check out any books besides the ones he approved. Do you like *Star Wars* too?"

"Sure. But more to the point, I work for a video gaming company, and we're working with Lucas Arts to develop some games. What was his name? If I clear the mentor bar I'll try to hook up with him. It would give us something natural to talk about."

Before I could answer, the Director of Camden School swept in, bringing the conversation to a close. Mark Henneman was a big, energetic bear of a man. He shook each of our hands firmly and plopped down in his chair to deliver a practiced speech about the mission and vision of Camden School. He talked about a typical student's background (Kyle was indeed an anomaly), teaching strategies, and goals of the mentor program.

"Did you know that teens with stable, loving adult influences in their lives are less likely to do drugs, drink, drop out, or engage in violence? But we've found our typical students have very few solid, grounded adult influences in their lives. Oftentimes they live in a single-parent family, or there are two parents who are not around much or not emotionally available for whatever reasons—maybe the parents are dealing with substance addiction themselves. The public school system isn't meeting the needs of these kids because it doesn't have the bandwidth to fill in the gaps in these students' lives. We try to do that here at Camden with on-site addiction counseling, life counseling, access to rehab programs, more one-on-one instruction and attention. And now we're adding this mentor piece. We envision matching up each of our students with a mentor, someone who will hang out with them or at least have some phone contact with them once a week, someone who will pray for that student, be a role model, do occasional special activities with other students and mentors. We'll have monthly trainings to cover topics like building trust, understanding addiction, safety and boundaries, and so on. You don't need to be an expert in anything. Can you love someone and invest in him or her? Can you try to build a relationship of trust? Can you applaud that student when he makes good choices and keep believing in him even when he makes bad ones?"

We were all inspired by now and sitting forward in our seats; even I felt like I might be able to manage, since I only had to be dedicated, rather than impressive.

Mark Henneman answered a few questions that arose and wound up by giving each of us an application to fill out and return. Once they'd checked references they would work on matching us up, schedule the monthly trainings, and invite us to the kick-off group activity.

We briefly went around the circle introducing ourselves—name, occupation, how we got interested in becoming a mentor. I stumbled some on the "occupation" part and said "freelance writer." Hopefully the School would recognize you could hardly beat freelance writers for dedication, and I couldn't quite bring myself to confess I was an unemployed widow doing housework for reduced rent. As for how I became interested in being a mentor, I could only say, "When the student Ellie gave her testimony in church, I felt very strongly that this was something I was supposed to do." Never mind that I did my best to ignore that strong feeling until circumstances cornered me today.

The woman I had chatted with was named Louella Murphy, and she was altogether more honest and brave than I was. "I'm retired, of course, but I used to be a nurse. Recently I lost my husband Frank after fifty-one years of marriage, and I want to see what God has for this new stage of my life. Frank and I used to go on medical mission trips to Central America, but that gets harder with age. I figure I can still get around and talk and love and pray, so here I am." What did I tell you? The woman made me look pathetic.

When we got around the circle, the young man introduced himself as "James Kittredge, project manager at a video game company," and I only managed to keep my mouth from popping open in surprise. Could this be Chaff James? The cute new guy who had all the sharks circling, as Joanie would say? Wait till she heard this! James, too, seemed more excited than intimidated by the mentoring thing; he had volunteered with Young Life all through college.

As everyone gathered their things to go, I saw James hanging back. Like Kyle, he unceremoniously relieved me of my pile of books and checked out the titles. "I definitely need to meet this kid. He knows his stuff."

"His name is Kyle," I volunteered.

"Kyle," he repeated. "I'll remember that. So what exactly are *you* doing with a pile of expert *Star Wars* books? Some of your freelance writing?"

I suppressed a squirm. My project sounded dumber each time I had to explain it. "I've mostly done grant writing and wanted to try some fiction, so I'm trying a movie novelization. You know, those dumb books they sell with the actors' photos on the cover. This way I thought I could compare my novelization to an existing one and see if I'm any good at it. Kind of like when you try to break into screenwriting, and they make you start with writing episodes for existing shows. Kyle actually promised to read it and tell me if it was crap."

James grinned. "I like this kid! The world doesn't need any more crap. If Kyle thinks it's any good, you should let me take a look. We're always looking for writers to do the game narrative and dialogue."

My eyes widened. "Really truly?"

"Really truly—if it's not crap. And on a related note, have you ever done any acting work?"

If I had heard Daniel ask someone that, I would think it was a creepy pick-up line. "Acting work? Not really, unless you count high school drama," I confessed. "I was Hermia in *A Midsummer Night's Dream* and Rebecca Gibbs in *Our Town.*"

James laughed. "We most certainly count high school drama. I don't know if you play many video games, but they don't exactly call for Oscar-winning performances. I know it's a weird question, but we need actors to record game dialogue, and you have a nice voice, kind of low and sweet."

That absolutely floored me. After a moment I managed to joke, "So I wouldn't be Chewbacca, then?"

We were outside by now, standing by a motorcycle. When James handed me my books back and unhooked the helmet, I realized this bike didn't belong to any student. My husband Troy had been a bike fanatic for as long as I'd known him, only giving up riding after Min was born, and it took me only half a beat to recognize that James rode a pretty sweet Ducati. "Is that a Monster City?" I breathed.

It was his turn to stare. "You a Ducati fan too, or just doing some freelance writing about them?"

I shook my head. "No. My husband had an M750, a couple years ago, and I—I remember him reading about these." I hoped I wasn't blushing when I mentioned Troy. It was one of the awkwardnesses of widowhood. Should I be saying "my late husband"? It sounded too ominous and opened up a conversational can of worms for which I didn't have the time or energy.

"Another guy I'm going to have to meet," said James, swinging his leg over the bike. Oops, probably should have mentioned it, then. Well, presumably they'd meet in heaven, and it was too weird to clarify now. He held out a hand to me. "It was great meeting you, Cass. I'm sure I'll be seeing you at that first group activity."

We shook hands—his grip was more assertive than Kyle's limp fish—and he was off, leaving me to walk home bemused. What did Phyl mean by calling him too tame? I would have thought working in video games and tooling around town on a Ducati Monster would have gained some traction with her. I picked up the pace, suddenly eager to run my day past Joanie.

• • •

"Chaff James? It was Chaff James?" Joanie's voice rose with excitement. "And he liked your voice? He must think you are so cool, knowing about *Star Wars* and motorcycles! Didn't I tell you he was cute? And taller than you, am I right?"

"For the last time, Joanie, I'm not thinking of meeting anyone right now. I still email my mother-in-law almost every day, for crying out loud!" She sighed exaggeratedly and went back to dusting the bookshelves. After a moment I couldn't help adding, "Besides, he thinks I'm married."

The duster paused. "Because of your ring, you mean? He probably didn't even notice it."

"Noooo…" Sheepishly I recounted my misleading comment about Troy. "And I'll just have to leave it at that, not that it matters. If we get to know each other through this mentoring thing, it'll just come up at some point."

"Yeah, and he'll feel like an idiot for saying he'd like to meet Troy and you not mentioning that, oh by the way, Troy is *dead*."

"Oh, well," I said helplessly. "It's done already, so stop picking on me." As it happened, Joanie would turn out to be right, but that was months in the future, and I don't want to get ahead of myself.

CHAPTER SIX:

Meeting Nadina

The next week was my turn to clean the Lean-To. I'd never been inside Daniel's place, and it was pretty spare. The kitchen was practically empty and untouched, since Daniel did all of his eating at the Palace—only a few wine glasses and coffee mugs in the sink which he hadn't bothered to return. In the bathroom I found one meager hand towel and bar of soap, and in the laundry room there wasn't even any detergent—I would have to bring it over from the Palace.

There was, however, a cozy living room with built-in bookshelves surrounding a fireplace. When Daniel was home, he spent his evenings in the Lean-To, even if Missy wasn't over; I assumed he watched television or worked when he was alone, but there didn't appear to be any television here, while his book collection was vast. People's libraries are irresistible to me, so my dusting went pretty slowly. He seemed to be a fan of the classics, and I ran my finger fondly over leatherbound editions of my favorites, but there were other, more unusual offerings: *The Complete Works of Francis Bacon*, volumes of travel essays, polar exploration, history of science, presidential biographies, British editions of *Harry Potter*. Ancient and contemporary maps hung on the wall, but the only photograph I saw was one of him as an adolescent beside a little Joanie on a fishing boat, holding up an impressive salmon. They were more wiry but recognizable and already hinting at their future extraordinary good looks.

When I went upstairs to get the laundry, I was relieved to find that Daniel was as much of a neat-freak as Phyl. His closet, like hers, looked like it had just been organized by a professional, and all the laundry was in a hamper, rather than on any available surface, floor to ceiling, like Joanie's. Even though we each did our own personal laundry, it was challenging even to dust Joanie's room, as everything lay buried beneath a thick layer of clothing and clutter. I stripped the bed, trying very hard not to think about the hard usage the sheets had been put to, and had just started the load when my cell phone rang.

It was Mark Henneman. I had only turned in my mentor application the day before, so maybe my recent history set off auto-rejection flags.

"Is this Cassandra Ewan?" he boomed. "This is Mark Henneman of Camden School."

"Hello, Mark. Yes. Please, call me Cass."

"Cass, it was great to meet you last week. Your application looks perfect, and your references checked out, and I would love to hook you up with one of our students."

I felt a butterfly in my stomach. They must be more desperate for volunteers than I thought. "You already talked to my references? I mean, that's great news."

He hesitated. "I talked this morning to Margaret Russ, and that was good enough for me."

Margaret Russ was the Congregational Care pastor at church who had led my Grief Recovery class last winter. I had listed her unwillingly—what could she say besides, "She was younger than most in the class but equally grief-stricken and angry at God"?—but in such a big church she was the pastor who knew me best. I guess if Camden School still wanted me after talking to Margaret, who was I to say no? I cleared my throat. "I can't wait to meet her—my student, I mean."

"You're going to love her!" declared Mark. "Her name is Nadina Stern, and she's a sophomore. She just joined the school this year. All the kids have heard now about the mentor program, but we haven't told them more than that because we don't know how many mentors we'll have. But you can give her a call and explain who you are, and she'll understand. Do you have a pen and paper?"

I scrambled through Daniel's empty kitchen drawers until I found a stubby pencil and an old receipt. "Shoot."

He rattled off her cell number and then told me the first optional group activity for mentors and their students would take place the Saturday after this one: a sailing trip on Lake Washington followed by a barbecue. "I'll send you that information in an email, but we're encouraging our mentors to hang out with their student before that."

"Absolutely," I said. "At least, I'll call Nadina and try to set up some times to hang out and get to know each other."

"That's the spirit! Give me a call or shoot me a message if you try to contact her and can't get a hold of her. She's got a kind of fluid living situation at this point, but she's making it to class. And remember, you don't need to solve any of her problems, just love her. Call us if you feel something's over your head."

"Okay," I said weakly. He hung up, and I sagged against the kitchen counter. What did "fluid living situation" mean? Why exactly had I thought I was qualified to do this? I remembered Kyle complaining that all the other students were druggies. Were those the problems Mark had referred to? Oh, well, too late now. But at least I could procrastinate until I was finished with the Lean-To.

On auto-pilot I put on fresh bedding and changed the towels and gave the shower stall a good scrubbing. In a hall closet I found a nicer vacuum than we had at the Palace, but after I finished the carpets, I couldn't find a broom anywhere. Guess Daniel's condo hadn't had any hardwood floors, but what had he used in the kitchen and bathrooms? I borrowed the Palace broom but made a note of everything we would need to buy for the Lean-To to make this easier in the future.

Finally there was nothing left to do, and I locked up and went back. I debated whether I should wait till after school to call Nadina, but I chickened out: voice mail would be easier to begin with. That way she could call me back when she felt like it.

To my dismay, Nadina picked up her cell phone. Glancing at my watch I saw it must be lunch. "Hello?" came her voice, high-pitched and slightly skeptical.

I cleared my throat. "Hello, Nadina. My name is Cass Ewan, and I'm calling because I signed up to be a mentor, and Mark Henneman paired us up. Have I caught you at a good time?"

"What?"

"Is this a good time to talk?" I clarified.

"Yeah, I mean I'm eating lunch."

"Oh, great. Well, I'd love to meet you and get to know you. Would you have time to get coffee after school one day this week? I could meet you at school, and we could walk to Tully's."

She must have covered her phone because I heard her voice, muffled, and some laughter. She came back on. "Yeah, okay. You wanna do today? I'm working tomorrow and Thursday, and Friday my boyfriend and I are busy."

Butterflies. "Sure, Nadina. Today would be great. What time do you get out?"

"Two forty-five."

"Okay, I'll meet you in front then, by the handicapped ramp."

"Okay, bye." She hung up before I could respond.

Crap! That was in two hours. Scrambling to my mirror, I made a hasty assessment: hair in a sloppy ponytail, smudges of dust on my face, World Vision t-shirt I'd thrown on for cleaning duty, frayed jeans. One of the consequences of being a young mom was that I hadn't bought any new clothes since before I got pregnant with Min; the most I could hope for from my existing wardrobe was vintage-three-years-ago cute.

It occurred to me that Phyl was roughly my size—a tad taller—and much better dressed, but I didn't know how she would feel about me rifling through her closet to borrow something. With Joanie I would have raided and pillaged without hesitation, as I'm sure she would do in my situation, but we didn't wear the same size. In the end I kept my faded jeans but managed to locate a more form-fitting top in a shade of brown, Troy had remarked, that exactly matched my eyes.

. . .

With five minutes till school got out, I was sitting on the bench by the entrance, clean and presentable. I'd stuffed a chapter of my novelization in my handbag, just in case I ran into Kyle. Presently students began spilling out, laughing and joking with each other in some cases, sullen and darting away in others. It wasn't hard to spot Kyle because he emerged on his own, his lanky form hunched defensively as if he couldn't wait to get away.

"Kyle!" I hollered, surprised by the surge of delight I felt in seeing him.

He glanced up, expressionless, but when he recognized me, he made his characteristic, "Huh," and came over to me. "What are you doing here?"

"I took the plunge and decided to become a mentor, so I'm meeting my student today. How are you?"

A shrug. "You working on your book?"

I nodded, scrambling to open my handbag. "Here, Kyle, you promised to check it out and tell me if it's crap. It's just a chapter, and I'm afraid I got intimidated and started with a not-too-technical one, but let me know what you think. I put my email address and phone on the last page."

He accepted the pages wordlessly and stuffed them in his backpack.

"How was school today?" I asked.

"Sucked, like always. I thought about cutting out again, but I think I want to go out for basketball, and the coach is a real hard-ass. You can't play if you have too many absences."

"Oh! That would be great! I could come watch you play," I tried to encourage him. "And so could your mentor, if you get one. I met a guy at the meeting who might be okay. He works for a video game company. They put me with a girl named Nadina Stern—do you know her?"

Kyle's mouth compressed, and he nodded. He looked around behind him at the students and gestured vaguely at a clutch of girls talking together. "She's over there." I peeked nervously around him. No one in that group seemed to be looking around for me.

"Which one?" I whispered.

"Blonde, with the loud, squeaky voice." At just that moment, the blonde smacked the girl next to her and shrieked, "Shut up! Are you *shitting* me?!"

I took a deep breath. "Okay, then, I guess I'd better introduce myself. What are your plans?"

"Kill some time at the library, then do some yard work for the basketball coach. Might have time tonight to read your crappy chapter." He almost smiled at me and then sloped off. Greetings and leavetakings were just not his thing.

Time to bite the bullet. It only took about three seconds to walk over to the group of girls, but they must have been on the lookout after all because they were all silent and staring when I reached them. "Hi," I said. "I'm Cass Ewan, and I'm supposed to meet Nadina."

"Were you talking to Kyle Bateman?" demanded a dark-haired girl. "He never talks."

"He doesn't?" I asked. "I mean, I've only just met him, and he talks to me, a little."

"Nooooo…" said another girl. She had fake black hair and large silver hoop earrings. "He thinks he's too good for this place or something because he's not a pothead, but he totally got busted for armed robbery."

"We call him Bandit," put in the third friend, while I tried to contain my astonishment. So that was the mysterious "other stuff" Kyle had dabbled in, to get kicked out of Bellevue? Armed robbery?!

I was dying for more details but forced myself to change the subject. If Kyle wanted to tell me his story, he would. "Anyhow, where can I find Nadina?" The other three girls backed away, giggling, leaving Nadina and me to stare at each other.

She was tall, taller than I was, and a little on the heavier side, though it was hard to get a clear idea of her figure because she was buried in an oversized barn jacket of brown corduroy. Pale blue eyes inspected me, framed by highlighted blonde hair, cropped short. "Henneman said your name was Cassandra."

"It is, but no one calls me that. Do you have a nickname, or is it always Nadina?"

"Always Nadina. My mom was watching TV when she was in the hospital to deliver me, and there was a soap character with that name. Before that I was going to be Brittany. Lucky she changed, though. I know about infinity Brittanys my age."

"Yeah, and I know about infinity Jennifers and Amys my age," I agreed. "You want to get a coffee or hot chocolate or something?"

She nodded, and we started walking. Nervously, I said, "So Mark Henneman said you're new to Camden School this year. How do you like it so far?"

I could tell by her expression that this was exactly the kind of question grown-ups ask and kids have to endure. "It's fine. The teachers are nice. Some of the kids are cool. I dropped out of my old high school."

"Which high school was that?"

"Winslow Homer." Winslow Homer was about twenty minutes south of Bellevue. "I dropped out because I got pregnant. I was doing lots of drugs, and my boyfriend told me the baby would be retarded or deformed or something, so I got rid of it."

Nadina had lapsed into a matter-of-fact, flat voice that I later learned was a product of having told her story so many times. Camden School relied on donations, so most students who were at all presentable were used to giving their personal histories at the drop of a hat. Nadina didn't seem embarrassed either. These were the facts.

"Then I just lost interest in school. My boyfriend thinks I should work." The knight in shining armor was still in the picture, then.

"Then how did you get here?" I prompted.

"My mom. She agreed not to hassle me about living with my boyfriend if I would go back to school. Not that I have to do what she says because she couldn't stop me, but it makes things easier if she's not pissed off at me."

That made sense to me at least, even if the choices didn't. "Do you have brothers or sisters?"

Nadina shook her head. "Nope. Just me and mom."

"She must miss you, then, if you moved out."

"I come by a lot, especially if I'm fighting with Mike."

By the time we got to Tully's, I learned that Mike was her 20-year-old boyfriend who didn't have a job at the moment and who spent a lot of his time with friends Nadina wasn't too crazy about, but she claimed they had some good times together. She and Mike were living in Mike's dad's basement, not too far from the apartment Nadina used to share with her mom. Although Mike was unemployed, he didn't seem to have any objection to Nadina working, and she had gotten a part-time job cleaning out cages and sweeping the grooming floor at a local Petco. Mike had bigger ambitions, though. "He wants to be like a music producer. He's totally into music, and he spends a lot of time in Seattle researching bands and stuff." I wondered how he supported this exploratory phase of his life but decided not to ask yet.

"How did you meet?" I said instead, stirring my tea to melt the honey. Nadina had ordered a complex, postdoc-level coffee concoction, caffeine being the licit, Northwest drug of choice for all walks of life.

"My girlfriend and I went to a party her brother was throwing. Mike and his buddies were doing some heavy shit that they shared with us. I totally threw up and passed out, and when I woke up, just Mike was there, listening to some music. I said I had this monster headache, and he made me this drink that made me feel better, and we got to talking. About a month later I got pregnant."

I thought of my own high school days; they seemed so Mayberryish that I was glad Nadina didn't ask me about them. My friends and I had gravitated toward the nerdier activities: band, yearbook, drama, youth group, journalism, French Club. There were of course kids at Bellevue who drank every weekend or got stoned or even just smoked, but they had their clique and we had ours. And my relationship with Troy—so gradual, so solidly based in friendship and mutual enjoyment and respect. It was like Nadina and I didn't come from the same universe.

Maybe because, for a brief time, I had been a mother, I found myself wondering if Nadina's mom had pictured this story for her daughter. "What does your mom do?"

Nadina spun one of her many silver rings around and around her finger. "She works in some assisted-living place. It stinks in there, but the old people are kind of sweet. Nobody visits them much because after about ten minutes you want to get the hell out. My mom works the graveyard shift. I see her mostly weekends."

"Do you still hang around with your friends, now that you live with Mike?"

"Not as much. Mike likes me around when he's around. I like the girls at this school, though. Some of them. I think we're going to see a movie this weekend."

"Do you like movies?" I asked. The Twenty Questions was getting a little old, but heck, that's getting to know adolescents. "It'd be fun to hang out a little every week, and we could see a movie or get coffee again or walk the lake or whatever."

"That'd be cool," said Nadina. She even smiled a little at me. "I like all those things." For whatever reasons—maybe we never get over high school emotionally—approval from teenagers feels ten times more rewarding than approval from other age groups.

I smiled back at her. "And they've got some kick-off activity planned for us and some of the other mentors and students next Saturday. Sailing, I think, and a barbecue."

"Fuck that!" Nadina exclaimed, quickly clapping her hand over her mouth. "Sorry, but I wanna hurl even when I go on the merry-go-round. No way am I going on a boat."

"I get seasick, too," I assured her, "But Dramamine works really well." I blushed, thinking she probably could tell me all about drugs, over-the-counter or otherwise. "I'll bring some for you, but you have to come totally sober. No mixing drugs on my watch."

"Ay ay, Captain," Nadina saluted me.

In the meantime we agreed to go for a walk the following Tuesday, and I promised to try to borrow a dog, so she could lay some of her Petco knowledge on me. I couldn't honestly say I was looking forward to it—would I have to think of another 150 questions to hold us through another hour? That meant if we spent an hour a week together, I would need to generate…let me see…over 5000 questions before school got out in June.

My thoughts in a whirl, I headed home, wondering what on earth I had gotten myself into.

CHAPTER SEVEN:

Of Cheesecake and Stained Glass

When I woke Wednesday morning, there was an email from Kyle with the poker face subject: "Your chapter." It took me a while to work up the nerve to open it; I showered, ate breakfast, answered some other messages, including two from Raquel, even cracked open one of the many books on grief or widowhood or losing a child that everyone under the sun had given me. For open house that week I'd knuckled down and invited our old couple friends the Luckers, and I figured I needed to do emotional prep. It was slogging through the "Old Friends, New Beginnings" chapter that chased me back to the email.

No salutation, of course.

> Reason everyone thinks about technology and special effects so much. Scenes without them suck big time. Chapter okay. Agen Kolar—dude with the horns who looks like he had a bad tanning session, not Confucian conehead.
> Check out links. Or give up and do kids' version, so all the friggin diehards get off your back.

Friggin' diehards like Kyle. He listed at least ten websites which would take me days to read through. The kids' version sounded like a good option. Hadn't I chosen this project so that I wouldn't have to waste time working out a plot? Instead it looked like I'd have to waste time doing enough research to make it plausible.

> Mentor guy called. One you were talking about? Said something about you too. Meeting Wed.
> Lawyers are moneysucking blowhard vampires!
> Later

He must have had a discouraging development with his lawyer. My mind wandered back to Nadina's friends' comments—how much of it was true? It wasn't like Kyle was secretive. I would just ask him.

> Kyle,
> Thank you for reading my chapter and for your corrections and suggestions. I'll take a look, but I am beginning to think this is over my head, and maybe I should do a *High School Musical* novelization instead.

I laughed out loud to think what Kyle's reaction to that would be.

> Hope you like your mentor James. Nadina and I plan on going on the sailing event—see you there?
> I know a couple lawyers. If you don't like yours, maybe they might have another they recommend. I think you said you're trying to get felony vandalism charges knocked down? Anything else?
> Cass

After a day spent reading Clone Wars back stories, it was a relief to escape to the kitchen. Dinner was a reheat-friendly, homemade spaghetti sauce with Troy's favorite twist: spicy linguiça replacing half the Italian sausage, hot enough to make Phyl's nose run.

"This is not good," she complained, blowing her nose. "Joanie and I have singles tonight, and now my nose will be red."

"The Predator might think you're drunk and an easy target and try to hit on you," Joanie said mercilessly. The Predator was the fifty-something man who attended Chaff religiously, preying on any new young women. "Remember, a quick knee to the groin and palm heel to the nose."

"Wouldn't 'no, thank you' work as well?" I asked.

"Phyl would find the self-defense moves easier than saying no to someone."

"That's not true!" Phyl laughed. "I'm getting better at it, and I actually have managed to turn the Predator down before. It wasn't even super hard because he reminds me of Jason—or what Jason will be like in twenty years." Jason was Phyl's ex-husband. "Only Jason will probably be hitting on women in bars instead of church singles groups, since he quit the church when he quit me."

Joanie and I never had nice things to say about Jason, so we usually bit our tongues. Joanie turned her attention to me. "What are your big plans tonight, girlie? Sure you don't want to come with us?"

"No way! I may be old, but if the Predator gets desperate enough he might go for me. Besides, I wanted to make that cheesecake for tomorrow. Do we have a head count?"

"Don't bother asking us," said Joanie. "Better ask Daniel when he comes home."

● ● ●

Cheesecake was something I hadn't made in years, but I had a good recipe, the kind with sour cream topping that covered any surface cracks. I was pulling the baked graham-cracker crust out of the oven when Daniel came home. I hadn't seen much of him this week; the couple times he came home at a normal hour he had Missy with him, and Missy made it clear that she didn't want to socialize. It made me slightly uncomfortable to have him catch me in the kitchen with an apron on. Too Mrs. Cleaver or something. At least when Missy was with him, I felt more like Alice on *The Brady Bunch*.

"Smells great. What is that?" he asked, dropping his briefcase and gym bag by the barstools, and running his hand through his hair. He must have just showered because the blond spikes were still damp.

"It's the spaghetti I made, but this here will be a cheesecake for tomorrow. By the way, should we be expecting the barbarian hordes? Joanie wants to grill salmon, but we don't want to put it on the endangered species list."

"I'll rein it in, then," he answered lightly, taking the plate and glass I offered him. "I think just Michelle and me."

"You mean Missy. Her name is Missy, for Pete's sake." I pushed the spinach salad toward him.

"No, actually, her name is Michelle. Missy and I are…taking a break."

"Oh," I said, blushing. Turning away, I dumped the cream cheese and eggs in the mixer and switched it on. Sugar, vanilla, lemon zest. Once, when I had been using my stand mixer, I lifted Min up to see the beater rotating. When I put her down, she turned round and round across the kitchen floor, to show me what she'd seen.

"Are you sorry to see her go?" Daniel broke into my thoughts. For a second I was confused and thought he meant Min.

I shook my head to clear it. "No. I mean, it's none of my business. I'm sure Michelle will have her…strong points as well." Knowing Daniel, I'm sure she'd have at least two very strong points. Wanting to change the subject I added, "Do you know much about criminal law?"

"Why, have you done something naughty?"

"No, a…a friend of mine did." His flirty tone made me uncomfortable, but I couldn't help grinning when I said this. "Do you know, for instance, if vandalism can be considered a felony?"

"You were going to repaint your room, weren't you? Are you trying to tell me something? Should I go take a look?"

What was the deal with him? "I promise you it's not me, and my room looks fine. Be serious and answer the question."

He sat back thoughtfully. "Well, I'm going off of two quarters of criminal law years ago, but I'm pretty sure that vandalism is considered a misdemeanor until you exceed a certain dollar amount in damage. I don't know Washington State's threshold."

"Does it make a difference if it's a minor?" I pressed.

"It makes a difference in who has to pay for it. The minor's parents are probably liable, but the minor himself would be the one arrested or doing time or facing charges."

"So then, what would it mean if the prosecutor diverted? Would that mean you wouldn't face charges?"

"If it's a first-time offense, oftentimes the prosecutor will want to give the kid a chance to rehabilitate and make restitution, without getting a ding on his record. I imagine a property crime would fall in that bucket." Daniel's mouth twisted in characteristic amusement, his heavy-lidded eyes meeting mine. "Quite the conversation. I wouldn't have let you live here, you know, if I didn't think you were a good church girl. I hope you're not falling in with the wrong crowd."

"Yeah, and I thought you said they weren't coming to open house this week," I retorted. It annoyed me that Daniel seemed incapable of conversing with a woman without having that flirtatious edge. It was only absent when he spoke to Joanie or Phyl. Joanie was obviously, but why not Phyl? I pondered this while pouring the filling into the springform pan. Did he suspect flirting with Phyl would make a giant mess of things, but I was safe? I was a broken-hearted widow, for crying out loud—show some respect.

Gingerly I placed the cheesecake in the oven and set the timer. Between the spaghetti and the dessert, I'd managed to dirty every bowl, pot, and utensil in the place, and it took me some time to clean up. When I finally finished, I snuck a peek at Daniel. To my surprise, he was perusing my *David Copperfield*, which I'd left on the table. He must have felt my eyes on him because he looked up. "Yours, I gather? Joanie only reads books which are sub-200 pages."

I nodded. "Mine. I'm kind of a Dickens nut. When it comes to good books, I think the longer the better. I even like his long-winded descriptions. The only thing I don't like is that every book seems to have at least one character I can't stand."

He waved *David Copperfield*. "Uriah Heep?" he guessed.

"He's awful, too," I agreed, "But it's Steerforth who drives me nuts."

Daniel's gaze flicked away, out the bay window. "Because he's a seducer?"

Was that a *conscience* smiting him? I smothered a giggle. "No! I mean, it's bad that he ruins Little Em'ly, but what really bugs me is how David is so trusting of someone who only uses him. It's the same reason that I want to wring Mr. Skimpole's neck in *Bleak House*." I couldn't quite believe I was having this conversation with him. Apparently discussing literature could effectively jolt him out of perpetual flirtation mode.

"Steerforth takes advantage of David Copperfield, and Skimpole takes advantage of Mr. Jarndyce, but does it necessarily follow that the users don't love the ones they use?"

"That isn't love," I objected. "That's…fondness…for someone who indulges your self-love without giving you any trouble. Real love is thinking about the other before you think of yourself. Thinking about the good of the other, even if it puts you at a disadvantage or costs you something." He didn't answer, and I felt suddenly embarrassed by my earnestness. Cripe, I'd be quoting the Bible at him next.

It appeared to have bounced off the Teflon, however. He laid my book back down and gathered his things. "Well, I've got some trade secrets to protect before I hit the hay tonight," he said lightly. "Enjoy your book, Cass." That sly look returned. "Unless you'd rather hold my pens."

"Your what?" I gasped, almost dropping the tub of sour cream.

"Pens. *Pens*. Like Dora Copperfield does for David. What on earth did you think I said?"

"Never mind," I muttered, turning away to hide my scarlet face. I heard him laughing softly as he let himself out the back door.

• • •

Our second open house was much quieter.

Dave and Sandy Lucker showed up, looking as awkward and nervous as I did, at first. We hadn't really spent much time together in the past year, and when I congratulated Sandy on her new pregnancy, she stammered and teared up, assuming I was feeling terrible about Min, which I actually hadn't been until she made me think I ought to, and then I teared up, too, confirming her fears. Ugh.

Sandy and I had never been total kindred spirits, but we had gotten along well enough to make the Luckers our closest couple friends. Dave and Troy were much more compatible: they met on a church service day when they were both assigned to carpentry, and found additional common ground at work and weekly pick-up basketball. Sandy and I bonded over our daughters: little Claire Lucker was a girl exactly Min's age. Ordinarily Sandy could talk indefatigably about Claire—something I had found tedious when I still had a daughter of my own—but now, with the emotional embargo on the subject, Sandy seemed at a loss.

"Do you have Claire signed up for anything?" I asked.

"Oh, yes!" Sandy glowed. "I found this great Mommy & Me ballet class at the Arts Center. Claire just loves it and wants to 'practice' with me all the time, and she even wanted her leotard to match mine. It is the cutest thing… It's—that is—we like it." She trailed off uncomfortably.

As for Dave, he and I couldn't get much beyond how his job was going, and he took frequent refuge in talking to Roy or Daniel, while shooting me occasional furtive looks. If my anxiety for their anxiety hadn't been so exhausting, I might have pitied their pity for me. As it was, I was grateful for my new house and housemates because they didn't excite any painful compassion, and we could converse as a large group without having constantly to avoid emotional landmines. Phyl's sangria didn't hurt, either.

Roy was on a roll that week with Joanie because he had scraped together several first-round interviews with different companies. His unemployed status was cramping their dating style, and they had only seen each other at church and Chaff because Roy didn't want Joanie to treat. Even for the open house he had done his part, showing up with a respectable orzo salad that was his own creation.

Phyl was 0-for-2 on the invites, and I was secretly hoping the Luckers would go home early and leave us free to play another game of Scrabble.

Missy's replacement Michelle was the assertive brunette I remembered from last week, and I preferred her to Missy, if only for the fact that she didn't seem so desperate for attention. She was an architect in a firm that shared Daniel's office building in downtown Seattle, and she was refreshingly smart and confident. When I whispered as much to Joanie, Joanie only cracked, "Yeah, and I bet Daniel's been studying her form and function." He looked willing to learn, turning on the full charm for her, and she was smart enough to hold herself a little apart.

After yesterday's odd conversation with him, I was relieved that he hardly seemed to notice my presence, although I might have preferred disrespectful flirtation to walking on eggshells with the Luckers. Phyl, however, was a little cast down by Michelle's superiority and was trying to make up for it by being extra nice to her.

"I think that's wonderful, that new high-rise your firm designed going up on Camden and Northeast 6th," Phyl said warmly, "Did you play a part in that?"

"They actually gave me the atrium," Michelle answered. "I had a great vision for this multi-story waterfall dropping down the center of the grand staircase against a stained-glass backdrop, but alas—cost-cutting measures. The glass made it in, but the waterfall had to go, and the staircase turned out to be much more utilitarian." She gave a graceful shrug.

"I love stained glass," Phyl enthused. "The company that did the glass for our new church building did a beautiful job."

"It's probably the same company the builders are using. There aren't many in the area—Ascensions and Crucifixions aren't such a growth industry anymore." A hint of condescension tinged her voice. "In fact, I wanted my design to reflect a new, secular spirituality, a yearning for transcendence. You know, the human race, kind of, *outgrowing* the chains that held us back."

Phyl looked abashed, but I saw Joanie sitting up a little straighter. "What kind of chains?" she asked innocently. Joanie loved philosophical discussions.

"Well, chains like religion and old ways of thinking," Michelle said, with an apologetic smile at Phyl.

"That sounds good," said Joanie. "No more religion and old ways of thinking. What are we growing toward? What is our new source of transcendence?"

Michelle sat up a little straighter. "I would say…compassion. And peace based on tolerance for people's differences. Growing toward… our potential…Love, I guess."

"Love? Oh, I thought you were describing toleration," said Joanie. "What kind of love? What do you mean by love?"

Michelle threw a glance at Daniel, as if to say *what's with your intense sister*? but he merely shrugged. One got the sense that she could throw around phrases like "secular spirituality" and "yearning for transcendence" at the office without anyone questioning her. "By love I mean love! We recognize our common humanity. I let you be you, and you let me be me, and we don't throw bombs at each other."

"But what if me being me hurts you? Or what if you being you hurts me? Or what if you being you hurts you? What would love do in that situation?"

"I'm not following," Michelle said impatiently. "Are we in college again? This feels like a freshman dorm talk."

"I don't get what you mean by love," persisted Joanie. "If people love me, I hope that would mean more than being nice and not throwing bombs at me. How much do you really love me, if you don't actually care what the hell I do or think, even if it's harmful? How much do I really love you, if I don't care what the hell you do or think, even if it hurts you? Is that really love I'm feeling for you, or is it just…just…"

"Fondness," interrupted Daniel, "for someone who indulges your self-love without giving you any trouble." It would be hard to say whose mouth fell open the hardest—maybe a three-way tie between Joanie, Michelle, and me. Briefly his eyes met mine, and I couldn't read his expression.

Michelle was done. "All I meant was I think it's possible as a race to be humane and compassionate and loving without all the religious baggage," she snapped.

"That would be a lovely development," Joanie mused. "And since religion and old ways of thinking haven't changed much about us as a race, I sure hope your stained glass will do the trick."

"Should we get started on the cheesecake?" Phyl piped up hurriedly, when Michelle looked ready to blow. "I'll get a pot of decaf on."

Dessert marked a philosophical truce, and deliverance came shortly after: Dave and Sandy invoked the twelve-year-old babysitter and left at 8:30, with vague assurances on both sides to get together again soon; Roy and Joanie plopped on the couch to watch a movie; Phyl and I got the Scrabble board out; and Daniel and Michelle left to enjoy what Joanie called "second helpings of cheesecake."

"I don't think she liked getting into it with me," Joanie remarked, trying to skip through the movie previews.

"Joanie, no one likes wrestling with their foundational beliefs like you do," I said. "You thought you were having an intellectual discussion, but I think Michelle thought you were trying to attack her. You make everything a contact sport."

"Oh!" Joanie exclaimed, genuinely surprised. "Well, it'll be a good opportunity for her to practice her compassion and tolerance for me, then. I mean her love for me. It'll make for better stained glass in the atrium."

"I wanted to hear more about the stained glass, like what on earth transcendence looks like," Phyl mourned, "but now it'll be such a touchy subject I can't bring it up anymore."

"We'll just have to go see it when it's done," Joanie said unfeelingly, "A little transcendence field trip."

I couldn't resist. "A—a—secular spirituality spree."

"An out-of-body outing," threw in Roy, to our delight.

"Think of the upside," Joanie said, when we stopped laughing. "Maybe I've irritated her so much that she'll dump Daniel before he can dump her."

CHAPTER EIGHT:

Icebreakers

A dog fell in our laps over the weekend.

When Phyl and her husband Jason divorced, there were no children to fight over, so they fought for custody of their apricot Labradoodle puppy, Benny. Like many a child of divorce, Benny shuttled back and forth, bewildered, alternate Saturdays, ears drooping as he listened to his "parents" argue over how best to raise him. Because Phyl and Jason wouldn't bend to each other, Benny was faced with learning completely separate sets of commands, all of which he now obeyed imperfectly. With time their acrimony faded, however, and Phyl was willing to give up shared custody to move into the no-pets-allowed Palace, with the understanding that Benny could make the occasional brief visit.

Joanie and I cordially hated Jason for how he had treated Phyl, and I suspect the feeling was mutual, but we all managed polite small talk when he came by with the dog. Benny fell on the bigger, fleecier end of the Labradoodle spectrum, and he vaulted out of Jason's sedan to leap up on each of us in turn, trying and mostly succeeding in getting in a good face lick.

"Down!" yelled Phyl. "Off!" barked Jason. Benny ignored both and wriggled and sniffed excitedly.

"You're looking good, Philly," said Jason, checking her out in a way that made me want to hit him. He turned to appraise the house while Benny capered about, tearing through Phyl's flower beds. "Nice place you got here. You say this is Joanie's brother's?"

She nodded. Jason was the only person Phyl ever spoke to with any sharpness in her voice. "That's right. So you'll be back from New York on Thursday?"

"Yep. Jessica and I will take in a few shows between my meetings, maybe check out the Met. She's the arty type." Jason was always sure to mention his latest love whenever he saw Phyl. We half-expected to hear her measurements. "I'll come by Friday for Benny. Glad this could work out."

Phyl set up Benny's bed in the utility room and his bowls in the kitchen. She had bought a couple new chew toys for the occasion, which Benny gnawed and growled over appreciatively, and things had calmed down somewhat by the time Daniel and Michelle made their appearance. Michelle had been a little cool toward us since Thursday night, and having Benny launch himself at her crotch for a sniff didn't seem to help matters.

"Down! Off! Leave it!" commanded Phyl, grabbing Benny's collar and hauling him off. "Sorry, sorry. He's just here for a few days while my ex is out of town."

"'Leave it' got Benny's attention, I think," said Joanie. "Leave it, Benny! Leave the crotch."

Michelle smiled sourly.

I sprang up. "Let's take him for a walk, Phyl," I suggested. "Get some of his energy out."

"Good idea," said Joanie, "Before he humps Michelle's knee."

That first walk was quite the adventure for Benny. He dashed after birds and squirrels, burrowed under neighbors' hedges, engaged in long sniffing encounters with fellow canines. After a solid forty-five minutes we returned, but Benny was rewardingly mellow the rest of the day. For the sake of household peace, I walked Benny on Sunday and Monday as well, and even pre-walked him Tuesday before meeting Nadina, so he would be calmer.

At 2:40 I was on the bench outside the school, and at 2:45 the students began spilling out again. As I hoped, Kyle slouched over to see me, squatting down to get face-to-face with Benny. He had never answered my email but now said without preamble, "I had this lame-ass computer science teacher who didn't know jack but thought he was seriously Bill Gates in disguise. If I tried to correct him, he got really pissed off, so he started always talking down to me in class, and I got pissed off too. One day I told him what he could do with himself, and then I broke into the classroom. I did some redecorating and hacked into his computer and gave the whole class A-pluses."

It was the longest speech from him yet, although he delivered it entirely to Benny's left ear while he scratched him. By the end of it, Benny was snuffling Kyle's long hair and whimpering ecstatically from all the attention.

"Oh, Kyle," I said, "I'm sorry you thought you had to do that. But that's all you did, right?"

His rare smile flashed. "Isn't it enough?"

I saw Nadina and her friends emerging and waved. The dark-haired girl leaned close to whisper something to the others, and they erupted in laughter. "More than enough—don't get me wrong. But did you know they have a nickname for you here?"

His stony face returned. "Yeah…'Bandit' or some dumb name like that. I ignore them."

"But why 'Bandit'?" I persisted.

Benny was licking Kyle's face, so Kyle shoved him away and stood up. "I didn't steal anything, if that's what you mean. Maybe they couldn't spell 'Vandal' or 'Trespasser.'" He shrugged off my puzzlement. "So what's your deal, Cass? Did you really sell out and switch to friggin' *High School Musical*?"

"Are you kidding? After mixing up Agen Kolar with Ki-Adi-Mundi, you think I'm going to risk losing even more of your respect?" I fumbled in my handbag. "Here. Here's another chapter. Check out my Clone Wars research and techno-wizardry and let me know what you think."

Taking it, he started to walk away, causing Benny to strain at the leash. I called after him, "Wait! Will I see you Saturday? Are you going to the mentor thing?"

Walking backward, he nodded once and headed off down the hill. I was still watching him when I felt the leash jerk again and found Nadina beside me, her friends moving away in the other direction. Like Kyle she bent down to love on that ridiculous dog.

"You like Bateman, don't you?" Nadina asked, letting Benny lick her ear.

"I do," I answered. "I like him a lot. More than this dog, for instance. But I brought Benny the Wonderdoodle for you. My friend's ex-husband dropped him off for a few days."

"He's a beautiful boy—who's a beautiful boy?" Nadina crooned at Benny, who rolled around on his back like a moron. She took the leash from me, and we started off toward the lake.

Nadina really did have a gift with animals, or dogs at least. She patiently ran through all the range of commands and variations and figured out which ones Benny responded to—Phyl would be irked to know most of them were Jason's—and then worked with him on walking properly on a leash. First she would set off in one direction down the paved path, and the second Benny's attention wavered,

Nadina would whip around and go another direction, yanking Benny along with her. After a few minutes of this, he learned to keep an eye on Nadina and save himself some discomfort. It helped that she was so tall and strong; I doubted I would have the same success when I walked Benny home.

"Where did you learn all this?" I asked from my vantage point on the park bench. "Petco ought to have you teach some dog training classes."

"Yeah, I've been kissing the dog trainer's ass for a month now, and I think she's going to let me assist her, next class," Nadina replied. She stopped and rewarded Benny with scratching around his floppy ears. "I learned it from my grandpa. He got a King Charles spaniel puppy when I was little, and I watched him train her."

"Did you spend a lot of time with your grandparents?"

"I lived with them till fifth grade. My mom was off finding herself or something like that, and I've never met my dad. But when Grandpa died, Mom had to come back and get me because Grandma was losing it." Nadina sat down next to me on the bench, looping Benny's leash around one of the slats. "I miss him."

Coming fresh as I was off of our first mentors' training ("Building trust"), I felt a thrill of eagerness that Nadina was already willing to show a little vulnerability. We were told that students typically were hesitant to trust, based on histories of hurt and abandonment, and we were not supposed to force their confidences. As casually as I could I asked, "What was he like?"

"Big guy—I'm built like him. And he smoked for fifty years, so he was always sounding like he was going to hack up a lung. He made me promise when I was nine that I would never, ever smoke."

"And do you?"

She looked insulted. "No! I promised him!" Her zeal made me sorry he hadn't also sworn her off of drugs, alcohol and loser boyfriends.

I waited to see if she wanted to say anything else, maybe tell me about her own vices of choice, but she didn't. We talked instead about incidentals: the movie she'd seen with Sonya and Carly from school, an irate woman at Petco, the book they were reading in English. Mike wasn't happy with Nadina being so busy, apparently, but neither did she seem willing to go into more detail. True to teenage form, she didn't ask me any questions about myself, apart from wondering what I kept giving Kyle. When I told her, she lost interest and didn't pursue it further.

After we had been sitting and talking for some time, Benny spied some ducks and almost hung himself trying to chase them, forgetting his leash was tied up. Laughing, we released him to shoot across the grass and flounder a few feet into the lake, where the ducks took wing and escaped. He trotted back, dripping and pleased with himself, and we took that as our signal to walk back to the school.

"See you Saturday," I reminded her at the bus stop. "I'll be the one with the Dramamine."

· · ·

Because late September weather can be hit or miss, I was relieved to wake up to sunshine. Nadina could hardly dread sailing more than I did; I think the last non-ferry boat I had been on was the tourist barf-o-rama from Naples to Capri, a cruise that made top-five for Worst Memories Related to Physical Discomfort (only outscored by childbirth and late pregnancy). At least today would be no storm-whipped cruise. There was nothing to do but pop my Dramamine and put a brave face on it and hope the boat would be big enough to leave me nothing to do.

Nadina and I agreed I would pick her up in front of the school and we would carpool to the yacht-owners' house on Hunt's Point.

When I pulled up I couldn't help chuckling because her look of disgusted misery mirrored the one I was hiding. Wordlessly I handed her the Dramamine, and she choked it down with her smoothie. "I didn't want to do a solid breakfast this morning, in case I puke later," she said morosely.

The Hillards were major donors to Camden School, and they had graciously offered to skipper us on their cruising yacht and then host a barbecue lunch afterward in their spacious backyard. Troy had often teased me that I raised getting lost to an art form; sure enough, we were fifteen minutes late after having missed the camouflaged turn-off down to the water a couple times.

The rest of the group had already gathered on the back deck. I recognized Mark Henneman chatting up a middle-aged couple I took to be the Hillards, booming out in his cheerful voice, while everyone else stood around in loose pairs of ill-at-ease mentor and sullen student. Way off at the end of the dock I could see Kyle's lanky form dwarfing James'. At least they seemed to be talking.

Catching sight of us, Mark exclaimed, "Cass and Nadina! Wonderful! We're all here now. Let me introduce you to the Hillards and get you some life jackets." I saw Nadina rolling her eyes as she fumbled into her purple-and-aqua number and slapped a dorky name tag on it.

Mark told me that not all students had mentors yet. For the time being it was mentor triage, with newer, less-established students getting them, to give them a firm foundation. Fortunately for Nadina's happiness, her friend Sonya was also there, accompanied by the sweet old lady of the appliqué jacket whose bravery had put me to shame, and the girls quickly went to stand by each other. After chatting briefly with Sonya's mentor Louella, I made my way down the dock to Kyle and James.

Somehow James managed to look jaunty in the ridiculously bright life jacket. He was saying something about Xbox versus Playstation, but when he saw me he broke off and reached out to shake my hand, grinning. "Hey there, Cass, good to see you again. Kyle was just telling me about how your book is coming."

I gave Kyle an accusing look, and James added hastily, "No worries. Kyle specifically assured me that it's *not crap*."

"Coming from Kyle that's almost like winning the Pulitzer Prize," I joked. Kyle said nothing, only giving his characteristic shrug. "Well, thank you, Kyle. I appreciate you reading it for me. I'm getting faster now; I think chapters four and five are ready for your discerning eye."

"And if you feel up to it, shoot me a chapter or two," James said. "We lost one of our writers to Nintendo this past week—maybe you could do a little for us on a contract basis." He fished in his wallet for a business card: James Kittredge, Producer, Free Universe. A little logo of the Milky Way floating above a hand.

"'Producer,'" I murmured, impressed.

"A fancy word for Project Manager," James said quickly. "I try to keep all the actual workers in line, on task and on time."

"Well, with Kyle's approval I certainly feel confident enough to let you see it. Maybe I'll send two chapters, one technical and one not?"

"Perfect. Then give us a little while on our end to pass it around the office to some of the different development teams, and we'll be in business."

Mrs. Hillard clapped then to get everyone's attention. "Welcome again, everyone, to our home. Before we get under way, we just want to go over some basic sailing terminology and safety requirements, so if I could please have your attention. How many of you have sailed before?" Puking in a bag on my way to Capri surely didn't count, so I kept my hand down. Only a few of hands were raised, Louella's among them. "Just so," said Mrs. Hillard. "We don't expect much from you all except to duck if we say duck and practice some basic safety measures." She went over these—the main one being to keep one hand for holding on to the boat so that we wouldn't lose our balance—and indicated which parts of the boat were good for clutching onto: rails, side stays, mast, lifelines.

Nadina sidled over to me and muttered, "This is too much to remember—I'm just going to hang on to you, Cass."

"Good luck with that plan," I replied shortly.

In the event, our little cruise didn't require us to test our new knowledge. The Hillards did most of the work, with occasional help from the few experienced sailors; the rest of us were free to enjoy the breeze and sunshine and sparkle off the lake. The mountains were out—Rainier glowed blue-white and almost within reach. Something big must have been going on at Husky Stadium; we saw the cars backed up on the bridge, and the traffic jam added to our feeling of freedom. It was impossible not to relax; Nadina shrieked with laughter whenever the boat heeled unexpectedly, Sonya spotted a flipping fish, the grumpy older man Ray pointed out landmarks familiar to us all from childhood, and I even saw Kyle smiling. Maybe because we were the only two mentors there under 50 years old, James and I frequently caught each other's eye when one of the kids did or said something humorous and would look away before we could laugh.

Too soon it was over, but the good spirits carried over to the barbecue. Mark Henneman had us play a game where each mentor and mentee had ten minutes to find all the things they had in common, the crazier the better, and he gave us a list of possibilities to get us going: favorite books or movies, places we had been, names of people we had dated, shared talents or physical characteristics.

Nadina whipped the list out of my hand and moaned, "We're gonna lose! We won't have anything!"

"How do you know?" I countered. "We just have to be creative. Where were you born?"

"Federal Way. How about you?"

"Bellevue. But they're both in the same county. We'll say we were born in the same county. And your boyfriend is Mike. I dated a Michael in high school for two weeks."

"That's two things. You're married, right? What's your husband's name?" Nadina asked, getting into it.

"Troy," I said, after hesitating briefly. Is there ever a good time to mention someone is dead? Surely I could be forgiven for not squelching all Nadina's enthusiasm for the icebreaker.

"No way! Before I met Mike I really liked this guy named Troy who was on the Winslow Homer basketball team. He kind of liked me too, for a while."

"My Troy played high school basketball, too," I said. Nice that her Troy was also in the past tense.

By the end of ten minutes, when Mark asked us to wrap it up, we had compiled a respectable list.

"Okay," said Mark, "how many of you pairs found at least ten things in common?"

Several raised their hands. Nadina grabbed my arm and held it up in the air with hers. "Fifteen things?" A few pairs put their hands down. "Twenty things?" Only we and Kyle and James remained. "Twenty-five things?" James put his hand down.

"Whoo hoo!" yelled Nadina, punching the air. Mark asked us to share some of the things we had discovered, but when I reached for the list to edit a few of them, Nadina whisked it away. "Let me see... Cass and I both thought we might puke today. We both have moles on our ass—" (She danced away from my hand.) "We both dated guys named Mike, but her Mike dumped her, and we both dated guys named Troy who played basketball, only my Troy dumped me, and hers married her."

At least her phrasing was vague enough that you didn't know if Troy was alive or dead. If I added any more people to the Elvis-lives list, I would have to stage Troy's death on national TV to set the record straight. Mark Henneman must have noticed my quandary because he quickly moved on to the others. Nadina and I unearthed the most things in common, but not the most unusual, unless you counted the mole. Sonya and Louella could both tie a cherry stem in a knot with their tongues; Ray and his student Tan were both in a hot-dog-eating contest; and Kyle and James each won the same geek-sta rap CD at some video game conference in Seattle last month.

"If you both won the same CD at the same conference, did you run into each other there?" I asked.

James slapped Kyle on the back, I kid you not. "I dunno, Kyle—were you one of the eight hundred guys wearing glasses and a fanny pack?"

"Dude," rasped Kyle, "I thought that was you." He actually smiled again—twice in one day!—while James laughed heartily.

• • •

"I didn't know Bateman ever talked," Nadina remarked on the ride back. "He never talks in school. He must like his mentor guy."

"I think he does," I answered, smiling to myself. "They're both smart and know lots about video games and *StarWars* and such."

"Yeah…" she played with the window control, up down up down. "Mike doesn't talk much to me, but he talks to his guy friends about the music stuff. Does Troy talk to you?"

I took a deep breath. Time to take the bull by the horns. We were pulling up at the school, and I deliberately waited to answer until I shut down the engine, so that I could look at her. "Nadina, this is kind of weird, but Troy doesn't talk to me at all. Because he died about fifteen months ago. I'm a widow."

"Shut *up!*" she shrieked. "That is not even funny to joke about."

I grimaced apologetically but didn't know what to say. For some reason, maybe because my secretly-dead husband was beginning to loom comically large in my Camden School doings, I didn't feel that treacherous tightening in my throat.

Her mouth popped open, then shut. She made several attempts to speak, all unsuccessful. I put my hand on her arm to reassure her. "It's okay. I don't know what to say either. He had a heart condition no one knew about, and he just died very suddenly while he was driving. We had a little girl, who was with him in the car, and—and—she's gone too." Nadina's mouth continued to work, and some objective part of my mind noticed she looked a little like a fish after it's been landed on the boat deck.

"You're all alone?" Nadina finally managed. "That really sucks."

"Not all alone," I said hastily. "I was alone for a while, but now I'm living with some good friends, and I still have them and family and church and even my in-laws."

She looked at me skeptically. "Really," I persisted. "The last month has been the best since the accident, and today was so fun I almost forgot about it. Let's not end the day on this note. Are we hanging out Tuesday?"

Nadina continued to stare at me, and I wondered if she would want a mentor trade-in. Maybe it was too much to ask: not just— surprise! I have a dead husband—but wait, there's more! My daughter also died! I underestimated her, however, and what she had been through herself.

After another moment Nadina shrugged and started to get out of the car. "Works for me. See you then."

CHAPTER NINE

Going Deeper

"So what was your daughter like?" Nadina asked me one afternoon, some weeks later.

It had taken her some while to return to the subject, but I discovered talking about Troy and Min to someone who didn't know them was unexpectedly easier. I found myself lifting the lid on those boxes of memory I tried to stuff under the bed: what Min had been like and what I had dreamed of for her; how Troy had been my husband and best friend.

We were at the lake again, having walked Benny. Nadina and I spent most of our weekly time going for walks, with Benny whenever I happened to have him—Benny, who showed improvement for every hour spent with Nadina. (Phyl remarked on it, and even Jason complimented Phyl on finally showing dominance over Benny: "I've always told you, Philly, you weren't aggressive enough. You've got to show dogs you're the alpha. Glad to see you're finally getting some backbone.")

When it rained we got coffee at Tully's or walked to the Palace. No one was ever home at that hour, and Nadina got a kick out of exploring my natural habitat. "It helps me to picture you," she said, "Not sobbing into your pillow every night but living in a big house with a view." This October day was glorious, however, clear and blessedly dry. Clyde Hill's many maple trees had flamed into gold and russet, and we were perched on our favorite bench looking across the water to downtown Seattle.

"Min was a split between Troy and me," I remembered. "Everyone said she looked like me but she acted like Troy. Even though she was so little, she already liked to tease me. Like how I was about pacifiers. She would hear me preaching to my mom or someone about how I didn't like pacifiers, so whenever she came across one at someone else's house, she would instantly stick it in her mouth and come show me, just to torture me. She'd be grinning so hard around it that it would almost fall out."

"Cass, you're such a hard-ass. What's wrong with pacifiers?" Nadina asked.

"Oh, I had ideas about not messing up her orthodonture. I had lots of ideas you'd call hard-ass: no pacifiers, no sweets, no television, but it all didn't matter after all, did it?"

"If you had another baby, would you still say no pacifiers, no sweets, no television?"

In my stomach I felt a sudden tensing, like the tensing I felt when Joanie bugged me about dating again, only more severe. "No more babies," I said, before I thought.

She stared at me. "What do you mean, 'no more babies'? Weren't you just telling me all these things you liked about Min? You don't want to have a kid again someday?"

That airless feeling was back, and I found myself stretching my chest to fight it off. "It's because I liked Min that I don't want any more babies," I said. "It doesn't matter anyhow—I'm not married or even wanting to date again—" I trailed off when I realized I was saying this to the girl who had been both unmarried and pregnant. I don't know if she made the same connection, but she was silent for a long time.

To change the subject I asked, "How has Mike's music research been going?" Although I'd never met him, I pictured him as a giant oaf, taller than she, with hair hanging in his eyes and matting the backs of his hands, the kind of savage beast only calmed by music. This imagined-Mike lumbered around Seattle, haunting nightclubs and pubs from Belltown to Pioneer Square.

Her face closed off, and she shrugged. To give her time to think, I gingerly picked up Benny's slobbery chewy and launched it down onto the beach for him to fetch. This was an activity I used to avoid at all costs, even when Benny would come and bludgeon me repeatedly with whatever toy was on hand, but it was less onerous now that, when he returned, he would drop it on command.

"He hasn't talked about it lately. Sometimes I'm not sure if he even likes me anymore," Nadina said finally.

Like he liked you before? I thought sarcastically, thinking of him urging hard drugs on her, knocking her up, and then convincing her to get an abortion. Out loud I said, "Why is that?"

Another long pause before she answered. "He tells me I'm a drag now because I'm in school and I've been trying to use less."

While my first urge was to find stupid Mike and wring his neck, I realized this was the first time Nadina had ever mentioned her drug habit to me, and I had to tread carefully. "What would he like you to do?"

"He says I was more fun when he met me. I would do the hard stuff with him, and I wasn't going to school, so I was making more money and hanging out with him more. He doesn't like that I do stuff with girls from Camden and that when I'm home I haven't wanted to party unless it's the weekend. Drop it, Benny." Nadina threw his toy for him again, while I waited for her to continue. "And he—he doesn't like that I hang out with you."

"Me?" I exclaimed, "He doesn't even know me!"

She looked a little sheepish. "Yeah, but I've told him about you. He thinks you're the reason I've started being a drag."

At another time I might have laughed at her teenage tactlessness. "What do you mean?"

"Well, he thinks I might be trying to use less because you're trying to make me be a goody-goody like you."

Resisting the urge to swell up with indignation, I said as calmly as I could, "That's weird, considering I've never said one picking thing to you about using or not using. We haven't even talked about it until now. What do you think?"

She squirmed a little. "I don't know. I guess you haven't talked about it. It was more the counselors at school."

"Then why would he think I'm a goody-goody? What have you told him about me?" I persisted.

Nadina tugged on the toy in Benny's mouth, and he gave some delighted growls.

"I don't know, Cass. He doesn't like you or the school. Let's go because my butt is getting cold on this bench." Clearly, the borderline-intimate talk was over, and I kicked myself inwardly for pressing too hard. But at least I had learned a few things: she was trying to cut down her drug usage, she was committed enough to school to irritate Mike, and somehow I was becoming a lightning rod in their relationship.

. . .

Only Phyl was home when I got back, sorting through the recycling in the garage. Joanie and I were not completely clear on which items went into which bin, and Daniel didn't even try, so Phyl was always digging Starbucks cups out of the recycle and tossing them in the yard waste, or picking Tetra-Paks out of the trash and throwing them in the recycle.

My relationship with Nadina was not the only one to deepen that fall: Joanie and Phyl and I grew closer as well. I hadn't realized how friendships suffer after you have a baby. Everything with Min was so new, so all-involving; not only had my marriage shifted and re-adjusted around the new person in our lives, but my friendships unconsciously dropped in priority. Certainly Joanie and I had managed to see each other or to talk every couple weeks—once a month, at the worst—but I spent most of what little social time I had in playgroups, mom's groups, stealing a little adult conversation while the kids toddled around, fighting over toys and swapping germs. Renewed friendships weren't a replacement for my loss, but they were a precious gift in themselves, that daily involvement in each other's lives and concerns.

"Hey, Phyl," I greeted her, holding tight to Benny's leash so he wouldn't topple her in his eagerness. "Need help?"

"Nah, it's all done," she replied, taking the unrecyclable lids she'd removed from the gallon milk containers and tossing them in the trash. "Come talk to me while I finish dinner, though." I went, feeling slightly guilty because I knew Joanie and I were planning to ambush Phyl tonight at dinner.

As we had feared, Phyl's predictable attraction to Daniel had blossomed with time into a full-blown infatuation. Although she hadn't yet progressed beyond mooning over him, it had not escaped his notice. Joanie told me confidentially that Daniel had finally asked her what the hell Phyl's problem was.

"I told him she always fell for bad boys, including her ex-husband, and he should just ignore her till it blew over," Joanie reported to me late one evening when we were holed up in my room. "He said it was bugging the hell out of him how he couldn't be in the Palace without her gawking at him and dropping dishes and acting like they were in junior high."

"Isn't he used to it, by now?" I asked in exasperation. "I thought all women react to him that way."

"Yeah, but he can get away from other women when they act like that. He hates clinginess and possessiveness and adulation. It's hard for him to have to live with Phyl. Didn't you notice how much more time he's spending in the Lean-To lately?"

I hadn't, since I only saw Daniel occasionally anyhow, and when he found only me in the kitchen he would sit and eat dinner there, as often as not.

"What does he want us to do?" I asked. "He's a grown man. I think he should buck up and ignore her, or if he's too scared, tell him to bring in a girlfriend as a human shield." Nevertheless, we agreed to try to talk sense into Phyl at the next opportunity, which is how she now found herself cornered.

"Phyl," I began, "We need to talk."

She had been pushing around her Caesar salad absent-mindedly, her soft blue eyes thoughtful. "Did Jason tell you, when he picked up Benny?"

"Tell me what?" I asked.

Phyl made a face. "He and this Jessica are engaged now—can you believe it? And he's always telling me how she's so good with Benny. I hope Benny is peeing in his car as we speak."

Joanie and I always laughed when Phyl griped about Jason because the contrast between her gentle voice and mean words was so comical, and we wondered who, if not for Jason, Phyl would ever have pictured when Jesus told us to "love our enemies."

"He didn't mention it, and Jason never usually passes up an opportunity to brag," I marveled.

"That's because impending tragedy is nothing to brag about," sniffed Joanie. "I give it eighteen months. That marriage will have everything going for it except that Jason is in it."

"Oh, I don't care," Phyl said dismissively, "And I don't even much mind if the marriage works—it's just frustrating that I don't have any wonderful news to counter with. I'm not even dating anyone."

"You've been gone the last several Friday nights on dates," I pointed out.

"I mean I'm not dating anyone I'm interested in," she clarified.

When Phyl didn't continue, Joanie bugged her eyes out at me significantly, and I started in again. "So are you interested in anyone, Phyl?"

She stabbed a crouton with her fork, causing it to explode into little crouton bits. "You guys will kill me if I tell you." We waited. "I—I kind of like Daniel."

It was worse hearing it said aloud. "Phyl," I said, "Honestly, have you played the scenario to its conclusion? What do you think would happen if tomorrow, say, Daniel asked you out? How long do you think it would last?"

"Especially if you wouldn't sleep with him," put in Joanie. "Daniel needs lots of sex, not to mention variety. You'd have to wear different wigs and disguises to hold him more than a couple weeks. Do you still have your old high school cheerleader outfit?"

Phyl got a stubborn set to her jaw. "I wouldn't sleep with him, of course, but if he did ask me out, it would be because he recognized that there's more to life than those meaningless encounters. Don't you think sometimes he looks at our lives enviously? He sees we have people we know and really love and who know and really love us."

"I've caught a few expressions on his face, and I don't think any of them were envy," I said dryly. "More likely he thinks we're prudes who don't have sex because we can't get any." Phyl's lips compressed mutinously, and I pressed ahead. "But never mind what Daniel thinks—we can't do a thing about him. Phyl, if you marry a guy who sleeps around, you get a guy who sleeps around. I thought you learned this. Marriage wouldn't change him."

"Jesus could," she rallied.

"Exactly," I said. "The only one who could change Daniel is God Almighty, not Phyllida Levert, so why don't you just pray for Daniel while you think about someone else? Someone who wouldn't require an act of God to become a suitable husband."

"Besides," Joanie spoke up again, "Daniel said he'd have to kick you out if you keep staring at him and breaking the china."

"He noticed?" gasped Phyl, blanching.

"Everyone noticed, Phyl. Why do you think we're talking to you?" Joanie reasoned. "Be a good girl and say yes to the next nice and boring guy who asks you out. We like having you in the house. You don't want to end up with another Jason, do you?"

"And try to get some guy to come on Thursday," I urged, "so you can show Daniel you're over him. What about that Wayne who you went out with last week?"

"Wayne!" she moaned. "He's an engineer who has dinner with his mom once a week."

"You don't gotta marry him," said Joanie. "Ask Wayne. Your birthday's coming up, and if you ask Wayne I'll make you your favorite cake."

Phyl slumped in defeat. "Fine, I'll call Wayne. And you owe me one Red Velvet cake with cream cheese frosting. I know you two mean well, but I hate being ganged up on. Why should only Joanie get to like somebody gorgeous?"

"For all the good it does me," Joanie said disgustedly. "I can't believe how long it takes these big companies to do their hiring. Roy's in, what, his fourth-round interviews with Cingular and Microsoft? At this rate, they should go straight to negotiating his retirement package." True to form, Roy had continued to insist they only do things he could afford to treat, and Joanie was growing tired of dates limited to walks and open houses. "If he doesn't relax and let me pay for something, I may have to trade him in for an ugly guy with a paycheck."

Phyl got up to dish out the lemon pudding. "How about you, Cass? Are you thinking you may want to get out there again anytime soon?" Joanie's eyes lit up over this question, and I sympathized with Phyl's irritation at being "ganged up on."

"My hands are full, for the time being," I replied evasively. Briefly I told them about my afternoon with Nadina. "What do you think she uses? And what does she mean by 'hard stuff'? And why do you think this repulsive Mike is getting bent out of shape about me?"

"I thought you said you get mentor training," said Phyl. "Haven't they covered the whole drug thing, if so many students struggle with it?"

"We've only done trust-building," I said. "The big drug talk is up next."

"Well, if she still has all her teeth and isn't stealing catalytic converters I'm guessing she's not doing meth," said Joanie.

"Yeah, she's got teeth. Maybe I can ask her if Mike has teeth."

"Maybe she drinks and smokes some joints," suggested Phyl.

"Or they raid Mike's dad's medicine cabinet," said Joanie. "But what do we know? We're church girls. You should ask that Director guy or Daniel. I bet Daniel tried half the stuff in college."

After having already asked Daniel about felony vandalism, I wondered with amusement how he would respond to me now asking about hard drugs. "Well, I don't want to ask Mark Henneman before that next training because it might get back to Nadina. I'll give Daniel a try later. But what do you think about the dumb boyfriend? Why is he giving Nadina a hard time about me when I haven't said a single thing?"

"Isn't it obvious?" said Joanie. "Nadina must be talking about you a lot, so you must be making some impression. Since you came on the scene at the same time as all these changes in her behavior, he thinks it's you reforming her. It may be the counselors talking to her about the drugs, but she probably doesn't go on and on about school counselors. So it's all your fault." I hadn't thought of this—I knew Nadina didn't seem to mind spending her weekly time with me, but she never said anything to make me think she really felt strongly one way or the other.

"In for a penny, in for a pound," said Phyl. "You may as well talk to her about the drugs now, since you're already being blamed for it."

"I guess so," I agreed reluctantly, "Not that I have any idea what to say besides, 'Drugs? Don't do them.' I'm glad I'll be out of town next week, just in case Mike decides to off me for my supposed influence."

Little did I know, when my first opportunity to weigh in on Nadina's life choices came, it would almost end our relationship then and there.

CHAPTER 10

Employment

(September 22, 1:00 p.m.)

James—

The mentor sailing event turned out to be a pleasant surprise, since, as Nadina confessed for us, we thought we'd be "puking." Glad to see you and Kyle seem to be hitting it off.

Per your request, I've attached two of my novelization chapters for your review. Let me know your thoughts.
Cass Ewan

(September 22, 3:15 p.m.)

Cass:

Got your files and will keep you posted. I will probably pass them around the office if I think they're promising.

Kyle's a great kid and a smart one (except for doing the dumb things that got him kicked out of school). Hope you and Nadina are getting along.
James

(September 30, 4:00 p.m.)

Cass:

Several of us took a look at your Clone Wars chapter—
your writing and Kyle's "fact" checking make an
unbeatable team. Would you be interested in coming
in and meeting with some folks on one of our game
development teams? I'm not directly on the Star Wars
game, and they may not need additional help, but other
teams might. And we could talk about possible voiceover
work.
James

P.S. Speaking of voices, Kyle has a great, raspy one, but
I've never heard him emote! Think he'd be capable of it?

(September 30, 9:55 p.m.)

James—would I? Are you kidding? I would love to. Let me
know date and time. I'll be out of town for a few days Oct
7-10, but other than that am totally flexible.
    As for Kyle, I've heard him emote more than once—if
you need contemptuous or deadpan, he's your man.
Cass

(October 2, 2:30 p.m.)

Cass:

Can we try to get you in before your trip? I think I can
pull most of the pertinent people together for this coming
Monday at 3:00 p.m. If it doesn't work, let me know ASAP.
    If you've never interviewed with a video game
company, let me just say don't bother dressing up.
James

Easy for him to say. When it came to job interviews, being told not to bother dressing up didn't simplify matters. Should I wear jeans and a t-shirt? Corduroys and a sweater? Lederhosen?

Then there was the panic over how—come to think of it—I didn't know the first thing about video games, and my *Star Wars* knowledge was a mile-wide and an inch deep, and how exactly did I think writing a few chapters of a chintzy novelization translated into a skill for which I would be paid?

Promptly at 2:45 on Monday, the express bus dropped me a block from the high-rise downtown where Free Universe rented a floor. I had opted for the corduroys and sweater, and Phyl had lent me a messenger bag to hold my few writing samples and a notebook. Going in the revolving door, I checked my watch: 2:46. Too early.

Across the atrium I spotted a Starbucks, however, and headed over to kill ten minutes. It would never do to arrive with coffee breath or even to go in carrying a drink, but I could get a bottled water and slip it in my bag when the time came.

"Frak me!" exclaimed the tubby guy two people ahead of me in line. "Lewis, that's why I won't come down and order your Starbucks drinks—you drink girl coffee. Guys don't do flavored syrups."

"God, Riley," said the thin, rather monotone girl in front of me, "would you quit with the *Battlestar Galactica* cusswords and the sexual harassment. I take black, drip coffee just like you do."

"My point exactly," said Riley, earning an exasperated huff from her. "You're a guy with the best of them, Jer, not like Lewis here with his sugar-free vanilla."

Lewis was not an undersized guy, and Riley's attacks on his manhood didn't seem to faze him. "Don't knock it till you try it, Ri."

"Are we going to get James or Murray anything?" the girl spoke up again after she and Riley had ordered their tall drips.

"No way," declared Riley. "If we get them something, then everyone sits there with a drink except new girl."

"It could be okay," 'Jer' insisted. "Intimidating, like, 'we all have a drink and you don't.'"

"You gonna bully her, Jeri?" asked Lewis.

Jeri scrunched up her nose and looked grouchy. "No, but I don't see why we need another writer. I was glad Mindy left. Hope she likes it over there at *Nintendo*."

"We need another writer so you won't be a total bottleneck," said Riley. "I'm sitting there and I'm magic. I'm spinning out the ideas as fast as they come. You can't keep up with my moves." He started bobbing and weaving around her like a boxer, shooting out a hand every once in a while to bip her on the head.

Sighing dramatically while she tried to bat his hand away, Jeri said only, "Frak me."

By this time I had put two-and-two together and figured out I was seeing most of the interview team, but I was spared having to decide whether or not to reveal myself when I heard my name called. Lewis, Riley, and Jeri turned as one at James' voice, and I caught Riley and Lewis cracking up and nudging each other out of the corner of my eye. Jeri seemed to be turned to stone.

"Hi, there, Cass," said James. "I was just going to grab something to take into the interview. Can I get you something?"

"Just a bottle of water, please," I answered.

"Did you meet the team?" he asked, gesturing at the trio. When no one answered immediately, James made the round of introductions. "And Murray will join us in the conference room. Our office doesn't have one, so we'll use the building's, one floor up."

When the drinks were in hand, he led the way with his characteristic quick stride, and I found Riley next to me. He looked unembarrassed and unrepentant, as far as I could tell, and even grinned at me. "Down the crapper with Jer's 'we all have a drink, and you don't' strategy, huh?"

• • •

After such a beginning, it was hard to be nervous anymore for the interview itself. I suspected James wanted everyone on their best professional behavior because he looked mildly irked when Riley referred to him once as "Jimbo" and then couldn't find any business cards except a crumpled one that had made the trip through the wash in his pants pocket. Not to mention when Riley told me to quit saying Free Universe: "Just call it F-U, like the rest of us do."

Jeri was stiff and silent throughout, probably from having said the most incriminating things; I tried to put her at her ease by asking her questions, but she didn't unbend. Another tough case was Murray the sound designer—I don't think he cracked one smile and spent most of the hour making notes on his pad that, on closer inspection, looked more like a flow chart than anything to do with the matter at hand.

Lewis was friendly enough. When I admitted my general ignorance of Free Universe games—("Just say FUG," corrected Riley)—he whipped out his laptop and walked me through the two that had actually made it to market, while James explained how the pieces came together. "Good as Riley's ideas may be, or those of our other developers," he said, "only a percentage of games will finally see the light, depending on circumstances. Everyone works their hearts out—developers, programmers, artists, sound engineer, writers, testers—but there's no guarantee that project will make it to the shelves. It's pretty cut-throat, but it's a creative work environment and a stimulating one." (Here Jeri snorted.) "The good news is our first couple games have done pretty well, and we're looking to ride that wave with our next product. We have one we were hoping to ship in November, but it's looking like that's going to slip."

"Good-bye December," put in Riley.

"Yeah," agreed James. "Looks like December will be crunch time, unfortunately, but that wouldn't really affect you, Cass. We were thinking of trying you out on some games still in concept stage. Riley's got a lot of ideas swirling around in his brain—"

("Bip!" went Riley, pretending to box Jeri again. She slapped his hand away and I saw the infamous "frak me" form on her lips.)

"—so we figured that would be the best team to start you out on. Jeri's trying to cover for three teams at once, and it's getting a little much."

Rather than looking eager for the additional help, Jeri merely sniffed. Murray also looked up at this point from his flow chart and said colorlessly, "Do you think you need me anymore, Kittredge? Vil isn't happy with the Elf Archer's voice—he says it's too Munchkin and wants me to take it down a register."

James nodded. "No problem. Catch you later, unless Cass had any last questions for you."

If I had, I wouldn't have had the nerve to ask them, the way Murray was tapping his pencil impatiently. As it was, James wrapped up the interview fairly quickly after that. "This was great," he assured me, shaking my hand as I stood up. "Thanks for coming down. We'll be in touch."

You would think I'd never met the guy before, but I happened to glance back as I was shutting the door behind me, and he gave me a conspiratorial wink.

(October 6, 5:30 p.m.)

James, Lewis, Riley, Murray, and Jeri:

Thank you for talking with me today. I appreciate your time and the thought and imagination inspiring Free Universe games. It would be a pleasure to work with you all, whether in writing or voice work or both. I look forward to hearing from you.
Cass

(October 6, 6:42 p.m.)

Cass:

You were a total hit today! I know Riley went right back to his cube and burrowed in, trying to figure out which storyboard he wanted to go over with you first. He drives everyone here off their nut from time to time, especially Jeri who sits next to him, but he's probably the most creative guy we've got.

Speaking of Jeri, don't worry about her weird vibe—since our other full-time writer left she wants to be Queen Writer and will brook no rivals. However, we've got too much going on for her to do all of it, so she's just going to have to deal with a Writer Princess. Or should I say "goddess"? That's the other thing—Murray agrees with me that you are the perfect voice for the Snow Goddess in *Tolt*! He'll be following up with some script that he'll want you to come in and read for him. It's pure tripe, but I think I warned you that game writing isn't Shakespeare, right?

Have a good trip. We'll try to pull things together in the meantime, and maybe we can set up some times for the week of the 13th. You'll probably hear from Riley before then. And Keri our HR person will mail you some paperwork.

By the way, I think I'll see you before then for the Camden School mentor bowling thing, right, on the 11th? If we thought the sailing event was humorous, I can't wait to see the bowling.

Cheers.

(October 6, 10:15 p.m.)

James—

Thanks for the feedback. I am so excited to work with you all at Free Universe. Kyle is going to be amazed! He might even emote! I'll look forward to hearing from various team members soon then and seeing them when I return.

And yes, Nadina and I will be at the bowling event on the 11th. If you think I'm a gifted sailor, wait till you see me bowl.

Cass

Clicking the "Send" icon, I sat back with satisfaction. I was once more a (somewhat) gainfully-employed woman.

CHAPTER 11:

Cornered in the *Marché*

For at least an hour after losing Troy and Min, I considered moving down to California to be closer to family. Make that half an hour. It wasn't that I didn't love them and wish I wasn't the only member of my immediate family still in Washington—and heaven knew I had no objection to more sunshine—it was that California had never been home. Dad and Mom had moved to Washington before I was born to take up professor jobs at the U, back in the day when such jobs went begging, even in fields like Classics (Dad) or Comparative Literature (Mom). Ours was the only branch of the McKeans to leave the San Francisco Bay Area, so all growing up, visits to extended family involved fifteen-hour car trips down I-5, with the requisite stop in Ashland to take in a play if the Shakespeare Festival was going.

When Troy and Min died, just about every one of those McKeans made the trek up to attend the memorial, a gesture I appreciated, and I saw several of them in the intervening year, but the thought of seeing them all again this week for Mom's 60th aroused more dread than eagerness. There was going to be crying and fussing, no doubt about it.

Mom was worried about other things. She had called the week before to say my little brother was occupying their spare room again, his attempts at supporting himself screenwriting still not paying off, and his wife having gotten sick of financing him.

As children, Perry and I had fallen into the roles of high-achieving, well-behaved oldest child and low-achieving, family-clown youngest child, and those roles carried into adulthood. Where I went right to college and graduate school and worked until marrying a respectable man, Perry took two years off after barely graduating high school, meandered through an expensive college in five years, and then married someone he met on Spring Break in Cabo. He had dabbled in local theater, local radio, culinary school, and waiting tables before convincing his wife to move to Los Angeles so he could try screenwriting. As Betsy had thrown him out before, we didn't know if this was for real, but my mother sighed, "It would be nice to turn sixty without a son at home as if he'd never left."

Exasperating as he could be as a son, husband, or brother, Perry had been the very best of uncles. He had spoiled Min silly, buying her huge, noisy toys that drove me nuts and would always "mysteriously" disappear or run out of batteries; he would carry her around on his shoulders and feed her even more sweets than Raquel or Mom, and she adored him, calling him "Peh-wy." One of the worst moments after Troy and Min died had been seeing Perry. I couldn't even bear to call him in my state and foisted the task on Mom, and when he and Betsy flew up, he just sat on my sofa holding some talking bear he had given her, weeping silently.

Mom sent Perry to pick me up at San Jose International, not fifteen minutes from where she and Dad lived in a modest condo on Santana Row. They had finagled jobs at San Jose State University when Perry and I both ended up at California schools, only to have the two of us move away again right after graduation. By then they were too established with their friendships and church to relocate, and they'd gotten used to all the sunshine and drought.

Perry was right on the other side of security to meet me—a surprise, given he'd always been more of the curbside and fifteen-minutes-late kind of airport ride. My brother had never been exactly handsome, just as I had never been a knockout, but he had my father's big frame and engaging, elastic features. He was looking tanned and had grown his hair out longish, and I saw heads turn when he enveloped me in a giant bear hug.

"Cass!" Loosening his grip slightly so I could breathe, he studied my face intently. "You look good, Cass. Way better than the last time I saw you."

I cleared my throat and smiled weakly. "Yeah? Well same to you. And what's with the big Public Display of Affection?"

He grinned and relieved me of my carry-on bag. "What? Haven't I always been big on PDAs with you?"

"Not that I can recall."

"Well, my loved ones have been dropping like flies lately, and I'm determined to hang on to the ones I've got left. What with Troy and—and Min—and I'm guessing Mom told you that Betsy has kicked me out again..?"

I felt the catch in my throat when he mentioned Troy and Min, but I had been prepared and swallowed it down ruthlessly. "Will she take you back this time? You could surprise her by getting a real job and cutting up that credit card you share with Mom and Dad."

"I could," Perry said noncommittally, "not that it would do much good. Betsy says it's for good this time."

Not for the first time did I offer the usual comforts. "Well, she's said all that before, hasn't she? I'm sure she'll come around. A few months of nightly take-out instead of your Academy cooking, and she'll be begging for mercy. You'd better just hope she doesn't meet someone gainfully employed—it might be more temptation than she could withstand."

So much for the new affectionate side of Perry—he put me in a headlock and growled, "Go easy, Cass."

Heads were turning our way again, so I cried uncle quickly, but I couldn't help adding, "Perry, really, I went easy on you both the first few times you separated. Can I help getting a little jaded? After losing Troy, it's hard to put up with people who can't decide if they want to be married or not."

He nodded. "I told her we should just take the divorce option off the table, but she told me she was seeing the lawyer this time. And she was really careful to check Mom and Dad's address. I think she's going to serve me papers." His shoulders slumped, and I could only pat him wordlessly as we watched the luggage carousel rotate.

Betsy and I had always gotten along, without exactly being kindred spirits. It was hard to get too close to someone who was always kicking your brother out of the house, even if that brother was often aggravating and still showed no signs of wanting to sell out and get a real job. However I might sympathize with her, he was still my brother, and while he did pursue careers with infinitesimal chances of success, at least he pursued them wholeheartedly and tirelessly.

In silence, Perry hauled my suitcase off the carousel, but somewhere on the shuttle between the terminal and the parking structure I could see his irrepressible spirits beginning to lift. Honestly, it was only after Min died that I think I saw him depressed for more than a few hours running. As we got in the car and started driving, I could almost hear his brain switch gears and start ticking.

"The good thing is," he began abruptly, "suffering produces character, as we know, as well as better art. We just have to see if the genre ends up romantic comedy or tearjerker. And then, it's not at all a bad time to be out on my ear, on the verge of divorce."

"You mean there's a good time for divorce?" I asked skeptically.

"It means all bets are off. If I've got a few months of being on my own, I may as well spend them in Portland."

"Portland? Why Portland?"

Perry got a mischievous look in his eye. "Because an old director friend there broke up with his dramaturg, and now he needs a new one ASAP for an upcoming musical production. It's about aspiring actors in Hollywood, and who would know more about that than me?"

I made a face. "It can't be any good, can it, a musical opening in Portland? Sounds like a rehash of *A Chorus Line*."

"I'm hoping not. I think Sam said it's called *Waiters: the Musical*."

Then I did laugh. "What? To differentiate it from *Waiters: the Board Game* or *Waiters: the Epic Poem*?"

"Cass, look, I don't know if it's any good or if it will even pan out, but I might as well explore it. And if I'm in Portland I'll be able to get up and see you." Given Perry's propensity for unannounced visits of indeterminate length, I didn't know if this was a good idea. We had never discussed Daniel's policy on house guests, and I was reluctant to have unpredictable Perry be my hypothetical case.

When I told Mom she gave me no sympathy; I think she secretly saw it as an easy way to get rid of Perry for the time being, or at least until Betsy took him back again. "What's the worst that can happen, Cass? He might come up for a few days without telling you ahead of time, but if he's employed in Portland he'll have to go back sooner rather than later." As with most things completely out of my control, I put it out of my head, to be dealt with later. After all, Mom's birthday dinner was more than enough to be going on about.

Dad had gone all out and reserved Marché in Menlo Park for her private party. Between the five-course wine-pairing menu and a guest list upwards of forty family members, I couldn't help teasing him that he'd better hope Mom didn't make it to her 70th.

It wasn't a bad evening, apart from the forty times I had to have someone take my hand, eyes full of tears, and tell me, "I've been thinking about you all the time, Cass. How are you? Are you okay? Do you think you might move down here? What are you doing all by yourself up there?" Their sincere concern made me cry with them until my head ached, but at least sympathy was preferable to Aunt Judy. Being the oldest of my father's siblings, she was used to managing all.

"Cassandra, how long will the insurance money last?" she demanded. "Have you thought about how you'll support yourself when it runs out? I know you quit work to stay home with Min, even though I told your father a woman should always keep one foot in the workplace. If you need help updating your resumé, have your cousin Greg take a look at it. I had him look at Janie's, and it really helped her get that job. Of course, you are the spendthrift branch of the family. Just look at you and Perry, without two pennies to rub together. Look at this restaurant! My 60th was at Chef Chu's, and I'm sure that was fancy enough for everyone. You'd better eat more of this expensive food because you're still looking too pale and thin. Like Troy. I didn't mention it, but I had my misgivings when you married Troy—he always did look a little peaked."

The whole family put up with Aunt Judy, but for once I found something refreshing in her matter-of-factness; the tone in which she discussed the complete wreckage of my life was no different from how she had tsk-tsked over the sunburn I got when I was twelve, after ignoring her sunscreen offer.

That was the worst of it though. Once the sit-down dinner began, I was safely flanked by two teenage male cousins who never thought once to ask me a question about myself, and I was free to pop some ibuprofen and have an extra glass of wine. Who knows? Given the choice of getting it over with in one evening, or having the sympathy and tears trickle in whenever I happened to meet each of them, I'm not sure I would have chosen otherwise.

The rest of the visit passed pleasantly enough. We got in some golfing and walks and a trip to the City. Mom and Perry and I would stay up into the night playing cards and catching up; they were as thrilled as I had hoped about my new work at Free Universe, and full of questions about Nadina. Before I knew it, it was Friday, and I was headed back up to Seattle.

My taciturn father surprised me by taking me aside shortly before I had to head back to the airport. "Cass, your mother and I are so happy to see you looking well again." He fumblingly rubbed me on the shoulders, and I turned to hug him.

"Perry said the same thing when he saw me. I must have really looked terrible at Easter," I joked.

"We were very, very worried. We had the whole church praying for you," he said soberly, and much as I cringed to think of my name and story trumpeted in their church bulletin, I was touched.

"Thanks, Dad."

"Are you still going to church?" he asked. I understood the indirection: he meant, did I still believe in God?

Kissing him on the cheek, I answered, "Yes. Tell Mom not to worry. I love you, Dad."

. . .

Joanie and Phyl had lots to catch me up on when I got home. Cingular had offered Roy a job at last; Jason had run into a door chasing Benny and broken his nose ("It's swelled up like a football!" beamed Phyl); and Wayne was improving slightly in everyone's estimation.

"It turns out he visits his mom so often because she's disabled and he wants to check up on her, since his dad died a couple years ago," explained Phyl. "But his mom is always telling him to get a life and says that, if he really wanted to make her happy, he'd get married and produce a few grandkids."

"Ooh, yes, caring son sure beats browbeaten mama's boy," I agreed. "And if you married him, at least your future mother-in-law sounds like she would have a sense of humor." Phyl made a face.

"How was the open house last night?" I asked. "Even while eating at my favorite Thai place from college I was sorry to miss it."

"All right," reported Joanie. "There was lots of Rock Band, but it was kind of flat without you."

"I don't even play Rock Band," I laughed. "If anyone missed me, it would be Phyl, to have no Scrabble partner."

Phyl added in a slightly hurt tone, "As a matter of fact, I think Daniel missed you too. He even asked Joanie where you were, and when she told him he looked almost disappointed. I bet he'd be thrilled if I were gone."

"Now, now, remember how you're trying not to give a rip about my brother. If Cass was always sighing and moping over him, he'd be thrilled to have her gone too," Joanie explained for the hundredth time. "Daniel's fondness is inversely proportional to yours."

"Heart-warming, I'm sure," I said dryly, "Wait till he hears my brother Perry is going to be in Portland and swinging up here to stay whenever he feels like it. Do we know how Daniel feels about house guests that aren't his?"

"Oh, he probably wouldn't even notice," Joanie said dismissively. "We'll just stash Perry in our spare room, and chances are he won't even run into Daniel. If I were you, I wouldn't even bother asking."

Not being as unscrupulous as Joanie, I decided I would ask Daniel whenever I managed to have the conversation about hard drugs. Between his travel and my own I had only seen him a few times in passing, and usually with other people around.

"What are you guys up to, tomorrow?" I asked.

"The singles group adopted a few families in East Bellevue, and tomorrow is the extreme home makeover for the first family," said Phyl. "I think they put me down for heading up the landscaping."

Joanie moaned. "I didn't have any skills to list: can I use power tools? No. Have I done any painting work? No. Landscaping? Never. Which means they'll put me on cleaning detail. I hope this isn't one of those super pack-rat families with newspapers piled floor-to-ceiling and dirty dishes from three different decades." She looked at me suddenly, and her voice took on a wheedling tone. "Wanna come help me, Cass? It's Chaff-sponsored, but we'll all be too busy and grime-encrusted to hit on each other."

"Tempting, Joanie, but I'm going to have to say no. I wanted to get started on some Free Universe stuff, and then there's a mentor bowling thing in the afternoon."

Phyl and Joanie exchanged a glance, and Phyl said, "I guess that means James Kittredge won't be at the home makeover tomorrow either. Lots of ladies might be disappointed."

"Lots?" I echoed. "Isn't he still with Brooke Capshaw?"

Joanie snorted. "That is way-old news. They only went out a few times, and she says she had to call him for two of them. After that he made the rounds with a few other ladies, but I don't think he's looking to get serious. Does he get flirty with you?"

"Not a bit. He's charming and all, but totally polite and professional." I paused, frowning. "Maybe because of the mentor thing and working together in future—or maybe he just doesn't find me attractive."

"Idiot!" said Joanie scathingly. "And maybe because he thinks you're married, remember?"

A grin broke across my face. "Oh, yeah, I'm sure he'd be dying for me, otherwise. I'm certainly not going to enlighten him. I'd rather be friends—friendships usually last a whole lot longer than romances."

CHAPTER 12:

Too Much Information

On Saturday I got up early, wanting to have some Free Universe work under my belt before I saw James that afternoon at bowling. Riley had sent me three scenarios, of which I found the Antarctic exploration concept the most intriguing, but it would also require the most research. Thinking ruefully of my *Star Wars* novelization, I wondered if I was always drawn to whatever I knew the least about.

Riley had only basic notes. Players could choose an actual historical expedition to lead or create one of their own. If they chose an actual historical expedition, they could see if their own leadership choices, coupled with a hundred years of hindsight, could alter outcomes: could Robert Falcon Scott beat Roald Amundsen to the South Pole? Or, failing that, could Scott's ill-fated team survive that final trek and make it to that last cairn? For those who preferred epic sea voyages there was even an option to play Ernest Shackleton and captain the *Endurance*. I spent some time online, but flipping back and forth between various sites and scrolling across maps and photos limited by my 15-inch computer screen grew tiresome, and my mind kept returning to that shelf of polar exploration books Daniel had in the Lean-To.

I looked at the clock: 9:30. Surely he must be stirring by now, reading the paper and having his coffee in the Palace kitchen. Alternatively, he and a girlfriend might still be snoring away or otherwise engaged. There was nothing for it but to go see.

The kitchen was deserted, but the coffee pot was hot, and there were a few mugs in the sink. No telling how many of the mugs were from last night's tea. After loading them in the dishwasher I checked in the garage for Daniel's Corvette—not there. Maybe he'd gone golfing. Grabbing the key to the Lean-To, I zipped out the back door and went to let myself in. His place was spotless, bare and silent, as usual. Phyl was a better cleaning lady than I because the kitchen was sparkling, but perhaps love and frustration led to harder scrubbing.

An hour later I was lying on the floor, books spread in every direction, having taken several pages of notes. It was hard to confine myself to getting down facts—dates and jumping-off points, ponies versus dogs, sledding versus man-hauling—when I kept getting absorbed in the stories themselves. I had just read Scott's farewell letter to posterity and was wiping away tears when I saw motion out of the corner of my eye and glanced up to see Daniel standing at the bottom of the stairs in nothing but a tan and boxer shorts.

"Good heavens, you're home!" I shrieked, sitting up hastily in a flurry of paper. Trying to look anywhere but at him, I began gathering all my notes and pens. "I wouldn't have barged in uninvited if I'd known, obviously. I checked for your car and didn't see it in the garage, and I figured it was already stinking 9:30 and—"

"Cass, it's fine," Daniel interrupted, his voice amused, as it always seemed to be when he addressed me. "I lent a friend the car for his wedding today—I'm just hoping it doesn't come back to me covered in Silly String or trailing cans." He didn't seem in a hurry to go put some clothes on, so I focused on putting my notes in order and getting them clamped on the clipboard.

After watching me a minute longer he said, "I feel like I haven't seen you for weeks—and you've taken up a new hobby. Fascinating books, aren't they? I wasn't aware Antarctic exploration was one of your interests, too."

Not surprising, considering he didn't know what any of my interests were, beyond church and Dickens and Scrabble, but I bit back this ungraceful comment and only said, "It's for a little work I'm doing. Would you mind if I borrowed a book or two and took them back to my room for a while?"

He padded over and crouched down next to me. "Your place or mine."

He was so near to me I could see his muscled arm and feel heat coming off his body, and I blushed furiously, shaking my head. "Oh, no, that won't be necessary. I've—I've got enough notes to get started." Blindly I turned away and started shoving books back on the shelf, and I heard him chuckling under his breath as he began to help me, rearranging them where I'd put them in the wrong order.

"What's this?" came another voice from the stairway. It was Michelle the architect, whom we hadn't seen in weeks, draped in a too-big bathrobe that must have been Daniel's, her long dark hair loose around her shoulders. "Do you guys even clean his place on weekends, when he has company?"

Even in my confusion and embarrassment I was aware of the muted hostility in her question. What had I done to warrant this? Another mystery for the ages, I supposed. "I didn't mean to intrude. I'm so sorry, and I'll get out of your hair now." Before I could take a step, Daniel was in front of me, and when he didn't move aside I was forced to meet his eyes. They were still laughing at me.

"At least take this book with you—a good comprehensive overview of polar exploration," he murmured. His voice took on that familiar, baiting note. "Something about the…frigid…cold is irresistible to some men; they can't stay away from it. Must be all that untrampled, virgin snow. The purity of it."

I scowled at him then, snatching the book. "Not that you would know, having spent all your time where 'generations have trod, have trod, have trod.'"

Daniel laughed outright. If Michelle hadn't been standing there on the stairs, arms crossed and looking daggers, I might have added a few choice words, such as, he was the most disrespectful, conceited, insensitive man I'd ever met, and could he please confine his flirting to the masochistic women who were interested in it? As it was, I turned on my heel with what dignity I could muster and shut the door just shy of a slam.

• • •

The rest of the morning, I hid in my room, writing, and not going down for lunch until I saw Daniel and Michelle leave. Daniel was wearing a suit, so I assumed they were going to the friend's wedding and I would be spared his presence for the rest of the afternoon.

By two o'clock I had rough drafts of the game introduction and one scenario, enough to talk about if James asked, and my thoughts turned to bowling. At least I had been to Tech City Bowl before, so when I swung by to pick up Nadina at the school, we made it on time. She was not noticeably more excited about bowling than about sailing and greeted me with, "Dude, do you think they'll let me have the bumpers up?"

I patted her arm. "Hey, there. How was your week?"

"Okay. Not much happened. School. Work. Blah blah."

"How did your math test go?" I persevered.

Her face lit up suddenly. "I got a 77%! And I totally forgot I was going to email you and tell you that Kyle Bateman helped me with my math!"

"Kyle did?" I asked, pleased. "How did that happen?"

"I was sitting outside Tuesday after school, and since you were gone I was trying to go over my stupid pre-test which I totally bombed because I did not have a clue what was going on, and Kyle heard me cussing and saw me throw my math book on the ground, and he came over and was like, 'Dude, that'll break the binding.' And I said, 'Fuck the binding'—sorry, Cass—'it's not like having a nice binding is gonna help me understand what's inside.' And he looked like he was gonna walk away, but then he didn't and he said, 'Did you want help with that?' And he sat with me for like almost an hour and explained stuff to me, and I almost got it! 77%!"

Not only was I glad for Nadina, who struggled with most subjects besides science, but it gave me a thrill to think of Kyle reaching out for once to one of the 'druggies' he despised. "Let's try to get a lane with Kyle and James," I suggested. "I'd love to thank him and talk to him."

"Whatever, Cass. As long as you don't get embarrassing on me," agreed Nadina. "And let's try to get Sonya and her old lady with us, too."

Although it was dark in the bowling alley, it was easy to spot Kyle sloping toward the shoe rental counter, James alongside him. Kyle was wearing his characteristic three t-shirts and low-slung jeans hanging by their last threads, and James was his usual dapper self in a snug charcoal gray sweater and dark corduroys. I sent Nadina to wait in the check-in line and let Mark Henneman know we were there so I could catch them.

"Guys!" I called. "Mind if Nadina and I bowl with you?"

James turned with a big grin on his face and shook my hand heartily, and Kyle even got the ghost of a smile. "Cass! How was your trip?"

"Not bad. It was my mom's 60th. She and my dad moved to the Bay Area when my brother and I were in college, so it was great to get some sunshine." I turned to Kyle. "And I hear from Nadina that you helped her with her math this past week. She even passed a test she was sure she would fail." As I suspected, Kyle merely nodded and shuffled his feet, letting his long hair fall in front of his eyes, and grunting when James slapped him approvingly on the back.

It was a riotous afternoon. To Nadina's disgust, the bowling alley had a maximum age limit on bumper usage, and she didn't qualify. She and I were wretched, barely breaking seventy, and James was hardly better. The overall lane champion turned out to be Sonya's mentor Louella, putting us all to shame, but no one minded.

Having not seen him for a while, I was glad for the chance to talk to Kyle. Louella was bowling her third strike in a row and Nadina and Sonya had gone to get everyone drinks when he said abruptly, "So you're not writing your novelization anymore?"

"Nah," I admitted. "I hope you're not too heartbroken—I know I didn't leave you in suspense—but did James tell you I'm going to be doing some writing work for Free Universe? And you helped me get the job because you fixed all the mistakes that would have made me look like an idiot."

"Yeah," Kyle answered vaguely. "James invited me to come see his office, too. I got to beta test some of the games and tell them if they were lame."

"Oh—and were they?" I asked awkwardly. I could see that James must be listening because he turned away to hide a smile and made a big deal of looking for his bowling ball.

"They were okay. They didn't suck." Now I was grinning. Obviously faint praise wasn't so damning when it issued from the mouth of a teenage boy. In fact, it was downright thrill-inducing.

James must have shared my opinion because he turned back to throw an amused look at me. "It's our company motto," he declared, "'We just don't want to suck.'"

"Then I'll fit right in," I laughed.

When Kyle was up bowling, I asked James if he'd spoken to Kyle about doing voiceovers yet. "I mentioned it when he was in, and he tried to hide it, but I could tell he was excited by the idea. Maybe after you work with Murray some, Kyle can come watch you do some recording."

"Let him see how the pros do it," I teased.

After the game was over, and we were up in the snack bar having pizza, Sonya accosted Kyle with "Hey, Bandit, what's going on with your court case? Are you going to juvy?"

Louella, who hadn't heard of Kyle's situation, choked on her soda, and Sonya had to thump her on the back. Kyle was very still for a moment; I knew he was no fan of giggly girls who talked about people for entertainment. He seemed to be weighing his options in his mind but finally answered, "My sorry-ass lawyer and I just signed my diversion agreement with the prosecutor." He ignored me clapping my hands, thrilled, and continued, "I've got to pay the stupid school back and do a shi—do a load of community service and write an apology to the friggin' computer science teacher."

"You're lucky, dude," crowed Sonya. "I was thinking you'd have to go on Judge Judy, and she would so kick your ass!"

Kyle was spared having to respond to this asinine comment by Nadina. "Sonya, you friggin' retard. Judge Judy does small claims. Kyle, like, trashed hundreds of dollars of stuff and hacked some dickhead's computer—he didn't run over somebody's dog."

I hardly knew where to look—looking at James would make me laugh, and looking at Kyle would make him feel even more uncomfortable—but it did occur to me that Kyle and Nadina must have talked about more than math that one afternoon, if she knew something Sonya didn't. Sonya appeared to have reached this same conclusion because she raised her eyebrows at Nadina and dropped the subject, probably intending to dig for more details when they were alone.

• • •

The sun had nearly set by the time I came home. It was too early for dinner, not that I was very hungry after the bowling-alley pizza, and I didn't feel up to doing any more writing or research, so I made myself some tea and went to lounge on the porch. Phyl had transitioned all the planter boxes to ornamental kale and coleus and arranged a little display of white and orange pumpkins by the door. I hadn't been there more than twenty minutes when Daniel pulled up, still in the swapped car. It was dark now, and I thought briefly about sneaking around the corner of the porch to avoid him and Michelle, before I decided that was juvenile.

As it turned out, he was alone, and with my mind full of Camden School I realized this might be a good time to hit him up about hard drugs. "How was the wedding?" I called, as he came up the steps. Although he had taken off his tie, he was still more dressed up than I'd ever seen him, and I had to admit Phyl wasn't totally nuts always to be staring at him.

Daniel surprised me by smiling a little and coming to throw himself in the chair across the table from my glider. "It was a wedding. Have you ever noticed that, in Shakespeare, all the plays that end with a wedding are comedies, and all the plays that begin with a marriage are tragedies?"

I mulled this over. "You're probably right. And all the ones with couples who are separated are half-comedy, half-tragedy. Shakespeare and you must be kindred spirits." And Michelle had definitely been channeling Lady Macbeth that morning. "Do you and your friends hold a wake every time one of you gets married?"

He looked at me with a wry expression. "I'm not against other people getting married, Cass. I've just never seen the need myself."

"What about the Francis Bacon I saw on your bookshelf—what

does he say? 'Wives are young men's mistresses, companions for middle age, and old men's nurses.' Maybe you're right, Daniel. Who needs a wife? You've got girlfriends for now, golfing buddies for middle age companionship, and you'll probably be able to afford a really nice assisted-living place when the time comes."

"Who says I can't have mistresses at every stage?" he challenged.

"Good point," I replied caustically, "I can't speak for other women, but I know I've always been a sucker for lecherous old goats in wheelchairs."

Daniel laughed. "I didn't mean you, Cass. I could never aspire to you." He delivered this last remark mockingly, and I felt my cheeks warm. He was hopeless.

Making my tone sternly business-like I said abruptly, "Now that we've settled that, I have two quick things I wanted to discuss with you." He waved his hand as if to indicate I should go on. "One was that my brother Perry might be dropping by unannounced some time or times in the future because he'll be working in Portland for a few months. I don't imagine he'd stay more than a couple days at a time, if that's okay." Daniel nodded, so apparently Joanie was right and he didn't care.

I hesitated then a little over the drug question but decided there wasn't any nice way of going about it. Better just to plunge ahead. "You don't still do drugs, do you?"

He stared at me, his mouth twisting in amusement. "I never can guess what you'll say next, Cass." Watching my blush deepen, he finally said, "Was that still part of the first item on the agenda, or was that item two? Does your brother need a local dealer when he visits?"

"Umm…two. That was related to item two," I clarified.

"The answer is no, I don't still do drugs. I haven't since college. Why?"

I fidgeted nervously. "Well, in college then, did you just smoke pot?"

"No," he replied unhelpfully, appearing to enjoy my discomfiture.

"Then what did you do?"

"A variety of things."

"LSD?"

"Once."

"Ecstasy?"

"Several times."

"Cocaine?"

"Several more times." He leaned forward in his chair to read my expression. "Is this about another 'friend' of yours, Cass?"

"Yes, I have a ... *friend* ... who's trying to cut down on the hard stuff, and I just wondered what 'the hard stuff' might be."

"For a church girl, you keep some strange company."

Waving this off, I persisted. "If this friend's boyfriend were in the Seattle music scene, do you think those are probably the drugs she's exposed to?"

Daniel shrugged. "Probably all those and more. The drugs and permutations of drugs keep multiplying. I would bet she's seen speed and ketamine and GHB, poppers—ah, to be young again." I knew he said this last just to irk me, so I ignored it. After a pause he said, "If she's not too addicted, she may find it's easier to quit the drugs than the company and the culture."

Troubled and thinking of Mike, I asked, "But is it possible to quit the drugs without quitting the company?"

Picking up one of Phyl's little pumpkins, he spun it by its stem, setting it whirling like a top. It bumped off the porch into the rhododendrons. "It's pretty difficult," he answered finally. "Depends how close you are with the company. If she's just using with strangers she sees on weekends at some rave it can be done, but if the company is closer than that—good luck." Bending down gracefully, he plucked the pumpkin out of the bushes and replaced it on the pile. "She might just find the company doesn't want to let her go."

CHAPTER 13:

Shootout at the Petco Corral

Phyl's birthday fell on a Friday, but we decided to celebrate Thursday at our regular open house. True to her promise, Joanie's masterpiece of a red velvet cake stood under its glass dome, and while she worked on a lasagna, I made a quick dash to the mall to pick up a little birthday gift. I figured I could kill two birds with one stone and drop in at the Petco to see Nadina at work.

It wasn't hard to spot her tall figure pushing a broom around, bizarre though she looked in the work-issue blue polo shirt. Min and I used to be frequent Petco visitors, it being the low-maintenance, Eastside alternative for moms who didn't feel up to the half-day Woodland Park Zoo trek.

"Do these guys ever do anything?" I asked Nadina, pointing to the snoozing, dog-piled ferrets. "Every time I've been here they're all piled up asleep like this."

"I've seen 'em move," she said imperturbably. "They get really active around dinner time, but they sleep 18-20 hours a day. Also, they're probably depressed because they really ought to be able to run around outside their cages. Come check out this dog I groomed totally by myself."

"By yourself? Did you get a promotion?"

Nadina snorted. "Nah, we just had a lot of dogs today."

She led me into the separate, glassed-off grooming center and pointed proudly at an immaculate Cocker Spaniel. All the dogs began barking their heads off when we walked in, and I watched bemused as Nadina went from cage to cage, murmuring to each one with a tranquilizing effect.

"Nadina, you are amazing!" I marveled. "First Benny, now this. You really ought to think about becoming a veterinarian."

Her eyes lit up briefly, before doubt shadowed them. "Man, Cass, I don't even know if I'm gonna make it through high school. But, hey, being a vet would give me all kinds of access to drugs. Did you know lots of dog drugs and people drugs are basically the same, only the dog drugs are cheaper because they don't have to get FDA approval?"

I frowned at her. "That knowledge will come in handy when you're stricken with heartworm. What a criminal mind you have! Besides, if you get through high school and college and veterinary school, it'll be because you managed to kick the drugs and alcohol."

She rolled her eyes. "You sound like all my teachers and counselors now. Look, I told you I don't hardly use now, and if my friends and I want to get stoned on a weekend or go to a party when there's nothing else going on, it doesn't hurt anyone. I'm going to school, right?" When I didn't answer, she groaned, "God, Cass, haven't you ever even been drunk or anything? Your idea of fun is going to church and working on that dumb *Star Wars* book." She opened the Cocker Spaniel's cage and plopped him on the stainless steel grooming table so that she could clean out his crate.

"I have too been drunk before—a few times," I objected.

It was true, but I hadn't thought about it in at least a decade. When Troy and I graduated high school, I insisted we head off to college unencumbered. He wanted to stay together, but I wanted to break up. While the hiatus didn't last long—we were back together by Thanksgiving—the few months apart were more than long enough for me to get into trouble. "I got drunk in college," I said, "because that's what everyone did freshman year in the dorms, and I wanted to fit in and try it out, so I got drunk."

"See?" said Nadina, slinging the dog waste in the trash can. "Sometimes you just need stuff to relax. Even smart people in college. That's all I'm doing, relaxing and having a little fun with my friends. I mostly stay away from the heavy shit now, even when Mike and his friends do it—"

"I didn't think getting drunk was fun or relaxing!" I interrupted. "I would wake up smelling like barf or with my shirt on backwards, feeling totally used and trashy the next day. I could hardly look at anyone because I had fuzzy memories of acting like an idiot. Not to mention making out with guys my sober self wouldn't even consider. If it was fun at the time, it didn't seem worth it later. After a few nights like that I kept it to one drink per party, and I found different friends who wanted something else out of life. Don't you want something else out of life?"

"Like what?"

"Like—like purpose and meaning," I floundered. "Like becoming the person you were created to be."

"What?" Nadina looked stumped. "I don't know! I haven't thought about it," she said defensively. "What's wrong with my life and my friends?"

"I just wonder if your friends always want what's best for you. Like, do you have any friends who don't use?" When she didn't answer, I ventured, "Do you and Sonya use together?"

Scowling, Nadina began brushing the Cocker Spaniel so hard that he whimpered a little. "Sonya says she's gonna do what the counselors say and go to rehab. We didn't do anything together—we just got hammered a few times at her house with her brother. Just beer and stuff from her parents' liquor cabinet. What all teenagers do."

"So if Sonya goes to rehab and decides she's going to be sober, how are you going to help her?"

Nadina exhaled loudly, suddenly angry. "I don't know, Cass! Why are you riding me today? Just keep out of my fucking business, okay? I already have enough people trying to tell me what to do!"

So much for my Trust-Building training. I obviously needed remedial lessons, and in the meantime, my blood pressure was rising. "I'm not trying to tell you what to do, Nadina. I'm just asking you questions because I don't understand why you would—"

"You don't know anything about my life," she exploded, setting some of the caged dogs whining. "You think because you're my 'mentor' and spend a little time with me you can start judging me and my friends? You think you know what my life is like? You think 'cause you went to your fancy college and live in your fancy house and have all those goody-goody friends that you're better than me?"

"Better than you?" I echoed, keeping my voice as steady as I could. We had learned in our last mentor training that addict behavior could involve irrational aggression, lying, and fighting, but it was still hard to let it roll off me when Nadina was so in-my-face with it. I held up my hands to interrupt: "Just hang on right there, Nadina—where do you get off thinking that about me?"

She responded by slamming her own hands down on the grooming table. I don't know if she even heard me. "You think you have better friends and a better life?" she shrieked. "Just because you don't use? You use, Cass. You just call it different things. Mike says—Mike says—your church and all your do-good stuff is just a—a crutch to make you feel better about yourself. He says you're just a lonely, sorry-ass person with a dead husband and a dead kid!"

Any well-trained mentor detachment I had cultivated to this point fell away from me sharply. Aggression, fine. Irrationality, fine. But this was below the belt. She was panting now, and I was panting, and we faced each other across the shiny grooming table like enemies. The dog between us whimpered nervously, but neither of us bothered to comfort it. I could feel rage and pain clawing their way from my stomach to my throat, and I wanted to lash out at her. Stupid girl! Stupid, vicious, hurtful, ungrateful girl! Feeling that old tightening in my chest, I gripped the table to stay upright. Count, Cass. Count to twenty. Make that fifty.

When I finally managed to speak, my voice was shaking. "Yes, Nadina, Mike's right. I am a lonely, sorry-ass person with a dead husband and a dead kid, and I am no better than you or anyone else on this planet, and I'm worse than some. All of us need a little help to get through life: I know it, and you know it, and Mike knows it, and God knows it. Everyone's got a crutch, but some of the things we use for crutches are God-given gifts, and other things are just going to break off in our hands and make us hurt worse than ever. The drugs don't love you. The alcohol doesn't love you." I wanted to say that I was pretty sure Mike didn't love her either, but my courage and my anger failed me there. I felt my shoulders sag as the emotion drained, and I just felt defeated. "I'd better go."

Nadina was still glaring at me, but suddenly her eyes were welling up. "So that's it? I pissed you off and now you're not going to hang out with me anymore?"

"What?"

She hammered on the table with her fist and the dog yelped and peed. "You heard me! I pissed you off, and now you're not going to be my mentor?"

"God almighty, Nadina—you want me to be?" I demanded, perplexed.

Some of her tears overflowed, and she dashed them away angrily. "I'm not going to see you anymore, am I?"

She was incomprehensible. After turning on me like a wild animal and laying me open, she tells me that, actually, she'd like to keep me? Shaking my head, I put a tentative hand on her arm, which she instantly flung away. "If you want to see me, you'll see me." What did she want? What did I want? With an effort, I added, "And, Nadina, I apologize. I didn't mean to come across like I was judging you and your friends. I—I don't know you very well yet, and I certainly don't know your friends, and trust takes a long time to earn. I meant it out of concern. I'm sorry."

To my alarm, her face crumpled, and she started crying in earnest, burying her face in the fur of the now-truly-anxious Cocker Spaniel. I tried to pat her shoulder. "Shhhhh. Nadina, it's okay. For Pete's sake, you'll mess up your nice grooming job. Put the dog back and clean up the pee and calm down. I think your manager's coming over."

"That bitch?" Nadina screeched, hiccupping. She thrust the dog back in its cage and wiped her face quickly on a towel, seconds before a tall, wizened woman with huge glasses and long red fingernails let herself into the grooming center. "BLAISE," the nametag on her chest proclaimed: "I'm here to help."

"Nadina?" she asked, in the grainy voice of a seasoned smoker. "Everything okay here?" Her eyes took the scene in, from Nadina's puffy red eyes to my frazzled expression to the pee on the grooming table, and she added, "Everything okay, ma'am? That your dog?" Indicating the Cocker Spaniel.

I shook my head. "Oh, no. I'm just a friend of Nadina's. I popped in to say hello, and she wanted to show me what a great job she did on that little fellow. I'll be going now."

When I revealed my non-customer status, the manager put her hands on her hips and turned on Nadina. "You know we're not supposed to let folks wander around the grooming center, and I thought I had you sweeping up that spilled cat litter on 7. You better clean this up and get back out there."

Considering how Nadina had just torn me to pieces, I didn't have much hope she'd spare Blaise, but I shook my head warningly behind her manager's back.

"All right. Sorry, Blaise," Nadina muttered gruffly to the floor. "See you later, Cass." I followed Blaise out of the grooming center, relieved to be rescued from my emotional evisceration.

• • •

Though I took some time walking around the mall to decompress, it was hard to throw off a general feeling of lowness. Nadina's boyfriend had a point, though I hated to admit it, since I liked him sight-unseen as little as he liked me: I had volunteered to be a mentor partly to feel better about myself, by trying not to think about myself. Instead I seemed to be thinking about myself more and more, especially when the person I thought I was "helping" seemed so alert to my shortcomings. Was I any help to Nadina? This was the first time I tried to weigh in on her choices; prior to this I only listened and asked questions. But I must have done it badly, to get her so angry and defensive. And if it came down to my opinions or Mike's, it looked like she was going to go with Mike. And why not? Who was I to her, but some woman she hung out with, once or twice a week for a couple months?

Not only was I hurt by Nadina and feeling blue, but I was mad at God again, to tell the truth. After all, wasn't it his fault I was a "lonely, sorry-ass person, with a dead husband and a dead kid"? And then, when I try to obey him and get over myself and help someone, that someone, instead of being grateful, sticks a knife in me? I was being melodramatic, I supposed. And being angry that Nadina wasn't grateful just went to show that I was in it for myself, after all. Case closed.

Having worked myself into an even more anxious state, I decided I would email Mark Henneman before I went to bed that night. Let him know of our disastrous conversation and see what he thought I should do, if anything. He had said early on that we were there to love and encourage—and love didn't sit around letting someone destroy herself, I knew that in my heart of hearts. How could I let Nadina hurt herself without trying to intervene?

I was in such a dither that I didn't notice the time passing until it was already past six. Grabbing some random bar of scented soap and lotion for Phyl, I returned home to find all our guests already there and Joanie shooting me questioning looks.

The evening passed in a blur; unlike the Apostle Paul, I was present in body, though absent in spirit. Phyl had dutifully invited Wayne—who, truth be told, did not make much of a first impression in my present state of mind—along with her sister and some of her close friends. Roy was gone to Atlanta on a training trip, having started Monday at Cingular, but Daniel showed up triply buffered against any lingering adoration on Phyl's part: Wyatt and Delia Collins came, Daniel's odious friend Tom who had hit on Phyl long ago and was now officially divorced, and a new girlfriend whose name I can't remember, and since she didn't even last the typical two-to-three-weeks, I didn't have a chance to learn it.

For some reason, I found Tom next to me much of the evening. I hadn't even been watching to see if he'd already tried his luck with Phyl's other friends or sister, but given my distraction, I rather appreciated his indefatigable willingness to talk about himself. I had only to ask a question now and then and nod and say "oh!" and "hmm…" at the right moments, and he was content to take it from there, while

I returned to composing my mental email to Mark Henneman or thought of things I should have said to Nadina. Or things I could say, should we ever speak again. In any case, Tom must have mistaken my preoccupation for fascination because, when Joanie sent me to poke around in the pantry for birthday candles, I was startled to find him following me.

"That's great that you love backpacking," he said, leaning an arm nonchalantly on the cereal shelf and blocking my exit out. Backpacking? Me? I thought we'd been talking about him—and the last I recalled, hearing about his recent promotion. I must have really been blanking out. "Maybe you and I should do a little overnight hike on the Peninsula," he suggested.

I suppose some women would have found Tom attractive. He was wiry and athletic, with skin that was unnaturally tanned for late October in the Northwest. Could he possibly go to a tanning place? Whatever the source, it made his teeth seem particularly white and his eyes quite blue. Clutching the little pack of twisty birthday candles I took a step back from those teeth. "Backpacking? It's practically November," I said nervously.

"What's a little rain or even snow, if you've got a nice little campfire and a cozy tent?"

"Did—did your wife like to go backpacking too?"

He looked bewildered. "My ex? What does she have to do with this?" With a wave of his hand he consigned his wife to oblivion and took another step toward me. I could smell the appletini on his breath. "I thought we were really hitting it off tonight, Cass. I know I'm a little out of practice, but I'm trying to ask you out." Out of practice indeed, when I knew very well I'd seen him tailing Phyl at our first open house! And could he honestly not tell my mind had been a million miles away during his virtual monologues? I'd have to tell James that I really was quite impressive in the acting department, after all.

Trying to eke around the side of him I said hastily, "Oh, thank you very much, but no thank you. I—I—my—actually I lost my husband fairly recently, and I'm not dating."

His other arm came down like the barrier arm in a parking garage, blocking my escape. "Well, that's strange," he said, "considering how you've been coming on to me all night."

Outraged, my voice rose a little. "'Coming on to you'? *Coming on to you*? Look, Tom, I've been sitting and listening to you talk, and that's about it. Now excuse me—" I pushed on his arm, but it didn't budge. I pushed harder. Nada. It was indefensible, I know, but being cornered and accused of more bad behavior by a predatory guy I hardly knew was the last straw, after the day I'd had, and to my own horror I dissolved in angry tears. "Let me out, Tom!" I shrieked. "Get out of my way!"

Before he could even gather his wits to respond to my crazy outburst, a hand reached in and yanked him out of the pantry. "What the hell are you doing, Tom? Leave Cass alone." Of course, on a day that seemed to go from worse to worse-and-worse, it had to be Daniel. Gasping and sob-hiccuping ridiculously, I tried to wipe off my face before he could see me, but no luck. I heard Tom grunt something apologetic as he left the kitchen, and I expected Daniel to follow him, but he didn't.

"You all right?" he asked. I nodded in answer, turning away to blot the last embarrassing tears. When I didn't say anything, he added lightly, "You could hardly blame Tom, you little tramp, the way you were daydreaming and agreeing with everything he said, while he droned on and on. He's come to mistake that glazed expression for adoration."

Despite all, I giggled a little. "If that's all it takes, he should see me when I do the laundry."

"I couldn't answer for the consequences."

"Hell-o, Cass!" Joanie called. "What the heck is going on with those birthday candles? And where was Tom going in such a hurry? It's time to do Phyl's cake."

. . .

It was almost 10:30 when the party finally broke up and I could dash upstairs to email Mark Henneman. After Tom's ambush I couldn't remember half my mental composition, so I would have to start over, but when I sat down at my computer, there was a text from Nadina in my inbox. Lobbing more emotional grenades at me? Anxiously I tapped my fingers on the desk, trying to work up the nerve to open it.

She must have wanted to make sure she would be understood because the message was in English, rather than her usual texting patois.

> Cass,
> Sorry I said those things. I know you weren't trying to be mean. See you Tuesday?
> Nadina

My relief was so great I burst into tears again—happy ones this time. Maybe I was going into early menopause. Joanie found me fifteen minutes later, still wet-faced but in good spirits, typing my response:

> Nadina,
> Thank you for your message. You are my favorite wannabe pet groomer in the whole world!
> Next week it is.
> Cass

"Cass, what on earth is going on with you?" Joanie demanded. "You acted like such a zombie tonight! I couldn't believe it when I looked over, and you let that stupid Tom glom on to you and bore your ear off."

"Was I so bad?" I sniffled, smiling. "I hope I didn't put a damper on Phyl's birthday."

"Phyl was trying so hard to act like she didn't care about my brother that she was probably the only one who didn't notice. Sheez, your weird behavior even penetrated Daniel's narcissism; he asked me after you went up if you were okay." We laughed, and she threw an arm around me. Now that my fight with Nadina was no longer the end of the world, I found I could talk about it and even find some humor in the poor Cocker Spaniel's ordeal.

Joanie fired up with indignation when I got to what Nadina said, but after I had—with some difficulty—talked her down, she huffed, "Well, if you're going to forgive her I guess I have to. You may get over being called a lonely old sorry-ass on emotional crutches, but it's going to take me a lot longer to forgive being called your 'goody-goody friend.'"

CHAPTER 14

A Bad Year for McKean Marriages

"Yeah, yeah, this stuff on Scott is great, but what is with your little digs at Amundsen?" Riley demanded, jabbing the paper with his stubby forefinger.

We were crammed into his cubicle at Free Universe, going over some of my latest revisions for *Antarctiquest!* Because there wasn't room for two chairs, I was perched on the end of his work table trying not to wipe out his action-figure diorama with my behind.

"Does it show?" I asked sheepishly. "It kind of bugs me that Amundsen only beat Scott to the South Pole because he was gunning for that and nothing else. Scott, on the other hand, was thinking science and exploration and responsibility to posterity."

"That is crap. That is total girl-think and girl-speak," declared Riley.

"Well I'm a girl. So sue me," I retorted.

"Yeah, well, you're gonna have to put on your boy hat, if you wanna work at Free Universe, because 90% of our gamers are boys. Jeri puts on her boy hat every day, don't you, Jer?" He raised his voice to deliver this zinger, and Jeri leaned around the wall of her cube to flip him off.

"Amundsen made it to the goal; he kept his eyes on the prize. Besides, we market our games around the world—or we want to—so you can't be knocking Amundsen and pissing off everyone in Denmark."

"Norway."

"Whatever." He handed me back half my sheaf. "So I'll take the Scott and Shackleton stuff, but don't give me Amundsen until you've declawed it. Think guy, Cass. More guys are gonna wanna play the Amundsen and Shackleton scenarios than the Scott one—who wants to be the guy who dies like a popsicle?"

This was maybe my fourth visit to the Free Universe office downtown. Since I did all my writing at home and was in frequent email contact with other team members, I didn't really need to come in, but the game developer world was proving irresistible. The forty or so employees of Free Universe occupied office space that I would wager was designed for twenty, jammed up next to each other in high-walled cubicles which provided some visual privacy but no sound protection. If anyone really wanted to get something done, they stuffed in their earbuds and cranked up their MP3 players; James even had some of those fancy noise-cancelling headphones for which he'd taken truckloads of flak until other people had tried them on. Riley, however, a Game Designer, thrived on the constant interaction and noise and provided much of it himself, to his immediate neighbors' irritation. In the few weeks I'd known him, he'd quickly become my new favorite person, from his bald-but-ponytailed head to his ridiculous t-shirts ("Squirrel— the other White Meat") to his Tevas with socks. But it wasn't just his looks: I also loved the unapologetically geeky collections that littered his cube, with his petrified candy museum topping the list.

I dug in my jacket pocket for a minute. "Oh, hey, Riley. I saw you didn't have one of these—I used to eat tons of these in college because they were made nearby."

"A Big Hunk! Yeah, baby!" Riley quickly popped it out of its wrapper and positioned it tenderly on his cube's fraction of the window sill, the better to be quickly petrified by the forced air running up underneath. Then he carefully smoothed out the wrapper and placed it in his top drawer. Once the candy petrification was complete he would fashion the wrapper into some delicate origami creation and display them together.

"Aw, Cass, no, don't encourage him." James had appeared, his noise-cancelling headphones around his neck. "We finally got him to agree that he can only display ten moldy bits—"

"Artifacts!" corrected Riley.

"Ten artifacts at a time," James agreed. "Ri, are you sure you want that one enough to part with one of the others when it's done?"

"Of course I want it. Cass gave me this one—and don't think I didn't get your subtle message, babe. A Big Hunk for the big hunk." He slapped his generous gut with satisfaction.

I burst out laughing. "I knew I couldn't slip that by you, Riley. It was between the Big Hunk and a Sugar Daddy."

Jeri leaned out again. "I gave him Nerds last Christmas, deluxe size." She was warming to me, if only slightly, since I showed no signs of wanting to steal her full-time job.

James cleared his throat. "Cass, if you and Riley have wrapped it up, Murray wants you to drop by Lockdown before you leave." Obediently I rose, waving my goodbyes.

Lockdown was Murray's office. As the Sound Designer at Free Universe, he was the only one in the company who got an actual office with walls and a locking door, thus the nickname. Murray was a pale, skinny guy with long, stringy blond hair to match his overly-long limbs. He wore round little glasses, and altogether he reminded me of an albino grasshopper. Because Murray's office doubled as the recording studio, the walls were covered with chunks of foam, and countless cords snaked their way across the floor, hooked up to various pieces of mystery music and sound equipment.

Murray looked up from his little desk in the corner when I came in. "Hi, Cass. Did you get the scripts Jeri sent?"

I nodded.

"Everything make sense? You think you'll be ready to record next Friday?"

"Sure—I don't have to memorize, right? I just sit there and read?"

"You just sit there and read."

"And did James tell you that that kid Kyle was going to come after school gets out and observe?" I asked.

Murray nodded. "If he can keep his mouth shut, he can come." That wouldn't be a problem for Kyle, at any rate. For a guy who did sound for a living, Murray had a strange aversion to it, viewing banter and small talk as unnecessary at best—which might explain why he and Riley got on each other's nerves frequently—and this terse warning signaled the end of the interview.

I flipped through Jeri's script on the bus ride home. There wasn't much to it: one introductory monologue of sufficient corniness and various discrete lines of dialogue and random interjections, including such jewels as "Freeze flame!" and "Die, Varlet!" James was right about not needing an Oscar-winning performance; the real trick would be recording such silliness without giggling. Hence Murray on the job, I supposed. No one in that office made you feel less like laughing than Murray.

Walking up the hill from the bus stop I was surprised to see a strange man raking leaves in our front yard. Most of the leaves had fallen long ago, and the remaining stragglers were rather blackened and damp, but the man was doggedly scraping them from where they clung to the grass. Something about his movements drew my attention, and then I was running.

"Perry! Why didn't you call me?" I demanded. "I was at Free Universe and could've gotten here sooner."

Slinging an arm around me, he shook his head. "I did call you, idiot. Your phone must be dead. Come on, let me in and give me the tour."

As we did the circuit of the Palace, Perry filled me in on the latest. It turned out he had moved up to Portland at the end of October to start work on *Waiters: the Musical*. He was sharing some tiny place with a couple other people he'd found on Craig's List and loving it. "Not that it won't be great to spend a night up here in your huge spare room. This place is great, Cass!"

"Is that all you're staying? The one night?" I prodded when we were at the kitchen table, sharing some of Phyl's molasses cookies and tea.

Perry looked shifty. "That's it this time, but, hey—what are your Thanksgiving plans? Want me to come up and make the best stuffed turkey since Grandma McKean died? Or were you going to go hang out with Troy's family?"

I suppressed a shiver. "No way. I'll probably see them all the weekend before, but I told them I had other plans that day."

"And do you?"

"Well, we have a standing open house on Thursdays, so I guess that counts. Phyl will probably have her sister over, if they don't take off to see her folks, and I think Joanie and Daniel are around. I'd love to have you." Perry looked so happy about this that I hated to wreck it, but I had to ask: "So what's going on with Betsy? Have you heard from her?"

Sure enough, his face fell. "I've heard from her lawyer." When I gasped, he nodded grimly. "Yep. It's official this time. Betsy is divorcing me."

"You have to talk to her," I insisted. "She doesn't mean it. She's always taken you back. Have you talked to her?"

"I have, I have." He held up his long hands defensively. "I even offered to drop it all and get a real job this time, the more boring the better."

"You did?" I was amazed, Perry never having made such an offer during any of their previous separations. Before this it had been enough that he take on a second slacker job. "And Betsy didn't take you up on it?"

He'd dunked his cookie so long in his tea that it had broken up like the flotsam of a shipwreck. "She didn't even consider it really because I think she's dating the lawyer."

"Dating the lawyer?" I screeched. "Which happened first? Dating the lawyer or serving you papers?"

"I think it was simultaneous," he sighed.

Pressing my lips together, I tried to prevent saying anything too regrettable, but the effort was too great. I had to bolt up from the table and cover my stream of furious muttering with kitchen clatter: pots and pans, pantry rummaging, slamming the refrigerator drawers open and shut. Perry must have thought I was too dangerous to be wielding a kitchen knife because, when I smacked an onion down on the cutting board, he wordlessly disarmed me and began chopping it himself.

On ordinary occasions—meaning, when I wasn't so upset I thought I would explode—I loved to watch Perry cook. That fancy Culinary Institute of America training he'd done in San Francisco had never led to any longstanding desire to be a chef, but it had made him more stylish and skillful than your average home cook. Not that he hadn't been more skillful to begin with, I had to admit.

Needing to do something aggressive, I started ripping up the head of romaine. "That lawyer should be disbarred!" I finally exclaimed. "How can you be a divorce lawyer and hit on your clients? It's conflict of interest! It's—"

"Betsy said she'll switch lawyers," Perry said soothingly.

"Betsy!" I raged, tearing the heart of romaine off the base, "Changing lawyers is the least she can do—don't get me started on Betsy—

what's wrong with you, Perry? Why are you so calm about this?"

"I've had a couple more months than you to get used to the idea," he explained. He had moved on to slice the carrots in a flawlessly uniform julienne. "Don't get me wrong—I'm mad too, but I've been suspecting this was it since September. I just didn't want to drop the bomb when you were down last month for Mom's birthday."

"Oh, Perry, I'm so sorry," I said helplessly.

"Yeah. I mean, I know it wasn't easy to be married to me. Though you'd have thought that meeting me in Cabo like she did, Betsy would've had a little more patience with a freewheeling kind of life, but she says she wants kids now and that I can't seem to grow up myself."

Nothing I hadn't occasionally thought myself about Perry, so I had to bite my tongue again and just murmur sympathetically. Shouldn't he, at 31, be getting a little sick of the self-important theater scene and of sharing apartments and medicine cabinets and refrigerator space with strangers he found on the internet?

"What do you think, Cass? Am I as hopeless as she says?" He paused in all his slicing and dicing to study my response. Having always been a wretched liar, I managed not to squirm, but a telltale blush rose in my cheeks. "You do!" Perry accused. "You think I'm hopeless! You would have divorced me, too."

To mollify him and hide my own face, I threw my arms around him and hugged him from the back. "No, Perry! I mean, I wouldn't have married you in the first place because you know how rigidly I had my life planned out. But Betsy married you with her eyes open." I rested my forehead against his shoulder. "You're a good guy, Perry."

He turned and swallowed me up in one of his giant hugs, and I was appalled to see he had teared up—it reminded me of how he had looked after we lost Min. We were quiet for a long time, and then he gave me another little squeeze and released me. "It's been a bad year for McKean marriages, I guess."

I blew my nose. "You can say that again, even though I'm a Ewan. Did you tell Mom and Dad? Looks like it's your turn to dominate the Please Pray For section of their church bulletin."

"Why do you think I'm hiding out in Portland?"

. . .

To my surprise, Daniel was the first one home that evening. When he strolled into the kitchen he stopped short and glanced sharply at Perry, who was expertly plating the fricasseed chicken and showing me how to garnish it with fennel fronds, but his expression relaxed when Perry chided, "No, idiot, don't put all the green in the same place on the dish."

"Perry," I said quickly, "This is my housemate Daniel Martin. Daniel, this is my brother Perry who's up visiting for a night." They nodded at each other, and I added, "Perry cooked the dinner tonight, and you're just in time—in fact, you're early. What are you doing home so early?"

He grinned at me. "Remember Josh, the one on family leave? He's back. Looks like he didn't sleep the whole time he was off, but he's back." Helping himself to a beer, he offered Perry one. "So how did Cass get the fancy Greek name, and you got named Perry?"

I snorted. "He actually got the fancier Greek name because Perry is short for Pericles."

Smirking at each other, Perry and I added in unison, "Of Athens, not of Tyre."

"Perry always used to say that to people when he was introduced," I explained, "until I finally told him that probably only ten people in America had heard of either Pericles, and two of the ten were our parents."

That evening was our first household dinner all together and almost alone since who knew when. Since I knew Perry was only staying one night and that Daniel didn't mind, I could relax and enjoy having him around, and I'm sure Perry appreciated talking about something other than his impending divorce. Daniel also seemed glad of a male buffer, and he was the least tense he'd been around Phyl since the early days. We talked culinary school and Portland, since Daniel and Joanie had grown up there, Perry's screenwriting efforts, and, of course, what was going on with *Waiters: the Musical.*

"That was so delicious," Phyl said, at last, laying her silverware across her plate. "And beautifully presented, like in a restaurant."

"Yeah, and not the restaurants Jason took you to," cracked Joanie, pouring us each a last sip of pinot grigio to empty the bottle.

"Or Wayne, for that matter," added Phyl regretfully. "Give Wayne one of those all-you-can-eat buffets, and he's a happy man."

Joanie looked skeptical. "You've gotta be kidding me—isn't he a little young to like all-you-can-eat buffets, or is it his mom who's hooked on the canned peas and mac-and-cheese?"

"Ooh! Ooh!" I broke in. "'Canned peas and mac-and-cheese'—I feel lyrics coming on! Perry, does *Waiters: the Musical* have any songs about 'Wayne at the all-you-can-eat bu-u-u-u-u-ffe-e-e-e-et?"

Perry punched me in the arm, but Joanie instantly began dinging her glass rhythmically with her knife: "Those tater tots really hit the spot/ jell-o mold, worth its weight in gold/ frankly, my dear, I don't give a damn/ just slice me up some honey-baked ham—"

"And there'd be a chorus line of 250-pound retirees crossing the stage—"

"Banging their canes and walkers, like a production of *Stomp*—"

"And the end of the song could be a spotlight on one guy in plaid golf pants singing, 'Waiter, can I have the check, ple-e-e-e-e-ease?'" I finished. Joanie and I collapsed, cackling, and Phyl was trying not to laugh, to spare Perry's feelings.

Perry, however, after aiming another smack at the back of my head, only laughed and said, "Yeah, so *Waiters* isn't going to win any Tony Awards, but it's not as bad as you two think."

"You're right, Perry, it couldn't possibly be as bad as we think," I agreed readily, sending Joanie and me into more gales of laughter.

He rolled his eyes at Daniel. "How can you stand to live with them? Cass has been cutting me down to size since she was six."

"No surprise there," said Daniel, smiling. "I've only known her a few months, and I can't count how many times she's given me the rough side of her tongue." Though his tone was light, he gave me his usual wicked look, in case I might miss his *double entendre*, and I resisted the urge to stick that tongue out at him. Chuckling, he went on easily, "And we gave up on Joanie early on. Joanie will say what Joanie will say, or sing, as the case may be."

Joanie made an apologetic face at Perry. "I somewhat apologize. I don't really know you well enough to mock you, and I was presuming on Cass's relationship with you."

Perry nodded graciously, and Phyl piped up in her soothing voice, "And of course we would love to come down to Portland and see your show when it opens."

"If you give us free tickets," I put in.

"And reimburse our mileage," added Joanie.

There was a general chorus of screams as Perry reached his limit of endurance and tackled me, knocking Phyl off the end of the bench. I kicked at him, but I was laughing too hard to fight effectively and had to cry "uncle" when he had me on lying on my side while he sat on top of me. "Remember this technique, Martin," he advised Daniel. "If Cass ever gets too much for you, a little manhandling puts her in her place."

Daniel's amused grin widened when he heard my resentful huff. "I'll make a note of it."

CHAPTER 15:

Back on the Wagon

There was a text in my email inbox Tuesday morning. Nadina had given up on texting to my phone, since it was dead half the time. With the practice I'd gotten from her cryptic messages and Riley's emails, and some additional help from online glossaries, I came up with this respectable translation:

Cass—

In class. So boring. Math makes no sense again. What do you suggest? Can we go to your house this afternoon? I wanted to make Sonya some cookies and mail them. Don't bother coming to get me. I'll come to you. Let me know if that's not okay. See you later.

Nadina

Since our fight and electronic reconciliation, things between us had been both better and worse. Better because we hadn't had any other arguments, but worse because we had avoided any controversial subjects, meaning most of Nadina's life. While I wasn't sure what to do about it, I knew I didn't want to force intimacy and trust on her.

Nadina's friend Sonya had indeed decided to go away to rehab, but I knew no further details—not what it was, where it was, how long it lasted, anything. Throwing some butter on the counter to soften, I hoped that Nadina wanting to work on a care package together indicated she was ready to talk about it.

The doorbell didn't ring until 3:30, and Nadina burst in without waiting for me to get it. "Cass, hey."

"What happened to you? Did you get lost?"

"You'd be proud of me because I cornered Bateman after school and actually asked him for math help!" Nadina exclaimed, throwing her damp rain jacket on one of the cushioned benches and tossing me a bag of chocolate chips.

"Since you're late, I assume Kyle said yes?" I asked.

"Yeah. You know what? He's okay. I mean, he's a smart-ass and doesn't try very hard to talk to people, so they all think he's full of himself, but he's actually okay. I've been telling other people he's cool."

I stopped my clanging around with the stand mixer to go over and squeeze her arm. "Oh, Nadina, that's great. Thank you!" She rolled her eyes exaggeratedly, to let me know I was being embarrassing and corny, but I also knew she wouldn't have told me except that she knew it would please me.

Talk about school got us through the mixing of the dough, and I waited until Nadina was dropping the heaping tablespoonfuls on the cookie sheet to broach the Sonya subject: "So how far away are we mailing these suckers?"

"Not far. The place is only in Bellingham."

"How long will she be there?"

Nadina shrugged. "I dunno. Henneman says it depends on the

student. Maybe another few weeks? But like, she couldn't even bring her cell phone, and there's no computers. You can only mail things."

"You mean you two can't spend eight hours a day texting each other like you usually do?"

"Nope," said Nadina. "She gets a little regular phone time once a week, but she has to use most of it talking to her mom and dad. For me she had to send a postcard."

Taking the cup of tea I offered her, Nadina perched on the counter to dry dishes as I washed. "Dude, she says there's a workout room and a game room and stuff, but they have to meet with all these counselors, and she says sometimes they try to get all religious on them."

I paused. "Is Sonya religious?"

"Her grandma's Catholic, or something," Nadina answered carelessly. "They do religious stuff at our school, too. It's fine. I mean I believe in God and everything; I'm just not very religious." She was drying the same bowl without really seeing it, round and round the rim. "You're not very religious either, are you, Cass?"

"Why do you say that?" I asked with some trepidation, not really wanting to hear her answer.

"You never say things like, 'I'll pray for you,' and you never talk about church and Jesus and stuff. I know you go to church, but that's it. Sonya said her mentor Louella was always going on about, like, God this and Jesus that, and praying for different things and asking if Sonya wanted prayer and crap like that. Awkward."

Awkward indeed. I was beginning to worry that my tombstone might read: *Well, she was no Louella Murphy*. "Nadina," I said after a moment, "I don't talk about prayer much because I haven't been praying much, honestly. I used to pray all the time, but since Troy and Min died I've kind of been keeping to myself. But I am religious, if by religious you mean I believe in God. Believe that God made me and…cares about me. You know, the only reason I know you is because I couldn't help it one morning in church, and I was praying about what to do, and I felt like I was supposed to be a Camden School mentor."

She stared at me like I had lapsed into another language. "Seriously?"

I described the nudge I'd felt and the entire string of events that had led to her being in my kitchen that afternoon. "I guess I don't talk about God or religion with you because I'm in such a weird place spiritually. It would feel fake. It reminds me of the time in high school when my brother Perry was trying to sell his car. He put an ad in the paper because there was no Craig's List then, but when his best friend offered to buy it, Perry didn't know what to say. I mean, it was an okay car to sell to a stranger, but you would want the car to be perfect, if you were going to sell it to a friend." Cripe, now I was comparing God Almighty to a used car.

Nadina thought about this. "So you still go to church and believe in all that Jesus-God stuff, and you still think he talked to you enough to make you a mentor, but you wouldn't want to sell me God because he let Troy and Min die?"

I smiled wryly. "That about sums it up. The car runs, and you'll get where you're trying to get eventually, but there's no guarantee it's not going to break down on you and cost a lot of money to fix." Taking some cookies from the cooling rack, we sat down on the barstools to eat them.

Nadina took a big swig of milk before asking, "Where are you trying to get to? Heaven?"

I chewed meditatively. "To be honest, I never thought much about heaven until Troy and Min died. It was always about wanting to know God here and now. If He made me, and He loved me, like they told me in church, and He sent his Son to come looking for me—"

"What do you mean 'come looking for you'?" she interrupted.

"Isn't He God? Doesn't He already know where you are?"

I grinned. "You're right. Maybe I should have said He sent his Son to come after us. We ran away from God, so he sent Jesus to ask us to come back and hang out with Him. I guess that makes knowing God the destination, and Jesus the car that gets me there. If God loved me and went to all that trouble, I wanted to see what He was about."

"And you think that's what Jesus was about? God trying to get us to come back to him? That sounds totally lame and desperate to me, Cass. If you're God, why wouldn't you just be cool kicking it in heaven with a bunch of angels and blowing things up when you felt like it? Why would you care if a few billion little ant-people don't want to hang out with you?"

"I guess because you can't help who you love."

Nadina ate another cookie, breaking it in quarters. "So now what? You decided you wanted to hang out with Him, so you got in your little ant-person car and headed off, but it broke down and now you don't know if you want to get back in?"

"Oh, I'll get back in eventually. I just want to get out and kick the tires and slam the doors and pound on the hood and cuss for a while. I don't really have a choice."

"You could walk."

"It's too far."

"Take the bus?"

"None of the bus routes go anywhere near. For me it's Jesus or nothing."

She sighed. "I changed my mind. You're even more of a Jesus Freak than Louella, and you're worse because you're trying to be sneaky about it. I don't even buy all that Jesus-loves-you crock, and you've got me wanting you to get back in the car." When I put an arm around her shoulders to squeeze her, she shrugged me off casually, adding, "I don't want to be the only one with the lame mentor who doesn't pray for her."

"Look at me, Nadina," I commanded. Her blue eyes met mine skeptically. "If you would like me to pray for you, I will pray for you. What do you want me to pray?"

She was done with our almost heart-to-heart, however. "Use your imagination."

• • •

After Nadina had gone, I spread out my Amundsen research materials at the kitchen table but ended up staring out the bay window for an hour or so, lost in thought until I heard the front door slam.

"Cass! Oh, Cass, guess what?" Phyl rushed in, her wavy brown hair flying and her eyes snapping with excitement.

"What on earth, Phyl? Are you okay?"

She flung herself down on the cushioned bench opposite me and grabbed my hands. "The tackiest—you are never going to believe—" Out of breath, she nevertheless managed to succumb to a giggling fit.

"For the love of Mike, Phyl, spill the beans!" I urged, giving her hands a squeeze.

"Okay, okay. Wayne proposed to me!" She enjoyed my dumbfounded expression for a second before barreling on. "He proposed to me today at lunch *at a hot dog stand.*"

Recovering my voice I said, "There are so many things wrong with that sentence I don't know where to start."

"I know," Phyl laughed. "When I called Joanie, I could barely get her to understand. I tried to call you, but your phone was dead, as usual. Wayne proposed! At lunch! At a hot dog stand!"

"You've only known him a couple months," I wondered aloud. "He even beat Roy to the punch. Did he bring his mom along? And what did you say to him? No, or hell no? Give me details."

"To make a long story short, I said no," Phyl began.

"Come on, Phyl. Make a long story long—start at the beginning," I insisted.

"Well, okay. He messaged me at about ten o'clock and asked if I could have lunch today at Seastar, but I had a meeting at 11:00 and another one at 1:00, so I didn't think it could happen. But he must have promised himself he was going to ask me today because he wouldn't let me beg off. All we had time for was the hot dog stand on the corner by my office. So there I am, loading up on the Gulden's Spicy Brown, when all of a sudden he grabs my hand off the dispenser pump and says, 'Phyl, I'm in love with you. You're the girl I've been waiting for. Will you marry me?'"

I clapped my hands, thrilled. "Go, Wayne! Imagine—he couldn't even wait till you were spooning on the onions. Is it too late to change your mind? Lesser men would have aborted the mission when it got moved to the hot dog stand, but not our man Wayne."

Phyl giggled. "I'm not sure he even noticed. Probably his mom told him to ask me at a nice restaurant, but when he had to go to Plan B he probably didn't think it would matter."

"Nor did it, in the event," I pointed out. "Were you sorry to say no? Even the littlest bit?"

She weighed this for a moment. "You know, Cass, I was! You know how I've been kind of lukewarm on him all along—lukewarm at best. He's nice-looking and employed and kind and even interesting, once you get him talking—did I tell you he's a World War II buff?"

"You don't have to sell me on Wayne, Phyl. As Elizabeth Bennett said to her sister Jane, 'You've liked many a stupider person.' Jason, for instance. And Daniel, for another." She looked sheepish, and I asked hesitantly, "If you think he's not so bad after all, do you think you could learn to love him? We really don't know him very well, at this point, but he seems to be a quality guy." She grimaced and shrugged her shoulders. "You didn't turn him down because of…of Daniel, did you?"

"No-o-o," Phyl answered unwillingly. "I still like Daniel—I can't help that—but he's clearly not interested in me, and I'm not just going to pine over him the rest of my life. I just wish Wayne were a little more exciting. The whole engineer thing, and the dutiful son thing just don't do it for me. I can always guess what he's going to do or say."

"That is total bunk, Phyl," I protested. "You had no idea he was going to propose to you so soon—today—and the hot dog stand was pure bonus unpredictability."

"Good point," she amended. After a pause Phyl asked, "Troy did engineering, didn't he? But you didn't think he was boring."

"He could be vastly boring, if he was talking about one of his work projects," I said encouragingly, "but I could bore him right back when I talked about my dull days staying home with a baby. For every exciting milestone Min hit, there were lots more hours spent talking about what brand of diapers I liked, or what my friends had read about baby food, or Min's sleeping habits. Life has a lot of boring in it. Maybe the trick is marrying someone with your sense of humor, so that even when you hit all the boring, you can joke about it. Troy and I could. Didn't you find with Jason that marriage was at least 85% companionship?"

"Not really. Being married to Jason was about 85% fighting and 10% sex and 5% companionship."

I winced. "Ooh, that's bad. And I bet if you married Daniel it'd be 85% sex, 10% fighting, and 5% companionship, until he dumped you."

"I could go for those ratios," Phyl grinned incorrigibly. "Until he dumped me, that is."

"So did Wayne go away completely demoralized, and you've seen the last of him, or is he asking to keep seeing you?"

"To keep seeing me," Phyl answered slowly. "And—I didn't even tell Joanie this—after I said no, and he said he was going to keep trying, if I didn't mind, he grabbed me, hot dog and all, and kissed me in front of everyone."

I whistled appreciatively. "Wow! I'll hardly be able to look at him this Thursday without blushing." I teased. "And think—next time you see Jason, you'll have some bragging rights. When's the last time Jessica kissed *him* over a hot dog?"

$$\bullet \quad \bullet \quad \bullet$$

When Joanie got home we hashed through it once more.

"Cass thinks I shouldn't rule him out until I get to know him better," Phyl concluded. "What do you think?"

"Quality people improve on acquaintance," I explained. "Flashy people like Jason get worse the longer you know them. I think Wayne falls in the first bucket."

Joanie considered. "Well, dear Wayne is probably never gonna set the Thames on fire, even if you know him for years—"

"Who wants a husband who sets the Thames on fire?" I insisted. "Thrill-seeking guys do not make good husbands. They dump you right off, like Jason, or they dump you when they hit their mid-life crisis and run off with the first aerobics instructor who compliments their receding hairline." Joanie and Phyl didn't look entirely convinced. Flustered, I continued, "I'm not saying boring is beautiful— I'm just saying that thrilling is overrated. Troy and I had humor and mutual respect and compatible outlooks on life... If he hadn't up and died on me, I think we could have gone the distance."

Hearing my voice tighten up a little, Joanie put a hand over mine. "Aw, Cass..."

"It's okay, Joanie," I said quickly. "All I mean to say is that Wayne is a good man, and he has serious long-distance potential, Phyl. Don't rule him out."

• • •

My conversation with Nadina and Wayne's proposal made it difficult to fall asleep that night. After an hour or two of staring up at the ceiling, I found myself praying before I realized it. When it did hit me what I was doing, I stiffened and tacked on a surly, *Don't think I've forgotten about what You did to me—I'm just praying because I told Nadina I would.* But after a space of time I even dropped that. *Fine. I'm praying. Who else am I going to ask?* And there was so much to ask for Nadina: I prayed she would dump Mike and move back in with her mom; I prayed she would be able to stand up to him and keep off the hard drugs; I prayed for the people around her to make good choices; I prayed for wisdom and self-control when I spoke to her; I prayed she might begin to think about her life and what she was doing on earth.

Prayers for Nadina drifted into other prayers, for Phyl, for Perry and Betsy, for Kyle, for myself. Maybe what I had told Nadina was no longer relevant: sometime in the past few months I had gotten back in the car. My Bible still sat gathering dust on the shelf, but I occasionally flipped through Joanie's or Phyl's, if they left it lying around.

In church, too, I had begun to invest again. I now recognized many faces at the early service and even made chitchat with those who regularly sat around me. This group included Louella Murphy, whose bright appliqué jacket I had spied one Sunday from up in the balcony and whom I gravitated toward thereafter. Along with the faces, the hymns had grown familiar, and I began to sing again because I had always loved to sing. There were still the services where I was out of sorts and would spend the hour trying not to burst into tears, but they were getting less frequent. If Louella would catch me on one of those mornings, she would reach over and squeeze my hand encouragingly. Once when she did this she whispered, "I miss my Frank, too."

"How—how did you know?" I gasped under my breath.

"Nadina told Sonya, and Sonya told me," she said simply. "I'm sorry about your little girl, too—oh! Shhh…it's okay."

Really, though, those days were getting fewer and farther between. As I drifted off to sleep, one final prayer flitted across my mind: *You're still there, I guess. Thank you.*

CHAPTER 16:

Virgin Territory

"You want to try it again, Cass? You're getting that hitch in your voice."

Murray's own hitch-less, dry voice came over the headphones, and despite his long-suffering tone I knew he was impatient with me. I was perched on a stool, the script on a towel-draped music stand in front of me, surrounded on three sides by jury-rigged walls covered in geometric, acoustical foam. A microphone hovered in my face, covered by a pop filter to catch any overexuberant "p" or "b" or "s" sounds. When I had jokingly recited "Peter Piper picked a peck of pickled peppers" to test it out, Murray didn't even give a perfunctory laugh. But it wasn't Murray or my strange setting that was throwing me.

After one more unsuccessful take, I pulled off my headphones and said, "James, you've got to go. You're throwing me off."

"Who, me?" he protested, grinning. "I'm not doing a thing." Murray and I had been doing just fine getting some of the one-off lines down, including that ridiculous, "Die, Varlet!" But then James had let himself into Lockdown, cup of coffee and clipboard in hand, drawn up another stool not ten feet from me, and proceeded to observe, a half-smile playing about his lips.

"These lines are corny enough. I absolutely can't say them when someone is watching me," I insisted. "So buzz off, or at least go sit by Murray where I can't see you."

Instead, he pulled his stool closer. "Cass, where's your professionalism? Pretend I'm not here."

"If you wanted a professional, you should have forked out the money to hire one," I retorted. "You hired someone who's only been in high school plays, so go away."

James laughed but threw up his arms in surrender. "Fine, fine, I'll go away. But I thought you invited Kyle to come and watch. What are you doing to do when he gets here?"

"I'll tell him he has to sit by Murray."

"Speaking of Murray," said Murray loudly, "Can we respect Murray's time here and get back to recording?"

James and I smiled sheepishly at each other, and he shot Murray a Cub Scout salute. "Need anything?" he whispered before he left. "Drink of water? Snack?" Shaking my head, I watched him slip out. His movements were always so quick and precise; he reminded me of one of Lewis' animated characters in *Tolt*—the Elf Archer, maybe. Not that I would ever say that to him, though, men not generally liking to be compared with elves.

With James gone and only the dour Murray's voice in my ears we made more progress, and when I finally emerged from the recording booth, it was to find that Kyle had been there quite some time. He was sitting beside Murray, wearing identical goofy headphones and responding to Murray's murmured comments monosyllabically. Trust Kyle to cotton on to all things technical instantly. He pointed to one of the thousand knobs on what looked like a black dashboard in front of Murray and asked a question I couldn't hear. Given how unexcited Murray had been at the prospect of having an observer, I was astonished to see him nod and launch into a lengthy explanation. The two of them reminded me of the Sorcerer and his apprentice brewing up some dark magic together.

When I was right next to him, Kyle looked up at last and nodded. I heard him say, "Thanks, Man," before removing his headphones.

"Peace," answered Murray, barely glancing at me as we left.

After I shut the door behind us, I burst out, "Sheesh, Kyle! How did you ever manage to charm Murray?" He looked at me questioningly. "I couldn't get two friendly words out of him all afternoon, and there he was talking to you and showing you things!" Kyle only gave his usual shrug, and I added resignedly, "I guess it was all downhill after I asked him what some of the 'doodads' in the recording booth were. He seemed offended by my technical jargon. Come on, you want to get coffee with me?"

"James said to grab him when we were done," said Kyle tonelessly.

"Oh, okay then," I agreed. We didn't even make it as far as James' cube, however, because we found him crammed in Riley's, where the two of them were having an animated discussion.

"Dude, everyone knows there's no sound in space," Riley exclaimed, holding up a hand to greet me. "You put sound effects in the spacewalk sequence, and nerds around the world are gonna flame us in their blogs."

"Ri, you can't have an extended silent sequence," objected James. "Everyone's going to think their console or their TV or computer is on the fritz. It's a convention to have sound effects in space. Think of every space movie you've ever seen. Even nerds suspend their disbelief. It's like when you call someone—you know the ringing sound you hear has nothing to do with the ringing sound the physical phone generates. Kyle, you with me on this one?"

Before Kyle could respond, Riley blurted, "Think about it, Bateman. It's not a battle scene—it's a spacewalk sequence. You know, the astronaut's got to fix the friggin' mirror that isn't pointing the right direction anymore and that kind of crap. What do you want, power drills and hammering?"

"Silent," judged Kyle.

James threw up his hands in mock despair. "Overruled by a 15-year-old. Who's mentoring this kid anyhow? He should be fired instantly."

"How about music?" I suggested. "Floating-in-space kind of music. Fixing-mirrors-and-tightening-screws-in-space kind of music."

Riley gave a loud guffaw. "God, Murray will be all over it. All his crap-o music sounds like synthesizers falling into bathtubs—perfect background music for spacewalks."

"Or you could do loud, in-helmet breathing," I went on. "You know, the spacewalk from the astronaut's perspective. I could record some breathing sounds for you."

"No way," said Riley. "If we put in girl-breathing, the game won't get an 'E for Everyone' rating. On the other hand, if we could get Jeri to record the breathing, it would be more androgynous." Predictably, Jeri's hand appeared over the cubicle wall, flipping him off.

"Riley," I protested, "no one can tell the difference between girl- and guy-breathing—and I didn't mean panting breathing, you pervert."

"We'll give Murray the final say on the sound," said James, cutting off any further debate. "But there will be some kind of sound. Let's get some coffee. You coming, Ri?"

• • •

The coffee break was a riot. Riley and Kyle got into a big argument over some bit of *Star Wars* arcana that I couldn't follow, even after the hours of research I put in on my novelization, with James throwing in his two cents' worth from time to time without measurable results.

"You hide your nerdiness well," I remarked to James, when Riley and Kyle escalated to drawing dueling diagrams on the unbleached paper napkins. I couldn't recall ever seeing Kyle this lively.

"You wouldn't say that if you saw me in high school," James answered easily. "It'd be another few years before I finally grew into my head, got contacts, changed the wardrobe. A girlfriend made me over freshman year in college."

I smiled. "It'll do. You could pass easily now for someone who did tennis team in high school."

"You mean it? The marching band and Academic Decathlon don't show anymore?"

"Not a bit. But tell me how the Ducati fits in—all the nerds I knew in high school didn't tool around on any cool bikes."

"Yeah, my motorcycle interest was something I had to hide from my friends and my enemies, since they both would have given me grief for it," James admitted. "Lucky for me my parents wouldn't let me have a bike in high school. Riley and the guys still give me hell for it when I get it out in the spring—it's like I bring up bad memories for them of being stuffed in lockers."

"Stuffed in lockers?" I gasped. "It's hard to picture Riley ever being able to fit in a locker, even with some determined jock pushing on him."

"You may be right about Riley," James conceded, "but I was the perfect size to stuff in a locker." When I groaned and covered my eyes in dismay, he added laughingly, "I've told Kyle he doesn't know how lucky he is to be tall—if he ever got folded into a locker, he could at least see out the vents at the top."

Hearing his name, Kyle looked over, his rare smile lighting his face.

He was having a grand time. If he hadn't been sold on the mentor program to begin with, he was a true believer now. Suddenly dispirited, I wondered if James had ever had a knock-down, drag-out fight with Kyle like I had with Nadina. Doubtful. On the other hand, it was equally difficult trying to imagine them talking about God and prayer—not James so much as Kyle. For all Nadina's volatility, she plainly had a deep streak to her that she would let me glimpse occasionally; it was like staring down into a crevasse and seeing something bubbling down there. But Kyle was such a hard read. What would James use as an analogy for faith?

Riley slammed his hand down on the table to make some point, jarring me from my reverie, and I was surprised to find James' eyes on me, a troubled expression on his face. When I raised my eyebrows questioningly, he suddenly looked extremely uncomfortable and, fumbling for his cell phone, said abruptly, "Oh, I think that's Murray, wanting to know where we went, Ri. We'd better get going. Cass and Kyle, great work today. We'll be in touch."

"Tell Murray to keep his wig on," said Riley without budging. "I'm on coffee break."

James hesitated, then knocked on the table. "Okay, then. I'll see you back at the office." With his usual quick movements, he was gone.

• • •

Riding the bus home later I reflected with satisfaction on the day. Though Murray hadn't said one word of approbation, I assumed with him that if he didn't make me redo it, the voiceover work met his standards. Riley had likewise been content with my last revision of the *Antarctiquest!* Amundsen sections and just wanted me to edit for length. Free Universe might pay their contractors peanuts, but they more than made up for it in sheer fun. James' odd behavior at the end was puzzling, but maybe he really did have to dash back. And his frowning, thoughtful expression might have been no more than a reflection of mine, as I thought about how comparatively disastrous I was as a mentor.

The bus turned the corner, heading past the park and up the main arterial into Clyde Hill, and I forgot about James when I noticed that they were already putting up the tent for the seasonal skating rink. I'd skated for years in elementary and middle school when we lived closer to an ice rink, but when we moved downtown it had become too much of a hassle. It would be fun to try it again now and see if I could still do any of my old tricks.

Friday evenings were usually very quiet around the Palace, since everyone usually had a date or, in Daniel's case, someone to wine and dine before he slept with her. Heating up some leftover enchiladas, I brought my laptop down to check email while I ate. Two from Raquel, one from Nadina. Predictably, Raquel was reiterating her Thanksgiving invitation, and I was grateful to have Perry coming and a legitimate place to be, but to throw her a bone, I promised to visit the weekend before. Nadina, for her part, had two entirely new bits of news for me:

> Cass:
>
> Guess what? Got a 2nd job at that skating rink in Downtown Park! I'm a cashier elf. They can work around my Petco schedule. Wanted me to start day after Thxgiving, but mom and I will still be in Ohio. Tell you more Tues.
>
> N

Ohio? What on earth would they be doing in Ohio? Not that I wasn't glad that Nadina was going with her mom and getting away from Mike for a little bit. I had thought briefly of inviting Nadina and her mom to Thanksgiving dinner, weird though that would have been with my housemates, but had abandoned the idea when I figured I might also have to invite Mike and his dad. Although Nadina had been very quiet about Mike's attitude toward me since our fight, I still had visions of him bludgeoning me to death with a turkey drumstick.

Shutting down my computer I moved it away and reached for my new library book about Captain Cook's travels. Next to 19th-century novels, I loved a good armchair voyage with the Royal Navy. Before long my surroundings were forgotten, and I was stepping ashore in Tahiti, the air smelling of flowers and my footprints appearing and disappearing in the black sand.

I had just gotten to the part where the Navy men observe the Transit of Venus when I heard the garage door opening. Frowning, I glanced at the clock: 7:30? That could only mean someone's Friday night had gone awry.

It was Daniel. He gave a curt laugh when he saw me, dumped his usual gear by the barstools and went right to the sink to start scrubbing his hands.

"Doing a little surgery tonight?" I asked dryly, after his unusually vigorous hand-washing went on for some time.

"Kelly vomited at dinner with me," he said shortly, getting another pump of soap.

"I hope you didn't take it personally."

He smiled to himself in response and reached for the dish towel to dry his hands.

"Did the poor girl at least make it to the bathroom? Tell me she didn't throw up at the table." If she did that might be the new winner for World's Worst Date.

"She made it to the bathroom. We were just finishing up," he answered carelessly.

"And she didn't barf all over your Corvette?" He didn't bother replying. Coming over to the table instead, he made to reach for my Captain Cook book, but I scooted it away. "How do I know you're not still contagious? You might have kissed her."

"Are you flirting with me, Cass? Because, seeing that I just washed my hands for five minutes, the only way I could then infect you would be if I kissed you." When my eyebrows zoomed together in response, Daniel said softly, "Easy there." He sat down opposite me and very deliberately took the book from my hand. "More of your Antarctica research?"

I shook my head. "No, he's only reached Tahiti." I couldn't resist adding, "You would have been in your element there—all those topless women rowing out to meet your ship."

"Yes, too bad the Christian missionaries ever had to get to them," he replied. "Taking something natural like sex and calling it dirty."

"Oh, I don't know," I considered. "Do you think it did more damage to have Christian missionaries come and ask people to slap a shirt on and get married before they had sex, or to have people like Cook's sailors come, who loved 'em and left 'em in every port and brought venereal disease and prostitution to Tahiti?"

"Point taken," he conceded, "but I've wondered about you church girls. Tell me that even church girls nowadays don't wait till they're married to have sex." If he had once told me he never knew what I was going to say, I could now return the compliment, except that his surprising comments could usually be tied back in some fashion to sex.

"I bet you could find lots of church girls who would have sex with you."

"Sex with guilt," he clarified. "Girls who would have sex but feel guilty about it."

"No, I'm sure you could find lots of church girls who would have sex with you without feeling the least twinge of guilt, if they thought you loved them and they loved you."

"But not girls like you," he persisted. My predictable blush came and went, and he added, "I mean, you don't sound like you'd put yourself in that category. Women who think like you, or Joanie, or Phyl, for that matter, wouldn't do even the sex with guilt. What's that about?"

I couldn't suppress a squirm. Embarrassment-wise, this was about on par with the junior high Discussion with the parents. I hoped Daniel wouldn't say "penis." After a pause I said cautiously, "Well, what girls like me think wouldn't make any sense to you."

"Try me."

I sighed. "Okay, but I know you hate this stuff, so remember that you asked me." It took me a minute to gather my thoughts. "In the Bible, marriage is an analogy for our relationship with God. It's total: body, mind, and spirit. You love a person your whole life long with all you've got inside you, and they love you the same way, just like God asks for total commitment, and he offers total commitment. You can't be intimate—really, truly known and loved—if there's always the fear that the other person doesn't love you and might leave you. You'll always hold back. Having sex outside of marriage is like giving precious, intimate parts of yourself to someone who's just going to throw it all in the trash when he's done."

"Plenty of church people get divorces and throw all kinds of stuff in the trash," he pointed out.

I sighed again, thinking of Phyl and Jason and now Perry and Betsy. "Yeah, well I was giving you the ideal situation. Just because it sometimes fails doesn't mean it's not worth shooting for."

His cell phone rang, and he pulled it out of his pocket, turning it off without glancing at it. Holding it in his hand, he flipped it over and over absently. "So you think, when I sleep with different people and then move on, I'm throwing precious parts of them in the trash."

Well, wasn't he? I remembered Missy's unhappiness months ago at our first open house, but I couldn't speak for all of them. Michelle had seemed as content as Daniel to sleep together when it suited them. "Daniel, you asked me what I thought, and I told you. I guess if both people don't care it doesn't make much sense." If only he were Mom and Dad—then I could whine, "Now can we *please* change the subject?" Instead I said, "So anyway, what's your Plan B when Plan A gets the stomach flu? Do you whip out your little black book?"

"I've got to trash somebody's heart tonight," Daniel responded, deadpan. He sat back, looking like he was debating whether or not to let me sidetrack him. My wary expression must have decided him because he said, "Actually, I was going to ask you if you felt like playing a game of Scrabble."

I stared. "Are you joking?"

"When am I ever not serious with you, Cass?"

"You mean besides all the time?" I felt relieved, at any rate, to hear the teasing note back in his voice. Before having this uncomfortable sex conversation, I would never have imagined I would welcome that sound. Scrabble was tempting, although it meant another hour hanging out with him. By his own admission he was no expert. A smile played around my mouth, which didn't escape his notice.

"I thought you might be interested," he said mildly. "You never do pass up a chance to crush me."

CHAPTER 17:

Lust in the Afternoon

A crash downstairs startled me.

Sitting back on my heels, I brushed stray hairs out of my face with the back of my rubber-gloved hand and listened.

Thumping, followed by laughing shrieks and giggling. Good Lord, please don't let that be what I think it is.

It being my week, I had been on my hands and knees, scrubbing the floor of Daniel's shower stall in the Lean-To, a bucket of soapy water beside me and a scouring pad in my hand. The towels and sheets were tumble-drying downstairs, but thankfully I had already made the bed. I say thankfully because, if I guessed right, Daniel and some girlfriend were dropping in for a lunchtime quickie. Please please please don't let them come upstairs!

Getting noiselessly to my feet, I peeked around the bathroom door. Still downstairs. Could I possibly sneak out without being noticed? I couldn't lurk in the bathroom and risk being found after having heard everything—should I hide in the closet? Under the bed? Picturing myself flat under the bed while they bounced around on top was too farcical, and heaven knew I never moved the bed to vacuum. All the dust under there might make me sneeze at an inopportune time, and being discovered under the bed sounded even more humiliating than being discovered in the shower stall. Nor did I want to be forced to hear the entire proceedings. At least in the closet I could shut the door to muffle the ruckus, but what if Daniel wanted to put on a fresh shirt after his exertions?

There was nothing to do but try to make my escape.

While the giggling and groaning and bumping around continued downstairs, I quickly and silently stripped off my rubber gloves and stashed them with the bucket under the sink. Slipping off my shoes, I stuffed them in the pocket of my apron and tiptoed out to the landing.

"Oh, Daniel," someone moaned appreciatively. "Oh, *Daniel!*" Yeah, I thought, I'd like to Oh-Daniel him for putting me in this ludicrous situation.

Step by step I crept down the stairs. It sounded like the action was happening in the kitchen—unfortunate, since the only door in and out of the Lean-To was there, but fortunate in that a wall separated that room from the stairs. On the last step I peeped one eye around the wall, only to retreat a split-second later, my fist crammed in my mouth so I wouldn't laugh out loud. From my vantage point, Daniel had his back to me—he was ripping off his button-down shirt but was otherwise still clothed, thank God—and he had deposited his long, lithe, fake-redheaded girlfriend on the kitchen counter, her leg hitched over his hip. In contrast to Daniel, she had hardly a stitch left on, though articles of clothing formed a trail back to the door, in case she should forget the way out. He was kissing his way down her neck while she growled and purred and whimpered like a one-woman children's petting zoo. If they weren't going to make it out of the kitchen, this was going to be a problem.

Dropping to a crawl, I scurried across the floor and hid behind the island. Although the door had shut behind them—the crash I'd heard, presumably—the lock wasn't turned, and maybe if I waited for my moment I could zip out and close it oh-so-quietly. It only took me another ten seconds to decide that this woman was so darned noisy they probably wouldn't hear anything if the ceiling caved in, and I'd better go for it. Scrunching my apron up around my waist I began squat-creeping toward the door and had just emerged from behind the island, reaching silently for the door knob, when I felt an insidious vibrating in the back pocket of my jeans. In that position, there was no way I could get my phone out of my pocket to shut it off before I heard the ringtone building: dah dah dah dah DAH DAH DAH DAH dah dah dah dah DAH DAH DAH!!! Stupid Beethoven's *Ode to Joy* on my stupid cell phone that is only charged ten days out of any given month, and this had to be one of them? I slapped my hand over my pocket, but the sudden silence told me I needn't bother. "Dah dah dah dah DAH DAH DAH DAH dah dah dah dah DAH... DAH DAH!!!" sang my phone again, enjoying my mortification.

"Are you planning on getting that, Cass?" came the dreaded voice. Cringing, I turned to look up at them. Daniel was leaning over the counter, bare-chested at this point, and the girlfriend peering over his shoulder, outraged. He was rather flushed, but I had no way of knowing if that was from his recent labors or embarrassment or anger or all three. Those piercing blue eyes traveled from my disheveled hair, swept back under a red bandanna, to my ratty World Vision t-shirt to my gingham half-apron with shoes stuffed in the pocket.

Wordlessly, I rose to my feet with my back to them and dug my trilling phone from my pocket. Nadina. I quickly switched it off. "Excuse me," I croaked. Before anyone else had to think of something to say or do, I was out the door and across the deck without a backward glance.

. . .

"Dude, why do you look so thrashed today?" Nadina demanded, when she met me outside the school a few hours later. I was still in my housecleaning get-up, minus the gingham apron which was stuffed in my purse, having fled the Palace as quickly as I could yank a coat from the closet and pull my shoes back on. I hadn't had the presence of mind to grab some leftovers on my way out, so my stomach was growling, but it had seemed more urgent at the time just to get out of there.

I didn't know why I felt so perturbed, but I had been walking the big gravel loop at the park ever since, trying to figure out what my problem was. To be sure, it was awkward being an unwilling witness to other people's sexual shenanigans, but Daniel could hardly be upset with me for it, since I had just been innocently cleaning his place, and I'd never before known him to pop in midday for a tryst. Besides, before my stupid phone exposed me, I had been trying to sneak out for the dignity of all.

Was it because I had somehow expected something different from him, after our conversation Friday night? This troublesome question had halted me in my tracks, my third time around the loop. Of course I hadn't imagined Daniel would hear my opinion on the meaning of sex and suddenly have his eyes enlightened, but, to be honest with myself, I had hoped it might make him reflect just the tiniest bit. Since that clearly wasn't the case, I guessed the lack of "house guests" the entire weekend must have been merely the product of Kelly's continuing stomach flu, rather than any growing awareness on Daniel's part.

And, while I was being honest, I had to admit that my thoughts kept flitting back to what I had seen. It had been, what, nearly seventeen months now since Troy had died? And it wasn't like we had been having tons of sex before then because I was usually exhausted from my day with Min, but occasionally was still more often than never. Daniel's bare chest came to mind again, and I blushed scarlet. Did I really need to have that picture in my mind? It would be so easy to go there, to let physical attraction override my better judgment—to do exactly what I had told Phyl was foolish. Even easier for me to do it than Phyl because Daniel kept his polite distance from Phyl, while baiting me seemed to be one of his favorite pastimes.

By the time I headed up the hill to meet Nadina, I had resolved that I would avoid Daniel for the time being, giving the images of the morning time to fade until I could be sure of behaving rationally.

"Oh, I had to leave the house in a hurry," I answered her vaguely. "I can't always look drop-dead gorgeous. What were you trying to call me about earlier?" Although the day was overcast and lowering and we had no Benny with us, we fell into step and headed toward the lake.

"The best, Cass!" Nadina crowed. "You remember stupid Blaise, my Petco manager?" It was unlikely I could forget the horny-clawed Blaise, whose eleventh hour entrance had cut short our unpleasant scene, and I nodded briefly. "She says that this Saturday I finally get to help out at the dog training class!"

Stopping short, I gripped her arm excitedly, and such was Nadina's good mood that she permitted it. "Finally! That's great, Nadina. They are going to be so blown away by your skills. Does Blaise do the training?"

"Her?" she scoffed. "I don't think she knows which end of the dog is the front. Nah, it's some perky chick named Katie. She's hella full of herself 'cause she's volunteered at the friggin' SPCA since she could walk, or some b.s. like that, and she annoys the hell out of me, but I'm dying to do this."

"And you're going to be cooperative and do what Katie says, right?" I prodded. "Even if she gets on your nerves and bosses you around?"

"Y-e-e-e-s, Cass," groaned Nadina. "You're supposed to be my mentor and encourage me, not nag me all the time."

"I am encouraging you, you idiot. I'm encouraging you to be your best self. You're the most gifted person I've ever seen with dogs, so don't screw up this opportunity just because perky Katie makes you want to slap her."

She giggled. "Most people make me want to slap them. I even want to slap you sometimes."

"That's called being a teenager." On such a day the waterfront park was deserted, but we sat on our usual bench. "How are you going to swing this dog training thing, if you're also supposed to start working at the ice skating rink?"

"It'll work. I close on Saturdays at the rink, so I don't have to be there until 3:00, and the dog training is in the morning. You wanna come skate?"

"Sure, I'll come skate," I agreed. "How about the Saturday afternoon after Thanksgiving? Speaking of which, what's this about you and your mom going to Ohio? What's in Ohio?"

"My great-aunt Sylvia." At my questioning look, she added, "It's my grandpa's younger sister. She's always hated my mom and talked lots of trash when Mom left me with Grandpa and Grandma to live, so my mom was all pissed and cut her off, and they haven't talked for years. But a few weeks ago Sylvia called out of the blue. Who knows why, but she invited us to come out for Thanksgiving."

"And your mom wanted to go?"

Nadina pulled on some threads hanging from her barn jacket sleeve. "I wanted to go. Mike and his dad would probably just sit around and have TV dinners, and I haven't hung out with my mom for awhile, so she said she'd suck it up and go if I wanted to."

"Wow. So have you been there before?"

She shrugged. "A couple times with my grandpa. Sylvia lives in

Cleveland. We're gonna fly out on Wednesday and come back Friday. Mom doesn't want too much of a good thing, I guess."

"How does Mike feel about all this?" I asked in the most casual voice I could muster. Nadina was too alert for me, however, and she shot me a sharp glance.

"You don't like Mike, do you?"

"I don't know Mike," I replied carefully.

"But what you know you don't like," she repeated.

Cornered, I tried to pick my way through the landmines. "I only know what you tell me, Nadina. So that means I know that he's older than you and that he likes music and—and drugs, that he…likes to spend time with you, and he likes you to do drugs with him."

"And I know your opinion on drugs."

"And you know my opinion on drugs," I echoed. Turning to face her head-on, I said, "Nadina, are you trying to pick a fight with me? What do you want? Since I don't know Mike, and I only know what you tell me, why don't you tell me what you like about him?"

Maybe my question was too bald, but really, when Mark Henneman talked about trust-building he wasn't using Nadina as the case study. She seemed to want to lure me into intimate conversations, only to trap me into saying something she wasn't going to like. I had to outflank her.

"I like—I like—" she floundered, "He's been there for me." Her knee started jiggling nervously. "Times when no one else has been around. Grandpa's dead; mom's working. Friends at my old school don't even call me anymore. He came with me when I got my abortion."

At least he finished what he started, I thought sourly. When I could trust myself to speak I managed, "Dependable people are hard to find."

"Yeah, they are," she agreed. "I can depend on Mike."

"So what does dependable Mike think of Ohio?" I asked again, drawing another suspicious look, though I hadn't thought any sarcasm leaked out. What do you expect? I'm a video game actress.

Nadina cleared her throat a couple times and popped to her feet, her usual signal that the conversation was over. Surprisingly, she said, "He doesn't like it. He says he doesn't want to be alone with his dumb dad over Thanksgiving and that I should think about him more."

"Oh!" I exclaimed lamely, amazed that she had shared this with me. "What do you think?"

"I think he'll live." She tugged on my arm to get me walking.

"Where are we going?" I protested. "It's only 3:30."

"To get a snack, Cass," Nadina laughed. "I can hardly hear you over your stomach growling."

• • •

Joanie came home that evening with her phone glued to her ear. "Yeah. Yeah. Uh-huh. No, no that's okay. That'd be great," she said unenthusiastically. "Sure—I mean, we'll have at least one other overnight guest, but there's plenty of room. Okay, love you. Bye." Clicking her phone shut, she groaned and threw it on the table before pushing me along the cushioned bench and slumping down next to me.

"Don't block me in," I complained, wanting to make a hasty escape whenever Daniel happened to come home.

Ignoring me, she laid her red-gold head on my shoulder. "Don't be grouchy, Cass. Can't you see I'm in dire straits?"

"Is someone coming for Thanksgiving?" asked Phyl. Joanie nodded, her eyes shut. Phyl and I exchanged glances. "Someone you find unpleasant?" Joanie nodded again.

"Well, come on and tell us and stop being such a martyr," I chided waspishly. "Is it one of your ex-fiancés?"

"Worse," she moaned. "It's my mother." Phyl and I gasped, horrified. Although we had never met Mrs. Martin, we knew her chief pleasure in life came from criticizing Joanie and that, whatever preparatory praying and planning Joanie did, it all went up in smoke the second Mrs. Martin opened her mouth.

Repenting my hardheartedness, I put my arm around her. "That's awful news, Joanie. How long is she coming for?"

"Wednesday, leaving Saturday," came Joanie's muffled voice.

"Maybe it'll help to have us and Daniel here," said Phyl hopefully. "And Perry, too. We can all distract her. Be a buffer."

"Nothing will distract her from her one goal in life: torturing me," declared Joanie.

"Does Daniel get along any better with her?" I asked.

Joanie sat up, sniffing. "Oh, Daniel's her golden boy. She never has anything negative to say to him."

"Well, you're not sharing a room with her, in any case," I decided. "We'll put your mom in the spare room and put Perry in my room, unless Daniel offers to have your mom over in the Lean-To."

Joanie rolled her eyes skeptically. "That'll be the day! Although— although—he may agree if you ask him, Cass, just to be polite. He'll be more polite to you than me."

"I'm not asking him!" I exclaimed, feeling my cheeks get warm. "It's your mother—besides, I have to go upstairs and work on something." I tried unsuccessfully to push her out of the booth but froze when I heard the garage door opening. Too late.

"Please!" whispered Joanie urgently. "Please please please, for me, Cass." I jabbed her furiously in the ribs, and she gave my hand a hard pinch. When Daniel came in the door, the three of us were sitting in unnatural silence: I was looking determinedly at the table, Joanie was goggling her eyes meaningfully at me, and Phyl was still shy and embarrassed around Daniel after her ill-fated crush. Strangely enough,

Daniel was also silent, and I was on the verge of peeking at him out of curiosity when Joanie cried, "Terrible news, Daniel—Mom's coming up for Thanksgiving!"

He didn't respond right away, and I heard him putting down his things and starting the microwave. "Is that what you're all so quiet about?" I did peek at him then, but finding his eyes on me, I hastily looked away. Then it occurred to me he probably thought I'd been blabbing about my adventure in the Lean-To, and I felt a surge of resentment. Of all the pots ever to call a kettle black—as if he could accuse me of being indiscreet! Shooting him a dirty look, I shook my head infinitesimally.

Joanie had sprung up and gone to hang appealingly on him. "Yes, Mom dropped the news like a bomb on me, and I dumped it on Phyl and Cass. We don't know quite what to do because, you know, Perry is already coming to stay. And Cass has already told Perry he could have the spare room, but now with Mom—"

"Perry can stay in my room," I said to a spot between Daniel and Joanie. "Your mom can have the spare room."

Joanie scowled at me. "Well, but you told Perry, and he asked first. Maybe Mom can go somewhere else."

"I could put Perry up in my spare room," suggested Daniel. "If Cass thinks that would be okay."

I wondered briefly if Daniel planned on more weekend antics, now that Kelly was clearly over her barfing thing—assuming that was even her I'd seen today. Perry probably wouldn't bat an eye, given how he was living with all those randoms off of Craig's List, but did anyone really want to listen to that all night? Of course, putting Mrs. Martin out there probably would cramp Daniel's style considerably, and I didn't see how he'd go for it, polite or not.

"Umm," I hesitated. "Perry likes his sleep, so I think I'd better keep him with me. We shared a room until we were in middle school," I added irrelevantly.

"I can't see how sleeping in my guest room is going to be less restful than sleeping on your floor, Cass," said Daniel. Still not looking at him, I merely raised my eyebrows, and when he spoke again, his voice had a steely note in it. "And really, you do such a beautiful job cleaning my place. Why waste all that hard work on me?"

The man was unbelievable. Apparently shame was not part of his emotional lexicon. Goaded, I snapped back, "Well, actually, your shower stall might not be up to Perry's standards because I got called away before I could finish scrubbing it today."

"Too bad. I hope the interruption was worth it." Daniel must have seen my hands curl into fists because he sounded like he was trying not to laugh. "Maybe if you allow a little extra time next time."

"It wasn't something I could have planned for," I retorted, "because it was dirtier than I thought."

"Well!" interjected Phyl, looking alarmed by the hostility I was putting out. "Don't worry, Cass, I'll take care of it next week. Maybe it just needs some of that OxyClean stuff."

Joanie launched back into bemoaning her mother's impending visit to Daniel while he ate, and I took the chance to steal up to my room. If Mrs. Martin harassed Joanie anywhere near as constantly as Daniel seemed to enjoy harassing me, not only did Joanie have my full sympathy, but I was beginning to think maybe spending the Thanksgiving weekend in tears at my in-laws' might have been the wiser choice.

CHAPTER 18:

Persona Non Grata

The turnout for the third mentor training meeting was unexpectedly good, considering it was the Monday of Thanksgiving week. I, for one, was determined never to miss one of these, given my ignorance and the continued drama of having Nadina in my life.

From the doorway of the fellowship hall I spotted James and Louella in conversation and made my way quickly over to them. "Hello, you two!" Giving Louella a hug, I asked, "Did you have a nice lunch with your daughter after church?"

"It was wonderful," Louella beamed. "She took me to that delicious crêpe place, and we had three kinds of crêpes, including chocolate-banana, and a big pot of tea. Thank you for asking."

"And how was your weekend?" I turned to James. To my surprise, he avoided my eyes, looking ill at ease. "Are you okay, James?" I asked uncertainly.

"Yes, great, thank you," he replied hastily, looking over my shoulder. "Ah, there's Mark Henneman—I had a quick question I wanted to ask him before we got started. Would you excuse me?"

Frowning in puzzlement, I stared after him. "Did I interrupt something, Louella?"

"I don't think so," said Louella. "Why don't you come sit next to me? I can show you the card I want to send Sonya in Bellingham, and you can tell me if it's too sappy." Shrugging, I let her lead me away.

I thought James might come sit next to Louella and me for the session, but when I turned around later to look for him, I saw him at the back, next to Ray. Maybe I would chat with him afterward.

Mark Henneman spoke more on neurological changes in the addicted brain, making me wonder how much of Nadina's erratic behavior stemmed from continued substance abuse. From there he went on to describe the basic practices of Camden School's chosen drug rehabilitation center and to answer questions from mentors whose students were currently in rehab, wrapping up with his usual reminder: "But don't think we expect you to solve their addiction problems or even know how to handle every situation. Please just give us a call if something comes up you're uncertain about. Remember, all we ask of you is that you spend regular time with them. Make them feel special. Give them bragging rights with their friends. If there's something particular you can share with them, be it your hobby or your workplace or your favorite foods, go for it. At first it may feel like you're giving and giving and getting nothing back, but building relationship with these kids is a slow, cumulative process. Plus, they're teenagers—they're not always going to let you know what they're thinking and feeling or even act in ways we would consider normal responses. Keep at it. Have that coffee with them. Ask their opinions on things. And—we can't stress it enough—keep praying for them."

This last bit of our pep talk made me think of the funny Free Universe coffee we had last Friday, and I looked back to see if James was thinking the same thing. I felt like I just missed catching his eye, because suddenly he was very absorbed in the handout, and when

Mark finished speaking, James murmured a quick word to Ray and bolted out of his chair for the exit.

What on earth did this behavior mean? Had I done something to offend him, or why else would he avoid me? I thought back to that passing troubled expression on his face on Friday. Maybe Murray had texted him to say, "Whatever happens, we have got to fire Cass. She SUCKS." Bewildered, and more than a little unhappy about it, I decided I would pop into the office tomorrow to see if I could unravel this mystery.

· · ·

The elevator doors had barely closed behind me when Riley popped up over the cube wall. "Cass, the Big Hunk will last for eternity now. Come check it out." To my untutored eyes the candy looked the same, but he had fashioned the wrapper into a miniature pinwheel, so I made admiring sounds.

"What I really want to know, Riley," I said, "is where you got that awesomely rude t-shirt."

Riley proudly thrust out his chest, on which was emblazoned, in full-on *Jeopardy!* lettering: "Suck it, Trebek!" It was well-known around the office that Riley had taken the online *Jeopardy!* test three times and still not received an audition call. "Last night was a crime," he complained. "Can you believe that question about high explosives was a Triple Stumper?"

"Riley, I told you, I don't watch *Jeopardy!*" I said for maybe the fifth time.

"I'm thinking about changing my name to Marcia—did you know it's easier for women to get on the show than men?"

"Don't you think, when you showed up for the audition, they'd cotton on and figure out you weren't a woman?"

"By then it wouldn't matter to them," he declared. "With my

winning personality, they would already love me and have me pegged as America's Next Sweetheart." He rocked back in his Aeron chair and held out his hand, waggling his fingers. "Okay, what do you got for me today, Cass? Have you stopped stalling on my truffle-hunting pigs?"

I pulled the flash drive out of my purse but paused before handing it to him. "Riley, do you think my work is going okay? I mean, it's working for you all?"

"Aw, Cass," he groaned, "Are you gonna go all girl on me? You need more pats on the back? If we don't say it sucks, you're doing great."

"And no one has said it sucks?" I persisted, holding the drive out of reach.

"No one has ever said it sucks except me," Riley said with exaggerated patience, "and when I think it sucks, I tell you to your face." That was true enough. I relented and gave him the drive, which he leaned over and popped into his USB port.

We were watching him copy my files over when James' head appeared over the cube wall. "Oh, hey, Ri, Lewis was wondering where—" Catching sight of me, he broke off. I gave him a tentative smile which he barely returned before continuing, "You're busy. I'll catch you later."

"James, you dashed out of that mentor training before I even had a chance to talk to you," I said in a rush to his retreating back. He paused and then turned and looked back at me questioningly. I didn't want to be shouting this through the office, so I said as quietly as I could, "Has Murray said—did he say—was the voiceover work I did Friday all right?"

"Cass is suffering a crisis of confidence," put in Riley.

James took a few steps back toward me. "He hasn't said anything, so I assume it's fine."

"Like I said," muttered Riley.

"Oh, great," I said lamely. James' face was still shuttered, and when he was about to turn away again I added, "Did you and Murray decide whether Kyle could do some voice work?"

"Yeah. He'll be in Wednesday, I think Murray said," he answered shortly. "Anything else, Cass?" When I shook my head, he was gone, throwing "Happy Thanksgiving!" over his shoulder.

Well, that was enlightening, I thought sarcastically. Holding out my hand, Riley slapped the flash drive back in it, and I hopped off his desk. "Have a good holiday, Riley. I'm off to buy pie ingredients."

"Save me a piece, Cass," he called after me.

• • •

Clearly, James was avoiding me. I mulled this over as I rolled out my pie crust, patching the unsightly gaps in the dough. I knew Perry planned on making an apple pie when he came up, but Thanksgiving called for pumpkin and pecan as well.

If he was avoiding me, I had two options: I could give him some space and wait till he either got over whatever it was or brought it up with me; or, I could try to bring it up myself and possibly make it a bigger deal than it needed to be. It didn't take long to decide. Thanksgiving would be a natural break, and I just wouldn't go in to Free Universe until sometime later next week.

Crimping the edges of my homely crusts, I smiled to myself. James should consider himself lucky—it was a lot easier to avoid someone whom you only saw once in awhile than to avoid someone you lived with. Case in point, consider my past week trying to avoid Daniel.

Since the whole Lust-in-the-Lean-To incident, I had imagined I would just stay out of his way until the vivid memories had time to fade—try to avoid any one-on-one conversations—but this had proved unexpectedly tricky as he seemed to be spending an inordinate amount of time around the Palace. Whenever I heard his car pulling into the garage, if Joanie or Phyl weren't with me I would suddenly dash upstairs to my room, even if it meant abandoning a kitchen mess till the coast was clear.

At our weekly open house I'd had other worries. Kelly had shown up, considerably more clothed but understandably not very pleased to see me. And on top of how awkward I felt seeing her with Daniel and envisioning the last time they were together, that Tom had shown up again. Just when I was thinking I might spend the evening hiding under the couch, Tom managed to corner me for a second time.

"Ahem. Cass?"

"Yes..?" I said warily.

His overly white teeth flashed as he grimaced uncomfortably. "I just wanted to apologize for how I acted a few weeks ago and for—for making you feel threatened. Ahem. It won't happen again and I-hope-we-can-be-friends," he finished hastily.

The apology was so entirely unexpected that I tried not to gape and quickly said, "Oh, of course. It's all right. I was on edge that night and a little nuts myself. Thank you for apologizing."

"Didn't have much choice," he muttered. "Dan said he'd kick my ass if I didn't. Not that I didn't mean it," he added hastily.

"Yes. Yes, thank you, Tom." My eyes drifted unwillingly to Daniel, who was lounging in the recliner with Kelly draped on the arm. He'd been reading some article Roy had given him about networking something-or-other, but I had the feeling he'd been listening to Tom's apology because he gave me a little smile.

That was Thursday, and then I'd spent Friday and most of Saturday with Max and Raquel and others of Troy's family at the cabin in Cle Elum, since I wouldn't be there for Thanksgiving. It was exactly the time I pictured: lots of reminiscing over glasses of wine, a slideshow of our dead family that Raquel had put together—God help us—

and everyone ending up in tears more often than not. The crashing headache I got as a result was still with me Sunday evening as I sat in the kitchen playing with my dish of leftover spaghetti. With so much else on my mind I'm not surprised I didn't think fast enough to get up from the table when I heard the garage, and sure enough, I had found myself alone with Daniel for the first time since the Incident.

"Well this is unexpected," he said lightly. "Are you sure you don't want to go tearing upstairs?"

Had I not been emotionally spent I might have mustered a blush. As it was, I didn't bother denying it. "I'm too tired."

He looked at me measuringly. "You are. Better eat that spaghetti. You'll need your strength because I've been wanting to talk to you."

Tell me he was not planning to sit down with me. He was. Rubbing my temples, I obediently took a bite. "You have?"

"I wanted to apologize for putting you in that situation on Tuesday."

Well blow me down. First Tom, and now this. Though I suppose Tom had only apologized because Daniel made him, so really this counted as the second apology I could attribute to Daniel. With a mixture of amazement and embarrassment I stammered, "Oh. Oh… uh… thank you. You didn't—er—do it on purpose. Sorry to have interrupted." I managed an uncomfortable smile.

He grinned back, looking genuinely pleased. "So we're okay now, and you'll stop avoiding me?"

"Okay"? Were we anything? I wasn't aware we had enough of a relationship to warrant adjectives. Not knowing how exactly to respond, I managed to nod and tried to focus on my spaghetti. Daniel seemed in no hurry to go anywhere, even leaning back against the wall of the booth and crossing his ankles.

"Joanie and Phyl at church?" he asked presently. I nodded again. Silence.

After a few minutes he tried once more. "Still reading about Captain Cook?"

"Finished," I said between bites.

"Cass, let me get a word in edgewise, what do you say," he said in mock exasperation. "If you don't start talking, I might suspect you're still angry with me."

I marshaled a weak laugh, rubbing my pounding temples. "I wasn't angry with you," I said slowly. "I was embarrassed."

"You were angry when I referred to it in front of Joanie and Phyl," he pressed.

"I was," I admitted. Carefully I crossed my knife and fork on my empty dish. "Because you have absolutely no shame."

"And you do." It wasn't a question.

The familiar annoyance flared. "You would call it shame; I would call it modesty. Daniel—can we argue about this another time? I'm not up to it right now."

He tapped his fingers on the table, debating whether he would let me off, but the better angels of his nature won out this once, and he said in a different tone, "Agreed. How about a Scrabble rematch, then? I might be able to beat you if you're tired."

I cracked a real smile, then. "Not tonight, dear. I have a headache."

• • •

So Daniel and I were "okay" now—maybe James and I would be again soon.

While the pecan and pumpkin pies were baking, I ran upstairs to check my email one last time. It was odd, I thought, that Nadina hadn't bothered to let me know how her first dog training went. Usually with her, no news was bad news, and I found myself getting a little anxious about it.

At 2:45 sharp I was on the bench outside Camden School, a miniature pie in each hand, but Nadina didn't come dragging out until fully five minutes later, a knit cap pulled all the way down to her ears and a sullen expression on her face. I held out the little pies, and Nadina received them blankly. "I was going to tell you, Cass," she began without preamble, "I have ice rink training today, so I can't hang out."

"Oh!" I exclaimed, a little crestfallen at her attitude. "What time is the training? I'll walk down there with you."

Nadina heaved a sigh, which I interpreted as if-you-must-you-must, and we set off. Something was definitely wrong because she answered my warm-up chat monosyllabically: School? Fine. English paper? Needed revision. Did she prefer pumpkin pie or pecan? Both fine. How about her mom? No idea. Packed for Ohio? Not yet. Had I told her we were going to have Benny for the whole Thanksgiving weekend? Nope. I could almost hear Mark Henneman's advice in my head: "Let them tell you things on their own time, when they're ready." Forget it.

"Okay," I barked suddenly. "Spill it. What is bugging you, Nadina?"

She kicked at some straggling clumps of lamb's ears next to the sidewalk. "You're going to be so pissed when I tell you, Cass." I said nothing, waiting. Finally she burst out with, "I got fired from Petco on Saturday—and don't say anything because I know you're going to say I told you so, and I don't want to hear it. It's all that friggin' perky Katie's fault."

Groaning inwardly, I concentrated on swallowing all the things I wanted to say, which did in fact include *I told you so*. "What happened?"

We were outside the skating rink tent at this point, so I indicated that we should walk the gravel loop.

"It was all going fine," she began, "but then this lady showed up late with two German Shepherds. One of them charged the group, so stupid Katie tried to keep that dog next to her while she went on with the class. But then that dog didn't like that and got all tense, so the other German Shepherd started freaking out and growling and snapping at the other dogs, and next thing you know everything's going to hell. All the dogs are barking and whining and running around in circles with their leashes, and owners are panicking and yelling at the German Shepherd lady to control her dogs *for Chrissake*, and she's yelling back at them in some friggin' heavy accent no one could understand, and then they're all yelling at Katie and me. Craziness. I tried to tell Katie—in a nice voice 'cause I really was trying to do my best, Cass—that she just needed to show that first German Shepherd who was boss and then it would stop sending those stress signals to the second one, but by then Katie was all freaked out and ready to pee her pants anyhow, so she told me to shut the hell up 'cause who was teaching this class, and it-sure-as-hell-isn't-you-Nadina, and I told her fine, she could just shove the friggin' class up her ass if she had it all under control, and I took off out of there, and Blaise caught me and said I'd better get back in there if I knew what was good for me, and said I was sick of her fucking telling me what to do all the time and I QUIT! And she yelled, 'Too late to quit 'cause you're fired!'"

Well, that would explain why Nadina hadn't texted me that weekend. After a minute I ventured, "Do you think Blaise really meant it?"

Nadina turned on me furiously. "Who the hell's side are you on, Cass?"

"Yours," I said with deliberation. "I am on your side, so don't bite my head off."

"Well then don't ask me about Blaise, 'cause it doesn't matter 'cause I'm never gonna see any of them again. I am through with them. I've got this job now."

"You have got to be kidding me," I couldn't help saying. "Seasonal rink elf? That'll show 'em."

For a second I thought Nadina might hit me, the way her head whipped around and her fists clenched, but after glaring at me hard for some moments, her lips twitched. Then she snorted, and then suddenly we were both laughing. When she caught her breath she gasped, "You should see the stupid hat I'm going to have to wear! It has a friggin' *bell* on it, and I was too big to fit the girls' costumes, so I have to wear a men's large."

"Speaking of your brilliant career, what time are you supposed to be at your training? You don't want to lose the only job you have."

"You're one to talk, Cass. You clean some guy's house and hang out with nerds writing video game lines." Nevertheless, she flipped up my wrist to see my watch. "I totally gotta go. Thanks for the pumpkin pie, Cass. I feel better now."

"Have a good trip to Ohio," I called after her. "And we're not done talking about this."

"Yeah we are!" she retorted. "Have a good Thanksgiving!"

CHAPTER 19:

Thanksgiving

Benny was the first visitor to arrive for the long weekend; Jason dropped him off Wednesday morning on his way to the airport. Perhaps because he associated me with Nadina, Benny behaved himself circumspectly around me now, and after nudging me for some preliminary patting and scratching, he obediently lay on his bed.

My underemployed brother came next, around midday, and we had a ball getting a jump on the Thanksgiving meal: cranberry sauce, rolls, apple pie, green-bean casserole. Perry had been given complete charge of the turkey, and he had ambitious plans for it, involving brining and subcutaneous infusions and stuffing made from the bread up. The two of us were just struggling to lift our 20-pounder from the cooler and exchange the cold water—a procedure which greatly interested Benny and kept him underfoot in hope of windfalls—when Joanie burst in, shoulders slumping and looking like a child forced to donate all her birthday presents to Toys for Tots.

"T minus 45 minutes," she sighed, barely managing a greeting for Perry. Mrs. Martin was taking the Amtrak Starlight from Portland,

and Joanie had to go pick her up from the station.

"Why can't Daniel go pick her up?" I demanded. "It'd buy you another half hour."

"I was desperate enough to ask," admitted Joanie. "But he has some stupid client meeting. What kind of client wants to meet the Wednesday afternoon before Thanksgiving? I think he scheduled it on purpose so he could have another couple hours of peace." Or the client was some woman, I thought, and Daniel wanted to get one more fling in before Mom showed up.

"I could go get her," Perry spoke up from where he had plunged the turkey back in its bath. "Just describe her to me. Heck, if I'd known she was coming from Portland, we could have carpooled."

Joanie looked at Perry as if he had just offered to donate her a kidney. "Thank you so much. That is such a kind offer, but if I passed Mom off on someone else, I would never hear the end of it. She wouldn't care if we had an earthquake and I was pinned under an overpass—she would say it was my poor planning."

I gave her a hug. "Well, Joanie, I know it's really painful for you, but Phyl and I are dying of curiosity to meet this woman. We've never seen you so cowed by anyone."

Phyl came home shortly after Joanie headed out, laden down with cocktail ingredients. "I found a recipe for Pink Verandas that I want to test out tonight. What's for dinner, Cass?"

I grimaced. "You know how Joanie says her mom is a vegan? I figured, since only a few of the Thanksgiving dishes are vegan, we could do vegan tonight. I've got coconut-curried vegetables in the slow cooker."

"But Daniel always makes that face when we cook vegetarian," Phyl reminded me, her brows knitting.

"He'll survive!" I said dismissively. "It's his mother, after all."

"He and I can pop out to Burgermaster later," said Perry helpfully.

"Only if you take Mrs. Martin with you," I warned him. "We promised Joanie there'd be safety in numbers for her this weekend."

• • •

When Joanie returned with the long-awaited harpy in tow, I could only blink in shock. I didn't know what I was expecting when I pictured Daniel and Joanie's mother, but Angela Martin was not it. Joanie had described her as artsy and vegan and very left-wing, and I had vaguely imagined your typical aging hippy: overweight, with long, gray-brown hair, Birkenstocks, art jewelry, and loose, unbleached clothing. However, rather than being the last woman in America wearing a Summer of Love t-shirt, Mrs. Martin turned out to be one of those amazingly beautiful women of a certain age, tall and erect, her silver-white hair twisted in a neat chignon, and her muted black clothing so form-fitting and tidy that I immediately felt frumpy. Maybe Joanie's and Daniel's dad had run off so many years ago because he couldn't bear to be the only ugly one in such a family. On the other hand, there was a lot of Daniel in Mrs. Martin's looks, so gorgeous Joanie must take after her long-lost father.

It appeared from their body language when they walked in the door that Joanie and her mother had gotten their first tiff out of the way. Joanie's mouth was pressed in a thin line, and she thumped her mother's bags down in the entry way as if she would rather be drop-kicking them. Mrs. Martin, without looking back at her daughter, smiled serenely and held out her arty leather handbag for Joanie to take. As her eyes took in her new surroundings, her smile became positively beatific. "What a beautiful house Daniel has! And what a nice job he's done with it."

Joanie flared up instantly. "That's just it, Mom, he *bought* the house. I did most of the decorating downstairs, and Phyl did all the plants inside and out, and Cass—Cass—" She was spared having to think up a specific way I had contributed to the house aesthetics by her mother's nonchalant interruption.

"Yes, Joan, but your brother has always had an eye for beauty." She continued right over Joanie's derisive snort. "This house has very good lines—excellent *feng shui*. I love how the *Qi* flows up the curved pathway into the entrance—just the right size entrance, and the window above it giving all that light. Remember your last apartment? That tiny entryway, and the back door straight across from it? Energy could hardly find its way into your place, and what energy did make it in went straight out the back door."

"So that was my problem," said Joanie, pokerfaced.

Mrs. Martin bore the many introductions bravely, declaring, "Please, call me Angela," and giving a slight "hmmm…" when she heard my name, whatever that meant. She gave us each a cool, dry handshake, and we invited her into the kitchen while Joanie took her bags up, a task which took her an inordinately long time, though she came down looking ready for another round. On her reappearance, Phyl considerately slipped her a Pink Veranda.

"And how is it that a nice fellow like you isn't married?" Angela asked Perry. She had been enthusiastic to discover her Portland connection to him and their mutual interest in the arts, and I think this was a roundabout way of asking Perry if he was gay.

"The same way a nice fellow like Daniel isn't married," Joanie interposed.

Perry, sharing half my genes, flushed. "Actually, Angela, I am married—or was. We're separated now, my wife and I."

"Oh, I'm sorry," Angela replied conventionally. She turned to look at me. "And Joanie told me about your loss. This must be a difficult couple years for your family, one divorce and one death."

"Almost as bad as two kids who never married," put in Joanie.

I frowned at her. For a girl who had spent the last week complaining about how her Mom riled her, she wasn't exactly an innocent victim.

"Now, Joanie, you know I've never held up marriage as a goal for either of you. You're a modern woman. We live in a modern world. No one needs pieces of paper or anyone's blessing to tell them whether they're in love or not. Look where marriage got your father and me. I'm convinced that if I hadn't pressured him to marry me, he wouldn't have felt so trapped. He wouldn't have run off to Venezuela or wherever, when you both were so little."

"You're right, Mom. He probably would have taken off right after you got pregnant with Daniel."

"Another Pink Veranda, anyone?" broke in Phyl, getting up to mix a second batch.

Angela patted Joanie's stiff arm. "No, thank you, but I wouldn't mind a glass of wine with dinner. That curry smells delicious. Do you have any Sauvignon Blanc? A dear friend I've been dating is a sommelier, and I've become rather particular with my wine pairings."

Joanie rolled her eyes, and to forestall any comment from her I sprang up saying, "Phyl, I'll go down cellar for it. You keep working on the drinks."

The Palace didn't really have a wine cellar, but we had jokingly designated one corner of the three-car garage thus. Mostly it was Phyl's territory, and it took me several minutes to figure out her classification methodology: by country, by region, by variety, by year. There were several bottles of Sauvignon Blanc, and not being much of a wine connoisseur myself, I was just regretting having volunteered to choose when the rolling door started going up and Daniel pulled in.

"I'm so glad to see you!" I exclaimed, when he opened his car door.

"You are?" His voice held a mixture of pleasure and wariness.

"Yes, very. Come help me. Your mom is here, and she wants a

Sauvignon Blanc with the vegetable curry tonight. Which one would she like best?"

He came over to inspect the bottles, and I peeked sidewise at him. Yes, there was Angela Martin's straight nose and high cheekbones and easy, self-contained grace. I wondered if she had been blonde as he was. Or if Mr. Martin had found anyone better looking in Venezuela—I'd heard Venezuelan women were as beautiful as they come. No one bragged much about Venezuelan men, however, so I was pretty sure they couldn't hold a candle to Daniel. He plucked the 2002 bottle from Healdsburg off the rack and handed it to me, catching me in my furtive stare. Of course I turned scarlet and was ticked with myself when I saw the answering gleam in his eye.

"Anything else I can help you with, Cass?"

"No!" I snapped, making his mouth curve in amusement. "Oh, but actually, yes. If you don't mind. Joanie is pretty on edge, and she and your mom have been getting on each other's nerves. If you could run interference these next few days, it'd be lovely. For Joanie's sake."

"I'll do my best, though I've never seen them relate in any other way. Anything for…Joanie."

Hearing that familiar note in his voice, I bit back an exasperated sigh and headed back inside, trying not to be self-conscious about him right behind me. While Daniel might distract his mother and sister from their favorite pastime of mutual aggravation, I didn't know who was going to distract him from his.

Mrs. Martin sprang up the instant he came through the door, taking his hands and holding up her cheek for a kiss. "Mom," he said simply, after he had complied, his eyes flicking over to check on Joanie.

"Darling," she cooed. "It's been months. Thank you so much for the flowers you sent for my birthday. I brought them to the gallery to show them off. You remembered how gardenias are my favorite."

"Actually, Joanie remembered," Daniel said easily, "But don't you think I did a nice job signing the card she picked out?"

His mother made a little pouting face and punched him playfully on the arm. "You can't fool me." She went on to repeat her praise of his beautiful house, tell him how well he was looking, enumerate some of his most recent accomplishments, and so on, while I made myself busy serving up dinner, getting Joanie to help me. In fairness to him, Daniel did try to shut her up a few times, but she seemed to assume he was just being modest and that, if he wasn't going to toot his own horn, someone must.

After an hour in Angela Martin's company, it made a lot more sense to me how Daniel had come by his sense of entitlement where women were concerned, not to mention his bulletproof self-assurance. His mother's adulation, coupled with his extraordinary good looks, had ruined any chances he may have had to see himself in any but the most glowing lights. He was a man with no need of grace— not from God, not from anyone.

With her daughter, however, Mrs. Martin took the gloves off. It wasn't that she didn't love Joanie as well, but somehow mother-daughter love came out as a constant urge to improve the daughter. As if Joanie reflected on her in a way Daniel didn't. No wonder Joanie had struck out on such a different path in life. "Joanie, why on earth did you cut those layers in your hair? You know your hair is too wavy to begin with, and the layers just make it stick out more."

"The rest of us would just kill for Joanie's hair, Mrs. Martin," spoke up Phyl. She was absolutely the most loyal person I knew, and indignation for Joanie here trumped her natural gentleness.

"Oh, I'm sure," said Mrs. Martin placatingly. "And do call me Angela. You know mothers and daughters. We just can't help picking at each other." She certainly couldn't, because not ten minutes later she accosted Joanie with, "Honey, did you read those books on atheism I sent you?"

"Cover to cover," said Joanie expressionlessly. Clearly her love of philosophical discussions did not extend to debates with her mother.

"Very thought-provoking, I found them," continued Angela blithely. "Especially the parts about how we have evolved to engage in social, ethical behavior without recourse to religion, and the connection between religion and warmongering."

"Mom, considering how the majority of people at this table are religious, and you're eating their food, you may want to rein in the atheist proselytizing," said Daniel dryly.

She gave him a mild *et-tu-Brute* look. "Daniel! Did you read them? I asked Joanie to pass them on."

"She did. And she was pretty speedy about it, too. But I have to confess, I didn't care for them either. Ranting ideologues from either side of the fence don't do it for me." That put a cork in her, as Joanie remarked to me later.

Perry neatly turned the conversation to Angela's art gallery and art in general, where we doggedly kept it until the end of the meal. Despite my request, I half-expected Daniel to bolt off to the Lean-To at that point, leaving the rest of us to close ranks around Joanie until Angela chose to retire from the field, but he surprised me by coaxing his mother to sit down at the piano with him. It turned out Joanie wasn't the only musical Martin. Daniel and his mother knew a number of easy duets, and when there were lyrics, Joanie sang along.

"I didn't even know he played," Phyl said to me under her breath, as we cleaned up after dinner.

"It's kind of too much, isn't it?" I replied. "The Martins! They sing! They dance! They sit around looking beautiful!"

Perry jabbed me in the ribs. "We McKeans better think of our act. You didn't tell me about the talent portion of the evening."

"Dinner was the talent portion of my evening," I retorted, "Unless someone wants to hear my Snow Goddess monologue. Phyl, you could score big points with Mrs. Martin by telling her about vegan composting."

"Speaking of vegan," said Phyl, "What on earth are we going to feed her tomorrow? Won't we have butter in absolutely everything?"

"Everything that doesn't have chicken broth," said Perry.

"Or whipping cream," I added. "We'll just have to dish out portions of the vegetables before we add all the dairy. Anyhow, given how this evening has gone, don't you think Angela's diet is probably the least of our worries?"

. . .

With such dismally low expectations, Thanksgiving could only prove a pleasant surprise. Daniel was true to his word, running interference between the other Martins, and turning his considerable charm on his mother, who hardly required this effort to be delighted with him. Seeing that her brother meant to pull his weight, Joanie relaxed, and even managed to overlook a few of her mother's jabs. And it did help to have all of us there; when Angela insisted on a morning walk to get the blood pumping ("Have you put on a little weight, Joanie, since I last saw you?"), Benny and I came along as the welcome third wheels and managed to defuse a few tense moments. Tense moments such as when Angela asked me, "Do you also work at the church, dear?" in a tone equally suited to questions like, *Did you always want to be a garbage man when you grew up?*

By the time we came back, blood now circulating satisfactorily, things were in full swing in the Palace kitchen. "Well that's something I never thought I'd see," said Joanie, when she caught sight of Daniel at the stove sautéing onions and celery and sausage for the stuffing. "Quick, Cass—go check out the window and tell me if you see Jesus coming again."

"I'll have you know, Joanie, he chopped the onion, too," said Perry. He was engaged in loosening the turkey's skin and slipping pats of herbed butter underneath.

"How come you never get off your butt and help when we cook?" Joanie demanded.

"Perry beat me at cards last night," answered Daniel laconically, flipping Benny a hunk of sausage which the beast caught in mid-air.

"I've beaten you at Scrabble," I pointed out, and he grinned at me.

"Name your price, Cass. But you'd better be aware that, if I beat you in the future, I'll name mine."

Perry had been put in charge of the day, and by dint of keeping everyone busy we managed to get through it with a minimum of tension, although Mrs. Martin and Joanie seemed able to whip it up any time they were in the same room.

"Tell me more about this Roy you're dating, Joan," Angela began at one point. We were taking a break from our kitchen labors at this point and playing a few hands of hi-lo at the dining table, while Daniel and Perry parked it in front the television to watch a game. "I was so fond of that Keith, if you insisted on getting married at some point." Keith had been Joanie's first fiancé.

Joanie bristled immediately. "Keith and I had unresolvable communication issues, Mom. We bickered a lot, kind of like you and me."

"Well, who was that next one, then? Paul? Patrick?" her mother persisted, laying down the queen of spades.

"Peter," Joanie ground out. "The one with the overbearing mother, if you can imagine. And then there was Steve, who was too clingy. Do we really have to talk about this? If you think I've run up a list, why don't you ever quiz Daniel on his love life?"

"Daniel is a particular, restless man, and he's always had the good sense not to take things too far," said Angela, casting him a fond look while Joanie pretended to gag. "Like your father. It would have been better if your father and I had never married."

"So you've said," replied Joanie dryly. "The real truth is that, if you wanted to keep up with Daniel's love life, you'd have to run a ticker, rather than an annual update." Either overhearing or sensing that we were talking about him, Daniel came over for another of Phyl's stuffed mushrooms.

"I was just asking your sister about this new boyfriend Roy she has," Angela beamed up at him. "She's being evasive. I don't even know what he does for a living."

"Fine, Mom," replied Joanie, goaded. "I met him at church. He's a network engineer, okay? That is, when he's not warmongering and bombing abortion clinics. And before that he worked for World Vision in Cambodia, teaching English."

"Oh!" exclaimed Mrs. Martin, making a little face. "Network engineer—what on earth is that? It sounds terribly dull for a creative girl like you. Are you two very serious?"

Seeing that Joanie had fire in her eyes, Daniel gave me a wink and said, "It's actually a very nuts-and-bolts, visual-thinking kind of job, Mom. Not very different from your beloved *feng shui*. You're thinking how to capture the *Qi* and keep it circulating through your home, and they're thinking the same thing about electronic connections in a company's network."

"What a load of crap," muttered Joanie, but I didn't think it was such a bad way of thinking about it, and Mrs. Martin was completely appeased, as Daniel had intended.

• • •

We sat down for dinner at four. Phyl had set a beautiful table with her best glassware and china, pillar candles glowing and an autumn garland running its length. By then some stragglers had joined us—a couple of Phyl's co-workers, her sister Mary, and good old Tom, now a model of deportment.

When all the dishes had been produced, and the sideboard nearly groaned under the weight of them, Joanie rose from her seat at the foot of the table and farthest from her mother. "I'd like to propose a toast," she declared, raising her festive glass of Blanc de Noirs. "To family and friends and the hands which prepared this food. May we be truly thankful."

"Here here!"

I clinked glasses with Perry and Phyl and Mary across the table, and we were all about to dig in when Daniel spoke up. "No grace, Joanie?"

A little silence fell—Mrs. Martin froze in spreading the non-dairy butter alternative on her bread—and then Phyl hastened to smooth it over. "Of course. Maybe Cass, since Joanie gave the toast?"

Shooting Phyl a reproachful look, I quickly bowed my head and shut my eyes, so everyone else would. I had never been much of an out-loud prayer, and my months-long hiatus didn't build my confidence, but too late now. "Father," I began hesitantly, "we are grateful for your blessings large and small. For the friends and family around this table and the ones who aren't with us. For this wonderful food and this beautiful house. For health. For love, especially your love, which never gives up on us. Amen."

A few "amens" and rather more awkward throat-clearings greeted this, and we dug in.

CHAPTER 20:

Rinkside Revelations

"One grande with whip caramel macchiato, extra hot, and in the seasonal red cup," I announced, pushing it across the counter at Nadina.

It was the Saturday afternoon after Thanksgiving, and I was glad to see she'd made it back from Ohio. Both Perry and Mrs. Martin had left that morning for Portland, and while the visit had come off better than Joanie had thought possible, she still cheered when the door closed behind them: "I feel great! Must be all the extra *Qi* in the house!"

The hot coffee concoction was meant to be a surprise for Nadina at her skating rink elf job, and it looked like my timing was just right. She was perched on the stool behind the cash register, her jingle-belled felt elf hat at a cocky angle, and a decidedly belligerent look on her face.

"Whoo hoo! Cass, you're the best! I've been sitting here freezing my ass off and thinking I should go crawling back to Petco." She held the cup up to breathe in the steam appreciatively. "Mmmm…"

"One coffee drink doesn't rule out crawling back to Petco," I admonished. "In fact, if you drink my drink it means you agree to go back and talk to your manager. You can't leave it like that, Nadina. Besides, you are totally gifted with animals, and you don't ice skate. Who needs an employee discount here?"

"Blah blah blah, don't nag me, Cass. I can guess what you think now, did you know? I can even hear your voice in my head telling me what I ought to do sometimes."

"That might not be me—it could be your conscience waking up after all this time. But I'll give it a rest for a minute," I conceded. "How was Ohio? Tell all."

Nadina took a tentative sip and sucked in air to cool her tongue. "It was tense," she said. "Everyone took turns fighting: me and Mom, then Mom and Aunt Sylvia, then me and Aunt Sylvia because I thought she was being mean to Mom. And then we'd start over again with me and Mom."

"Bummer. What all did you fight about?"

"Let me see…me and Mom fought about me living with Mike, and Mom and Aunt Sylvia fought about Mom not raising me right, and me and Aunt Sylvia fought because I told her I wasn't a friggin' baby—"

"I hope you said 'friggin,'" I interjected.

"And Aunt Sylvia said I sure acted like one, and Mom told Aunt Sylvia to mind her own stinking business—"

"I hope she said 'stinking,'" I interrupted again.

"Knock it off, Cass!" Nadina objected, laughing. "But the really biggest fight was when Aunt Sylvia told Mom she thought I should come out and live with her in Ohio."

"In Ohio?" I echoed. "Live with Aunt Sylvia in Ohio? What, because you were all getting along so well?"

"Because Aunt Sylvia said I need to make a clean start, and since

Mom couldn't control me, blah blah blah."

The thought of Nadina moving to Ohio made me feel oddly empty, and I couldn't get my voice to work for a moment. "Did— what did you think about all that?"

"What the hell would I do in Cleveland? I'd have to start over at some crappy new school and not know anyone except my seventy-year-old great aunt. If I don't even want to live with my own mother, I sure as hell don't want to live with her." I felt a wave of relief, and then guilt for my relief—a fresh start for Nadina far away from loser Mike wouldn't necessarily be a bad thing. "And I told Sylvia so, and she said to think about it when I wasn't all freaked out and when Mom wasn't around to gum up the works."

Sylvia was no dummy, it would seem. I supposed we had both learned the hard way what happened when you pushed Nadina past the point of rational thought. "Whew!" I whistled. "In between all the fighting, did you eat any turkey?"

"Yeah, but that was almost another fight because Mom said she would do it, and then she fell asleep in front of the TV, and Aunt Sylvia didn't wake her up because she wanted to say 'I told you so,' and so the turkey came out kinda dry."

"Oh, for Pete's sake!" I protested. "I should bring you some of my brother Perry's turkey—it was luscious. No, on second thought, I'll throw it in the freezer and hold it out as a bribe for when you've sorted things out with Blaise. How about if we do some role playing right now? I'll be your manager, and you come and tell me why I should hire you back."

"Because I'm the awesomest," said Nadina incorrigibly. Her gaze suddenly sharpened. "Oh, hey," she whispered. "Here comes Kyle's mentor with some lady."

I turned and, sure enough, saw them cutting across the grass to the rink entrance, James walking jauntily with a pair of hockey skates slung by the laces over his shoulder, accompanied by his tiny, adorable date, all curling blonde hair and blue eyes under a knit cap. Well, this would be interesting. Would this be the friendly, charming James, or the awkward, distant one?

It was both, as it happened. James caught sight of us the next instant, and his face lit up. "Cass! Nadina! I had no idea you worked here, Nadina—nice elf outfit. Did you guys have a good Thanksgiving?" We answered with the usual platitudes, and when I asked after his he answered equally vaguely. So...happy to see me? Apparently not, because the next moment he started looking around nervously until he remembered himself and added, "This is Rachel. Rachel, this is Nadina who goes to Camden School and her mentor Cass."

"You're a skater, too, then," said Rachel, as we shook hands and James fished in his wallet to pay. She gestured toward the figure skates I was toting. "This is going to be very embarrassing for me, I think."

"I've skated since I was in elementary school," I answered, "But it looks like James knows what he's doing, so you can hang on to him." Turning to him I added, "Was hockey another activity you had to hide from your high school friends and enemies?"

With such a pointed reminder of the last time we'd had a friendly conversation, James had the grace to look abashed. It seemed to help him decide something because he suddenly looked me square in the face. "So, hey, does this mean I finally get to meet this mysterious husband of yours? Trent? Or was it Troy? Is he here? We can make this a double date."

In the split-second I hesitated, Nadina's jaw dropped and she blurted, "Dude! Way insensitive. Her husband's dead, remember?"

James, of course, remembered no such thing, it having never been told him in any way, shape or form, and his eyes flashed to my face to see if Nadina and I were perpetrating an elaborate, if tasteless, joke. I felt myself go red, and that, combined with my mortified expression, was enough to tell him the truth. "Good Lord! Cass, what happened? I just saw you last week—" He apparently thought tragedy had struck in the interim—not an irrational conclusion, except that I was standing at a festive skating rink, skates in hand and, up to that moment, a smile on my face.

Had I not been so uncomfortable with having to explain myself, I might have laughed—it was so farcical: Nadina the oversize, affronted elf, James struck by lightning, and poor Rachel looking from one to the other of us, bewildered. "Nadina, he didn't know," I managed at last. "Umm…it was pretty sudden—Troy's death—but it happened almost a year-and-a-half ago. He had an enlarged heart and died in a car accident."

"Along with their daughter," put in Nadina breathlessly, now looking quite ready to forgive James and get into the spirit of the exciting revelation. I frowned at her. It was too much tragedy to throw at someone unawares. Nadina scowled right back at me. "If you don't come clean now, Cass, you'll just have to do it later, and it'll be even weirder next time." True enough.

"I'm sorry," I began. "I haven't figured out a graceful way of telling people I meet—I can't go around announcing that he's dead whenever his name comes up."

"Cass, please don't feel you have to apologize!" James interrupted, putting a hand on my arm to stop me. "I'm so sorry…"

"It's her ring," said Nadina matter-of-factly. "If she didn't still wear her wedding ring, she wouldn't have to explain anything to anybody."

"Men don't notice wedding rings," I hissed defensively. I turned on James. "Did you notice I wear a wedding ring?"

"No, but is that a trick question?" His gray eyes smiled ruefully. "I thought you were married because when I first met you, you mentioned your husband, and naturally I assumed he was alive."

"See?" I told Nadina. "It has nothing to do with wearing a ring." She raised her eyebrows, unconvinced, but had to turn away to help some new people at the cash register.

Rachel's pitying expression was beginning to be tinged with impatience, and I felt guilty about my miscommunication hijacking her date. "Here you guys, go skate," I urged. "Please." Rachel grimaced at me apologetically and then tugged on James' arm.

He was still watching me thoughtfully. "Are you going to skate, Cass?"

"Oh, I don't know. I brought my skates just in case. Mainly I came down here to hang out with Nadina and catch up. Please, go enjoy yourselves." Please! To my relief, he nodded, and they headed toward the skate rental counter. My own skates felt suddenly too heavy, and I thumped them down by Nadina's macchiato. "Well, that was awkward," I said to her, when she finished with the customers. "I'll be so glad when I've been widowed thirty years. By then I'll have more company, and people won't think I'm such a freak."

"They wouldn't think you're such a freak if you would just take off your wedding ring and admit you're not married."

I glared at her. "Maybe. Probably. Can we just drop the subject and go back to your Petco problem?" She sighed gustily but nodded and patted the stool next to her.

We spent the next fifteen minutes role-playing what she could say to Blaise, going over her apology and possible answers to objections, until Nadina knew the gist and could say it in a reasonably polite tone. During these discussions, my eyes wandered frequently to James and Rachel: he helped her lace up her skates, guided her by her mittened hands slowly around the rink while she squealed and slipped, and when she rested against the side he made a few high-speed circuits before doing a dramatic hockey stop next to her and spraying her with snow. Rachel laughed and pelted him with a chunk of it.

Nadina was nothing if not observant—it must be all her dog-whispering prowess. "Think he likes her?"

"Well, he asked her out, didn't he?" I said mildly.

"That might just be because she's shorter than he is."

I laughed. "You sound like my roommate Joanie, who is a towering 5'10" like you. He doesn't seem worried by his height like you and Joanie seem to be. Besides, Rachel is cute in her own right."

"Yeah, if baby bunny is your type."

I tried unsuccessfully not to giggle. "All right, girlie, I think my work is done here. You call your manager and let me know how it goes. Today or tomorrow, okay, before you forget what we've practiced."

When I was halfway down the ramp exit, I heard James calling me. Vaulting neatly over the half-wall surrounding the ice, he clumped across the rubber-padded floor. "Will you be coming in to the office this week?"

Seeing as he didn't seem to hate me anymore, I nodded tentatively. "I'm sure I will. I like it there."

He hesitated another moment. "Hey, Cass, I'm sorry again about your husband and about this whole weird situation where we had to dredge it up in public and all."

"James, really!" I groaned. "It's not your fault how it all came out or didn't come out until now. It's just sort of ridiculous and embarrassing, and I still haven't figured out how to go about telling people. I didn't mean to make you feel bad, for heaven's sake." I fiddled with the blade guards on my skates, but when he didn't respond, I ventured a glance and found him studying me with an unreadable expression.

"Can I call you later to talk?" he asked.

My voice took on an admittedly whiny note. "Oh, do we have to? I actually don't want to talk about this anymore. I'm sorry I let you think Troy was alive, and I'm sorry he's dead, and I really don't want to hash it out again."

"No, no. I meant talk about some other things."

"Oh. Oops." I blushed. "Sorry to snap at you."

He grinned. "I forgive you. I'll give you a call later." He backed up, waving at me. It occurred to me that James didn't have my phone number—there had never been any reason to call me before, and email had always done the trick—but I really didn't want to walk over there at this point. If it was that urgent, he would just have to figure it out.

• • •

All was quiet at the Palace. Joanie and Phyl were off at some Chaff-sponsored event, and who knew where Daniel was. It was a relief after the constant togetherness of the last few days to come home to just one Labradoodle. Benny launched out of his crate and tore around the downstairs twice before lapping up some water and whining to go outside. When he was taken care of, I flipped on the gas fireplace and curled up with some tea and a novel, but after reading and re-reading the same page a few times I gave up and shut my eyes.

A knock at the door, followed by Benny's mad barking, woke me up. It had gotten dark outside, and I struggled up from the armchair confusedly, fumbling to turn on as many lights as I could. When I managed to get Benny to lie down on his bed and stay, I pulled the door open, and to my dazed astonishment, James stood there. He was minus the hockey skates and Rachel, but wearing the same moss-colored Shetland sweater and uncertain expression. "Cass, hi—yeah—I didn't know if anyone was home."

"What are you doing here? How did you know where I live?"

He ducked his head rather sheepishly and gave me a lopsided grin. "You're going to think I'm some kind of stalker, but I realized I didn't have your phone number, so I ran by the office and got your address off your W-4."

"That *is* creepy," I said, but smiled back at him. "What was so doggone urgent that you couldn't just shoot me an email?" I stood aside to let him in and pointed toward the living room. "You've been acting weird lately, and I've convinced myself that you're going to fire me."

James laughed shortly and threw himself down in Daniel's favorite armchair. "Oh, you thought I was behaving oddly?"

"To say the least!" I answered. "One minute you're talking to me like a normal human being and then suddenly you're avoiding me like the plague. At the mentors' meeting, at Free Universe. I figured you needed to can me, but you were trying to work up to it."

He ran his hands through his curling hair, his gray eyes still not looking straight at me. "I didn't know you'd notice, much less put such an interpretation on it—"

"For Pete's sake, James," I interrupted impatiently, "Stop being so mysterious. What is it?"

Rocketing up abruptly and causing Benny to whine a little anxiously, James started pacing in front of the fireplace. After a few moments of this, I started to have the same urge to whine as Benny. What on earth was the matter? As if he'd heard my thoughts, James forced himself to stop moving, and I joked feebly, "I feel like you have some momentous announcement—let me guess—you're my father?"

Not even acknowledging my attempt to lighten the mood, he sat back down again. "Cass, would you go out with me?"

"What?"

"Would you—would you consider going out with me?"

"Out where?" I asked idiotically.

"Out on a date," he said patiently. "I've been making an ass of myself because, that day when we were having coffee with Riley and Kyle, I was sitting there enjoying myself, and then I realized the reason I was enjoying myself was that I was with you, and that I found you really attractive. I thought you were married, of course, so I've been trying to avoid you ever since, until I could think and behave properly."

Had I not already been sitting on the sofa, I think I might have collapsed onto it. "Oh," I said limply.

"And I know this is tacky," he continued hurriedly. "The second I hear you're not married I rush over here to ask you out. Poor Rachel—I couldn't get rid of her fast enough," he added, with a rueful chuckle.

Two urges were warring within me: one that told me to run screaming from the room because I didn't want to date anyone, and James was too young and too innocent and worked with me besides; and the other that told me it had been almost eighteen months, and if I was honest with myself I would admit that I liked him very much and found him attractive as well. I cleared my throat. "James— I haven't been dating because it's only been a year and some-odd months since I lost Troy and—and my daughter Min."

He sat down next to me, wincing. "I'm sorry. I know. This is bad timing on my part. It's just that I've been telling myself for days not to think about you, and so when Nadina spilled the beans this afternoon and I realized it was okay to think about you, it felt like it couldn't wait."

"Besides all that, I don't think it's a good idea to date someone you work with," I argued reluctantly.

He grinned at me. "Would it help if I fired you after all?" He must have been able to see from my face that I was wavering. "Okay, I'm rushing this. Just don't rule it out, Cass. Tell me we can spend a little time together, outside of the office and mentor training meetings, so you can figure out what you want."

"You could…come to our open house this Thursday evening," I suggested. "My housemates and I have an open house every Thursday night. That would be some low-pressure time together, sort of."

"Open house," James repeated thoughtfully, "they must be pretty common at this church because my friend Roy is always going to his girlfriend's open house."

Comprehension dawned on me, as I remembered vaguely that Roy and James knew each other somehow. "That's Joanie! His girlfriend is Joanie, and she's one of my housemates."

James stared at me. "Are you telling me I could have found out months ago that you were single? Roy's invited me a couple times, but I hate being a third wheel, and I barely know Joanie from YAF. He sure never mentioned who her housemates were, or I certainly would have come."

"Well, come now, at any rate," I urged. "And even if you'd known months ago that I was widowed, I really wouldn't have been ready even to hang out with you, back then."

He got to his feet again, stuffing his hands in his pockets and grinning at me cheerfully. "It's a deal. I'll be here Thursday after work. It's a long time to wait, though. You'll be sure and pop by the office before then, right? Or come with Joanie to YAF on Wednesday night?"

"That'll be the day," I scoffed, following him to the door. "Besides, Joanie would kill me if I came after you asked, since she asks me every week. I'll see you Thursday for sure, and maybe earlier—I promised Riley I'd save him a piece of pie."

CHAPTER 21:

Prince Charming at the Palace

Thursday afternoon before our open house I spent window shopping with Raquel, leaving myself plenty of time to get home. But the 5:15 p.m. bus was MIA, making the 5:30 too crowded to squeeze onto, and the 5:45 broke down with me on it. By the time the replacement bus came along, everyone was grumpy and frazzled, including me. For someone who was not dating, I felt suspiciously upset because I wouldn't have any time to primp. Fortunately, the walk from the bus stop gave me time to regroup and talk some sense into myself. This was not a date. It was hanging out. And given my mixed feelings and James' own flightiness in relationships, this might be the first and last thing we did together.

Halfway up the hill I could distinguish several people standing in our driveway, and after another minute I recognized them as Daniel, Kelly and James. For some reason Daniel's posture looked tense, but James appeared completely at ease, hands in his pants pockets, rocking on the balls of his feet. Kelly must have said something because they all three turned to look at me. James waved gaily, and I felt my heartbeat speed. Ridiculous.

"Cass!" he exclaimed, coming to meet me. "Check this out. I have a little surprise for you." He caught my arm to stop me and pulled his MP3 player from his pocket.

"You made me a mix tape?" I teased.

"Are you kidding? We haven't even gone out yet, much less broken up." He grinned at me, unwinding the earbuds from the player. "Ready?" I nodded, and he pressed the play button. I heard a swell of music and then my own voice: "Who gives you leave to enter here? Only he who wields the Shadow Blade can challenge me…"

I gasped and put a hand to my mouth. "James, it sounds incredible! Murray did a great job!" Incredulously, I listened to my monologue unroll, hitch-free, and found myself smiling hugely. 99% of all gamers would probably skip the hokey speech, but for the 1% who would listen, there I was!

"'It' sounds incredible? You mean *you* sound incredible," he said warmly, enjoying my enjoyment. "I knew I was hearing the voice of our Snow Goddess the first time you opened your mouth and lied to me about having a husband." I shrieked in mock outrage and punched his arm, but he only laughed. "And check out the next track."

I hushed up in time to hear Kyle's characteristic rasp: "Energy points low. Death awaits."

"James, this is great—has Kyle heard it yet?"

He pulled on the earbuds and rewound them. "I'm seeing him tomorrow. He'll hear it then. And I'll have you both in again when we've tied it to the animation. I got here early to give you the preview."

"Oh, no!" I said. "I'm ordinarily here all afternoon, but I was downtown with my mother-in-law today, and the buses were having issues. Wouldn't Joanie let you in?"

"Didn't even get a chance to ask, since Daniel and Kelly were just pulling up." He inclined his head back toward the driveway, and

I noticed with some surprise that Daniel was still there, now leaning against his Corvette. Kelly was rubbing one of his arms, but he wasn't paying the least attention and seemed, in fact, to be watching James and me. No, watching wasn't the right word—Daniel was glaring.

"Did you get in an argument?" I whispered as we approached.

"Not that I know of," said James.

I said hello to the lithe and gorgeous Kelly of the unnaturally red hair, but it had been hard for us to make eye contact ever since I'd seen her almost as naked as the day she was born in the Lean-To. As for Daniel, I would merely have nodded in his direction, except his steely blue eyes seemed intent on catching mine. What was eating him? I would have to quiz James later, but now was not the time, since he and Kelly were following us closely into the house.

It was one of the fuller open houses we'd had in a while: Roy was there along with the persistent Wayne, some of Phyl's friends, James, and Kelly. Joanie mostly had things under control, but she had me string snow peas. After all the rounds of introductions, James pulled up the stool next to mine and started helping me, Joanie goggling her eyes at me behind his back. I pursed my lips at her.

"How was your day?" James murmured, under all the general conversation. "Do you still see your mother-in-law a lot?"

"From time to time," I answered. "It's sort of an odd thing, to keep a relationship going when you've lost all the connections that bound you. I think Raquel works at it as a way to keep Troy and Min fresh in her mind, and I think that's the main reason I find myself wanting some space. I want to let them sleep."

"Was 'Min' short for some other name?"

"Minerva," I said unwillingly. "It was Troy's grandmother's name, and the name of Troy's sister who died young. I didn't want to saddle my daughter with all that baggage, so I had everyone call her Min, or Minnie at the most."

"How old was she?"

"About a year-and-a-half. Walking and even doing some talking. She would have been three next month." I smiled a little shakily. "At least she's with God now, and she didn't even have to go her whole life with people giving her combination birthday-Christmas presents." James smiled at me sympathetically, but I hastened to change the subject. "What were you and Daniel talking about before I came home? He looked a little irked."

James looked surprised. "Well, it was nothing I said. I'd just introduced myself, and he asked if I was a friend of Joanie or Phyl, and I said, actually, I was here at your invitation. Then you showed up."

I mulled this over. "Maybe Kelly said something to irritate him, then." Though, if that were the case, it didn't explain the dirty looks he gave me. Unless Kelly had said something about how uncomfortable she felt around me now after the Lean-To incident. Maybe she'd mistaken my embarrassed vibe for hostility.

Phyl tapped me on the shoulder and handed me and James each some fizzy drink. "My own creation," she announced. "And Cass, can you brave the Avalanche for my Christmas runner and napkins? I can't send anyone inexperienced. If you're lucky you can find them in time for dessert."

The Avalanche was another Palace joke. Combining three households' worth of linen had resulted in a towel, tablecloth, sheets, placemat, napkin, and dishrag collection of Bed-Bath-and-Beyond proportions, upon which the door of the closet could barely be shut. I was deep in the third shelf, bent over almost at a right angle and dug in to my shoulders before I felt my fingers close on the tasseled fringe of the stupid Christmas runner and simultaneously heard an amused voice say, "Can I help you?" Conscious of my ridiculous position, I stood up too quickly and slammed the back of my head on the shelf above. Everything spun, and I staggered, seeing nothing but stars and flashes. I felt myself crash into someone while two hands grabbed me by the upper arms to steady me.

"Whoa, there." I still couldn't see, but I recognized the voice as Daniel's and hastily tried to push off his chest, knowing how he hated women clinging to him. Unfortunately, this move ran me into the linen closet door. His grip on my arms tightened. "Cass, for God's sake, hold still."

Dizzy, I obeyed. After a few more blinks, everything came back into focus, and I was looking up at him. He didn't look angry anymore, whatever that had been about, and after a moment he slowly let go of me.

"Sorry I startled you," he said, the amused note back. "Did you find what you were looking for? I think you're going to have one hell of a bump." His hand gingerly touched the back of my head, where we both felt the knot rising. I winced, and not just with pain. I think in the months we had lived together, Daniel and I had never so much as shaken hands, and the contact made me uncomfortable.

"No sacrifice is too great for the Cause," I mumbled, turning away to stuff my arms full of the worthless Christmas linens.

He surprised me by relieving me of them. "I'll go figure out what to do with these. Why don't you get some ice for your head?"

Halfway down the hall, I suddenly remembered my Kelly theory. "Daniel, is Kelly okay with me? I mean, I don't make her uncomfortable, do I? I've never said anything to her about—about the whole…"

His look of genuine puzzlement answered my question. "Okay, then. Never mind. I'm going to go get some ice."

· · ·

We needn't have bothered with the Christmas linens; everyone had taken their bowl of chili and draped and perched on various solid surfaces in the living room. With so many extroverts present, Joanie suggested a game of celebrity charades after dinner.

She handed each of us a few pieces of paper, skipping over Daniel. To our surprise and Kelly's apparent irritation, he tugged on Joanie's sleeve and took a few. Each of us wrote down a few famous names, real or fictional and threw it back in the bag.

"Okay," said Joanie, "now we divide into teams. I think with Kelly sitting out there are ten of us. Let's just do this side of the room versus that side—we'll split right down the middle between Cass and James." She winked. "And, Cass, why don't you go first?"

Celebrity charades was more like $20,000 Pyramid than traditional charades, meaning I could describe the names I drew in the first round. The teams looked pretty balanced, since the people most likely to read each other's minds had been split up: Joanie and Daniel, Phyl's friends and their spouses.

When Joanie started Roy's watch, I drew out the first slip of paper: Oliver Twist. I hadn't put him in, so it could only be Daniel. I looked at him and said, "Remember, you can't guess your own celebrity in the first round. Umm… this Charles Dickens character runs away from the poorhouse and falls in with a gang of thieves." Amusement flitted across Daniel's face, and I knew it was indeed his. Everyone else looked blankly at me.

"I haven't read any Dickens since high school," complained Roy.

"Okay," I said quickly, "The last name is like in Phyl's lemon drop martinis, you put a—something—of lemon."

"A twist!" yelled Phyl. "Oliver Twist!"

I grabbed another name. "Umm…the president during World War I."

"Roosevelt!" hollered Phil's friend Kendra. I shook my head.

"Wrong war."

"Woodrow Wilson," said Daniel calmly.

I suspected Daniel was responsible for the next name, too. "Err... this was the explorer who was first to the South Pole."

"Peary!" yelled Wayne. I shook my head again. "Wrong pole."

Since Daniel wasn't allowed to answer his own this round I had to get to Roald Amundsen by way of Roald Dahl and almonds.

Next name. In James's cheerful scrawl: the Snow Goddess. I felt my cheeks warm and glanced over at him. He must have read my mind because he grinned and raised his glass to me. "All right... this is the character I do the voice for in James' video game." Joanie, on the other team, clapped her hand over her mouth and jumped up and down.

Phyl screwed up her eyes. "Oh! Oh, I can't remember."

"Those of us who know nothing about this will need some clues," said Daniel, his voice expressionless.

"Okay... the first word is the frozen stuff they get at Snoqualmie Pass." They guessed this easily. "And the second word is a word for a female deity, like Athena."

"I would have thought Aphrodite more appropriate," mused James, just to make me blush harder.

"Goddess," said Daniel in a voice of stone. "Snow Goddess."

"Time's up!" called Joanie. "Team One gets four points."

The game went quickly. Joanie led off for Team Two and crushed my four points with six, though Roy mock-protested that George W. Bush and Hillary Clinton were way too easy and should be thrown out. There was the usual arguing over whether a certain "celebrity" was too obscure, and the usual hilarity when someone mixed up different people—witness Wayne, who confused Barbara Kingsolver with Sophie Kinsella, and spent several minutes afterward groaning into his hands. James was the undisputed master of the straight charades round, his Pat Benatar and Brian Boitano drawing huge laughs. Altogether it was great fun, and only at ten o'clock did any guests make moves to leave.

James, however, hung back to help me tackle the dishes.

"This was a blast," he remarked, handing me the bowls as he rinsed them. "Thanks for inviting me."

"It was fun, wasn't it?" I said. "I'm glad you came."

"Well, I wanted to see you, didn't I? And this was all you would offer me." He waited for me to say something, but I couldn't think of what to say. "Not that it wasn't a nice evening, but how about if we go out for dinner next?" My slightly panicked expression caused him to backpeddle a little. "Okay, not dinner right away. How about if we get coffee or walk Green Lake or both? Come on, Cass. We're friends. We enjoy each other's company. Let's hang out."

Hanging out wasn't dating, I reminded myself again. I nodded hesitantly. When his face broke into a big grin, I couldn't help grinning back, despite the unease in my stomach. "But it's not dating," I added. "You're too young for me, and we work together, and you date too many people, so it's not dating. We'll go dutch on the coffee."

James rolled his eyes and dried his hands on the dishrag. "Any other qualms you want to tell me about? Because now that you've agreed to spend time with me, you can say anything you like."

I shook my head shyly. "No, that's all. Is there…is there anything you want to say to me?"

He laughed. "That I don't like about you? Give me some time, and I'm sure I'll come up with something. Right now all I can think of is what I like about you." He leaned closer to me, and I found myself holding my breath. He was too charming altogether. "Like that voice of yours and that quick wit and those brown eyes. I like how you—"

A crash of crockery startled us both, and we sprang apart to find Daniel had dumped the salad and dessert plates in the empty chili pot. "Excuse me," he said dryly.

Embarrassed, I went to get the dishes. I could feel his eyes on me, willing me to look at him, but I refused. James and I hadn't been doing anything, after all, and even if we had, it couldn't begin to approach what I'd unwillingly witnessed in the Lean-To. A thought distracted me: if Daniel hadn't interrupted, would James have tried to kiss me?

Phyl and Joanie came in, carrying linens and glassware, and the moment was lost. James went back to rinsing, giving me a little wink.

"What happened to Kelly, Daniel?" Joanie asked. "Did you send her home early because she wouldn't play Celebrity?"

"She left," said Daniel bluntly. "I don't think she enjoyed herself, and I found I wasn't enjoying her either."

"What wasn't to like?" asked Joanie innocently. "She was your favorite combo: big boobs and easy morals."

For some reason, Daniel's eyes narrowed when she said this. It was no more than the truth, and he usually would have given as good as he got, but maybe he didn't like her talking like this with James there, a relative stranger. Joanie, seeing her brother was not in the mood, flew to hug him and said contritely, "Sorry. None of my business." His expression softened, and she added mischievously, "Mom was right, you always have the good sense not to take things too far in your relationships."

"Good night, all," interrupted James, folding up the dishcloth and giving a general wave. "Thanks for having me." I walked with him to the door and helped him find his coat. He took my hand. "So I'll call you tomorrow? Remember, coffee and Green Lake, you promised." I nodded. I could feel my heartbeat speed up as his gaze traveled briefly to my mouth, but he turned lightly away. "Good night, then, Cass." I stood in the hallway for a minute, leaning thoughtfully against the wall. What was I doing? Should I be doing this? Would Troy have agreed to go for a walk with some other woman so soon, if it had been I who died with Min? On the other hand, it was just a walk. Nothing to get dramatic about. I remembered hearing in the Grief Recovery class that women tended to grieve alone, and men tended to grieve by getting someone else—if that could be called grieving. So presumably, were the situation reversed, Troy would be getting remarried about now.

In one of her mind-reading moments, Joanie peeked out from the kitchen and bounded over to give me a bone-crushing hug. "Don't over-analyze, Cass. James is great, and he likes you. Just have fun. You don't have to marry him. It's been over a year! *Way* over. It's high time you spent time with someone over 18 of the opposite sex." She tugged on my arm. "C'mon, let's go up to your room for a heart-to-heart."

I pulled away. "No way. It's 10:30, and if we have a heart-to-heart I'll definitely over-analyze. I'm going to bed."

CHAPTER 22:

Brain Damage

I dreamed that I was getting married.

I was wearing some floating white gown and standing at the head
of the Palace staircase. Joanie and Phyl stood at the bottom, bouquets
in hand, waiting for me to descend, a little flower girl with them. Min.
She looked darling, a crown of flowers on her light brown hair. Next
to her was a younger boy, presumably the ring bearer, although he
was no one I recognized. This is ridiculous, I thought in my dream.
Aren't I already married? But who am I married to? I looked around
for my father, so he could walk me down the stairs, but he was no-
where to be seen. Memory came back: I was a widow. Did that mean
I was marrying James? Or was I dead and going to renew my vows
with Troy, which would explain Min's presence? The opening bars of
Lohengrin's Wedding March sounded and, tentatively, I took a step
down. Looking past Joanie and Phyl and Min, I saw into the entry
way. The front door was open, and the senior pastor stood in the
doorway, beaming but waiting for me to get down there, already. The
groom had his back to me. My groom. Too tall for James. When I

took another hesitant step down, completely off the music, he turned slowly to face me.

I slipped and fell down the stairs.

When I woke up, my heart was racing, and it took me a second to realize where I was. Rattled, I flicked on the light. It was only 12:30 in the morning, so I hadn't been asleep long. Why on earth would I dream I was marrying Daniel, of all people? At least my subconscious sensed that such an unlikely scenario was actually closer to a nightmare. Must have hit my head harder than I thought. Throwing off the covers, I got up and pulled on a sweatshirt. Nightmares call for a cup of tea.

The Palace was eerily quiet. I hesitated at the top of the stairs, remembering my imaginary fall, but then gingerly descended them and padded into the kitchen. Dreams always make you wonder. When I was in grad school and TA-ing a 19th-century survey course, I once dreamed I was making out with one of the freshmen in the class, someone my conscious self never considered, of course—not being a cradle-robbing predator—and the next day in section I was so mortified I could hardly speak to him. I paused in my rummaging through the pantry tea shelf, struck by a thought: if I went out with James, we would have the same age difference as that freshman and I. Ugh. So much for my holier-than-thou attitude.

Joanie, Phyl, and I were all major tea drinkers, so the selection was vast. I stood holding Market Spice Tea in one hand and chamomile in the other, hardly seeing them because my mind was still going a mile a minute. I would worry about James later. Did dreaming I was marrying Daniel mean I secretly yearned to be the long-suffering, much-cheated-on, eventually-dumped wife of an atheist sex addict? It could at least get me on a talk show: "Atheist Sex Addicts and the Women Who Love Them." Or did the fact that it was a nightmare negate such low-self-esteem longings?

The click of the back door opening woke me from my meditations. The kitchen was dark, except for the little light above the stove which we left on all night and the pantry I was in, but I had been standing silently for who knew how long, clutching the stupid tea boxes, so a half-zonked, meth-addicted intruder could easily imagine he was alone. Heart hammering, I was just laying the boxes down and reaching for the self-wringing mop-cum-weapon when I heard Daniel's voice: "…Er…Cass?" He flicked on the overhead light.

I popped out of the pantry, furious, and found myself face to face with my dream groom. He looked rather less natty, given that he was wearing sweatpants and a t-shirt instead of a tuxedo, but I imagine he could say the same about my Oregon Shakespeare Festival sweatshirt over a knee-length flannel nightgown. "How many times today are you going to scare the pants off me?" I hissed.

Daniel's eyes fell pointedly to my bare legs. "With legs like those, I don't have much incentive to stop."

I blushed to the roots of my hair and scurried back into the pantry. Marry that guy? Maybe I didn't fall down the stairs in my dream—maybe I threw myself, to spare myself such a fate!

His voice came again, placating this time. "Cass—sorry—you handed that one to me. No, really, I am sorry. In my defense, you're pretty jumpy today. Please don't feel you need to hide in the pantry."

"I'm not hiding!" I lied. Stomping back out with the Market Spice tea, I went to get a mug, adding accusingly, "Do you always creep around houses in the middle of the night?"

Something flickered across his face, but he said calmly, "I'm not creeping, and this happens to be my house." He had me there. Sullenly I concentrated on making my tea. "I'm almost glad to see you having trouble sleeping," he continued in a smiling tone. "After such a knock on the head you probably should be woken up every couple hours to make sure there's no brain damage."

"Oh, there's been damage enough," I replied dryly, thinking of my nightmare. "What are *you* doing up?" Maybe he couldn't sleep without a bedwarmer and was regretting kicking Kelly out.

Daniel ran his hand through his blond hair, standing it up on end. "I had a lot on my mind," he muttered. "Mind if I have some of that with you?" I did, but one could hardly say so. He stared at me, perhaps absent-mindedly, while I in turn kept my eyes on the mugs of water rotating in the microwave.

By the time we plunked down at the table, I had decided that maybe spending some time in Daniel's head would give me relief from mine, and I accosted him with, "Did you have a hard day? You seemed upset about something when I came home." An understatement, when I remembered his chilling glare. To my amazement, Daniel turned bright red and shifted around uncomfortably. "Good heavens!" I said. "Did you rob a bank or something? Get Kelly knocked up?"

He took a long sip of tea that would have burned my tongue and replaced his cup precisely on the table. His eyes flicked up to mine. "I don't want to talk about it. Let's talk about you. What's this about you working on a video game?"

I blinked at him. I was used to his general evasiveness by now, the way he would neatly deflect personal questions, but he had never before resorted to feigning interest in his interlocutor. I wondered if that particular word combination, "let's talk about you," had ever issued from his mouth before. What next? He must really want out of his own head tonight.

"James is a video game producer for a little company called Free Universe," I replied at last, "I've been doing some writing for them on various games in development. One of his current projects is called *Tolt*, one of those fantasy-world kind of games, and they had me do some voiceover work for them as the—er—'Snow Goddess.'"

Daniel's fingers drummed on the table: tap tap tap. "Is that what he was playing for you when you came home? Your voiceover?"

I nodded. "Are you much of a video game fan, beyond Rock Band?"

He shook off my question. "And how did you meet James? Church?"

"No-o-o, though he goes to my church. He goes to the evening service, like Joanie and Phyl. And he also goes to the singles group on Wednesdays like they do. I met him because we're both serving as mentors at Camden School." I anticipated his next question. "Camden School is an alternative high school for at-risk youth."

"'At-risk' in what way?"

"Oh, the works. Drugs, alcohol, criminal records. Whatever might get them thrown out of public school."

"Comprehension is beginning to dawn on me," Daniel said, sounding amused. "This would explain some of the odder conversations we've had. What on earth made you think you could tackle these things?"

I sat up straighter, a little indignant. "Of course I didn't think I could tackle these things. I don't know anything about them—hence the 'odd conversations' with you. Camden School has counselors and teachers to help the kids with that stuff. I'm more like Nadina's friend and encourager. And she's mine," I added thoughtfully.

"Was it because of…Nadina…that you asked me about felony vandalism that one time and hard drugs?" His steel-trap memory really was impressive. It must help him out with all that law business. Speaking of which, from the way he could ask questions when he wanted to, he might have missed his calling as a prosecutor. This totally uncharacteristic barrage was freaking me out a little.

"No on the vandalism," I answered. "That was because of Kyle. Kyle is James' student. His case is unusual. But yes on the hard drugs. Nadina is more of your stereotypical Camden School student—lots of substance abuse and risky behavior."

"So knowing nothing about drug abuse or risky behaviors, what made you want to be a mentor?"

I hesitated. A truthful answer to the question would far outstrip his interest level, but there was no help for it. At least this wasn't as embarrassing as our sex talk.

"I've been up and down emotionally the last few months," I began, "and one weekend I was in church and the pastor talked about getting outside ourselves by serving others, and that sounded like a good place to be—outside myself. I tried to—to pray, and then a girl from Camden School stood up and talked about the mentoring program. As you pointed out, I'm totally unqualified, and I didn't want to do it, but for some reason I felt like I was supposed to. I…resisted for a while…ignored the feeling, but then I happened to run into Kyle at the library and got sucked in. You might call it coincidence, but I chose to see it as an answer to prayer."

His eyes gleamed at me. "How do you know what I would call it? I may have gone with 'power of suggestion' followed up by 'co-incidence.'"

I smiled. "All right, but then we would disagree on who was do-ing the suggesting. You might say the student or the pastor or the circumstances or my own head, but I might say it was God making the suggestion, through those avenues."

He didn't respond, and given his odd mood I didn't know what else to talk about. I was about to get up, put my dishes in the sink, and call it a night, when he said abruptly, "So does James know you're widowed?"

I gawped at him. "Do *you*?" I demanded. Daniel had never men-tioned or referred to my marital status, ever. And after months of his ceaseless bantering and flirtation, I had begun to believe he actu-ally didn't know about my Tragic Past, if only to excuse behavior I couldn't understand. Who would make a favorite hobby out of trying to make some poor widow blush whenever you saw her?

Daniel waved this away impatiently. "Of course I do. Joanie told me before you moved in." He waited for me to answer his question.

Well, then! I suppose if he'd known all along I was struggling with grief, his subsequent behavior meant only that he was, as I had often thought, insensitive, incorrigible and thoughtless. "If you knew, why do you always talk to me the way that you do?" I demanded.

"What way is that?" he asked innocently.

"You know very well what way!" I insisted. "You—you flirt with me. It's tacky of you. And shameless."

"You don't seem to find James tacky and shameless when he flirts with you. Does he know you're a widow?"

I pushed his question aside for a second time, distracted by his implied criticism of James. "He hasn't flirted with me from day one, like you have. And—and he isn't just trying to get a rise out of me to amuse himself. He actually likes me—or thinks he does," I ended lamely.

The blue eyes locked on mine. "What makes you think I don't like you?"

Now I was mad. "There you go again, Daniel. Knock it off!" Grabbing our mugs and tea paraphernalia, I dumped them in the sink with a clatter. When I turned to leave, he was right next to me, the silent snake.

"Does he know you're a widow?" he asked for the third time.

"Yes!" I hollered in frustration. "He thought I was married until a few days ago when Nadina said Tr—said my husband was dead."

"And then he asked you out?"

"Yes." I crossed my arms defensively over my chest. "It's no big deal—James is kind of a serial dater like you, not that it's any of your business. I'd give it a couple weeks. Now I'm going back to bed. You're kind of freaking me out, Daniel. You're not behaving like yourself."

"In what way?"

"Being nosy about my life!" I laughed shortly. "I'm not used to it. I thought we were fine being permanent acquaintances. I stay out of your life, and you stay out of mine."

"You don't think we've gotten to know each other a little better than that?"

"Not really, no. I mean, we can converse on lots of subjects, but I don't really know you, and you don't really know me. If you think you'd like to be friends now, that's great. Keep me posted. But I'm going now because this conversation is just too strange—maybe because we're having it in the middle of the night and I've banged my head and you're worried about something else. Good night, Daniel." It might have been cowardly, but I fled. If he had wanted to open up about whatever was bugging him I would have forced myself to listen, but if he just wanted a distraction—well, that's what books and television were for.

CHAPTER 23:

Luke, I am Your Father

"That's five bucks each, and don't be thinking I'll be letting you in for free just because I know you." Nadina cracked her gum and grinned at James and me from behind the ticket table outside the gym. It was the Camden School Cougars' first home basketball game and we were there to cheer Kyle on.

James reached for his wallet, but I slipped Nadina my money before he even had it out. "Dutch," I reminded him, ignoring his aggrieved sigh. "And I'll meet you in there in a sec." Pulling up a chair, I joined Nadina and Sonya, recently returned from Bellingham.

"How did you manage to get time off of Petco and the rink?" I asked. "And why on earth are you wearing Blaise's nametag? She didn't fire you again, did she?"

"Nah," said Nadina, patting the plastic 'BLAISE—I'm here to help' on her chest. "She bitched about me asking for today off and complained about how hard she has to work to make up for all the slackers, but I just pretended not to hear. You tell me I should try to look at things from the other person's point of view, so today I'm seeing what it's like to be an evil old hag who tries to kill everyone else's buzz."

I rolled my eyes. However useless I was in every other area of Nadina's life, at least she had minded me about asking for her job back. I would've liked to have been a fly on the wall for Nadina's sackcloth-and-ashes speech; Blaise had gruffly agreed to give her another chance, albeit not with opportunities anytime soon to assist Perky Katie the Dog Trainer.

"I'm glad you kept your cool," I said. "You don't have to take on every person who irritates you."

"What'd I tell you?" Nadina turned to Sonya. "Cass is totally about me behaving myself."

Sonya had only recently reappeared at school, although she'd come home from Bellingham right before Thanksgiving, and Nadina swore up and down that, instead of drinking together, they'd gone to the movies once, and Sonya had come with some other Camden School kids to the rink. In any case, I was glad to see the two of them helping out at a school-sponsored event.

"Thanks for the cookies you guys sent," said Sonya. "I hid them so I wouldn't have to share."

"Good, they were all for you," I responded. "Louella was telling me on Sunday how you thought the place served too many vegetables."

"Everything there had to be good for you," put in Nadina sarcastically. She had complained to me on our last walk that Sonya had started going to Mass with her grandmother and had gone so far as to mention God a couple times, not even in a swearing context.

Sonya's only reply was to bite off another hank of her licorice whip. Seeing the open Costco tub of them next to her, I assumed she was making up for lost time diet-wise, and could only hope the spiritual effects might prove more lasting.

When another group of parents and mentors and other school

affiliates crowded up to pay their entrance fees, I waved to the girls and went on into the gym. The teams were still warming up, and I smiled a little to see lanky, sloping Kyle lumbering through the drills. Not only was it odd to see him moving faster than usual, but I had never realized when he wore his regular clothes how very pale he was; in his green-and-silver team uniform he looked as pasty as Murray.

It was more crowded than I expected in the gym—it looked like most of the students and staff were there, as well as some parents and mentors—and it took me a second to spot James, chatting with the middle-aged couple next to him. When I took the seat he had saved me, he turned to give me his warm smile. "Cass, I'd like you to meet Mr. and Mrs. Bateman, Kyle's parents. Mr. and Mrs. Bateman, this is Cass Ewan, she's a mentor to one of Kyle's classmates."

"Oh!" I exclaimed, holding out my hand to shake, "I'm delighted to meet you. I'm a huge fan of Kyle's."

Knowing so much about Nadina's family situation and how it had impacted her life choices, I didn't know what to expect from the Batemans. Kyle was in so many ways a normal, smart, functional kid—his crazy actions the one-time anomaly, rather than the rule. I did remember, however, that Kyle hadn't expressed much fondness for his dad, the first time I met him months ago.

Mr. Bateman looked every inch the hard-driving businessman, from his thatch of thick, gray-streaked black hair above shrewd eyes to his thickening waistline and pristine Johnston & Murphy cap-toe lace-ups. I could imagine him twenty years ago, in high school himself, most likely the very sort of jock who stuffed people like James into lockers. After an appraising glance, he gave me a friendly-enough nod, but he held himself rather aloof from the people surrounding him.

It wasn't hard to figure out which parent Kyle resembled most: his mother was a long-limbed, pale, quiet creature, with hair exactly Kyle's shade of brown and her son's light blue eyes. Smiling faintly at me, she pulled her sweater closer around her shoulders.

"We were talking about some of the finer points of Kyle's diversion agreement," explained James.

"How much money does he have to repay?" I asked, deferring to Mr. Bateman, as I imagined the whole world naturally did.

He made a disgusted face. "In the neighborhood of two thousand dollars, which is more than that damned teacher's computer equipment was worth, if you ask me. Damned Bellevue High trying to update their equipment on my son's dime, after they've already kicked him out and hurt his chances of getting into any decent college."

Much as I liked Kyle, it seemed to me hard to blame the school for narrowing Kyle's college options. "At any rate, I am glad that this won't go on his record," I said peaceably. Mr. Bateman only harrumphed, staring straight ahead at the court, where the game was beginning, but Mrs. Bateman gave me another timid smile, and I suspected she agreed with me.

Stretching an arm along the back of my chair, James said, as if returning to an earlier point, "Well, we'll be glad to have him as an intern at Free Universe. He's a great tester for our games, plus our sound designer says he has a natural knack for that kind of work. He'll only manage a few hours a week, but in a year's time it could put a dent in that two thousand dollars."

Mr. Bateman sighed but managed a gracious nod. "My wife and I appreciate you taking Kyle under your wing and giving him some work he'll like. But that kid! Of course he has a knack for that stuff. There's nothing he can't do—if he hadn't been such a blasted idiot about that damned computer teacher."

"How much community service does he have to do?" I asked. I was hunching forward a little so I wouldn't touch James' arm, something he didn't fail to note, though he did nothing beyond raise a teasing eyebrow. "Does he have to wear an orange outfit and pick up trash along the freeway?"

"Hundred hours," grunted Mr. Bateman. "Ninety-nine more god-blessed hours than it took him to do the damage."

"And he doesn't have to pick up trash," James continued. "The county is pretty flexible about how he can earn hours—any of Camden School's service projects count, and I'm taking him to a couple of the church's home makeovers." (Mr. Bateman snorted at the word "church.")

The "model kid" was in playing center, and while I doubted Kyle's basketball skills would make any college overlook his high school shenanigans, he wasn't half bad. In some ways, Camden School had opened a door for him that wouldn't have been open at Bellevue, with its cut-throat athletics and embedded dynasties of jocks. And I'd forgotten how much I preferred high school basketball to the few professional games I'd been to. When Troy dragged me to the Sonics, I often wondered why anyone watched anything but the last quarter—the Sonics would score; the Trail Blazers would score; the Sonics would score; the Trail Blazers would score; the Sonics would miss; the Trail Blazers would win. At least in high school, and certainly in Camden School's oddball league, there was a lot more missing and blundering on both sides, making for a more suspenseful game. Nor did I mind the absence of cheerleaders, though Nadina and Sonya and Ellie were screeching their heads off on the sidelines. And, whether because of lack of interest or fixation on more pressing issues, the Camden parents had refreshingly low expectations. No worries that parents from opposing teams would get in any ridiculous shouting matches, as occasionally happened at Troy's Bellevue High basketball games.

After the first quarter the Camden School Cougars were up 12-9. Kyle was on the bench for a breather, so I leaned across James again and asked Mr. Bateman, "Did you do any sports in high school?"

He grimaced, but the pale Mrs. Bateman surprised me by laying a gentle hand on her husband's arm and speaking up. "Rich played just about every sport, you name it," she said softly, her voice having just the tinge of an untraceable drawl. "And lettered in all of them. It hasn't always been easy for Kyle to find his own path. Basketball is about the first thing he's wanted to try that his father also did."

"Never told him he had to do anything I did," muttered Rich Bateman, a trifle defensively.

"You didn't have to," his wife responded. One got the sense this was not a new topic between them. "Every boy has to differentiate himself from his father."

"Yeah, and getting himself expelled was one way to do it," retorted Mr. Bateman. "Regular pioneer, our son."

James cleared his throat. "What are Kyle's plans for college, by the way? I haven't asked him, since it seemed like such a tiresome, mentor-y thing to do." His tact made me blush, thinking how I just the other day "casually" mentioned to Nadina some of the undergraduate prerequisites for veterinary school I found online.

"No chance for Stanford or Cal or the U anymore. I may still be able to pull some alumni strings and get him into Charlottesville—"

"Though Kyle didn't have any interest in going to Virginia, not even before all this happened," pointed out Mrs. Bateman. "He's no business school glad-hander." Clearly, classifying her as timid was a mistake—she must have learned, after so many years of marriage, just to wait for her opening and then thrust home. Her husband shut his mouth with an audible snap and returned his attention to the game.

While the Cougars' opponents rallied in the second half and eventually prevailed, the game was close, and they would be rematched a couple more times over the course of the season. Kyle scored twice, drawing disproportionately loud cheers from James and me, and managed a couple key blocks. Mr. Bateman had appeared to find the level of play somewhat painful to behold, but I was pleased when, after the game, he pounded approvingly on Kyle's pale, sweating shoulder. Before they left, Mrs. Bateman shook my hand again and gave James' a more heartfelt squeeze, saying in a low voice, "Thank you for helping my son."

For his part, Kyle accepted our praise and congratulations with his usual shrug, and I tried to rein in my tendency to be overly effusive, which Nadina had told me frankly was "friggin' embarrassing." The students planned on hitting Dairy Queen after the game, so James and I headed out to the parking lot.

"Give you a ride home?" he asked.

I shook my head. "Thanks—it's not raining. I think I'll walk."

"Can I walk with you, then?"

Hesitating, I nodded shyly, and we started up the hill. Since the open house we had seen each other a few times, once for the promised walk around Green Lake and coffee, and the other times briefly at work or Camden School events like today's basketball game or last week's mentor-student indoor rock-climbing activity. James had behaved himself more circumspectly than even I would have wished, I had to admit. There had unfortunately been no need to ask him not to fawn on me in public—putting his arm along the back of my chair at the game had been the most audacious thing he had attempted—and on our walk he had devoted himself to getting to know me better, asking about my family, my childhood, my likes and dislikes. Taking my cue from him, I had done the same.

Unlike Troy, who was the youngest of three brothers, James grew up sandwiched between a pair of sisters. Both of these sisters were married, one living in Spokane and one in Richland, just a few blocks from his parents, and I gathered from some of the comments he dropped that he was the petted family darling, something for the women to worry about and focus on. How was poor James? When would he settle down and move back to eastern Washington to be near the rest of the family? Never mind that there was no video game industry in the Tri-Cities; in his mother's opinion, James could do just as well working as an engineer in Hanford's vitrification plant. "Technical is technical," she declared. "Or you could drive UPS like your cousin Ashley's husband. They have a great benefits package." James relayed this remark good-humoredly. "All the people who tormented me in high school still live in Richland, working the gas stations and Jiffy Lubes—I'd be afraid whenever I had to gas up my UPS truck."

It made me squirm to think I was probably a couple years ahead of his big sister in high school, not to mention imagining what his womenfolk would think of James dangling after an unpromising, older widow, when I'm sure they thought most women not half good-enough for him. At least I wasn't twice-divorced with three children from different fathers. Sigh. And "dangling" didn't really describe his behavior. Maybe he had taken to heart my claim that I wanted to hang out as friends and was already dating someone else. When I had made such a claim, I'd thought in all sincerity it was what I wanted, but it didn't stop me from feeling regret mixed with my relief.

"Were Kyle's parents what you expected?" asked James, breaking into my dissatisfied thoughts. It was a chilly, misty day, and I was glad to have the uphill walk to warm me up.

I laughed. "Not at all! If it weren't for Mrs. Bateman's obvious resemblance to Kyle, I might have suggested they switched babies on them at the hospital. Imagine Kyle having such a hard-nosed businessman for a father—one who must have been a lord of all creation in high school."

"It makes sense to me," James countered. "Kyle's been pretty clear that he doesn't want to fill his father's shoes. Maybe fear that he couldn't turned into an effort to sabotage himself."

Pondering this, the pieces clicked together. "You're right. That's almost what Mrs. Bateman was saying—that Kyle had to differentiate himself. He wasn't going to be a star athlete; he has no interest in business; and his dad seemed to have big college expectations for him. Well, Kyle took care of those, though it sounds like he's traded in one kind of burden for another. I think Mr. Bateman isn't going to let him just go do whatever he wants now—he'll just give up on those top computer-science schools and shoot for one tier down."

James nodded. "At least Mrs. Bateman isn't afraid to speak her mind—she's definitely all for Kyle choosing his own destiny. I think she'll keep pushing back on her husband."

"That surprised me," I wondered. "She looked so fragile and retiring. I would've guessed Kyle's dad wore the pants in that family, but I think she may have at least one leg on."

After a beat, James said, "Who wore the pants in your marriage?" He had such a natural way of asking things that it was rather like talking with Nadina. There would be no uncomfortable tears shed on my behalf, no awkward shoulder pats.

I grinned. "It was like there were several pairs of pants in our marriage, and depending on what it was, sometimes Troy wore them and sometimes I wore them and sometimes we both had a leg on. I did all the money stuff, but in lots of other areas, I felt comfortable letting him cast the deciding vote." I laughed shortly. "And sometimes we still fought over the pair of pants and ran different directions and split them down the seam."

"Something funny?"

"We were married eight years, and the holidays never did get sorted out," I explained. "In fact, it got even worse after Min was born because then our families *really* wanted to monopolize us. We would end up trying to please both sides and getting in huge fights ourselves."

"So where will you be this Christmas?"

"Don't tell Daniel, but I think Perry and my parents are planning to congregate up here, and I'll probably have to do some time with my former in-laws as well, with and without my family. Should be a blast," I added, unable to keep a note of sarcasm from my voice. "What about you? Will you head across the pass to Richland?"

"Yes, ma'am. Go bounce my nieces and nephew on my knee, hear about my mother's latest career plans for me, and probably get introduced to at least one homely friend of my little sister's who has a great personality."

"You're awful!" I cackled, pushing him.

Quick as lightning, he grabbed my hand and hung on to it. "Want to get some dinner tonight? I could skip singles."

For all that I'd been worried he didn't like me anymore, I felt a wave of panic and pulled my hand away, balling it in a fist and answering lightly, "I cook on Wednesdays. And you should go to singles because you're most definitely single. How will you keep rejecting your little sister's homely friends, if you can't say you're making an effort to resolve the problem yourself?"

"I am making an effort," replied James dryly. "But sometimes the cure is trickier than the disease."

We had reached the Palace doorstep. Ignoring his comment, I asked, "Will you come tomorrow night for open house?"

"Do you want me to?"

"Yes," I said meekly. "Very much."

"Then I will." Before I could react, he leaned forward suddenly and kissed me on the cheek. My hand flew to my face, and I saw him grin, as he turned away, whistling, and headed back down the hill to Camden School.

CHAPTER 24:

Home Truths

Joanie was playing with her food and driving me nuts.

Phyl and I were verbally sketching out our Christmas decorating plans: who would get the tree, whose nativity sets we would put where, what the outdoor lighting scheme should be, and so on. Ordinarily Joanie would have plenty of opinions, but for the past ten minutes she sat in sullen silence, pushing food around her plate listlessly.

"What is the matter with you?" I demanded waspishly. "Are you not in the mood for Christmas or the hash I made or both?"

She looked up at me with hollow eyes. "Don't talk to me. You lack sympathy, Cass. Phyl, tell her."

"Tell me what?"

Phyl laid down the box of multi-colored icicle lights for which she'd been studying the energy usage graph. "I think Daniel won't object if I put up lots of these—the LEDs use so much less electricity, and I can run them on a timer." Joanie made an impatient sound, and Phyl added quickly, "Roy is giving Joanie a weird vibe."

"'Weird vibe!'" shrieked Joanie indignantly. "He's suddenly saying he needs some space!"

This was news. I tried, but couldn't recall, this ever happening in Joanie's dating history. Of course there was that guy who she claims dumped her freshman year in high school, but Phyl and I suspected she'd made that story up so that other women wouldn't find her too obnoxious. "Back up," I ordered. "What are you talking about?"

"Ever since he came back from Florida—you know, at Thanksgiving—he's been distant," she complained. "Before he left, he was starting to talk serious, asking me things like how I felt about kids and what I pictured when I got married."

"Well, no girl has had more opportunities to picture herself married than you," I interrupted. "Some women never even snag one fiancé, and you've had three."

Her eyes narrowed irritably. "This is what I meant, Cass. You lack sympathy."

"Roy knows about your three ex-fiancés, doesn't he?" I persisted.

Stabbing a chunk of sweet potato with her fork, Joanie confessed reluctantly, "I just mentioned Keith, and then I fudged the other two into ex-boyfriends."

"Ex-boyfriends!" I echoed scathingly. "You're like the Henry VIII of engagements. You can't blame Roy for not wanting to be Anne of Cleves."

"Who the hell is Anne of Cleves?" hollered Joanie, losing patience. "I want to talk about me!"

Phyl laid a cautionary hand on my arm. "Do you think he was going to propose then got cold feet, Joanie?"

"I don't know what happened," she snapped. "Yes. No. Maybe. All I know is that Sunday after church he tells me he wants to slow down a little, and I've been waiting for him to call since then, and here it is Wednesday."

"Do you even want to marry him?" I asked point-blank.

Not surprisingly, Joanie waffled. The first two times she began to speak, she thought better of it, and she finally even took a giant bite of dinner to stall. "Yes, of course I do," she insisted, after swallowing it down with a sip of water. "That is, not right straight away. I mean I like him a lot. Oh, hell, I don't know if I want to marry him, but I don't want him to break up with me! I want to decide. I want to dump him, if there's going to be any dumping."

"You," I replied, "are as bad as Daniel." Ignoring her indignant gasp, I pressed on. "You don't sleep around, but you have the same habit of holding back in relationships and shying off from commitment. To get out of real intimacy, Daniel tells himself he's bored, and there's always someone new and interesting around the next corner. You, on the other hand, flirt with real intimacy until it comes too close, and then you run away. But it's the same thing, in the end. You both just have the good fortune to be unnaturally attractive; otherwise you wouldn't have nearly as many victims to try this on."

Phyl's eyes were round and Joanie was sputtering by the time I finished my little lecture. It wasn't that I'd never laid it all out there before in our friendship, but losing everything had stripped me of patience and diplomacy.

I was pretty sure Joanie would let me have it in return, and she didn't disappoint. "I'm afraid of intimacy? Me?" Her voice rose an octave, and she was soprano to begin with. "Who the hell is it who's been hiding out in a cave the past year and a half? Don't tell me about those dumb teenagers you're hanging around with or those nerdy programmers at Free Universe. If anyone with potential tries to get closer, you're the ice queen—look at how you've been keeping James at arms' length! And don't give me that 'it's too soon' crap, Cass! You know perfectly well you're just afraid."

"Not without good reason," interjected Phyl, but I cut her off.

"So I'm afraid!" I conceded. "'Once bitten' and all that, but what on earth are you afraid of?"

Her temper evaporated, and she deflated abruptly. "I don't know. Probably of divorce. My family isn't really big on marriage, if you didn't notice. I guess I think if I could just find that perfect soul mate, divorce wouldn't even be a possibility."

"I don't believe in soul mates," I declared. "There are six billion people on earth, and about half are men. Are you telling me that out of three billion men, you think there's only one perfect person you're compatible with? I bet there are at least 100,000 I could make a marriage work with, but I'm pretty easygoing. Still, I bet there are at least 25,000 men who you could stand to have around for the next fifty years."

"You think Roy is one of the 25,000?"

"Sure, but I thought Keith was, and Peter was, and Steve would've worked, too. They were all good Christian men who loved you. Not ugly, not dumb, not mama's boys." I covered her hand with my own. "If you like Roy, and you haven't ruled him out, why don't you just ask him tonight what's going on? You're not usually afraid of being direct."

"Understatement," said Phyl.

Joanie fidgeted. "I've just never been in this position. But, yes—yes, I will ask him. Even if he breaks up with me, I'll be expanding my emotional horizons. Come on, Phyl, we better head over for Chaff. That Roy just better show up."

As Phyl was pulling her coat on, she ran over and added in a low voice, "I wanted Joanie to run our decorating plan past Daniel, but she's such a grump—if you get a chance—?"

Suppressing a sigh, I nodded. Things had been rather awkward between Daniel and me since our midnight conversation the other week, and I couldn't tell if I was the problem or if he was. He was quieter, to be sure, and I was uncomfortable, so the few conversations we had in the interim were stilted. But clearly his new interest in making normal-people conversation had outlasted the one night, and now I found that I was the one being evasive.

After the girls left, I cleared a space at the table for my Free Universe projects. Riley had made all kinds of edits on my truffle-hunting pig draft, and I riffled through the stack of pages, shaking my head. He seemed to be laboring under the assumption that gamers would appreciate each pig having its own distinct voice, realism apparently having its limits. An hour later, I had nothing to show for my time other than a few random pig exclamations ("Oinkreka!") and a whole lot of other lines I'd crossed out in frustration. No wonder farmers chopped them up and made them into bacon.

A rustling and thumping on the front porch drew my attention, and glad of the distraction, I hopped up to investigate. Peering through the safety glass I made out lots of greenery and a bright blond head, and throwing open the door, this strange sight resolved itself into Daniel, wrestling a six-foot Christmas tree up the steps. "Daniel!" I cried in delight. Had he been any other person on earth, and had he not been struggling with a heavy fir tree, I probably would have hugged him, but as it was I settled for clapping my hands and bouncing on my toes in excitement. It was a beautiful Douglas fir, and I inhaled the sharp scent with delight, squidging against the wall so he could get by. "I can't believe you did this! Phyl and I were just debating whether we should hit up Wayne or Roy to help us get one home."

Daniel looked absurdly pleased by my response. "You only had to ask me. I didn't know if you girls already had a stand, so I bought one too. Can you get it out of the passenger seat?"

Backing out of the driveway was a pick-up truck, which answered the question of how on earth he got the tree home, and I wondered how much extra delivery cost. Zipping back inside, I directed Daniel to the corner Phyl and I had chosen for our potential tree, and between the two of us we managed to get the trunk into the stand and adjust the screws so it wouldn't tilt. "It's perfect, Daniel!" I rejoiced. "Thank you so, so much."

"When were you planning on decorating it?" he asked.

"Well, we didn't even imagine we could get one before the weekend, but now that we have one, I'd better get started tonight, so everything will look nice for tomorrow's open house."

I don't know exactly how it happened, but the next thing I knew Daniel was in the garage with me, helping me get down various boxes of decorations. Nor did he beg off once we were inside; when I was lifting the lid off the first plastic container of ornaments, Daniel was perched on the arm of the couch, digging into his dinner.

Like an idiot I started with my own ornament collection—had I thought about it I would have consigned it to the attic for a couple years. "When my Grandma McKean died, I got her little glass birdhouse ornament—she was a big bird-lover," I said eagerly, rummaging through the top layer and not bothering to worry about whether or not Daniel gave a rip about my grandmother. "I hope it's not broken." Grabbing a likely-sized lump, I ripped the tissue paper off to discover, not a glass birdhouse, but rather a pair of ceramic booties emblazoned with "Baby's First Christmas," followed by the year and, handwritten, Min's birth date. Tomorrow.

Really, I had been doing okay about Min's approaching birthday. Okay, well, other than the one afternoon I spent on that website for kidnapped kids that takes a child's picture and computer-ages it, I had managed to tamp down any other emotions welling up. Having the ceramic booties roll out suddenly into my lap wasn't fair. Emotional ambush.

I don't know how long I sat frozen and mute with grief—it could have been one minute or ten; all I know is that after some stretch of time I felt someone gently pluck the booties from my lap, wrap them back up in paper, and replace the lid on the ornament box. "Cass," came Daniel's tentative voice. Some still-functioning part of my brain noticed that he sounded uncertain. "Cass, I'm sorry."

My face was wet. Oh, crap. Crying. In front of Daniel. It seemed to happen more frequently than I liked. *Do you mind?* I wanted to ask. *Your sympathy makes me totally uncomfortable, and I wish you would go back to acting like a shallow playboy.* Turning blindly, I flipped the lid off another random box. Phyl's stuff, thank God. Obviously hers, since it all looked either handmade-by-poor-people-from-various-developing-countries-to-foster financial-independence, or else store-bought but manufactured Responsibly and Sustainably.

To give myself time to pull it together, I went and fetched the step stool from the pantry, but when I climbed up on it, clutching Phyl's Ugandan woven-raffia angel, Daniel was on his feet. "Here, you fool, let me do it. Just show me where you want it." Grudgingly I pointed. After he hung it for me, he said casually, "So your grandmother liked birds?" Suspicious, I turned on the step ladder and found his blue eyes most disconcertingly just below my level. There was no nasty gleam in them, however, and I relaxed a little.

"Why do you want to know?" I asked cautiously.

Daniel gave a short laugh. "I'm not *dying* to know, to be honest, but you volunteered the information, and I'm trying to get to know you."

"But why?" I demanded, more aggressively this time. "Why do you suddenly want to get to know me?"

"And why are you so damned bristly?" he countered. "Why can't I want to talk to you?"

Because it made no sense, for one thing. Mutely I handed him some sort of carved star and pointed to another high branch. Why, after months of alternating evasiveness and inappropriate flirtation should he suddenly decide he wanted something meaningful? "I just don't get it," I said finally. "I've never seen that you put yourself out for anyone, except maybe Joanie, and you always treated me like I was some kind of—I don't know—some kind of challenge: let's see if I can make Cass blush today! So why change things now?" Handing him another ornament, I noted his grim expression. For a few minutes we were silent, as I continued to hand him ornaments and point to where I wanted them hung, until the highest reaches of the tree were complete. "Thank you for your help," I added awkwardly.

"You're welcome." I thought he would leave the room then, having better things to do than converse with bristly women, but he didn't. "You know, Cass," he began again, "It's not like you're the easiest person to get to know and it's all my fault for being such a cad. You have a way of…keeping people at a distance. You may not trust me, but I would say you're not likely to trust anyone."

First Joanie, now him? I might have been able to blow off Daniel's criticism, if Joanie hadn't said almost the exact same thing not two hours ago. I was cold? Untrusting? Had I always been, or was it because of what happened to me? And Joanie accused me of fearing romantic intimacy, but Daniel was saying I was even afraid of friendship. This was absolutely pathetic, that someone like Daniel—who had no wife and no friends any closer than collegial types like Wyatt Collins or golf buddies like that Tom—even Daniel found my ability to form deep bonds lacking. My immediate reaction was an urge to go hole up in my room and pout.

He must have seen from my face that his arrow had reached it target. "Hey," he said, more gently, with a smile playing around his lips, "if I hurt you, it was half in self-defense. I'm not saying I've behaved like a quality guy, or blaming you for being gun-shy. I guess I'm just asking if we could start over. I can—I can see why Joanie likes you, and I like you too. I like having you in my life."

"Oh," I breathed, completely nonplussed. Looking hard at him, I couldn't detect any false note. His expression was open, wary, watchful.

He really did want to be friends. This man who always had women hanging all over him and who didn't appear to lack anything the world had to offer. Maybe if everyone around you falls over himself to approve of you, you begin to welcome people who can still find your flaws. I wouldn't know, but possibly endless approbation got old.

I was spared having to think of something to say by the sounds of Joanie and Phyl returning. Joanie took one look at the trail of pine needles and Daniel standing there holding an Inuit crèche, and she flung herself at him with a screech. "Daniel, I love you! Thank you so much!" Around her strangling arms, his eyes sought mine. I nodded and gave a tiny smile. Friends.

With the girls home, decorating went quickly. Daniel retreated to the Lean-To, in the face of all the chattering and feminine arguments over where to place what, and I was glad because it gave me a chance to accost Joanie. "Well? Was Roy there? What happened?"

Joanie hesitated, distracted. "Phyl, you can't put the flipping stable animals so close to the Holy Family. We've got to keep an eye out for the barnyard *feng shui*." When Phyl docilely backed the camels and oxen and whatnot away from the manger, Joanie answered me nonchalantly, "He broke up with me."

"He—he what?" I gasped.

She slung herself on the couch, next to where I was perched on the arm, and put her arms around my waist, leaning her red-gold head against me. "He dumped me." Automatically I began petting her hair, as if she were Benny, all the while shooting Phyl incredulous looks. Phyl only smiled sadly and shrugged, waiting to let Joanie tell her story, which she did, after a few minutes. "He came to Chaff late and sat in the back, so I didn't even see him come in, but luckily I got up to get by the door before it was over, so I cut him off before he could escape, the blinking coward." At least she was sitting up in her remembered anger and had renewed fire in her eyes. "I said, 'Hey,

Roy, are you up for getting coffee?' and he just kind of mumbled and shuffled his feet, so I pulled him into the hall and was like, 'What the hell? You're acting weird.' And he said, 'Yeah, Joanie, it's like I said—I need a little time—and I'm thinking we should take a break.' And I said, 'Was it something in stinking particular that made you feel this way?' I can't cuss around Roy, of course, because he has ears like somebody's maiden aunt. And he tried to evade the question, and only by constant hammering did I get it out of him that he heard from that gossip-mongering, nose-in-everyone's-business hag of a hypocrite Lauren Potts that I'd had three broken engagements, like it was any of her blazing business to be talking to anyone about my life."

"So was it the number of broken engagements that freaked him out, or the fact that you didn't tell him and he had to hear from Lauren Potts?" I pursued.

"Oh, both, probably," snapped Joanie dismissively. "I told him he just should have been happy for me that I called them off before passing the point of no return, and for crying out loud, wasn't he glad that I didn't marry any of those guys? He just gave me this sanctimonious, I'm-so-disappointed-in-you look that made me want to hit him and said, 'I'm sorry you didn't feel you could be honest with me.'" Growling in frustration, she booted the 'Noel' throw pillow into the hallway. "I hate church people! I hate gossipy women! I hate men! Why don't we get a dog of our own? I need something to kick!"

Fighting back an urge to laugh, I gave her a firm hug. "What a crappy evening. What a stupid Roy. And whoever Lauren Potts is, she only talks about you because you're beautiful and everyone likes you."

Joanie kissed me on the cheek. "Thank you, Cass, for crumbs of sympathy. And you too, Phyl, for listening to me on the way home. I told Phyl I was dreading telling you because I thought you'd say 'I told you so,' since you did just tell me to come clean about the ex-fiancés."

"It did occur to me," I grinned, "but I figured I wouldn't mention it until the next guy asked you out."

"There will be no next guy," vowed Joanie impetuously. "I am, as of tonight, going on a dating hiatus—oh, well, except for this Friday because I was so pissed at Roy that I went straight back into Chaff and asked out the first guy I could find." In answer to my questioning look she added, "Some bald guy named Bo with an annoying, hissy laugh. Divorced, I think."

"Joanie made his Christmas, I bet," laughed Phyl. "He'll probably want to 'drop by' his ex-wife's place to show her off."

"Well if he does, you and Wayne are coming with," said Joanie. "I've convinced Phyl to double with us because I had barely asked him out when regrets choked all further utterance. I don't suppose you and James want to come, Cass?"

"Not on your life. You've used up all your allotted sympathy, and we've already made plans to go skating this Friday. Now come on, ladies. Let's see if between the three of us we can hang up the garland."

CHAPTER 25:

Show Me the Money

"Could you spot me some money until my next payday, Cass?"

After hurling the question at me, Nadina wadded up her elf hat nervously and then jammed it back over her spiky blond hair. James and I had agreed to meet at the rink that evening, and I had come early to see her. While waiting for him, I had been struck by Nadina's air of discomfiture. My wariness must have shown because, before I could formulate a response, she huffed, "Never mind. I knew you wouldn't."

"Now hang on a second," I objected. In our months of knowing each other, Nadina had never made a request like this, and beyond the usual uneasiness people feel when they're hit up for cash, the change in pattern disturbed me. "You work two jobs, and your mom pays your school tuition, so why are you feeling hard up?"

"When is James getting here?" she changed the subject. "Are you guys together?"

"Soon, and no," I answered curtly. "Answer my question."

She busted a roll of quarters open on the edge of the till. "Don't worry about it, Cass. I knew I shouldn't have asked you because you're so friggin' stingy and nosy." Before I could react to the injustice of this accusation, she barreled on. "Sonya was saying that Louella is taking her to *The Nutcracker*, and Ellie got a gift card for iTunes—"

"Are you saying you want a Christmas present?" I demanded. "I do happen to have one for you, and it's not a bunch of guys leaping around in tights. That can be arranged, however."

Nadina rolled her eyes but had the grace to look a little abashed. "No, forget that. That was stupid. I don't even want to see the friggin' *Nutcracker*. I'm just saying I never asked you for anything before, and you just shut me down."

"I didn't shut you down," I protested, "I asked you a question, which you haven't bothered answering, and I haven't even ruled out the possibility of—"

"Shhhh!" she hissed suddenly, slamming the till shut. "Just forget it, okay. Go skate." Bewildered by her abrupt about-face, I followed the direction of her anxious gaze. At first I couldn't figure out what she was looking at, but then, slouching out from behind a bundled-up family, I saw a slight young man making his way toward us. He was wearing a forest-green plaid flannel shirt over a black t-shirt and jeans even rattier and lower-slung than I'd seen on Kyle or Tan or any other Camden School boy. His towhead was whiter-blond than Nadina's, and his skin several shades paler. No tanning sessions for this kid, apparently. Light green eyes flicked over me with a dead curiosity, but when he reached the counter he had already put me from his mind.

"Did you get it?" He slapped his hand down on the glass-covered counter, and the silver rings he wore made metallic clinks. She shook her head mutely, not meeting his eyes. Judging from her strange tension and the obvious familiarity between them, a creeping suspicion was coming over me—was this ratty little fragile creature *Mike*?

Before I could ask, the bundled family bustled up to the cash register, the father waving a credit card at Nadina. In silence, she processed it, and in equal silence the off-putting young man stood his ground and stared fixedly at her. When the family was on its way, Nadina slammed the till shut and said, a note of challenge in her voice, "Mike, this is Cass. Cass, this is Mike."

I wasn't sure what I had expected, whenever this fateful meeting would take place—invective? violence?—but Mike did no more than nod infinitesimally at me and return his pale green gaze to Nadina. After hearing so much about how he disliked me and seeing repeated proofs of his power over Nadina, I realized for the first time that he was, after all, only twenty years old, and he might even be as intimidated by me as I had been by the imaginary Mike. Not only that, but if it came to violence, I think I could take him.

I took a step closer to get him to look at me. "Hello, Mike. It's nice to meet you finally." An outright lie, but a sacrifice to manners. I held out my mittened hand. He ignored it.

Uttering some kind of curse, heavy on the consonants, under his breath, Mike said to Nadina, "I'll give you a few more minutes." Without a backward glance, he took his delicate little self off to the snack bar to torture some other rink elf.

I whipped around. "What was that about?"

"None of your business," she answered automatically.

It took me a minute or two to bite back the first words that came to mind. I knew if I made any choice comments about her dear Mike, Nadina would turn on me. Choice comments like, *Are you ever worried you might accidentally sit on him and kill him?* Finally I settled on: "Was that why you wanted to borrow money?"

"None. Of. Your. Business!" was her infuriating response. "Here's James. Go skate with your boyfriend."

"He's not my boyfriend," I insisted, distracted.

"I'm not her boyfriend," came James' echo. I could hear the laugh in his voice. "Cass swears I'm not her boyfriend." Catching sight of my distressed face, his grin faded, to be replaced by a questioning look.

Nadina swiped the ten-dollar bill James held out, slapped it in the till and slammed the drawer shut without saying another word.

"Hey, what about my change?" James pointed out. "I thought Kyle's been helping you with your math." Scowling, Nadina punched the button for the drawer again. When it shot open, she yanked out two ones, threw them on the counter, and slung the drawer shut.

"Good thing you came early to butter her up," James teased, when we were out of earshot and lacing up our skates. "What's up with her?"

"I hardly know," I murmured. "But she tried to borrow money from me when I got here, and before I could even find out why, her boyfriend Mike showed up and then she wouldn't tell me." James whistled. "He's still here," I added. "He's that pale little hominid in the snack bar—don't look now!"

Obediently, James waited until we were out on the rough, divoted ice, circling leisurely, to look in the direction of the snack bar. Mike was hunched at a table, sipping a hot chocolate or something, his eyes fixed on Nadina.

"Him?" asked James incredulously. "I bet our Nadina could snap him in two. Did you meet him?"

"In a manner of speaking," I replied, recounting the uncomfortable introduction. "I just wonder if she wanted the money from me because she knew he was going to show up and that he was expecting her to have some."

"Good thing you didn't give her any then," said James practically. "Charming as he appears, I'm not sure he would have put it to the best use." He pulled on my hand. "Come on, you. Let's not let the 'pale little hominid' spoil our undate." Laughing, I tried to pull away, but he hung on and swung me around so that I was skating backwards in front of him. "Let's see some of these famed elementary school moves, Cass, that you bragged about in front of Rachel."

"Bragged about? I did not either brag about them," I objected, giving him a push with my free hand and spinning back around to skate next to him.

"Sure you did, so don't pretend to be outraged," he persisted, winking at me. "You know you wanted me." This time I gave him a harder shove and yanked my hand away, but he was too comfortable on skates to lose his balance and merely whisked around to my other side and took my hand again.

"Not in front of Nadina," I pleaded, feeling myself start to blush.

He looked at me out of the corner of his eye, trying to judge my mood, but then he obligingly dropped my hand and put his own behind his back. Relieved and yet mildly disappointed, I smiled my thanks, and we made a few more circuits in silence.

After a while, James began again. "I was going to be patient," he said. "I was going to be well-behaved and just 'hang out' with you until you got used to the idea, but I'm not a very patient person."

"So I see."

"It would be one thing to be patient if I needed to give you time to learn to like me," he continued, "but I think—I think you already have." Swinging out in front of me, he skated backwards so he could look me full in the face.

Well, here it was. James was a charming, attractive, well-liked man, and he liked me, for some reason, but he wouldn't wait around forever. And he was young and impatient, and I suppose two weeks in this relationship limbo had seemed long enough to him. If I put him off again, would he give up and move on? But if I said yes, what would it mean? He might lose interest in a few more weeks anyhow, but what if he didn't? Would we somewhere down the road have to wrestle with the question of marriage?

I thought back to my brain-damaged wedding dream, and it was no more natural to picture James waiting for me at the bottom of the stairs than it was to see Daniel there. It wasn't that James wasn't a good, faithful man or that he wouldn't make someone a good husband—it was that I felt so much older than he was, not only in years, but also in all the things I'd been through. As if I stood on the other side of some emotional chasm, and I didn't know how I could pretend life was simple and made sense anymore.

All of a sudden, Joanie's voice popped into my head, as if she had sprung up next to me: "For Pete's sake, Cass, don't over-analyze! You don't have to marry him. Just have fun. Get out of your scary cave." She had taken a risk, after all, to confront Roy; surely I could take a similar step to overcome my fears. It was true: I didn't have to marry him. All he wanted was to give going out together a try, and chances were he'd dump me before it even became an issue. And until that happened, it would be…fun.

I think James knew what I had decided, when I finally raised my eyes to his, because a huge smile spread over his features. "Good," he said simply, a note of excitement under his voice. "Good. I'd kiss you right here and now, but I think I can wait till Nadina isn't around since you're being so reasonable."

Funny what a difference it made, knowing I'd said yes. Although he didn't try to take my hand again, and only once touched me to brush some snow out of my hair, we may as well have parked it in the center of the rink and made out—I was so conscious of him. For the first time I let myself look at him as much as I pleased, and I couldn't seem to stop looking. The hokey music and flirting groups of teenagers and children screaming after landing smack on their heads—it all receded into faintness, and, like a bad '70s after-school special, I noticed only the laughing gray eyes and pleasant voice and quick, sure movements of the man next to me. Never mind that, at the age when I might have been watching after-school specials, James was still mastering potty training.

The rink was small; we probably went around and around at least two hundred times and would have blissfully racked up a thousand laps, had reality not intruded—reality in the shape of the Zamboni.

"At this time we'd like to ask all skaters to please clear the ice," intoned the infinitive-splitting, deep-voiced, snack-bar elf. "We will be resurfacing for the next ten minutes."

James took advantage of the ensuing hubbub to close the gap between us, and I heard his voice right at my ear. "Let's get some hot chocolate—my treat. Maybe if we're lucky, we can sit with Mike."

So much for my deep caring for Nadina—I'd completely forgotten about the whole Mike-money incident, and when I hastily glanced around now, I didn't see him anywhere. Giving James a quick smile, I said I would join him in line and clumped over to my girl.

She was slumped on her stool, staring into space, and hearing me call her name, she positively jumped.

"Jesus H. Christ, Cass!" Nadina yelled, turning red. "What the hell?" I might have asked the same of her, the way she began darting nervous glances over my shoulder. The rogue thought crossed my mind that, if she was this preoccupied, maybe I should have made out with James center ice after all.

"Didn't mean to startle you," I said apologetically. "Where did Mike go?"

"Away. Home. Away!" was her flustered answer. "I don't know."

"Did he get what he wanted?"

"What?" She was genuinely worrying me now, and I saw she was sweating. "He didn't want anything. I can't talk now, Cass—I have to work."

"So work," I responded evenly. Her lips were trembling. "Nadina… are you okay?" I tried again. "You seem stressed." Or guilty. Or both.

She wavered and said almost involuntarily, "Mike is stressing me out. I can't talk about it right now, Cass. Maybe I'll—maybe I'll tell you some other time."

I waited silently, hoping she would change her mind, but all that happened was that her eyebrows drew closer and closer together as I didn't leave.

She still didn't trust me, then.

I sighed. Mark Henneman was right—trust couldn't be forced, try though I might. I still did have one idea, though. Unbuttoning my wool coat, I unzipped the inner pocket and pulled out the forty-two dollars left over from hitting the ATM that afternoon.

"Here," I said, pushing it across the counter to her. "This may be a bad idea, but we'll talk about that later."

Stunned, Nadina unfolded the bills and counted them. Something flickered across her face, but it disappeared almost instantly. "Thanks," she muttered. "You better go. James is waiting."

He was leaning against the railing that wound up to the tent entrance. Ducking his head to catch my eye, he held the hot chocolate out to me. "Warning—it's the same terrible powdered stuff we have at work."

I took a tentative sip and made a face. "Ugh! We have the real deal at home—shaved bittersweet chocolate—because Phyl hates processed foods. I'd forgotten how awful fake food tastes."

Plucking the cup out of my hands, he dumped it along with his in the trash can. "Then let's go drink Phyl's," James suggested, "unless you think you need to stick around for Nadina."

I peeked at her one more time. She was slumped on the stool again but rubbing her hands restlessly on her legs. "No," I answered slowly. "Something is definitely up, but she refuses to tell me. I think she'd be relieved if we left." Still, I hesitated to have James come over. It was Friday night, and Joanie and Phyl were probably still out on the dreaded double date, but I didn't know, and I wasn't sure if I had a thick enough skin to stand Joanie's crows of triumph yet.

Reading my mind, he put his mouth close to my ear again. "It's kiss me there or kiss me here, Cass. You decide."

My heart skipped in response, half enthusiasm and half panic, and I squeaked, "I'll meet you there."

• • •

It hadn't occurred to me that Daniel might be home, but he was. I drove up to find the Palace alight and the sound of male voices and Dean Martin's Christmas album audible from the porch.

There was a poker game going on in the living room; the tree was lit, and so, apparently was Tom, judging by his raucous laughter. Wyatt was there, and two other men I didn't recognize. Leaving the door ajar for James, I was going to slip quietly into the kitchen, but Daniel spotted me and called my name. He was tilting back in his chair, grinning devilishly, piles of chips stacked in front of him.

"Cass, how nice of you to drop in. Come meet everyone. I thought you'd be home tonight, but I'd forgotten you joined the dating world." There was an unpleasant note in his voice which I couldn't place, but maybe he'd had a little too much to drink as well.

Reluctantly I came forward and met Josh from the office and Someone from somewhere-or-other, but before I could do more than say hello, I felt the draft of cold air behind me as the front door opened and shut and James came in. Being a guy, he didn't find the prospect before him intimidating and cheerily submitted to introductions, but when Tom invited him to join them, he begged off. "Thanks, but no. Good luck." And taking my hand, he pulled me into the kitchen.

I prayed earnestly that Tom wouldn't think to get up from the card table and forage for snacks because James cornered me in the very same pantry as I was getting the tin of chocolate. Who knew it was such a romantic spot? When I turned around, there he was, startlingly close. Slowly, he put a finger under my chin, lifted it, and kissed me.

Where did an ex-nerd learn to kiss like that? Maybe it was that college girlfriend who gave him the makeover, an idle part of my brain mused. I would have to ask him one day. Still holding the chocolate tin in one hand, I tentatively put my arms around his neck and let my free hand touch his curling hair. I was right to listen to Joanie—this was much more fun than being afraid.

When we paused to catch our breath, James leaned his forehead against mine. "Was that really so awful? I've never had to work so hard to convince a girl to do what was good for her."

"I'm glad you did," I whispered, but didn't get to say anymore before he was kissing me again.

We probably never would have gotten around to the hot chocolate, had we not heard sounds of movement from the living room. Daniel must have called the game prematurely because Tom was complaining that "Martin just doesn't want to let us win our money back." Joanie and Phyl came home as well, and soon the kitchen was full of people. James and I innocently made our chocolate and conversed easily with the others, but every once in a while he would give me a little smile, or his hand would brush mine. Of course Joanie noticed and raised her eyebrows, but I frowned at her quellingly and avoided James until people were taking their leave.

"Can I see you tomorrow?" he murmured. I nodded. With one more light kiss on my ear, he was gone.

• • •

Just as I was drifting off to sleep, my phone chirped on the nightstand. A parting thought from James?

Flipping over, I brought up the text. Not James—Nadina.

Cass—

Got fired tonight. Talk later.

N

CHAPTER 26:

Crime and Punishment

After her late-night text, Nadina made herself scarce. I gave her exactly one day to call me with further details, but when she didn't, I jammed her voicemail inbox with urgent messages until finally getting a hold of her on Sunday.

I couldn't help grilling her—desperate times calling for desperate measures—and when I wore her down, the story came spilling out.

"At closing time the till was short," she blurted out, sounding close to tears.

"How short?" I demanded.

"Almost sixty dollars—but it would have been a hundred dollars short, if you hadn't given me that money. The manager said he wouldn't press charges for $60, but that I was fired and better not show my face there ever again."

"Where did the money go?" I asked. There was a long pause, and I could hear her muffled sobs. Trying to make my voice non-threatening, I said, "Did Mike take it? Did he make you give it to him?"

More sniffling and hiccupping. "Mm-hmm. He's been—he's been

borrowing money off me for a while, but he told me this time he couldn't wait for me to get paid because he wanted to go out, and I better come up with the money. He waited until you and James were out skating and not looking and all, and then he came over and told me to open the f-fucking cash register and give him the fucking money. And I was like, 'Why don't get your own fucking job, for once, instead of taking my money or someone else's?' And he was all, 'Quit your fucking bitching and gimme the money!' His hands were getting all shaky, and I thought he was gonna freak out, so I opened the till, and Mike was all, 'Where the hell is all the money? Are you hiding it?' And I was like, 'Does this look like a fucking ATM? Most people pay with their fucking credit cards, asshole!' and then he reached in and grabbed all the twenties and took off."

They were no Bonnie and Clyde, that was for sure. When I recovered the power of speech, I prompted, "So what are you going to do?"

"Do?" she echoed.

"Do," I repeated. "Mike robbed the skating rink, and you were his accomplice."

She gave a loud, outraged gasp. "What the hell, Cass? Are you going to friggin' turn us in? If the shithole rink isn't going to bother about the money, what business is it of yours? I shouldn't even have told you, you friggin' goody two-shoes."

When the outburst had blown over me, I asked evenly, "Are you quite done?" She merely huffed, and I continued, "I'm not planning on turning you in or reporting you or whatever, although I think we should talk about restitution. I wanted to know what you're going to do about Mike."

Silence.

"What does he want the money for?"

Longer silence.

"Is it for drugs?"

"I think so," she answered unwillingly.

"And I would bet this won't be the last time he's going to hit you up for money," I pressed. "Plus, the trajectory is bad: first he just wants some of your paycheck, but he's willing to wait until you get paid; now he can't wait anymore, and he's even robbing your workplace and involving you in the crime?"

"What do you want, Cass?" Nadina demanded. "Just spit it out."

Good question. Quickly, I scanned through my mental file on How to Deal with Drug-Addicted, Live-In Boyfriends Who Push You to a Life of Crime—oh, that's right—I didn't have any such file. How on earth did I get involved in this, and what was God thinking? … God. Well, nothing better to try, and it was His fault I was mixed up in this after all. *What exactly do you want me to do here? I don't have a clue. Please, please, please, give me wisdom and the words to say. Help Mike pull his stupid self together, and help Nadina get free of him. I know you love them both—can't say I'm there with you on Mike, but I do love Nadina. Please, please, please help us.*

"Well?" growled Nadina. "This is gonna suck."

"How about," I said, "how about you go home and stay with your mom for a while, and you call Mark Henneman right after we get off the phone."

"No friggin' way."

"To mom or Mark Henneman or both?"

A pause. I waited, my fists clenched.

"I'll go visit my mom for the weekend or a little longer. But there's nothing to tell Henneman. I mean, I'll tell him Monday I got fired, okay?"

"But you'll tell him why you got fired, right?" I insisted.

She sighed. "He'll dig it out of me, just like you have, Cass."

I felt better already. "Do you need help? Can you get your stuff and go to your mom's?" She refused help, probably half-regretting she'd even told me about the whole thing in the first place, and when I ventured to ask if I could give Mark Henneman a call myself, she put her foot down outright. Fine. I could settle for her being out of Mike's basement for now.

. . .

When we met for our usual walk on Tuesday, Nadina was completely closed off. I managed only to discover she had gone to her mom's as she said and was still there two days later. As for Mark Henneman, they talked briefly, but more than that she wouldn't say. When I asked how Mike was feeling about it, she was evasive and tried to turn the subject to James and me, then Petco, then school. It was not one of our better times together, and she didn't communicate with me the remainder of the week.

After this many months of knowing her, however, I recognized that, whenever Nadina felt she had been particularly vulnerable, she always made up for it later by keeping me as far away as possible.

. . .

Despite the uneasy silence, I was unprepared for the shock awaiting me on the kitchen counter when I came down the next Saturday morning. For one thing, it was only eight o'clock, and the newspaper appeared to have been unfolded and flipped through, which meant that Daniel had already been and gone. I'd never known him to be an early riser on the weekend, but he hadn't brought a girlfriend home last night, so maybe he had cashed in on the extra hours of R & R. Come to think of it, when *was* the last time he'd brought a "friend" home? It had to be that woman at the open house the week after Thanksgiving. Could Daniel, like Joanie, have declared a dating hiatus? I smirked. If he had, I imagined it would last about as long as I thought Joanie's would.

Before I could spend any more time puzzling over this uncharacteristic behavior, however, my eye was drawn to the picture on the front page: policemen leading away a group of bedraggled, trashed-looking partygoers, among which was a suspiciously familiar, slight figure with white-blond hair and weaselly eyes. Mike, I would bet my life.

"Seattle House Party Turns Violent—Police Arrest Many for Mayhem, Drugs," blared the headline.

Quickly I scanned through the story to see if it named any names, but there was no mention of Mike. Still, I was certain there couldn't be two such identical creeps in King County. According to the story, someone had called at three in the morning on Friday to report that a fight had broken out at the house party next door and was spilling into the street. When the police arrived, they found complete chaos, what read like a cross between the Three Stooges and *Risky Business*, with people breaking furniture over each other's heads while others tried to jump from second-storey back windows when they heard sirens, and a third group too zonked to react, laying around with drug paraphernalia still in hand or spilling out of pockets. The end of the article reported that most of the suspects had been released on bail and would face arraignments on Monday.

Clutching the paper, I speed-dialed Nadina who, of course, didn't answer.

"Hi, girlie, it's Cass. Haven't talked to you since Tuesday, so I'm checking in. Give me a call when you get a chance."

The rest of the day passed with no word from her, but I expected that.

Then Sunday went by.

And Monday.

Had there not been a mentor training scheduled for Monday evening, I would have begun to badger Mark Henneman at the school.

As it was, I showed up early for the training, with the Saturday paper tucked in my purse, and made small talk with Louella and Ray over the cookies and coffee until I spotted the Director in the hallway and flagged him down.

"Have you spoken to Nadina—?" he asked.

"Did Nadina show up for school—?" I asked right over him. We both shook our heads, laughing, and I whipped out the paper to show him. "Is this who I think it is? Is this Mike?"

Without even glancing at it he nodded. "You got it. Here, I'm going to let Barry handle this training. You come with me, Cass, and we can bring each other up to speed."

Mark barely sat down behind his desk when I demanded, "Have you seen Nadina today? She hasn't been calling me back, and I've been trying ever since I saw this paper Saturday morning."

"It's okay, Cass," Mark assured me. "We know where she is—now. When she didn't show up for school Friday or today, we checked in with her mom and Mike's father and got the story between the two of them. As you figured out, Mike got himself arrested early Friday morning at that house party."

"For assault or drugs or both?" I asked, shooting for a concerned voice but ending up sounding somewhere between eager and thrilled—Murray certainly would have made me do it over.

Mark's eyes had a certain answering gleam that made me suspect he wasn't too broken up about it either. "Mike wasn't involved in the fight. He was one of the guys totally out of it on the sidelines, laying there with the goods on him—about 30 grams of BC Bud—so he got taken in." Seeing my quizzical expression, he added, "BC Bud is marijuana from Canada."

"Did he have to stay in jail?" I asked, the thrilledness getting more obvious.

"Not over the weekend. Mike's dad apparently bailed him out

Friday, and he got to go home until his arraignment today—"

"Oh, no," I said, "Nadina didn't go back there over the weekend, did she?"

Mark Henneman wadded up some paper from his desktop and shot a basket with it. "She says she didn't. According to Nadina, she didn't show for school on Friday because she was flipping out after she heard what happened. And today she wasn't in school because of the arraignment." Hmm... I didn't know if I believed that, and apparently Mark had the same doubts.

"Then what happened at the arraignment today?" I prodded.

"First-time offense," Mark sounded tired now. "He pled no contest, and for that amount of marijuana it's only a misdemeanor charge. The judge gave him a week in jail, fined him a few hundred dollars. He's required to attend a nonresident drug treatment program, and for two years he'll be on probation and submit to random drug tests."

"What if he fails the drug test?"

"If he fails a test or doesn't attend the treatment program, he could be up for more prison time, since they went relatively easy on him."

I growled. "That Mike!—'First-time offense' my eye! First time he got caught, that is, and they didn't even catch him with the good stuff on him. At least we don't have to worry about him around Nadina for a whole week." Smiling ruefully, I added, "I don't really wish they'd lock him up and throw away the key—it'd be great if he got better— but she's fifteen! If he would just disappear she'd have a chance."

"Yeah, well, with a kid like Nadina, there's always more going on," Mark answered. "Mike could disappear, but that wouldn't change the underlying situation, why a girl like her would take up with someone like him. We've got to keep building her up, supporting her. You're part of that, Cass, and so is her mom, the teachers and staff here, even this Aunt Sylvia of hers. The more support she gets, the less she's going to look to Mike."

His comments stirred a memory: sitting on the Palace porch with Daniel a couple months ago. I had asked him how difficult it might be for Nadina to break out of the drug scene, and he had said that it might be more a matter of those in the scene not letting her go.

Troubled, I said, "Mark, even if we get Nadina to trust us, and she begins to want good things for her life, what will prevent Mike from doing everything he can to undermine us and her?"

There was a thoughtful silence, while Mark shot a couple more baskets into the trash. "Some things are always going to be out of our control. Barry, our Substance Abuse Counselor, has told Mike's father that he would be willing to meet with Mike, and we've told Nadina that, too. But if you think Nadina has trouble trusting us, imagine Mike."

It wasn't hard to imagine, given Mike's months of groundless antipathy toward me. To my surprise, I heard my own voice after a minute. "I'm going to commit to pray for Mike." Pray for *Mike*? That slouchy little thieving creep?

Mark thrust his hand at me across his desk. "Let's shake on that, Cass. We're going to have to call in the big guns on this one. 'Be strong and take heart, all you who hope in the Lord'!" he boomed.

"And while God is working on Mike, I have an idea in the meantime," I ventured.

He leaned forward. "Lay it on me, Cass. I'm all ears."

• • •

My commitment to pray for Mike received its first challenge the next day when I finally saw Nadina, looking unnaturally perky for someone whose boyfriend was serving time. We agreed to go to the mall, a place we usually avoided, to get gingerbread lattés and enjoy the Christmas hubbub. The café tables looked out on the long, winding line of harassed parents and dressed-up darlings waiting to see Santa, and I thought, not for the first time, that I never would have imagined myself in this parallel universe. Instead of standing in that line with my own young child, I was getting coffee with a troubled teenager whose life read like a storyline from *Cops*. A storyline she was taking pains not to talk about.

After hearing her recitation of what she got Sonya and Ellie for Christmas and what they got her and what she bought her mom and then returned when she got ticked at her, I finally cut her off with, "Are you not going to talk about what happened this past weekend?"

Nadina's mouth popped open, and then her eyebrows rushed together. "Have you been talking to Mark Henneman?"

I rolled my eyes. "I saw Mike's stinking picture in the paper Saturday morning, Nadina, when he was getting arrested! And I gave you plenty of chances to tell me about it yourself. Can I help it if I had a mentor training last night, and Henneman wanted to fill me in?"

"Yeah, well, I didn't call you back because I knew you'd make a big deal out of it, just like I knew the school would," Nadina went on the offensive. "Chrissake, it was just some pot. Mike wasn't one of those friggin' crackheads going off on each other and smashing chairs on each other's heads. He was just asleep there, and next thing he knows, he wakes up and the cops are there busting everyone."

Keeping my hands under the table so she wouldn't see me balling my fists, I counted to twenty. "It was just pot this time, Nadina, which still happens to be illegal, no matter what you think, but you know and I know that Mike has had other drugs in his possession at different times which would have gotten him in way worse trouble. Not to mention the whole robbing-the-skating-rink-and-getting-you-fired incident." She began protesting, but I interrupted. "I'm just saying that it isn't the School and me blowing things out of proportion— things are out of proportion! Mike is in jail, Nadina."

Furious, she glared at the kids waiting to see Santa, and I waited. One of the dolled-up little girls in line dropped her hot chocolate, splashing her pristine red-velvet dress, and the girl's mother burst into frustrated tears, turning on grandma: "I told you to wait until after the picture to buy her that!"

In one of her whiplash-inducing, teenage mood swings, Nadina's sense of humor overpowered her resentment, and she grinned at me. "Ha! Cass, that could be you. Instead you've got me."

Relieved, I grinned back at her. "No joke. That probably would have been a big deal to me—chocolate stains on the Christmas dress. At least you do keep things in perspective."

She leaned back in her chair, stuffing her hands in the pocket of her sweatshirt. "I know what you and Henneman want, even though neither one of you comes out and says it. You all hate Mike and want me to break up with him and move back in with my mom and start being a good little girl, don't you?"

"We want to see you with people who love you and build you up," I said. "People who help you make good choices. You have so much going for you."

Nadina stifled a groan and rocked onto the back legs of her chair. "You want to go window shop?" Done with the serious conversation for the day, apparently.

I made a last-ditch effort. "One more thing, then," I said, ignoring her dramatic sigh. "I was going to get you a gift card to the movie theater for Christmas, so that you and Sonya could go watch something together, but then I thought maybe you'd like to go to Ohio again and visit your Aunt Sylvia for Christmas—this time without your mother."

All four legs of her chair slammed back onto the floor. "You bought me a plane ticket?"

"No, but my husband had some airline miles left over when he died, and I got you a ticket with some of them."

"But I have to work at Petco on the 27th."

"Give Blaise a call. I'm betting you can get out of it. If not, tell her I'll come in and cover for you."

"How do you know my Aunt Sylvia even wants me to come out there again?" she demanded suspiciously.

I knew because, when I made the suggestion to Mark Henneman, he called Aunt Sylvia then and there, but Nadina didn't need to know this. He and I agreed that it would be ideal for her to be a couple thousand miles away when Mike got out of jail; let them get more in the habit of being apart.

I dodged her question. "Give her a call. I booked the ticket departing Thursday, when school gets out, and returning the day before school starts." Fishing in my purse, I dug out the electronic receipt and slapped it on the table. "Merry Christmas. Hope this turkey comes out better than the Thanksgiving one did."

Nadina read the receipt incredulously, and I could see the desire to go warring with the desire to thwart annoying grown-ups' machinations. At least she wanted to go; when I proposed it to Mark Henneman I couldn't promise that she would take me up on it.

"Fine," she said, after some minutes. "I'll go to Ohio…thank you, Cass. But you and Henneman need to know that I'm not breaking up with Mike. I saw him this weekend after his dad bailed him out, and Mike swore up and down that he's gonna clean up and go straight and do whatever the judge tells him to do. He's gonna become one of those people who helps me make good choices and crap."

I didn't know whether to find this news encouraging or depressing. "But—but you're still going to stay at your mom's for now?"

"Nope. I told him that when he got out of jail I'd move back in to his dad's basement." Depressing, then. "You'll see—Mike's a good guy. He's just been crazy this last month, but he knows it too. Look!

For Christmas he gave me this ring."

She held out her pinky and wiggled a silver band at me. I made a feeble attempt to admire it, all the while thinking he'd probably ripped it off someone else's hand when they weren't looking.

But I would discover later that I was wrong—Mike was a real giver. And that Christmas, unbeknownst to us, he had given Nadina far more than a pinky ring and some tall promises.

CHAPTER 27:

A Mostly Merry Christmas

Christmas Eve was my favorite service of the year, and the later the service, the better. Even when I had Min we would go once as a family before dinner to the 5:00 Christmas Zoo, and then I would steal out again at 11:00 for the last service. Something about the candlelight and choir and carols—you didn't want to go from that moving "Silent Night" back to kids screaming and card tables with the in-laws. But if you got out at midnight, and it was just you in the solemn stillness, it seemed almost possible these thousands of years later to hear the angels sing.

Not that I was going to hear any of that tonight, I thought, as I looked doubtfully down the pew. Past Dad and Mom and Perry sat Joanie—no big surprise there—and then next to her, Mrs. Martin, and next to Angela, Daniel himself. I was glad to be clear down at the end, where I wouldn't have to spend the service trying to gauge their reactions.

It was Daniel's suggestion to go, amazingly. Everyone had been gathered in the Palace kitchen, grazing and talking, while some of us worked on the food for tomorrow's Christmas dinner, when he had turned to my father and asked quietly, "Which service were you all planning on attending?"

My mother choked on her cranberry spritzer, shooting me a look that needed no words to say, *Didn't you tell me he was an atheist?*

My father, who unlike me and Mom could keep his head about him, merely replied, "Cass prefers the 11:00 service. Probably more in keeping with Perry's night-owl tendencies anyhow."

"Oh yeah," seconded Perry. "Just getting started then."

"Suits me fine, too, Mr. McKean," said Joanie, "so I was going to tag along."

Mrs. Martin came to lean against Daniel. "I guess it'll just be you and me tonight, darling."

"Actually, Mom, I think we should spend the evening with Joanie," Daniel said lightly. "I'd like to see the service—I know her department has put a lot of work into it." Had Daniel announced his decision to get a sex-change operation and go on Oprah, I don't think he could have surprised us more, and no one could immediately think of anything to say.

"Oh!" Angela murmured, blinking her vivid blue eyes. "Certainly, dear. Whatever you like. I haven't set foot in a church in decades. I hope I'm not struck by lightning!"

So here we were. No stray lightning bolt took out Mrs. Martin when we entered the candle-lit sanctuary, but a metaphorical one hit Joanie and me when one of the ushers came striding up to Daniel, arm outstretched, calling, "Hey, Dan! Merry Christmas. Good to see you here. Can I show you and your friends a seat?" An unidentifiable expression flickered on Daniel's face, while Joanie and I glanced at each other, but before anyone could say more, the friendly usher was directing us into our row. A business acquaintance, perhaps?

I shut my eyes, putting the Martins out of my mind. *It came upon the midnight clear, that glorious song of old.* The senior youth choir had the clearest, most ethereal voices, and it felt natural that hearing them should make me want to pray. Prayers of thankfulness for family and friends and home and work and meaning. And James.

• • •

He had stopped by yesterday before heading over Snoqualmie Pass to visit his family in the Tri-Cities. The air had a bite of cold in it, and James said it had already begun to snow on the Pass. We hadn't managed to see each other more than a few times since the skating rink—the game James' team intended to ship in mid-November had indeed slipped until the third week of December, almost disastrous for Christmas sales but maybe not. As Riley pointed out, most guys didn't even start to think about buying Christmas presents until four o'clock Christmas Eve. Disastrous or not, the game finally shipped, but the team had been working around the clock. A couple times I brought by treats and once take-out for everyone, but the Free Universe office wasn't exactly conducive to private conversation, much less anything approaching a make-out session. Moreover, however much James might like displaying his affection in front of others (and I was always pushing back on this with him), in the workplace he was absolutely hands-off. Maybe you never get over your buddies' judgments of you.

"Can you come in for a minute?" I asked shyly, after I opened the door and he swooped me up for a hug and a resounding kiss. "I have a gift for you."

"A minute—the snow is supposed to get heavier as the day goes on, and they're not requiring chains at this point," he agreed, "but I also have a little something for you."

"When did you have time?" I marveled. "I figured you'd have to steal something off Riley's desk and wrap it up for me."

"The wonders of online shopping," he explained. Dropping onto the couch, he pulled me onto his lap, and I promptly crawled off, knowing all my housemates would probably cut out early from work and might appear at any moment. Seeing his reproachful frown, I scrunched up next to him and reached for the wrapped box he held out.

"Let me guess—some t-shirts to match Riley's," I joked. James only smiled, looking more and more smug as I peeled off the paper to find a GPS navigator for my car. "'A little something'!" I screeched. "This is not 'a little something'! You can't give me this—it's too expensive. You'll be sorry when we break up."

"You think I'm the vindictive type?" he asked, winding a lock of my hair around his finger. "That when you dump me, I'll suddenly be glad you spend so much of your time getting lost?" He tugged gently on my hair to pull me closer and kiss me.

Sometime later I rummaged under the tree until I came up with his present. "It's pathetic, compared to yours, but I thought it matched your eyes." I'd gotten him a merino wool sweater in stone gray, and James instantly ripped off the navy one he'd been wearing and donned mine.

"A perfect fit. I love it. Thank you, Cass." He couldn't stay long after that. I pressed some cookies for his family on him, and then he was gone.

• • •

O ye, beneath life's crushing load, whose forms are bending low, who toil along the climbing way, with painful steps and slow. I thought of Nadina and Mike and prayed for them. How much harder they were making their lives, and how everyone who cared about them wished for them to be whole and well and free. I had sent her a card, and she had texted me once to say she'd reached Aunt Sylvia's fine, but that was all I knew.

Nothing about Mike's jail time or how they were doing or what he thought of her being in Ohio when he got out.

For lo! the days are hastening on, by prophets seen of old, when with the ever-circling years, shall come the time foretold. The words of the song sank into me, and deep down I felt God's comfort. *When the new heaven and earth shall own, the Prince of Peace their king.* The years would keep circling; one day I too would die, but I would walk that new heaven and earth with Him and with Troy and Min. We would never lose each other. My father put his arm around me, and I leaned my head on his shoulder, my cheeks wet, but with comfort and even joy, not grief.

It was such a beautiful winter night, clear and cold, that we had walked to the service, but I would have wanted to walk even if it had been raining. Selfishly, I was sorry to have Daniel and Mrs. Martin there, because if they hadn't been I would have suggested singing as we walked home.

Mrs. Martin was even chattering away about the damage burning wax candles did to the interiors of buildings, but to my relief, Joanie read my mind, and out of the blue I heard her warm, bell-like voice lift: all four verses of the Sussex Carol, atheist family walking right beside her or no. It was hard not to love Joanie.

"All out of darkness, we have light, which made the angels sing this night: 'Glory to God and peace to men, now and forevermore, Amen!'"

"Honestly," sniffed Mrs. Martin when her daughter's voice finally died away and we only heard our footsteps once more, "think of your Jewish neighbors, Joanie."

• • •

Christmas morning the thermometer was right at freezing. Bundling myself in my flannel robe and pulling my hair into a quick ponytail, I zipped downstairs to start the cinnamon rolls on their last rise,

Christmas cinnamon rolls with eggs and bacon and grapefruit being a McKean family tradition.

After our late night last night, everyone had agreed to push back breakfast to ten o'clock—one of the luxuries of having no little children around—so I stopped short when I came upon Daniel in the kitchen getting the coffee going. These new early-bird tendencies of his still threw me. I guess if you don't spend half the night messing around with someone, there's no longer a need to sleep in. Briefly I considered turning tail and hitting the shower first, but I needed to get the rolls in the oven and, heck, he'd seen me looking worse.

"Morning," I said, slipping the cold pan out of the fridge and tossing it on the counter. "You're up early."

"I had an idea I might catch you if I got up," he said unexpectedly. "Coffee?"

Might as well, since I had to wait for the oven to preheat. He watched me dumping in the milk and sugar with the absent-minded distaste of someone who took it black.

"Was there something you wanted to talk to me about?" I asked, a few minutes later, when he showed no sign of continuing his thought.

"Two things, actually." He disappeared into the living room for a minute, returning with a wrapped gift. "Firstly I have something for you—Merry Christmas."

He held it out to me, and I backed away without thinking. "Oh, no! I didn't get you anything—I had no idea you were going to get me something. I hope it didn't cost much."

"A steal at twice the price," he assured me, forcing the present into my hands. "Open it."

Still feeling badly, I untied the ribbon. He must have paid to have it gift-wrapped. When I pulled the paper away I found myself holding a red leather volume, smooth as a well-worn Bible, with *Shakespeare's*

Romances stamped in gilt on the cover.

"Oh!" I said inadequately. I riffled the pages gently: *Pericles, Cymbeline, The Tempest, The Winter's Tale.* "Oh!" My own copies of these plays existed only in cheap, high-school paperback editions with yellowed pages, or in the ponderous *Riverside Shakespeare* of my college years.

"You remember our conversation?" Daniel asked after a minute. I looked up, still wondering, and saw that he looked pleased with his gift's reception. "Shakespeare's comedies end in a wedding, and his tragedies begin with a marriage."

"And the romances are somewhere in between," I recalled. "The couples spend a lot of time apart."

"I figured it was more like life—some tragedy but also some comedy."

"I should be about due for the comedy, then," I cracked. Cradling the volume to my chest, I added more seriously, "Thank you so much, Daniel. It's the nicest book I own. I wish—I wish I had something to give you back."

A mischievous grin appeared on his face. "Well, it just so happens that I've thought of the very thing you could do for me."

"What?" I demanded warily, holding the book a little away from me now. I didn't want to give it back, but who knew how much it would cost me?

Daniel looked insulted and pushed the book back toward me. "It's not conditional—the book is for you in any case. Just hear me out." He waited for me to give a tentative nod before continuing. "My office is throwing its holiday party on New Year's Eve, and I wondered if you would go with me."

"Me?" I squeaked. "Whatever for? You're Daniel Martin—just flip open the blessed phone book and call the first woman's name you see!"

"A brilliant plan," he said dryly, "but I've decided to change my dating habits."

"You have?" I asked incredulously. The oven reached 350° and beeped, causing me to jump.

He waited for me to sling the cinnamon rolls in and then said, "I have. I've decided not to ask women out if I'm not interested in them, and there's no chance of the relationship going anywhere." So never again, in other words? Why, then, was he asking me to go to the stupid office party? Reading my mind, he added, "I'd like to come with a date so it's all a non-issue there, but whoever I might ask would think I was interested in her. God knows you'd never get that idea, so I thought you would be perfect."

I hesitated, and he took that as an encouraging sign. "You and James didn't have plans for New Year's Eve, did you?"

I shook my head. "He'll still be in Richland. But Daniel, what kind of party is it?"

"Fancy," he said shortly. "Formal and expensive. Lots of alcohol, food, music. Right up your alley."

"I wouldn't have anything to wear," I stalled.

"Tell Joanie—she'll take care of that. Is it a date?"

Rubbing my finger along the soft leather cover, I thought about it. "I can have the book no matter what?"

"No matter what."

"Then I'll go."

• • •

It was a Christmas of odd pairings. Joanie flat-out refused to join her mother for the getting-the-blood-pumping morning walk, but my mother went enthusiastically. Instead, Joanie spent most of the day as Perry's sous-chef in the kitchen. Daniel horned in on the Scrabble game I was playing with my father, and, thanks to me drawing tray after tray of vowels, he won.

"Too bad, Cass," said Dad, patting my hand patronizingly. He was thrilled and disguising it ill, since he had lost to me nine times out of every ten since I was twelve years old.

Daniel wasn't even bothering to hide his triumph. Grabbing the score sheet, he declared, "I may have to frame this. Or hang it on the fridge."

"With an asterisk by my score!" I insisted. "Something to explain that I drew 90% vowels and you got the 'Z' and the 'X.'"

"Nonsense," he countered maddeningly. "The true Scrabble champion can play whatever he's dealt."

"And I did—witness 'luau' and 'oleo' for stinking four points apiece—but you had my dad sitting there feeding you Triple Word Scores—"

They both seemed to find this terribly amusing, and Dad even slapped Daniel on the back like they were in some cheesy buddy movie.

It turned out he wasn't the only one sucked in by Daniel that Christmas. After dinner, when Mom and I volunteered to clean up, she waited until I was elbow-deep in suds and scrubbing au gratin off a pan to say, "Cass, my dear, you gave me altogether the wrong impression of Daniel."

"What impression was that?" I asked, reaching for the nylon pan scraper.

"Well, you told us in October that he was an insolent, sex-addicted atheist," she explained. "Dad and I were a little concerned that you would be living with such a person, especially at such a sensitive time in your life—"

The pan slipped from my hands back into the soapy water. "You worried I would fall for Daniel? After being married to a quality guy like Troy?"

She shrugged off my indignation. "If he really was as handsome and unscrupulous as you said, there was no telling. But I only bring this up to say that this visit has set us at ease. I don't know what you meant by calling him insolent, and there hasn't been any parade of women, and as for the atheism—he's the one who suggested we all go to Christmas Eve service!"

With difficulty I refrained from rolling my eyes. It irritated me to no end that people like Daniel could behave like the biggest sleaze-bags, but all was forgiven and forgotten the second they turned on the charm.

"I'm glad you like him, Mom," I said. "I'm not holding my breath for his good behavior to last."

She patted me placatingly. "Yes, yes. I never meant to imply that you might be interested in him. I just meant we were happy to find you had such pleasant friends. Now tell me about this James you've been seeing. Perry tells me he's a lot younger than you…"

• • •

Hours later I lay in bed, thinking of this James who was a lot younger than I. He had texted me once since I'd seen him—a quick Merry Christmas and made-it-over-the-Pass kind of message—and I had to admit I was miffed about it. Not that he seemed to be the frequent-communicator type even when he was around. Granted, they'd been completely absorbed in shipping that game, and he seemed to like me well enough whenever he was with me, but was an occasional live phone call too much to ask?

I rolled over and buried my face in my pillow. I knew I shouldn't have started dating anyone! After all I'd been through, to subject my-self to these idiotic, junior-high, emotional gymnastics. Fine! Maybe he was already a little bored and forgetting about me, and I would just have to sit around waiting for the inevitable break-up text. Would he text? It would be so tacky.

Sleep obviously was not going to happen anytime soon. Sitting up, I flicked on my bedside lamp and reached for the book I had begun recently, but my hand stopped halfway to it since it was about a family of insomniacs who eventually died after their bodies broke down from lack of sleep. Not very soothing.

Next to the dying insomniacs lay my new book from Daniel. Picking it up gently, I fanned the pages, running my fingers across the stamped cover. *The Winter's Tale* would be just the thing for a sleepless winter's night; it had been one of my favorite Shakespeare plays ever since I saw it in Ashland at fifteen. Three bitter acts, followed by two of frolicking pastoral, as all was set to rights.

Only when I opened the front cover did I notice Daniel made an inscription on the flyleaf, and I wondered why he hadn't pointed it out before. There was no "Dear Cass" or "with fondest wishes," simply a few lines copied out in his minute, precise script. Paulina's speech, when she enchants to life the stone statue of Hermione, Leontes' long-lost wife whom he had imagined dead and past recall:

Bequeath to death your numbness, for from him
Dear life redeems you. You perceive she stirs.

CHAPTER 28:

Should Auld Acquaintance Be Forgot

"There! Okay, Cass, check it out." Joanie spun my chair around to face me toward the mirror. She had brushed my hair to a high gloss and twirled it up in an elegant chignon worthy of Angela Martin, only looser around the sides. She had also insisted on doing my make-up ("It's an evening occasion, for crying out loud!"), and I looked askance at my artificially longer lashes and sparkly eyelids.

Phyl clapped her hands gleefully. "Oh, Cass, you look lovely! I wish we could do this every day!"

"This is ridiculous," I complained. "I don't even want to go to this thing, and I don't know why I let you guys do me up. Not that it doesn't look nice," I tacked on hastily, seeing their hurt faces. Still grumbling, I let them stuff me into Phyl's burgundy satin dress, lent for the occasion. It really did fit me perfectly, and while the keyhole cut-outs in the neckline showed more skin than I was used to, it was otherwise modestly cut and not overly clingy. Joanie's strappy gold sandals complimented it nicely, but I didn't know how long I could last in those spiky heels.

"I need more tea," I declared, cutting short their fussing. "And I want to be downstairs before Daniel is ready—otherwise it'll be like he's picking me up for prom."

I didn't have to wait long for him, but in that short space of time I downed as many cups of Soothing Chamomile as I could, trying to ignore the mounting feeling of dread. Why on earth had I agreed to this?

When Daniel finally did pop in the back door, we stared at each other, stunned, for a minute. He was absolutely beautiful in a tuxedo. Dashing. Stunning. Good heavens.

"Good heavens," said Daniel, echoing my thoughts.

I looked at him warily. "Is it okay? I let Joanie and Phyl have their way with me."

"You look…lovely," he said finally. "That color really brings out your eyes and the lights in your hair—"

"Okay, okay," I cut him off, blushing. "Let's get going before I change my mind." I reached for Phyl's cashmere wrap, but Daniel plucked it from my fingers and laid it across my shoulders.

I had never ridden in his precious vintage Corvette before, and I hastened to open the passenger door before he could make any motion to—the prom feelings were getting a little overpowering.

"I feel like I need a corsage," I moaned. "What year is this thing, anyhow?"

"1965."

"I knew it! This is straight out of my parents' yearbook."

"I'd like to see that yearbook. You look a lot like your mom, you know." I made a noncommittal sound, not being in the mood for small talk, but he seemed unfazed, and for the entirety of our drive to the W Hotel in Seattle he kept up a running series of questions worthy of a Camden School mentor. When did my parents marry? Where did I grow up? What did Perry and I like to do as kids? What had our holidays been like, growing up? And so on.

Too soon we were pulling into the hotel garage. When I stumbled getting out of the low car, Daniel hauled me up by the elbow and didn't release me until the elevator doors were closing.

Someone from his office had knocked herself out decorating. The Great Room was alight with candles and Christmas trees, balloons and glittering centerpieces. The buffet table featured an ice-sculpted sled amidst platters and platters of food, and there were waiters everywhere, carrying trays of drinks and hors d'oeuvres. One side of the room by the windows had been carved out for a dance floor, and the DJ was already on the job. Must have been a good year for the firm.

Daniel drew my arm through his as we made our way in, and I obediently left it there, unsure of what to do with myself. He introduced me to someone who apparently made video animations for them as trial exhibits, and that man and I made dogged conversation about his work and the animation I saw Lewis doing at Free Universe while Daniel was engaged in greeting his boss and one of the chief clients. Eventually our talk petered out, and the man took himself off, leaving me free to look around once more. Call me paranoid, but it seemed like more than one woman was looking daggers at me.

All those cups of Soothing tea caught up with me then, and after bouncing from foot to foot for a couple minutes, waiting for a natural point at which to excuse myself, I finally hissed in Daniel's ear, "Gotta go to the bathroom—be right back" and took off.

Dancing around in the stall, I tried to hike every inch of Phyl's precious burgundy gown into the clear before I sat down. Because of my heels I was almost three inches taller, which I forgot to account for, and nearly tumbled down onto the seat. One day somebody will have to explain to me how drinking three cups of tea turns into a gallon of pee because I felt like I was at it for several minutes. Long enough to hear the clacking heels of several other women entering the bathroom.

"Did you see that girl Daniel was with?" asked the first voice.

"Oh my God, yes," replied the second. Only one of them went into a stall, so I imagined the rest were freshening up at the mirrored sinks. "His standards are slipping."

My mouth fell open in indignation. I wanted to press my eye to the door crack, but I feared if I got up from the toilet, the auto-flush would go off, and then the women would wonder why I didn't come out. Nor was I the type of woman who could sweep out of the stall, pin the gossipers with a steely eye and leave them shaking in their stilettos. Leave that to women who looked like Joanie.

"Her dress is nice," piped up a third, in a sweeter voice. I instantly pictured her as the Melanie Wilkes of the bunch and could almost hear her companions' eyes rolling. At least Phyl would be happy to hear her dress passed muster. "And her hair." Ditto Joanie's hairstyling skills.

"Yeah, but since when has Daniel been a dress and hair guy?" scoffed the second.

There was some muffled laughter, and then still a fourth voice said, "Exactly—women around him don't spend much time with any kind of clothes on. At least, I didn't." Fiona? Was that Fiona? I tried to scoot to the edge of the toilet, but no luck seeing out.

"You're awfully quiet, Kelly," prodded the first woman. "You're the only other woman here who's been with our Casanova. What do you think of his latest?"

Kelly was silent for a moment, and I knew her mind was returning to that same November afternoon in the Lean-To that mine was.

"She's always wanted him," she answered at last, provoking an affronted gasp out of me that I tried to play off by making lots of noise with the toilet paper dispenser. "I mean, I could tell from the times I was over at his place. She was always really flirty with him and kind of stalker-like. You know, he says she's a housemate, but she's actually more of the housekeeper."

That catty, rumor-mongering, fake redhead! What had I done to her? All these months I never spoke of what I saw that afternoon to anyone but Daniel, and she had the nerve to paint me as some kind of desperate scullery maid? I could feel my face, scarlet with anger and mortification. Really, it was another strike against Daniel's character that he would even sleep with women like this, but I suppose, with him, big breasts covered a multitude of sins.

"You know," came Melanie Wilkes' peacemaking voice again, over the snapping-shut of compacts and handbags, "I was surprised he brought a date tonight because I haven't seen him with anyone for weeks and weeks. And he's been different around the office, somehow. I used to always feel like he was secretly thinking of dirty jokes every time he talked to me." Despite my anger, I felt a twinge of amusement. I rather liked this girl—that was exactly the way I used to feel when Daniel talked to me.

"He has been less of a flirt," the second voice conceded. She sounded slightly disappointed. "I kind of miss it. It made me think one day I'd get my chance with him."

"You probably will," the first woman replied dryly. "If he's relaxed his criteria enough to go out with his stalker-housekeeper, I'll bet in another couple weeks an Accounts Payable rep fifteen years his senior won't be unthinkable."

"I'll be waiting!" sang the Accounts Payable rep, and I heard the clacking of heels again as the crew made their way back out.

I stumbled out of the stall, with the loud auto-flush drowning out the rushing of blood in my ears. Phyl's dress looked rather rumpled from its long stint scrunched up around my waist, and I tried to smooth it out before dabbing my face with cold water. Crap, I forgot I had mascara on. It took another three minutes to repair my make-up, then one more to gather my courage and slap on a calm face before emerging from the bathroom.

Daniel was at the bar, some woman awfully close to him, but when he spotted me, he excused himself and made his way to my side. "Good heavens—I thought I was going to have to send in the Marines," he teased, handing me a glass of some kind of white wine.

"Too much tea," I muttered, downing the wine. Better to let him think I had the bladder of a horse than to go into what really delayed me.

He raised an eyebrow as he watched me guzzle my wine but only said lightly, "I thought for a minute you might be meeting some other man here. You look pretty irresistible."

Thunking my empty glass down on a passing waiter's tray, I glared at him. "No, Daniel, that would be some of the other girls you've dated. And don't talk to me like that—I don't like it."

"Don't talk to you like what?" he demanded, knocking my hand down when I tried to reach for another glass of wine floating by.

"Like—like—" Melanie Wilkes' words popped into my head. "Like you're secretly thinking of dirty jokes. I'm here as a favor to you, so—"

"Thinking of dirty jokes?" he repeated, a low note of anger in his voice. "Actually, Cass, I was trying to pay you a compliment. You are the damned bristliest woman I've ever known."

"Well, I don't want your compliments," I snapped. I blinked at him, suddenly feeling the effects of chugging wine on an empty stomach. "I think I want food."

"I'll say you do, you little fool," he said. "Drinking a glass of wine that fast. If I hadn't stopped you from taking another, I imagine I could say or do anything I felt like with you in another ten minutes." Grasping my elbow tightly, he led me over to the buffet table, ignoring my tugs to rip it away.

Thankfully, some of Daniel's colleagues were also hovering around the food, and I was spared further conversation with him. Not further discomfiture, however. When he presented me to one of the senior partners, Daniel said, "Don, this is my friend Cass. Cass, this is Don Fields, the man who hired me."

"'Friend,' huh?" bellowed Don, winking at Daniel. "I've met a lot of your friends over the years, young man." Nodding at me, he added, "We had no idea when we hired him that he was going to cause so much turnover in our female staff, hey, Daniel? Had to ask him to lay off the paralegals, since they can be hard to replace, heh heh."

"Was that 'lay' the paralegals, or 'lay off' the paralegals?" I asked innocently. Don roared with laughter, beyond what my quip deserved, and I surmised I wasn't the only who had already had too much wine. Daniel, on the other hand, looked displeased and quickly changed the subject.

It was interesting to watch him in this environment, and I had plenty of opportunity, since no one seemed to expect much from me beyond nods and smiles when I was introduced. The male colleagues and clients were jocular but spoke to him with underlying respect and deference. Funny to me, since I had unconsciously adopted Joanie's sisterly forthrightness with him. I realized again that Daniel really was a smart, well-read man who could converse intelligently on any number of topics, something I hadn't dwelt on much, since my few serious conversations with him had been overshadowed by the many more about sex, drugs, and such. Or else I was too distracted by his dirty-joke tone to appreciate the actual content of our discussions.

The women's responses I could have predicted. When they saw I made no move to engage Daniel or keep him to myself, and as the evening wore on and more liquor got into them, some of them took to hanging about, flirting outrageously. At one point I was sitting at a bar table, resting my tortured feet and trying to give Daniel a little space to do whatever he liked. When he went to get a refill on his drink, two women scurried in his wake to try their luck.

"So, you're just a friend of Daniel's?" It was an older gentleman. I think he'd been introduced as another of the senior partners, but I couldn't remember.

I smiled politely. "Actually, I'm really good friends with Daniel's sister. I just…rent a room from Daniel."

"Then he probably wouldn't mind if I asked you to dance," he continued. "My third wife recently left me, and these holidays have been kind of lonely. Dancing with you would be a real treat for me." Ugh! Too much information, and when he got closer his breath smelt like vodka.

"No, thank you," I said firmly. "I borrowed my friend's shoes, and my feet are pretty sore. Good thing there are so many other lovely ladies here for you to dance with."

"Oh, come now, young lady," he pressed. "There are other ladies here, but I imagined you'd welcome it. It's always hard to be Daniel's date, the neglected wallflower."

"Ah, but she's not neglected, Jack," came Daniel's voice, and before I could react, his arm brushed across my bare shoulders, and he pressed his lips fleetingly to my temple. I turned the bright red of a cooked lobster and stared at him speakingly, keeping my mouth clamped shut until Jack shrugged and walked away.

"Just what was that about?" I demanded through clenched teeth.

"I was rescuing you from Jack," he replied calmly.

"For one thing, I didn't need rescuing, and for another, would you mind keeping your hands to yourself?" I could just hear the bathroom gossip that move of his would lead to, and my temple still felt warm where he had kissed it.

"You have a certain appeal to you, beyond your looks," he went on, ignoring my narrowed eyes. "It's an air of vulnerability—makes some men want to try their luck, like idiot Tom in the pantry or poor

Jack here, and makes other men feel protective of you…"

He trailed off, but I had no intention of continuing this subject. "Don't worry about me," I said dismissively. "You go and do your thing. I'm perfectly capable of sitting here and driving off any other knights errant." When he didn't move, I gave him a little shove. "Go on. Line yourself up some activity. You've been too long without any dates."

He hesitated. "I'm not interested in any of them."

I'd forgotten about his New Year's resolution to give up relationship dumpster diving. "Ha!" I scoffed. "That never stopped you before. You're getting picky in your old age. Let me see… how about her—over there by the chocolate fountain. Chocolate is said to be an aphrodisiac."

"Do you want to dance, Cass?"

"No," I said rudely.

Daniel leaned closer. "Dance with me, Cass."

"No!" I recognized the bull-headed expression dawning on his face and felt a little spasm of panic. "I borrowed Joanie's shoes, and my feet are killing me. I'm going to sit here until it's time to go. Go dance with chocolate lady."

"I want to dance with you," he said inexorably. "Take your shoes off if they're hurting you." Seeing that I was getting a mutinous look of my own he relented slightly. "What is so god-awful about dancing with me? Do you think James would mind?"

Would he? I doubted it. James wasn't the least bit the jealous type, and even if he were, he knew how I felt about Daniel. That I thought he was a womanizing snake, I mean.

"It's New Year's Eve, after all," Daniel went on. "I'll bet he's off at some party himself, making merry with a lovely Tri-Cities fräulein."

To my chagrin, I realized this probably was the case. James had said, after all, that visits to his family always involved at least one set-up with an amiable young woman, and what better night to set him up than New Year's Eve? I hadn't heard from him in days, moreover, not even any text messages, and I'd thrown my phone in a drawer in rebellion.

Pro that he was, Daniel sensed my wavering and pulled on my hand. "Come on, Cass, it's just a dance. You don't have to marry me."

This did draw a laugh from me. "You're right. No woman ever has that to fear from you."

· · ·

Dancing with Daniel turned out to be a pleasant experience because he knew what he was doing, and he had a natural, easy grace. Troy and I hadn't attempted much beyond the obligatory wedding dances, for which we prepared with six weeks of ballroom dance lessons, only to discover we could have saved our time and money—the billowing tulle skirt of my wedding gown covered every misstep. And I didn't even know if James danced—if he did I'm sure Riley would never let him hear the end of it.

It was a little disconcerting to have one of Daniel's hands on the small of my back—the burgundy satin wasn't terribly thick—but at least it never strayed anywhere, and he didn't squash me against him, like the sleazy guys in the movies. And holding his other hand wasn't too terrible either. He had warm, dry palms. I had been peeking over his shoulder to see how much damage this dance was doing to my reputation as stalker-housekeeper, and, judging from the various female eyes upon us, it seemed sufficient.

"What are you thinking, Cass?"

Startled, I met his eyes and found their expression puzzling. Intense, yes, they always were. But also—joyous? "Umm," I murmured, a little addled, "I was thinking how some of those other women are wishing I would drop dead. And that I'm—I'm enjoying this. You're not sleazy to dance with."

His short laugh wasn't entirely amused. "You don't have a very high opinion of me, do you? You always sound surprised when I don't act like the bastard you think I am."

"Oh, well, I—uh—" I dithered uncomfortably, "well, what do you care what I think? Everyone here thinks the world of you. The men have such respect for you, and the women are all gnashing their teeth because you brought me—even the ones whose hearts you've already broken!"

"Oddly enough, I've found that your good opinion means a lot to me," he answered in a low voice. "I've started to…want it."

I couldn't come up with any response to that statement, and we danced in silence. I began to hope the music would end soon or become something fast, so I could beg off and sit down, but the DJ blended smoothly into a foxtrot.

"How are you and James doing?" Daniel asked casually.

I was biting the end of my tongue, trying to concentrate on the steps, having always been foxtrot-challenged. Slow – slow – quick – quick – slow –slow . "Fine," I said shortly, in my best none-of-your-business tone.

"He's younger than you, isn't he?" I only scowled in response. "How old are you anyway, Cass?"

"Thirty-two."

"And didn't you tell me he'd lose interest in you after a couple weeks? It looks like the end date is slipping."

I trod on his foot and didn't bother apologizing. "Really, Daniel, if you want me to make it through this foxtrot without destroying your shoe shine, you'd better not make any more personal comments."

He smiled then and spun me around. "You're right. Let's not bother about all that. Let's just enjoy ourselves." Whatever he decided in that moment, it worked. He set himself to be brotherly and entertaining, and after a while I began to relax and joke with him as well. The increasing drunkenness of some of the partygoers made for plenty of good people-watching, and the foxtrot was followed by more waltzes and some swing. When the DJ moved into his Latin set, I tried to claim fatigue, but Daniel insisted on teaching me some basic salsa and merengue, and to my delight I found them much easier than the ballroom stuff.

When midnight came a few hours later, "Auld Lang Syne" blared out of the speakers, while balloons and confetti floated everywhere. I was perched on a bar stool by this point, with a defective blow-out favor that wasn't blowing out, laughing and demonstrating its lameness to him, when all at once Daniel put his hands on the back of my neck and pulled me toward him and kissed me on the mouth. It was a quick, chaste kiss, but so wholly unexpected that I just gawked at him.

"Of all the nerve," I managed weakly, but I couldn't maintain any convincing note of outrage after having such fun with him, and I found myself laughing it off.

He wasn't looking at me. He was looking at the people on the dance floor, kissing each other Happy New Year.

"Yes," he said after a moment. "Happy New Year, Cass."

CHAPTER 29:

DTR

I let my cell phone run down, I think accidentally on purpose. Nor was I checking my email. If my phone was dead and my inbox ignored, I couldn't expect James to call me or text me or whatever. Not that he was going to—with his initial text before Christmas and one on Christmas Day proper and one a few days later, that brought the total to three in almost two weeks apart. How was I supposed to interpret this? He buys me an expensive GPS navigator and then disappears? Maybe the "homely friend" his little sister picked out for him this visit turned out to be the girl of his dreams.

All I know is that I was in a funk. There's always the post-Christmas funk, for which New Year's is generally a sad attempt to make the descent less precipitous—and honestly I ended up having a wonderful time at Daniel's "office party"—but this was more than that.

"I shouldn't have kissed him," I complained to Joanie and Phyl as we worked on de-Christmasing the house. "Things were just fine when we were hanging out, but the second I let him kiss me, suddenly I'm depressed if I don't see him or he doesn't call me, which he doesn't."

"Where did you guys leave it?" asked Phyl, taking the ornaments after I re-wrapped them, and placing them in the box.

"I don't know," I said. "We exchanged presents, and his was very nice, but we've never talked about it."

"I'd say a GPS means you're dating exclusively," said Joanie, winding the string of lights around her arm. I knew I'd have to unwind them and do it again, or else it would be a hopeless snarl next year.

"I think the no-contact means he's just a generous gift-giver, and you're not dating exclusively," decided Phyl. "Who knows? The GPS could have been lying around his apartment, and he re-gifted it."

"It can't be a re-gift—it's too expensive!" I pointed out. "Only his mom or someone could have given him that, and you wouldn't re-gift something that your mom would obviously check up on later."

Joanie slung the clump of lights on the coffee table and started in on the paper village on the mantel. "I still say you're dating exclusively, but the guy is only 27. Meaning, he's happy seeing you or talking to you whenever he feels like it, and it hasn't occurred to him that you may feel differently."

"But even if he's only 27, and I see your point," I pursued, "don't you think that he'd want a little more contact? Especially if we've only been seeing each other in any sense for a month?" They didn't answer right away, and I knew they agreed with me. I sighed, "He's just not that into me, I guess."

"Sounds like you two need to Define the Relationship," said Phyl. When I groaned, she just shook her head and went on, "It takes too much emotional energy to wonder. After a good DTR you can decide if you like where you stand and want to stay in, or if you don't like it, and you want to get out."

"DTRs are too college for me," I objected. "It's already bad enough that he's too young—if I have to go back to college behavior, I'm out.

Besides, didn't you notice in college that whoever had to initiate the DTR was the one with more invested? It was always the initiator asking, 'We're totally in love with each other, right?' and the non-initiator saying, 'Actually, I can't even remember your name.'"

"Well, are you in love with James?" Joanie asked baldly. "If you are, I'd tell you to wait longer and make allowances for him being young and a guy."

A sudden silence fell, as everyone stopped fiddling with whatever was in their hand to listen.

"I don't think I am," I answered tentatively. "I mean, I like him a lot, and if I thought either one of us was interested in moving in that direction, it wouldn't be hard to—"

"Oh, Cass, you're so flipping practical!" groused Joanie. "Have you ever fallen for anyone in your life without weighing the pros and cons and giving yourself permission first?"

"Ye-e-es," I admitted, thinking of the Magdalen College tutor at Oxford, "but it was an unqualified disaster." Squashing the nativity-set Joseph back into his box, I let my mind roam back. "I thought I told you guys about Clive, my tutor during my study-abroad quarter. I was only 21, and he was redheaded and pale as a ghost and knew everything there was to know about Jacobean drama—" (Joanie made a face, and even Phyl looked concerned.) "And for six weeks we were totally nuts about each other, and I broke up with Troy over the phone and had my whole life in England planned out, but luckily we came to our senses."

"No, no, no," said Joanie. "No no no no. You're leaving lots out. How could you be this crazy about someone—crazy enough to break up with the guy you'd been going out with since senior year of high school—and then 'come to your senses'? And I'll bet it was you that broke up, not him."

Sinking onto the couch, I found myself smiling. "I was sitting in the little church I went to while I was there—it was freezing. I always think of Oxford as freezing because I was there during Hilary Term, and suddenly I thought of how church was warmer in America. Not just because it was in California but because I'd go with Troy, and we'd sit together, and he'd put his arm around me. Clive—stupid Clive!—he was named after C. S. Lewis, but he was a total atheist, and he used to tease me about being such a religious American. And it kind of came over me—what was I doing, dumping everything? My country, my boyfriend, my life plans—dumping everything for this brilliant, awkward man with crooked teeth, just because he wrote me notes in iambic pentameter? So I broke up with him, and when I came home I begged and begged Troy to forgive me, and he did."

"Wow," Phyl breathed. "That's romantic!"

"Except for the visual," Joanie interjected.

"So had he asked you to marry him?" Phyl pressed.

"Everything happened so fast—we just found ourselves talking about what we would do in the future, where we would live, where we wanted to travel—it was just assumed we would be married. Especially since he knew I wouldn't sleep with him. That was one of the main things he teased me about. I think I was one of the most unprogressive people he'd ever met."

"Have you Googled him? What's he doing?" asked Joanie.

I shrugged. "I did once. He's an assistant professor somewhere. Still brilliant, but I think if I'd met him outside the hallowed halls of Magdalen, I never would have lost my head like that. Those old buildings really give a guy an aura. Anyhow, can you imagine? No wonder I try to keep my head about me—I could have ended up the tweedy wife of an academic, pushing a pram through Bristol or wherever."

"Wayne writes poetry," Phyl volunteered, blushing a little.

"About what?" scoffed Joanie. "Closed circuits? Hot dogs stands?"

"Joanie, for Pete's sake," I said irritably. "In my opinion, Wayne has it all over Roy."

"Who doesn't?" she sniffed. "Sorry, Phyl. I guess I'm just in a snotty mood because I hate this dating hiatus. I might abandon it."

"It's only been a couple weeks!" I protested. "At least you've got to outlast Daniel."

"You mean he actually didn't hook up with anyone at the New Year's party?" Joanie asked incredulously. I'd given them a brief description of the event, leaving out Daniel kissing me, of course. It wasn't a real kiss, after all, not like stupid James'.

"Plenty of women were trying their luck," I said, "but I don't think he took any of them up on their offers."

"Do you think," began Phyl hesitantly, glancing at Joanie, "do you think he might…like you, Cass?"

The kiss flashed through my mind again. And dancing. And the Christmas book. "I think—I think he likes me as a person. As a friend, I suppose, and I think it's weird for him. He doesn't quite know how to categorize me, since the only boxes he seems to have for women are Family and—and—"

"Bed Clutter," supplied Joanie. Apt enough.

Our analysis of Daniel was interrupted by a knock at the door.

Phyl peeked out the safety glass and stifled a gasp. "Don't look now, Cass, but I think it's James."

"Crap!" I hissed, jumping to my feet, while Joanie ran over and started unwinding the Christmas garland I had draped around my neck and shoulders like a boa. "If I'm gonna get dumped, can't I at least look fabulous?" I complained. "If he dumped me New Year's Eve, when I was leaving the house with Daniel and all dolled up, he might have been a little sorry."

"If he doesn't dump you, what are you going to do?" whispered Phyl urgently. "DTR. Have your DTR."

"Stay here!" I commanded. "If you leave, I have to decide how to act, but if you stay, he has to." With one last smoothing of my sweater and hair, I went to get the door.

When I opened it, I quickly took a step back into the entryway, to moot the question of hugging or not hugging. "Hi, James." He was wearing the sweater I'd given him, which either meant he wasn't going to dump me or else that he was and wanted to be a jerk about it. When his gray eyes met mine, I thought he probably looked as uncertain as I did.

"Hey there, Cass," he said after a pause. "Your phone must be dead, or something. I've been trying to reach you the last couple days. Didn't you get my email?"

"Umm, no," I replied. Having totally shut down my computer in disgust, I hadn't received anyone's emails. "Did you want to come in? The girls and I were just putting away the Christmas stuff."

Awkwardly he followed me into the house where Joanie accosted him with a hearty greeting and Phyl smiled gently from up on the step ladder.

"Did you have a nice time in Richland?" I asked brightly, giving the tree skirt some smart shakes to clean off the pine needles.

"Oh—er—yes," he replied. "That is, it was a typical family visit: good to see everyone but maybe a few days too long. How was your time here with your family?"

"Fine. My parents and brother only stayed until the 27th, so there was lots of activity and then some peace and quiet."

"And then you had a pretty rousing New Year's Eve," put in Joanie, earning a dirty look from me.

"What happened New Year's Eve?" asked James.

I focused on the container I was packing, trying to think about innocuous things so I wouldn't blush. Things like organic broccoli and parking spaces. "Oh, well, Daniel had an office party, and I agreed to go along with him as a decoy, so he wouldn't be harassed by other women." Not that I was very effective, I thought. "What did you do New Year's Eve?"

Ah ha! From his averted eyes and shifting around, that was definitely a subject he wanted to avoid. "Went to a party as well. What would you girls like to do with the Christmas tree? Can I carry it outside for you?"

"Thank you," exclaimed Phyl eagerly, partly to cover the fact that Joanie was nudging me. "If you could just bring it out to the curb, I'll saw it up later for the yard waste bin."

"If you just show me where the saw is, I can do that too," offered James, coming forward with alacrity.

After he and Phyl got the tree out of the stand and wrangled it out the front door, trailing pine needles, Joanie pounced on me. "Did you see his face when you asked about New Year's? You better get to the bottom of that, girlie. Five bucks says he did something naughty and he's going to ask your forgiveness, and ten bucks says you'll give it to him."

"Shut up, Joanie," I growled. "He doesn't have to ask my forgiveness because we don't even have an official status."

"But if you made out with Daniel, New Year's Eve, wouldn't you feel like you had to say something to James?"

"I didn't make out with Daniel," I protested, unable to prevent a blush this time.

"Don't dodge the question."

"All right. Yes. I guess so. Go away, I'm going to vacuum."

"DTR," was all Joanie said, as she began piling up containers to return to the garage.

When Phyl and James came back in I was diligently running the vacuum cleaner back and forth, making a fearsome racket.

"Could we talk?" asked James. He had to repeat himself in a shout to be heard over the roar.

I flipped it off. "Oh. Yeah. In the kitchen? Would you like something to drink?"

"Actually, how about a walk?"

"Isn't it raining outside?" I hedged.

"Just mist. Nothing a good Northwest girl like you would mind." Crud. Phyl met my eyes sympathetically, but there was nothing for it but to put on my coat and go outside with James.

If we had ever found it easy to chat with each other, you would never guess it, watching us walk up the hill. He kept glancing at me, and I kept glancing at him, unable to think of what to say. Maybe Phyl was right, and we just had to have it out. Gathering my courage in true college fashion, I was on the verge of asking him what the heck was going on, if in fact anything was going on, when James spoke first. "So, you went to a New Year's Eve party with Daniel?"

"Technically, yes," I said. Inward cringes—what made me say that? It sounded defensive. Was I defensive?

"Where's he at today?" he asked randomly.

"Umm...skiing with some buddies."

"Are you mad at me, Cass?"

"Why would I be mad at you?" I countered.

"For not calling while I was gone."

I kicked at some fir twigs littering the sidewalk. "I was sorry not to hear from you very much," I confessed, not looking at him. "Not that you owed me phone calls or anything. I just—it would have been nice—I was just sorry about it."

"I was going to call you Christmas Day," he began, but I cut him off.

"Please, you don't need to make excuses—"

"Well, I'd like to explain myself," he said. "You can ignore me if you want to, but indulge me." He gave me his quirky little smile, and, suppressing a sigh, I nodded. "Like they always do, my family closed in on me the second I got there. Everyone was at the house: aunts, uncles, cousins, siblings, nieces, nephew, parents—and my little sister's friend Jen who—hey!—just happened to have moved back to town." (I could see where this was going. Looked like I owed Joanie five bucks.) "I'd actually kind of had a thing for Jen in high school because she was one of those cute, popular types that band geeks like me were always doomed to fall for. Well, Jen was back with her parents in Richland because she'd just gotten a divorce, and she and my little sister Amy are thick as thieves again. To make a long story medium, Jen confessed she'd supposedly always had a thing for me as well, and on Christmas Eve, in the general spirit of conviviality, we kissed."

The "general spirit of conviviality" my eye! I suppose I would have to say Daniel kissed me New Year's Eve "in the general spirit of conviviality," but that was just it. *He* kissed me. I hadn't kissed him and had, in fact, been taken totally off guard. If Nadina were here, she would tell James he was full of it. But maybe not. She took loads of it from Mike.

So this was a breakup conversation, then.

"I knew it was a stupid move," James continued, when I didn't say anything. "I told her right afterward that I was seeing someone." I made a noise in my throat, but he went on hurriedly. "But I was too embarrassed then to call you on Christmas because I felt like crap. I didn't want to lose your respect. Jen was everywhere the rest of the week. I didn't slip up again and even had an argument with my mom about it. You know how irrational they are about wanting to plan my life. Jen looked like a godsend to Mom and Amy and Melissa, and they didn't want to hear that I had other ideas." Especially if those ideas involved an older widow. Ugh.

"James," I said, stopping. We were at the top of the hill, from which you could see the lake and, in the foggy distance, the tops of the skyscrapers in downtown Seattle. With just this minor change in altitude, the mist had turned to tiny snowflakes. "Thank you for telling me, even though you didn't have to."

"Of course I had to," he replied, in a harder voice. He reached for my hand, but I took a quick step back.

"You didn't have to," I repeated. "You don't owe me explanations and phone calls and—and whatnot. It was, kind of crazy before Christmas, wasn't it? I mean, between us. I think it would be better if we just go back to being—being…colleagues. I mean, we're all wrong—" I didn't get any further in my breakup speech because James grabbed me by the shoulders and kissed me, hard. Gasping, I tried to shove him away.

"Cass, don't do this," he murmured against my ear. "Don't do this."

"Don't do what?" I demanded, jerking free from him.

He laughed humorlessly. "Don't dump me, for one. And for another, don't tell me I don't owe you anything. What I did was wrong. I wronged Jen by kissing her because I don't give a damn about her, and I wronged you because I never want to hurt you."

"James—"

"No," he interrupted. "No, I'm not going to let you be practical and rational and tell me we shouldn't be together. If you can stand me, I'm asking you to forgive me. Forgive me for losing my head for a minute and acting against my own interests. It won't happen again. Because I'm—I'm crazy about you, Cass."

• • •

"Well?" demanded Joanie a half hour later, when I came back in and was hanging up my coat.

I felt the warmth rise to my cheeks as I blushed. "I owe you fifteen bucks."

CHAPTER 30:

Service with a Smile

"Dude, this sucks," complained Nadina, collapsing on one of the walnut-stained pews lining the hallway.

"Get your muddy butt off of there!" I ordered. "I just wiped that one down."

"I'll wipe it again after I take a nap," she moaned. "God, I feel like shit. I think I must be getting the flu."

Camden School was kicking off the second semester with an all-school service project. Through the first couple weeks of the new year, heavy rains pummeled western Washington, leading to flooding in communities that fronted the many rivers crisscrossing the area. Rivers with delightful Native American names that tripped up newscasters and stymied those new to the area: the Puyallup, Stillaguamish, Duwamish, Skookumchuck. Among the many structures flooded was the tiny Community of Friends Church in Snoqualmie, and Camden School volunteered to do some post-disaster clean-up for them.

If Community of Friends' brisk, all-business Pastor Anne had any second thoughts when she saw the crew of pierced and dyed and otherwise ornamented teenagers getting off the bus, she kept them to herself, and Mark Henneman was quick to barrel out and get her all buttered up. It helped that we had almost as many adults as kids, counting staff and several of the mentors and volunteers.

Church members had already pressure-washed the exterior, but the receding flood waters had left a wainscoting of guck all through the interior of the building and covered the floors and furnishings in a muddy scunge.

"Gross!" said Nadina, two shades too loudly. "This place looks like hell. And what is that heinous stink?"

Pastor Anne only laughed. "Yeah, it's awful, isn't it? The Bible doesn't talk about what it must have smelled like or looked like for Noah and his family, after the waters receded."

"Who?" said Nadina.

"Noah, like in Noah's Ark, you friggin' idiot," supplied Sonya.

With that, Pastor Anne divided us into work teams. People with skills like Kyle and James got to stay clean and set up the church's new computer system, while the rest of us spent the morning slogging around with steam cleaners, wet-dry vacs, mops, blowers, and fans. Nadina didn't last long. By dint of constant prodding and nagging, I got her to help me move and clean off several pews before she collapsed in her present exhaustion.

"What on earth is wrong with you?" I demanded. "You're not usually this lazy."

"I'm telling you, Cass, I've got the flu," she whined. "Feel my head—am I hot?"

Since this particular pew was already messed up, I flopped on it beside her, pretty pooped myself. "Did you and Mike stay up late last night, doing anything you shouldn't have?"

Nadina groaned. "Not even. I was passed out by friggin' nine o'clock, and I told you, Mike's gone straight. He's done everything the judge told him, even gone to that stupid drug treatment thing and thrown away his pipes and stuff."

If this was true, it was good news. Maybe God was hearing my prayers for that knucklehead. "Did he talk much about his week in jail?"

"No, other than to say it sucked."

"How about the fine? How is he going to pay that?" I persisted. Glimpsing Mark Henneman passing by at the end of the hallway, I popped back up guiltily and started scrubbing at the pew again.

She shrugged. "God, Cass, you really got Henneman to dish the dirt, didn't you? You probably know more about it than I do. Mike's dad lent him the money for now, but says he's got six months to pay him back and to start paying rent, or he's kicking us out." Mike's dad was suddenly getting a backbone?

I had to tread carefully here, but at least in her flu-induced exhaustion, Nadina didn't seem to have her usual guard up. "So will you each pay rent, or will you pay the rent?"

Up went the guard. "Are you asking if he's going to try to steal from me again? Didn't I tell you he's going straight? He told me he might need to borrow from me now and then, but he's going to get a job and pay it all back."

"What kind of job?" I asked innocently.

Nadina seemed to be weighing her words. "Well…since he's so good with music and stuff, I was thinking maybe James could use him at his company, like he hired Kyle." Yeah, and at this rate, they might need to rename the company Felon Universe.

Keeping my voice noncommittal I said, "I'm sure Mike is welcome to apply, if they're hiring."

She sat up abruptly. "Aw, come on, Cass. You know you have an in with James because he's totally gone on you! I thought if *you* asked him, he'd be sure to give Mike a chance."

"He's not totally gone on me," I objected primly, hoping I wasn't blushing. "We've just gone on a few dates—"

"Bullshit, Cass! You don't think I've noticed you guys checking each other out whenever you're together? He always looks like he totally wants to jump you."

Now I was scarlet. "People like James and me don't go around 'jumping each other.'" I could have said more, but I figured now was not the time or place to go into Christian sexual ethics.

"Yeah, right," muttered Nadina.

"In any case," I said in a louder voice, "I am not going to interfere with how they run their business. I didn't tell him to hire Kyle—that was James' idea because he's Kyle's mentor and because Kyle had some skills they needed." Nadina threw herself back on the pew, muttering imprecations against me and covering her eyes with the back of her arm. "The most I'll do is pass on that Mike knows a lot about music—did you tell Mike you were putting me up to this?" I asked, as the thought hit me.

"Hell no!" she exclaimed with evident sincerity. "It's not like you two are super buddies. It was just an idea I had. I thought you might, for my sake."

"I'll mention it," I repeated. "Not just for your sake, but also for Mike's because, believe it or not, I've been praying for Mike, too. But no promises. It's not my business."

"Got it got it got it," said Nadina. "Now shouldn't you get back to work, especially if you have to do my part too? Look at Louella trying to wrestle that steam cleaner."

. . .

At the lunch break I brought Kyle and James their sandwiches, only to have James burst out laughing when he caught sight of my bedraggled, mud-spattered self. He, of course, was still pristine, not a fleck of dirt on his microfleece pullover. "Whoa, Cass—you look like they had to fish you out of the river!"

"Yeah, well, Mister, some of us have actually been working, while you and Kyle sit here pointing and clicking."

"Harsh," said Kyle. "Dude, I think I'm getting a repetitive stress injury."

"That means you need to take more breaks," James advised, winking at me. "Reconstructing their system from back-ups is painful and messy, but someone has to do it."

Kyle was inspecting his sandwich. "This has mayo. I'm gonna go see if they have one without."

The second he was out of the room, James was grabbing for my hand. "No, don't!" I protested, resisting. "I'll get mud all over you, and Kyle will know we were mashing when he was looking for no-mayo sandwiches."

"Would you be embarrassed?" he prompted.

"Yes, and so would Kyle, and so should you be. Our behavior hasn't escaped Nadina's notice either."

"Fine, then," James relented. "Just one peck on the—hmm... where could I actually kiss you where I wouldn't get dirty?"

"Probably no place that I'm going to show you, so just eat your sandwich."

After Kyle returned, we ate companionably, James and Kyle occasionally wiping their hands off to click some key or bypass some dialogue box. When I left them to check on Nadina, I found her outside with Sonya and Louella, sitting on the exposed-aggregate planter box and making a face over her bag lunch.

"What is it now?" I asked. "You're turning into a total princess-and-the-pea."

Thrusting her sandwich in my face, she demanded, "Does this smell right to you? Or is it going bad?"

I took a cautious sniff. "Smells okay to me, and surely it was made in the same batch as everyone else's, and they were all fine. Just eat it, Nadina."

Naturally, when faced with a direct command, she rebelled and pushed the lunch away decisively. "No way. Something is wrong with that sandwich. I'll give it to Tan."

"Oh, nice—poison your classmate," I said.

"C'mon, Cass, let's go wash windows."

It was handy to work with someone who was 5'10": she took the upper panes, while I handled the lower, but by this point her complaining reached a pitch that made me long to wring her neck. "Oh my God, I could never be a janitor because this fake Windex smells like pine puke... how come they only ever offer turkey or ham or friggin' vegetarian sandwiches—why not pastrami? ... Why the hell do we have to clean the windows when the water didn't even reach up here?... I don't see that friggin' Pastor Anne doing anything besides talking on the phone and bossing us around... How the hell did Kyle and James get such a lazy-ass job?... I am butt-tired—gotta go sit down."

I found her zonked on that same pew from the morning an hour later, snoring. Actually snoring! She really must have the flu. Quietly I reached out my hand and laid it to her forehead. Felt normal. Was she lying about Mike not giving her any trouble? Hiding something from me?

Waving my fake-Windex-infused washcloth above her nose, I waited for her to wake up, which she did suddenly, sputtering and slapping my hand away. "God, Cass—what the hell?"

"I am slightly concerned about you," I said. "Maybe we should ask Pastor Anne for some ibuprofen."

"No, I feel a little better now, since I got a nap. Are we done yet? Do we get to get back on the bus?"

"Soon, I think. Were you this much of a whiny lump when you were in Cleveland?"

"I dunno," she replied indifferently. "Ask Aunt Sylvia. All I know is that I got lots of sleep there because there wasn't much to do besides play bridge with her buddies and watch TV and eat. Plus, she didn't make weird food. In flipping Cleveland they don't put stinking hummus and pesto on everything."

"I give up. You go back to your nap, and I'll call you when it's time to get on the bus." That suggestion, at least, didn't draw a complaint, and she was stretched out with her eyes shut before I'd left the room.

· · ·

After we returned from Snoqualmie, James followed me to the Palace for dinner. It turned out to be one of those Saturday evenings when everyone was home, one of those Saturday evenings becoming more common, now that Joanie and Daniel weren't dating.

"Nadina was right—that fake Windex does smell like pine puke," said Joanie, helping herself to more of the beef phad khi mao she had whipped up. I had been regaling them with the day's adventures, including Nadina's litany of complaints.

"She's just never been much of a whiner," I mused. "Or lazy. Or a picky eater. Today was uncharacteristic for her."

"Did she say anything about how Mike was doing?" asked James. "Mike is Nadina's boyfriend," he added to Daniel, by way of explanation. "He got arrested and did time before Christmas for drug possession." Daniel said nothing, and I wanted to kick James under the table—he didn't know the Palace rule: we always assumed that, unless he gave us to understand otherwise, Daniel was not terribly interested in the minutiae of our daily lives.

"She didn't volunteer anything, of course, but I dragged it out of her," I answered. "I just don't know if it's the truth. She claims he's really walking the line: going to the drug treatment center, throwing away all the paraphernalia, saying he's going to get a job—everything!"

"Hooray!" cheered Phyl, ever the optimist.

"What kind of job, fresh out of jail?" asked Daniel, causing us to look at him in surprise.

I squirmed, thinking of the favor Nadina asked of me. Putting James on the spot in front of others was not my intention. "Oh, I don't know. I don't think he knew yet. Apparently he's very interested in music and the whole Seattle music scene, or he was, when he wasn't stoned out of his mind. Nadina thought – she suggested – she was thinking I could ask you, James, if you all needed any more help at Free Universe." Seeing him hesitate, I rushed on. "Of course I told her that you all had already taken on Kyle as your charity project, and that you're Kyle's *mentor*, for Pete's sake. Who knows anything about Mike, except that up until a couple weeks ago I thought he had no redeeming qualities?"

James leaned back from the table thoughtfully. "Not exactly a ringing endorsement. I'll have to think about it. I can't imagine Murray being thrilled to work with someone like Mike. I hadn't told anyone much about Kyle, except to say he was exactly our customer base and brilliant, besides."

"Is this important to you, Cass, to help Mike find work?" spoke up Daniel again. His blue eyes held mine steadily.

More fidgeting on my part. "Well, of course I'd love it if someone would give him a chance because then he could have some hope of succeeding in his new choices. His dad wants Nadina and him to start paying rent, and I'm worried it's all going to fall on Nadina. But on the other hand, I could hardly recommend him to anyone. He might rob you or come to work high or whatever. I'm kind of caught in the middle emotionally because ––well, I've kind of committed to pray for him, but then I'm afraid to be part of the answer to prayer. Like someone who votes for some public project but doesn't want it built in her backyard."

"So the answer is yes, it's important to you, but you're afraid of the consequences," said Daniel. This must be his lawyer tone. I shrugged and nodded, much as I imagine his clients did. "One of our clients owns a big recording studio in Lake City," he continued. "He started there years ago cleaning toilets. I could ask him if they need a toilet-cleaner. It'd be humble, but if Mike was serious about getting into music and serious about going straight, he wouldn't care how low he had to start out."

Halfway through this speech I had begun shaking my head emphatically. "No. Absolutely not, Daniel. This has nothing to do with you and less than nothing to do with your clients. Didn't I just say Mike could ruin everything?"

James laughed. "That's right. Let him ruin Free Universe."

Turning on him indignantly, I said, "You know that's not what I mean. I don't want Mike to ruin anything, but at least you have some idea of what it would involve." I shook my head again at Daniel. "How could you even suggest saddling a client with him? It could jeopardize your whole relationship. What's Hecuba to him or he to Hecuba, that he should weep for her?"

"Who the hell are we talking about now?" protested Joanie.

"Someone in the music business would have a better idea than most, about people like Mike," Daniel answered, ignoring his sister. "And I'm only suggesting he be the office grunt. You forget—I know exactly what I'm talking about. I was fired from more than one job in high school and college for either not bothering to show up or showing up stoned."

He was sincere. He meant it. And what he said actually made some sense, I thought reluctantly. I couldn't help worrying it would all end in the worst way—Mike stealing some software and equipment to get drug money, or showing up baked and trashing something valuable. Sad to think that, if Mike never showed up at all, that might be the best case scenario.

"You say your client has some experience in the drug scene?" I asked, after a moment.

Daniel merely raised an eyebrow and regarded me, amused.

"And you would warn him about all the possibilities for total disaster Mike would bring on his studio, if he said yes?" I persisted.

He folded his napkin and laid it beside his plate. "No, I think not. I think it would be better to bring you along when I talk to him about it. I'm sure I couldn't paint it in horrific-enough colors to suit you."

"Probably not," I admitted. I felt a rush of gratitude toward him—strange, unreadable man. Why on earth he should suddenly take an interest in the fate of the downtrodden was beyond me—maybe it really was sympathy he felt for Mike, a there-but-for-the-grace-of-God-go-I kind of thing. "Daniel, thank you. I still say your client would be nuts to take Mike on, but I appreciate you being willing to risk your working relationship to suggest it. You'd better not let the senior partners know."

Daniel didn't reply, but James leaned across the table to slap him on the shoulder. "Yeah, thanks, Martin. You've really taken one for the team."

For some reason, I felt an irrational twinge of annoyance. Not that I wanted James to take Mike on, but I wanted him to want to, if that made any sense. After all, James was the one familiar with the situation and all the players, and even Nadina assumed he would leap on a chance to help me out.

By the time I rejoined them mentally, the conversation had moved on to other topics, but I felt Daniel's eyes upon me. Raising mine to meet his, I had the funny feeling he knew what had just been passing through my mind.

CHAPTER 31:

Landlord Troubles

Daniel was as good as his word.

On Tuesday, just as I was starting a load of linens, I was startled to hear the door to the Lean-To opening. Feeling a stab of panic, in case this was November-with-Kelly Redux, I dashed out of the utility room to make my presence known before things got too hot and heavy.

It was only Daniel, immaculate and completely clothed in his button-down shirt and khakis, and my subsequent relief was not lost on him. "For God's sake, Cass—give me some credit."

"I'm sorry," I apologized hastily, seeing I had offended him. "I was going to break for lunch now anyhow, so I'll be out of your way."

"That's what I came about," he said, taking a quick step between me and the door. "I'm meeting Ray Snow at Yarrow Bay Beach Café and wanted to know if you could join us. It occurred to me this morning that I don't even have your phone number, so I had to take a chance and swing by."

"Ray Snow?"

"The client who owns the recording studio."

"Oh!" My hand flew to the bandanna covering my hair. "Cripe, Daniel—look at me! Give me five minutes, at least, or he'll never agree to Mike."

Fifteen minutes later we were pulling into the garage at Carillon Point. Although my hair was brushed and I raided Phyl's closet for a cute sweater, I felt as nervous as if I were going for my own job interview. Plus, as a sop to meeting someone hip enough to work with musicians, I had pulled on a crazier pair of Joanie's shoes, and they echoed loudly on the concrete. As did Daniel's shoes, but he didn't seem the least bit self-conscious about it. They must take some kind of class in law school like How to Ooze Self-Confidence and Totally Obliterate Other People.

I tried not to stiffen up as we entered the bar and I felt Daniel's hand on the small of my back, directing me. He needn't have bothered—the Yarrow Bay clientele tended toward upscale business types, and Ray Snow could only be the guy with the wild glasses and long shaggy hair and faded black t-shirt.

"Ray."

"Dan." They shook hands. "No charge for this, right?"

Daniel shook his head. "Not in the usual sense. Ray, this is Cass, a friend of mine."

Ray raised his bushy eyebrows, and I wondered how many of Daniel's "friends" he had met over the years. "Not that kind of friend," I said without thinking, and then turned pink. Fortunately for me, the waitress chose that moment to stride up, sling coasters on our bar table and ask for our order. It took a second to catch her eye, since she seemed more interested in checking Daniel out, but I managed to request my iced tea. Neither Daniel nor Ray ordered any food, so I was glad I hadn't either.

"How's business?" Daniel asked when the waitress left to grab our drinks. "Must be slow because you're on time."

"Little rough," said Ray. He had a rather raspy voice like Kyle, only about forty years older. "Seems like fewer and fewer bands want to shell out for a top-of-the-line recording studio anymore, even one with kick-ass acoustics like ours. More people would rather just record in someone's garage and mix it up on their laptop. But, hey, we still have our connections in the industry, which no software program can buy you. And we've got our expertise."

"And your proprietary technologies," said Daniel.

"Oh, yeah," agreed Ray, "those proprietary technologies that we pay your ass to protect."

"Bet it's worth every penny," interjected the waitress, sliding Daniel his pilsner and winking at him. Turning my head to look out the window at Lake Washington, I indulged myself in an eye roll. Really, didn't it get old for him?

To my embarrassment, Ray apparently noticed my theatrics and grinned at me. "So, Cass," he began. "Dan tells me you have a business proposition for me."

It would have been nice for Daniel to clue me in on this, but oh well. In my nervousness I dumped the whole sugar packet into my tea and had to fish out the paper. "Umm, yes, sort of. That is, Daniel tells me you got your start at your studio cleaning their toilets, so I thought you might have a heart for another kid who loves music and is looking to find some work—any work, I think."

"How old is this kid?"

"Twenty—so maybe not such a *kid* kid," I amended. "I'd better begin at the beginning, since I don't know what Daniel's told you—" (this, with a reproachful look at said Daniel).

Starting with Camden School, I explained who they were, how the mentorship program worked, my own relationship with Nadina, and finally her relationship to Mike. "Mike got busted before Christmas for marijuana possession and had to spend a week in jail, but in the weeks since, he's sworn to go straight. He's doing everything he's supposed to be doing, and now he just needs to find a little work to repay his debt to society. Apparently, what Mike loves best in the world is music. He spent most of his time trolling all the parties and clubs in Seattle, listening to different local bands. Nadina swears he's got a gift for it. It could be the best or the worst decision you ever make, Ray, but if you need a toilet cleaner and general grunt at the studio, I think Mike would be up for it."

It took me some time to get through my entire, impromptu spiel, with Daniel not opening his mouth once, and both of them had made significant headway with their beverages by the time I finished up. As James had pointed out, I couldn't in all honesty give Mike anything approaching a ringing endorsement, but I wanted Ray to be able to decide with all the facts before him.

Taking off his crazy glasses and laying them on the bar table, Ray rubbed his forehead thoughtfully. "Dan, you picked your man, didn't you?" When I looked puzzled, he went on to explain. "Martin knows that I did some pretty stupid things when I was younger. Done some time for drug possession myself." Looking out absently at the water, he seemed to settle something with himself and, after a minute, replaced his glasses. "Fine. Hell. What the hell. Kid'll probably burn the place down and steal all the technology I've been paying through the nose to protect. Have him call me. We can give him fifteen hours a week cleaning toilets and being the basic studio slave—minimum wage. One month probation. Take it or leave it." Ray threw his business card on the table and downed the last sip of his seven-and-seven.

Picking up his card, I held it as if it were a winning lottery ticket. "Thank you, Ray!" I breathed. "I'm sure you'll be sorry you did this, but thank you so much for being willing. I hope and hope Mike doesn't screw this up—"

Ray waved me off, laughing. "Whoa, Cass. You're gonna make me change my mind, after that great sales job you did. Better just leave it at thank you."

"Join us for lunch, Ray?" Daniel asked, looking rather smug.

"Not today, man. Got a paying customer coming in this afternoon. Gotta support my new charity work." Ray stood up, pulling on his leather jacket, and I popped up to shake his hand gratefully. He and Daniel slapped each other on the back, and as Ray left, he stopped to mutter something in Daniel's ear. Daniel only nodded, and Ray was gone.

"What did he say?" I asked curiously.

"He liked you, Cass. You did a good job today," he answered. I suspected he wasn't telling me all but got distracted when he added, "Do you have time for lunch, or do I need to get you back?"

I glanced at my watch. "I don't need to be anywhere until I meet Nadina at 2:45, but do you want to go somewhere else? Lunch here might be a little pricey for me."

"My treat," he said easily, throwing a bill down on the table. "Let's move to that booth over there."

"No way," I hissed, trotting after him. "You just did me the hugest favor. We should go dutch."

Daniel slid into the booth, signaling the waiter, who hastened over with menus. "Since I've known you, you've cooked me at least a hundred meals—I think I can handle this one."

"You pay me for those meals," I reminded him, "by reducing my rent, so we'll split this."

"Would it really be so difficult for you, Cass, just for once to say, 'Yes, Daniel' and leave it at that? I did just do you the hugest favor, as you pointed out, so the least you could do is not exasperate me."

Chastened, I nodded, though his logic sat ill with me. Maybe he decided to become a lawyer after he took some high school vo-ed test and scored high on Manipulating Others.

Having won his point, Daniel seemed satisfied and slipped into the easygoing, brotherly mode I remembered from the New Year's Eve party, telling me anecdotes about Ray's studio and some of the famous bands that recorded there in the past twenty-five years. He wanted to know more about Mike and Nadina, too, and I ended up filling him in on most of what had gone on up to that point, including Mike stealing from Nadina at the skating rink and how Mark Henneman and I engineered her visit to Sylvia in Cleveland.

The time seemed to fly by, and I was just pushing away my empty soup bowl, from which I swabbed up every last drop of butternut squash bisque with the bread, when I caught sight of the waiter leading a couple toward our area of the restaurant, and my mouth fell open in horror. One tall, rangy man with salt-and-pepper hair and a swing in his walk, and one petite, black-haired woman with an oversized handbag. "Oh, no!" Startled by my change in expression, Daniel threw a glance over his shoulder. When he turned back, I was scrunched low, trying to keep out of the couple's line of sight.

"Who the hell are they?" he demanded in a low voice.

Too late. "Cass? Is it you, Cass?" came Raquel's amazed voice. "Max, look—Cass is here!"

How could this be happening to me? I had the worst luck imaginable. Of all places and times, to run into my former in-laws when I was alone at a restaurant with Daniel! Sure enough, when the Ewans stopped in front of our table, Raquel blinked at him in astonishment. Even mild-mannered Max straightened his glasses and took a long gander. I hadn't known Raquel for going on fourteen years without getting pretty skilled in reading her expressions. This time, her face plainly said: "Ah ha! So she's gone from my son to a man like this? Probably Cass is glad Troy died when he did, so he wouldn't get in her way." Absolutely mortifying. My face was glowing like a sunset.

"Raquel, Max," I said in a wobbly voice that I tried to make sound perky. "Umm, Daniel, this is Raquel and Max Ewan, my mother-and father-in-law. That is, Troy's parents. And Raquel and Max, this is—this is Daniel Martin. He's my—my—my landlord." No sooner were the words out of my mouth than I realized how ridiculous they sounded. Which was sketchier—for me to be having lunch with some overly-handsome strange man, or for me to be having lunch with my landlord? "This is a business lunch," I added lamely.

"Cass apparently has issues with her wiring," said Daniel with a straight face. There was another note in his voice I couldn't identify, but I was too stressed out to worry about it. "How nice to meet you," he continued. "Won't you join us?"

Had he not been wearing his gazillion dollar Ferragamo shoes, I would have smashed his foot under the table. "Oh!" I shrilled, instead. "That would have been so fun, except that we've already finished eating and I need to get going. I was just going to run to the ladies' room before I left." Scooching along the bench, I stood up and gave them each a hug and a little shove to move them along after their waiter.

I managed to herd Max into their booth, but Raquel said, "I need to visit the ladies' room, too. I'll go with you, Cass." Sigh. Here goes.

No sooner was the door of the restroom shut behind us than Raquel said innocently, "My, what a handsome landlord you have. If I had one like that, I'd always be inventing repairs and urgent projects."

"Yes, well, he is certainly very handsome, but there's none of that going on. He's my best friend Joanie's brother, and he owns the house we all live in, remember? Except he lives off in the mother-in-law in the backyard, so it's not even like he lives with us." Definitely rambling now, and rambling with a defensive note. Not good.

"Oh, my dear," Raquel soothed, "you know we wish you all the best. And it would be absolutely natural for you to start dating again, but really—don't you think he looks a little…not your type? He looks like he must be quite the ladies' man."

"Yes," I agreed through gritted teeth. "Daniel is quite the ladies' man, which is only one of the million reasons why I would never date him, and why lunch today is not a date." She raised a skeptical eyebrow, and I knew the only way I could convince her would be to show my hand, something I'd had no intention of doing for months, if I could help it. "Actually, Raquel, I am seeing someone. Not Daniel. Just a nice guy from church."

Her dark eyes got very round, and I had a flitting memory of Min, the time I caught her stuffing the toilet bowl full of every roll of toilet paper she could find in the vanity. Min had her grandmother's eyes. "Oh, I see," Raquel murmured, the wind gone out of her. "Of course, Cass. It's been over a year and a half."

I felt the ominous tightening in my throat. "Don't say that, Raquel! I know what you're thinking—how could I possibly forget them so soon, but I haven't forgotten them! Not a day goes by—you don't think in a heartbeat I wouldn't rather have Troy and Min back?" I could feel heat behind my eyes, and her own were looking wet. Crap. Crap crap crap. "But they're not coming back," I pointed out needlessly. "I'm not trying to forget them—I'm just trying to get on with my life, what's left of it."

"Of course, of course," she repeated, her voice breaking. The next thing I knew, we were clinging to each other, crying all over the stinking place. At least the Café was upscale; they had complimentary Kleenex. Having gotten each other worked up, who knows how long we would have gone on, if another woman hadn't mercifully come in and interrupted our sobfest. Breaking apart, we laughed ruefully.

I splashed water on my face and dabbed it with a paper towel. "I've got to go, Raquel. Let's have lunch another time, okay? Love you guys." Not trusting her voice yet, she nodded and gave me a powerful squeeze before disappearing into one of the stalls.

· · ·

Daniel was waiting at the entrance. Feeling flustered and wishing I could just take the bus home, I blew past him out the door. How far would it be to walk? Two, three miles? I'd probably be late for meeting Nadina, in that case. Besides, in these crazy shoes of Joanie's I'd almost certainly twist my ankle and have to crawl home on my hands and knees. I rubbed my temples, feeling the post-crying headache building.

"Cass?"

I'm sure he thought I was behaving like a maniac and couldn't wait to get rid of me. Forcing myself to stop, I turned around slowly. "Sorry, Daniel. You must need to get back to the office. Do you still have time to drop me off? If not, I think the 231 goes down Lake Washington Boulevard."

"Get in the car."

Both relieved and reluctant, I obeyed. After buckling up, I waited for him to start the engine, but to my surprise, he put his key in the ignition and then just sat there. Peeking at him uncertainly, I saw he was looking straight out the windshield at the wall of the parking garage. "Are you okay?" I asked, finally.

"Am *I* okay?" he repeated in a tight voice. "Cass, what the hell was that about?"

What on God's green earth did he have to be angry about? I was the one who just got done crying her guts out in the ladies' room. "You mean me abandoning you at the table?" I demanded. "I had to go be cornered in the restroom by Raquel so we could have a good cry over our dead loved ones. Sorry if that bothered you."

He took a deep breath, as if praying for patience. "That's not what I meant," he said. "That must have been a lousy ten minutes."

"Then what did you mean?"

"I was asking you why you freaked out in the first place. Freaked out and introduced me as your damned 'landlord,' for God's sake."

"Oh!" I breathed, suddenly fighting an urge to giggle. Probably residual hysteria. "That was idiotic of me. I'm sorry. But I was afraid Max and Raquel would think we were there on a date, which is what Raquel ended up thinking anyhow, because I was so weird about it."

He was silent a moment, while I fiddled nervously with the strap of Joanie's shoe. "What would you have called James, if it had been James sitting there with you?"

Bewildered, I floundered around. "Good grief, I don't know. My co-worker, maybe, or church friend or something. I would have demoted him too, if that's what you're irritated about. I knew Raquel would get upset if I were dating already—especially if she thought I were dating you!"

"Why especially me?" He was still staring straight ahead, and it was starting to give me the willies.

"Because—because you're you!" I answered inanely. "You're not the kind of guy a good, ordinary girl like me goes out with. You hardly said one word to her, and Raquel already had you pegged for a ladies' man," I said, unable finally to repress the giggle.

"Why am I not the type a girl like you would go out with?" he pressed. This was reminding me of our strange, middle-of-the-night conversation that time after I banged my head. He was in the same federal prosecutor mode, putting me on the defensive.

The straight answer was that, after my misadventure with Clive at Oxford, I no longer had interest in being with someone who didn't share any of my foundational beliefs. When a believer and a non-believer got together, it was always the believer who gave ground. Added to his atheism, Daniel really left Clive in the dust when it came to being out of the question. All the women he slept with! My high school health teacher once said that, when you slept with someone, you effectively slept with everyone that person had ever slept with. Meaning, everyone who slept with Daniel was hooking up with most of North America. Ick.

Of course, none of this could be said to Daniel. I tried to give it a positive spin, as if his ego ever needed bolstering: "You're just way too handsome for me. You're out of my league." No need to go into Troy's theory of the Tiers.

"And that's all?" He brushed some lint off his pants. "Just my looks. If I were stricken with smallpox and disfigured, you'd be all over me?" Obviously he wasn't buying it.

"That's not how it works, Daniel," I objected. "You are who you are because you have been beautiful all your life. People have treated you differently your whole life long because of how you look. Getting smallpox at this late date would be a rude shock for you—you might have some trouble getting dates—but you've already become who you are." Hmm... not so good. I seemed to be implying that his character was the obstacle, and that it was beyond redemption. I resorted to whining. "Why are you doing this to me? I already apologized for calling you my landlord. Who cares what kind of guys girls like me date? You just stick to your kind—"

"My kind being..." he interrupted swiftly.

I exhaled sharply in aggravation. "Your kind being... beautiful and—and easygoing. Are you going to take me home or not?"

Without another word, he started the engine and backed out. It was a silent drive home, with both of us irritated with the other, though it seemed to me I had cause to be upset and he was just being ornery. When he pulled up at the Palace, I was already opening the door to get away, but no sooner was I out of the car than I turned and leaned in to look at him. "Daniel—thank you for lunch anyhow. And thank you so, so much for introducing me to Ray and making this opportunity for Mike. I am grateful, despite calling you my landlord and getting in another argument with you. You're a good guy—I'm glad I know you, George Bailey. Okay?"

His expression softened, even in profile. "'How far that little candle throws his beams! So shines a good deed in a naughty world.'" If he was quoting Shakespeare, he couldn't be too upset. Sure enough, throwing a wave at me, he half-smiled and called as he pulled away, "Have a good time telling Nadina."

CHAPTER 32:

Bumps in the Road

"What would you say to a little road trip?"

I had dropped in at Free Universe to get Riley's comments and suggestions—the truffle-hunting pigs material was finally going in a direction he liked—and to record a few enthusiastic "Oinkrekas!" for Murray to play with. When I emerged from Lockdown, James came skidding into the hallway on his Aeron chair and beckoned. Although he didn't mix business with pleasure, most of the office was on to us by now. Nadina wasn't the only one to notice us looking at each other a certain way.

"Road trip where?" I asked, squishing into his cube. Like Riley's, James' cube was wall-to-wall paraphernalia, but unlike Riley's, James' tended more toward freebies accumulated from several years' worth of game expos: mousepads, laser pointers, flash drives in a rainbow of colors, game controllers, posters, mugs, even a plastic Viking helmet and *Lord of the Rings* knockoff sword. Sweeping game-packaging mock-ups off the work surface to clear me a seat, James beamed at me.

"Richland. It's my grandparents' 50th anniversary Presidents' Day

Weekend, and I thought we could make a Valentine's getaway of it. You get to meet the whole family; they get to meet you. We could do a little wine-tasting to unwind afterward."

Wine-tasting indeed. I might need to suck it directly out of the barrel at that point. Choosing my words carefully, I said, "Do you think it's really appropriate for me to meet your family already?" Or ever?

James looked at me measuringly. "Well, we've been going out almost three months and known each other over five. Why not?"

"Well, why?" I countered. "Why don't you just go? I don't think you ought to subject girlfriends to family gatherings unless you've been going out at least six months."

James shot a quick glance out of his cube in both directions to see if the coast was clear before he stood up and pulled me to him. "I can see you're going to be difficult about this," he murmured. "I have no idea what your problem is. Trying to plan a romantic weekend here—"

"Ha!" I scoffed in an undertone. "It's not the least bit romantic to be trotted out for all the relatives, especially when I know all the relatives want you to be with cutesy Jen. No way. Go wine-taste by yourself. I'm fine with a card for Valentine's Day."

"Come on, Cass," he coaxed, dropping little kisses along my jaw up to my ear.

I could feel my resistance wavering, but I protested feebly, "Not only do I think it's inappropriate, but I'll be out of town the weekend after to go see Perry's musical."

"Then you really have to because it's too much time apart," he said softly, pressing his mouth to mine.

"Oinkreka! Yuck! So unprofessional!" came Riley's voice, followed by a wad of paper bouncing off James' head. We looked up to see Riley's own pony-tailed head and t-shirted torso over the cube walls, his hands planted squarely on his plump hips and an expression of fascinated distaste on his face.

"What the hell are you standing on, Riley?" James demanded, annoyed. "If you're on your flipping work surface, you're going to bust it off, and we're not paying for another one." On cue, we heard an ominous cracking sound, and Riley abruptly disappeared, to reappear seconds later standing outside James' cube.

"Just how am I supposed to get anything done, when I have to listen to you two lovebirds cooing at each other?" Riley complained. "I'm telling you, Kittredge, the working conditions are really slipping here. I knew we shouldn't hire any women. I let you get away with Jeri because she's on the fence, gender-wise, but—"

To cut off James' irked retort, I said, "You're right, Riley. I don't blame you. James and I can continue this conversation later and somewhere else."

"Like the Motel 6," said Riley, looking satisfied and ambling away.

• • •

Two weeks later, James and I were on the road, headed for the Tri-Cities.

Joanie and Phyl, the only two I told about it, had their concerns. "Cass, he has got to be thinking marriage," said Joanie. "What's your plan?"

"I don't know if he thinks that way," I objected. "He's only 27, after all."

"Are you kidding me?" she fired back. "He's 27, and he's not getting any sex till he gets married, so I'm thinking he's thinking marriage."

"I'm with Joanie," said Phyl.

Having expected Phyl to be more low-key, I went on the offensive. "What about Wayne, then, Phyl? He's pushing 30 and not getting any sex."

"That's why he asks me to marry him every couple weeks," she replied imperturbably. "Don't freak out, Cass. We just think you may want to be prepared."

"Prepared for what? You don't think he's going to propose this weekend, do you?" They exchanged glances which answered my question. Sitting down on the couch with a thump, I thought aloud. "We've only known each other a few months and we've been dating less than that, and Troy's only been dead for twenty months—he can't possibly ask me. He knows I'd say no."

"Does he?" said Phyl.

"Would you?" said Joanie.

I didn't know.

· · ·

"You're quiet," said James, taking my hand. We'd made it over the Pass easily and were already past Vantage, following the Columbia River through Mattawa and Desert Aire. The landscape was gray-brown in winter and the sky so wide on this side of the mountains—no hills and evergreens boxing you in, just the bluffs and the flat, high desert stretching away.

"We're getting there awfully fast," I answered. "You're sure this is okay with your parents?"

He looked amused and gave my hand a squeeze but didn't answer. No need. We'd already talked it to death in the last few weeks. Instead he changed the subject. "What's the latest with Mike? Has he been showing up for work?"

A good topic, and I felt myself untense. "Yes! Nadina says he can't stop talking about it. She claims he goes early, even, and hasn't complained once about bathroom duty or taking people's coffee and sandwich orders. And it's kind of like Cinderella—if Mike gets done with whatever chores they've come up with, they let him sit in the booth with them and watch them work. I'm so thrilled, James. So thrilled he hasn't shown up stoned or broken anything or stolen from the petty cash. And Nadina said Mike already knew some of the bands coming in. I don't know if that was a good thing or not, since the last time they saw Mike he was probably a mess."

"Maybe they don't recognize him all straightened up, then," James suggested reassuringly.

I gave him a skeptical look. "Little, pale, white-haired Mike? I guess if they were stoned too, then maybe not. Anyhow, so far so good. I'm so grateful to Daniel and Ray for giving him this chance. Nadina says they're going to pay Mike's dad some rent for the first time next month—a piddly amount but symbolic—and they're going to split it!"

"That's great, Cass. And how's our girl Nadina lately? Did you get her to agree to go to the doctor?"

My shoulders slumped. "Not yet. I'm working on it. She's still tired all the time and has lost a lot of weight because she thinks things smell bad. I'm worried she has something hideous like Chronic Fatigue Syndrome or Lyme disease or lupus or something. It's been over a month now. I may just have to kidnap her and take her to a clinic, so she can stick out her tongue and let the doctor have a look."

"I could ask Melissa's husband Pete this weekend," James pointed out. "He's doing his residency, and he might recognize general symptoms."

This reminded me of the unpleasantness ahead, and I sank back, silent, for the rest of the drive.

The sun set as we passed the turnoff for Prosser, and it was dark as we entered Richland. Too soon we were crossing George Washington Way and pulling up in front of his parents' late '60s split-level. The curtains twitched as James turned off the engine, and I wrapped my arms around myself as we darted through the chilly air to go inside.

Although the living room was crowded with people, as soon as our heads appeared at the top of the stairs, silence fell. Tableau of a lesser-known work: the Prodigal Son returns, bringing in tow his favorite prostitute. Then, "James!" shouted several female voices at once, and he was surrounded on all sides to be hugged, including by a couple little girls I took to be his nieces.

When he broke free, laughing, he pulled me up the last step, saying, "Everyone, this is Cass. Cass, this is my mother Peggy, my sister Melissa, my sister Amy, my best nieces Katie and Maddie—" they bounced in delight, staring at me with shy curiosity. The men were also there: James' father Hugh, his brothers-in-law Pete and Cody, his little nephew Buck. Buck was little sister Amy's first child, a boy almost exactly Min's age when she died. James greeted him by tossing him in the air, causing him to squeal with glee.

Dinner was laid out buffet-style in the kitchen for everyone to graze on, and I timidly presented Peggy with the box of Boehm's Chocolates I'd brought. She was a short, sturdy woman in her early 50s with curling, cropped brown hair and plenty of jewelry on. Peggy eyed the box. "Ah, Boehm's. Yeah, we can get them out at the Center," but she took the lid off and found space for it on the counter. "James tells me he met you through that kid he's helping."

I gave her the two-minute version, which she seemed to have heard before, and then she said, "So you're a widow?" There followed the two-minute version of that story. I had to walk a fine line between properly-bereaved and putting-it-all-behind-me, but Peggy didn't seem satisfied. "Not even two years, and you're already dating, huh?" Sigh.

After a moment, she shrugged. "James has always had a way with the girls," she said, shaking her head in a you-just-can't-help-it manner. This didn't exactly tally with what James himself had said about his high school years, but I suppose I had to make allowances for a mother's fondness.

And a sister's. When I made some overtures of friendship to little Buck, I found Amy watching. She looked the most like James, more than the taller and blonde Melissa, but Amy's gray eyes were narrower than her brother's and lacked his humor. "I had a little girl who was Buck's age," I said by way of explanation.

She nodded. "That's terrible. I'm sorry about that. I can't imagine what I'd do if that happened to me. Probably kill myself." Amy had a loud, flat way of speaking. An awkward silence followed this, and I wondered if my failure to slit my wrists was a strike against me. This was going to be a long weekend. "You're probably anxious to get married again and have more babies," Amy added, louder than before.

Blushing, I shook my head. "Oh, no. I'm not in a hurry to do either."

"James said you're older than he is."

"Yes," I conceded, "but I've got the rest of my life to get married again, and I don't think I want any more babies."

"No more babies!" echoed Amy. "If I were you, I would want to have more babies as fast as I could to help me get over it." Would that be before or after she caved to suicidal despair? Apparently she'd forgotten her dramatic declaration of a minute ago, and I certainly wasn't going to remind her of it. Amy shook her head resignedly in a fair imitation of her mother Peggy. "'No more babies!' You better let James know about that because he's always wanted lots of kids."

James either heard his name or caught the fleeting expression on my face because he broke off his conversation with Cody and came to put an arm around me. "Hungry? Let's get some food."

I was too old to beg him not to abandon me, but he stayed fairly close the rest of the evening. After dinner, when games were suggested and Melissa asked if I wanted to play Scrabble, James said, "You better not play, Cass, if you want to make a good impression. Cass cleans up at Scrabble," he added to the room in general. I joined the Yahtzee table instead, with Pete and Hugh and Pete's older daughter Katie. Pete and Hugh were content to let the womenfolk determine my worthiness or lack thereof, so they made for pleasant partners. As for Katie, she was sweet as can be. "You're pretty," she told me. "I like you." That makes one of you, I thought with a sigh.

It was a relief to go to bed and shut the downstairs family room door on the whole Kittredge and caboodle of them.

A text from Joanie awaited me: "Well?" Lying on the lumpy pull-out couch, I keyed in the dark: "Going over like lead balloon."

. . .

Things both improved and deteriorated the following day. Improved because everyone was so busy preparing for the anniversary celebration that no one had time to bother their heads with me; and deteriorated because cutesy Jen showed up at the party. All day long I tried to lay low, running errands with James, tying balloons, arranging centerpieces. The Kittredges reserved a ballroom at the hotel on the riverfront, so at one point I took Katie and Maddie to the adjacent park to play. It was only in the 50s, but the girls got us warmed up quickly, running around in their party dresses, chasing each other through the play structure, and begging for me to push them on the swings or give them a running start on the zip line. We were all three glowing and rather disheveled when we walked back to the hotel, only to find that the photographer and grandparents had arrived, and it was time for pictures.

"No way. Absolutely not," I declared when James tried to pull me into the family group picture. "That's all you need is some picture hanging on everyone's wall for the next fifty years and people pointing at me and asking, 'Who the heck is that?'"

"Who says you won't be around to tell them?" he replied steadily.

Good grief! Joanie and Phyl were right—James had marriage on his mind. My mouth popped open in surprise, and he managed to drag me within two steps of Melissa and Pete before I roused myself and dug in my heels. "No," I hissed through gritted teeth. "Stop it. You're embarrassing me. No! I'm not family." At least mom Peggy looked like she agreed with me.

As for Jen's arrival a half hour later, had it not been clear from Amy running over and greeting her with a hug and scream and James suddenly tensing up, I think I could still have picked her out. She had high school rodeo queen written all over her—4-H crossed with Ticktockers—all she needed was an embroidered shirt and a float.

"She's cute," I couldn't resist whispering to James. "I almost want to kiss her myself."

"Oh," Jen breathed, when James introduced her to me. "It's nice to meet you. James spoke so much of you at Christmas." Not a trace of rancor in her voice or wide blue eyes. Shouldn't I have guessed that James would never be attracted to any malicious hellcat? Sadly, I was probably the furthest he had ventured in that direction. Apart from me, he did seem to prefer what Nadina scathingly called "baby bunny."

So not only was Jen cute, she was kind and young and uncomplicated. If I were the Kittredges, I would have pulled for her too. These thoughts and other not-very-comforting ones ran through my mind as I sat at one of the tables, an innocuous expression pinned on my face, through the slideshow and celebratory toasts and inside jokes. I did enjoy watching James, although it contributed to my squirrely feeling that our relationship couldn't possibly work. He played with his nieces and nephew, made affectionate conversation with his relatives, kept bringing me drinks and food and holding my hand when he sat with me. Where did I belong? If this had been Troy's grandparents celebrating, I would have been like Amy—central, sure of my role, running after Min like she did Buck. It had been my paranoia the night before that made me think Peggy and Amy didn't like me. They didn't like me or dislike me; they were wary of me.

Jen ended up putting it best. She was sitting next to me shortly before the party ended, stirring as much milk and sugar into her coffee as I had. "You're probably used to more sophisticated kinds of parties, aren't you?" was her unexpected comment.

"Me?"

"James said your parents were professors, and you went to a fancy college in California, and you have a brother who lived in Hollywood, and you've lived in England. And he says you're a writer."

I frowned. "I guess all that is technically true, but it's not really that glamorous. Now I'm just kind of an underemployed housekeeper." And I wished James would keep his mouth shut. No wonder everyone kept looking at me like I was a newly-discovered species of rodent. "I'm not a big deal at all."

Jen smiled a little ruefully. "Don't try telling James that, Cass. I don't think you could ever convince him."

· · ·

On the way back home Sunday, we stopped for dinner in Ellensburg. It was windy there, as always, and in the dash from the car to the diner, my hood blew off and I slipped on a patch of ice, crashing into him and sending us to the pavement. "How much did you drink at the winery today, Cass?" he teased, brushing me off. "You've been punchy the whole drive back."

"I think I'm just so relieved to be done with it," I said, raising my voice over the wind.

He paused. "Or you could be just getting started with it." When I looked at him blankly, not sure I heard him right, he pulled me into the lee of the diner. "This totally sucks—it's not how I pictured this happening. But you know me—I never can wait for the right moment if I have an idea in my head. I think my family liked you, Cass. Do you think you could stand to have us all around, the rest of your life? I mean, what would you think of getting married one day?"

I exhaled in disbelief: were we seriously going to have this conversation outside a diner in Ellensburg, standing next to the *Homes and Apartments – Central Washington* dispenser? So much for making fun of Wayne's proposal at the hot dog stand. "I think your family would need more time to get used to the idea, and I think it's too soon to talk about it," I answered slowly.

"That's not a no."

"It's not a no," I agreed, "but it's not a yes either. I'm saying it's too soon to talk about it."

Taking a deep breath, James nodded after a moment. "But it must mean you're leaning toward yes—otherwise you'd flat out tell me no."

"I can't answer that. I can hardly believe I'm not saying no, flat out. I don't know. But James—I have to tell you—maybe Amy already told you because we talked about it Friday night—but I'm not feeling very open to the idea of having any more children."

This was an unexpected blow—I could tell from his face. Should've given Amy more credit for discretion, apparently. Was it a dealbreaker? The muscles in his jaw worked, as he tried to get his emotions under control. "How dead set are you," James said finally, "against children? Do you mean you just can't picture it now because it's too painful, or that you're positive you never want children again?"

"I don't know," I said again. "I know it's too painful to think about now, and I can't make any promises for the future. I'm sorry." Reaching for his hand, I held it between my ice-cold ones. "You can dump me now, if you want. I would understand."

Instead he grabbed me by the shoulders and hugged me to him, and I felt a fierce kiss to the top of my head. "You can't get rid of me that easily, my girl. I can wait a little longer. I knew it was too soon. I could've at least waited to ask you when your stomach was full— improve my odds." Releasing me with a final shake, he said casually, "So help me out here: you won't marry me—at least not yet—and you won't have my children, so why exactly are you going out with me?"

I looked at him helplessly. "James…"

"Tell me it's because you're in love with me—at least a little bit— like I'm in love with you."

What a mess I was. No wonder his family half-wished James would run away screaming into the arms of straightforward Jen. Did I love him a little? Of course. I wouldn't be here, otherwise. But would it do more harm than good to say so? I didn't think I could say it, at any rate. Finally, in a voice so low he had to lean forward to hear me, I murmured, "What's not to love?"

He smiled. It would do for now.

Taking his hand again, I let him lead me into the diner, but this roller coaster wasn't over yet.

"All this talk reminds me," James began again, "I didn't want to tell you this earlier because you seemed so much more relaxed today, but now that you're good and stressed—I mentioned Nadina's symptoms to Pete. He says he'd lay odds a thousand to one that she hasn't got any newfangled disease like chronic fatigue or lupus. He bets she just has the age-old one: she's going to have a baby."

CHAPTER 33:

Oregon Trail

Sometimes saying something out loud makes it real.

I went to Bartell's on Monday to pick up a pregnancy test for Nadina, but it felt like a waste of money. Don't tell me how I knew—I just knew Pete guessed right, and I was an idiot not to think of it. Did Nadina know? She'd been around the block before, after all, though I never asked her how far along she'd gotten in the pregnancy she ended. If she knew, had she told Mike? Had she told the school?

With Camden School on Mid-Winter Break, I wouldn't be seeing her tomorrow or even all week unless I could get a hold of her, and I certainly was not going to contact Mark Henneman without talking to her first. What could I do but text her a couple times, playing dumb and saying that I'd love to get together?

As the week passed with no word from her, I only grew more convinced. Nadina only fell dead silent when there was something she wasn't ready to deal with. By Thursday I even resorted to roundabout spying on Mike, sending Ray Snow a how's-it-going-with-the-studio-slave message. His everything's-fine response didn't comfort

me—it only meant she hadn't even told Mike yet. She wouldn't…
take steps…on her own, would she? Especially if Mike would be all
in favor. Or maybe the prospect didn't upset Mike—it wasn't like he
was super-emotive. Maybe he could abort his second child in the
morning and show up to scrub toilets in the afternoon without missing a beat. As long as I didn't know the outcome, I could pray, and I
did, all week long.

But I would be lying if I said that Nadina's possible pregnancy
was the only idea which had become real to me. Or even if I said it
occupied 90% of my emotional energy that week. Ever since James
brought up marriage and I instantly squashed the notion, I found
myself dwelling on it, allowing myself to entertain the possibility
openly for the first time. Was there any point in thinking of it now,
since I told James I didn't want children, and he clearly found that a
showstopper? And if he decided he would marry me anyhow, how
could I allow him to give up so much? No, if I truly didn't want children and he did, the right thing to do would be to break up with him.
And yet, maybe he was right, and in a year or two I might be able to
think about a baby again.

After much more circular, inconclusive dithering, I threw up my
hands mentally: I didn't have to decide right now. One emotional crisis at a time. Let me deal with Nadina first. If she would ever call me.

I hadn't been able to conceal James' proposal from Joanie and
Phyl, of course, since they practically tackled me upon my return.
True to form, Joanie thought I should accept him and trust that the
child thing would work itself out: "Half the couples who get married
turn out to be infertile anyway!" she exaggerated. "Getting married
doesn't automatically mean you have kids." And Phyl, just as true to
form, thought I absolutely shouldn't ask it of James but didn't want
me to break up either. No help at all.

For the time being, I was keeping my Nadina fears to myself. No need to get Joanie and Phyl going on that one, too, because maybe, just maybe, I still could be wrong.

What little emotional energy remained was devoted to the upcoming trip to Portland. As promised, Perry sent complimentary tickets to the opening weekend of *Waiters: the Musical*, and the girls and I were eager to see if it lived down to our expectations. The fourth ticket was unexpected—did Perry really think Daniel would be the least bit interested? And truth be told, having Daniel along would just put a damper on the car conversation and make hotel logistics more complicated.

"Just ask him," Joanie suggested, "and phrase it negatively, like, 'Daniel, Perry sent you a ticket to *Waiters*, but you probably have plans that weekend,' and then we can take Phyl's sister or someone. Besides, he's always gone at his mystery activity Saturday mornings, so maybe he won't want to miss whatever that is."

"Why can't you ask him?" I demanded.

"Because it's your brother and your brother's musical," Joanie replied. "Open and shut case. Just ask Daniel as he's on his way out the door. It'll take two seconds."

• • •

"Daniel, Perry sent you a ticket to *Waiters*, but you probably have plans that weekend," I spluttered one morning, when he seemed in a particular rush to fill his commuter mug and head out.

Glancing at his watch, Daniel said, "Yes, I know. I'm planning on going."

"You do? You are?" I asked, chasing him out to his car. "Wouldn't you miss whatever it is you do on Saturday mornings?"

He stopped for a second, his eyes raking from my fleece top to my ripped sweat pants, and then he grinned as he opened the car door. "I can miss whatever it is I do on Saturday mornings this once. Musical treat aside, I'm not passing up a chance to spend the weekend with my best girls."

Which is how it came to pass that, on Friday evening, we were all in Joanie's car, headed down I-5. The conversation was as stilted as you might imagine, since, with him along, most topics became off-limits. I don't know why—when I was alone with him I didn't feel reticent about any subject except James—but with Phyl and Joanie in the car I didn't feel I could approach him on the same level. Wouldn't they think it odd that he and I had something of a friendship by now? I had begun to believe that, for whatever incomprehensible reasons, he actually took an interest in my life.

Not that I could have conversed with him very easily on that drive anyhow, crunched as I was behind him in the backseat. I would have liked to ask him how his week had gone because he'd been terribly busy at work, gone long hours and on his laptop constantly when at home. It didn't surprise me when, somewhere past Castle Rock, his head drooped to the side, and he fell asleep.

"Thank God!" said Joanie, changing the radio station. "I can't imagine why he wanted to come."

"Did you call your mother and tell her we were going to be in Portland?" Phyl asked.

"Hell, no! It's bad enough we have Daniel, without Mom dropping her little snide comments. Only Cass and I are allowed to make fun of Perry and his musical."

"He got along with her pretty well at Thanksgiving and Christmas," Phyl pointed out. "What if he sent her a ticket, and we run into her at the show, and you didn't even call to say you'd be in town?"

Joanie gasped, but I waved at her. "On it, on it. I'll text Perry right now and check," I reassured her. "If he did, we can just call her right afterward and say—surprise!—we're coming down. He may not get back to us until really late, though, since this is Opening Night."

"Yeah," agreed Joanie. "It'll take time to greet all five people in the audience, especially if they're the same five friends and relatives who showed up to watch the dress rehearsal."

"Even if we're the only ones in the audience, it's nice to get away," said Phyl. "Wayne hasn't asked me to marry him for two weeks, so he's about due."

Joanie groaned. "If you're gonna say no to him every two weeks, why don't you just break it off? Or why doesn't he just break it off?"

"He asks me half as a joke now," Phyl laughed, "and I think he can tell I get closer each time to saying yes." We were agog, off course, and she continued, "You were right, Cass. He really has grown on me. After Jason, I'm not used to someone who's so kind and thoughtful, and for a long time I think I saw it as weakness. Isn't that sad?"

"We'll have to take his wonderfulness on faith," said Joanie dryly. "I still have a hard time getting twenty words out of him when he's over, but if you say he's solid, he's solid."

"That's because you intimidate most guys, Joanie," I explained. "Wayne talks to me just fine."

She pouted. "Don't tell me I'm intimidating! I just can't stand it when guys look timid around me—it makes me want to be mean to them. I think you're way worse. You look all sweet on the outside, but you're like the kitty who plays with her food before she eats it."

"What?" I shrieked. Daniel stirred, and I lowered my voice. "What are you talking about?"

"Totally," Joanie insisted. "Take James as a case in point. He wants to marry you, and you're afraid to get married again, but you want to string him along, just to torture him a little bit because it's fun to have a guy around."

"That's not true!" I hissed. "I told him he could break up with me and not wait around. No, no listen to me," I urged, when she made a skeptical sound, "and if I didn't honestly think I could ever marry him, I would have told him so straight out. I just said it was too soon for me to think about. And then, of course, there's the whole kid thing—"

"Uh huh," Joanie pounced, warming to her theme. "That right there. You know very well that someday down the line you're going to be okay with the idea of having kids again. Not today, no, but someday. So what if you're all pissed at God right now—each day you're getting less pissed, so why don't you just admit it? You're throwing up an obstacle and playing with that guy."

Folding my arms over my chest defensively, I stared out the darkened window in a huff. I could just make out the nuclear cooling tower in Kalama glowing faintly in the moonlight. Some minutes passed, but when Phyl tried peaceably to introduce a new topic, I cut across her. "You may be right, Joanie—I might be throwing up an obstacle that will go away eventually, but it feels real right now. And I'll have you know, this past week, I've been having crazy thoughts that maybe I could marry him. Even though he's stinking five years younger than I am, and I'm weird about kids, and his family is weird about me."

"Ooh!" exclaimed Phyl, reaching over to squeeze my arm.

Joanie merely sniffed. "Well don't do it just to please me."

She unbent a little at bedtime. Rather than sharing a room with her brother, Joanie opted to cram into a queen bed with me, and after I turned out the light, I felt her sharp chin digging into my arm. "I'm sorry, Cass. I'm just grouchy. I hate this no-dating thing. I think I'm going to give it up because I'm starting to look so unhappy that guys have stopped asking me out. But I swear—I absolutely swear—that the next guy I go out with will know all about my sad engagement history."

• • •

I woke up Saturday to a message from Perry: Angela Martin did not know we were in Portland. He sent it at 1:00 in the morning, so I knew better than to try to call him. Not that I would have anyhow, it being only 6:00 a.m. Instead, I donned my swimsuit and sweats and snuck out to do some laps in the hotel pool. As I'd hoped, I had it all to myself, and the soothing, monotonous activity gave me plenty of time to think.

I wondered if I could convince Nadina to have the baby and then give it up for adoption. How strange that would be, to think of your own flesh-and-blood running around somewhere on earth, and you not there to see it. Until that flesh-and-blood turned 21 and appeared on your doorstep wanting answers, as always seemed to happen in Hallmark specials and books. What would Nadina be like at 37? Would she step onto the porch of her two-storey house in suburbia and embrace her long-lost child, weeping? Or would she be with her latest loser in a dingy apartment, with too many other children underfoot to be glad of the one she thought she was rid of?

When my body began protesting the unwonted exertion, I climbed rubber-limbed from the pool and went for a little reward-time in the hot tub, turning the bubbles up high and sinking down to my chin luxuriously. By this point, the first family with early-riser kids arrived, replacing the meditative quiet with screeching and splashing and cannonballs that washed gallons of water over the sides. The youngest child was a girl, about three years old, in one of those darling swimsuits with the ruffly bottoms. Creeping to the side of the hot tub nearest them, I stared mesmerized as she jumped repeatedly off the side of the pool into her father's arms, crowing with fearful joy. *This sucks,* I told God. *Why would you saddle Nadina with a baby in her situation, and take mine from me?* The little girl got water up her nose, and I watched jealously as her face turned scarlet and scrunched up with tears, and her father comforted her.

"Mind if I join you?"

Who else but Daniel, for the love of Mike. I'd been so hypnotized by the little girl that I didn't even see him come in—straight from the hotel workout facility and pool shower, apparently, because he was dripping wet and clad only in gym shorts. Remembering that chest clearly, I kept my eyes somewhere over his left ear. Didn't he know that women don't like to be come upon in their swimsuits unaware, when they had no idea a man was going to see them? My suit was a harmless, navy-blue lap number, but I'm pretty sure he was more used to seeing the itsy-bitsy, teeny-weeny variety, with a much higher exposed-skin-to-Lycra ratio, the better to show off the tramp stamp. And speaking of skin, mine was getting a little pruny by this point, but no way was I going to climb out with him sitting there.

"I was just about to go up," I hinted.

Being Daniel, he ignored my hint, relaxing into the hot tub like he was there for the duration and watching me with those unsettling eyes.

So be it. "You look rested after your long week," I said.

"It was a long week," he agreed. "We were working up until the last minute on a settlement. I've spent enough time and thought on it these past few days. How was your week?"

"A little nerve-wracking," I heard myself saying, and then I told him what I hadn't shared with anyone. "I think Nadina might be pregnant, but I can't get a hold of her." It was a relief to tell someone. James thought I was worrying too much and should just leave it up to Mark Henneman to deal with, if Nadina even was pregnant, which he was willing to doubt.

Daniel leaned further back in the hot tub, resting the back of his head on the lip and looking up at the steamed-up skylight thoughtfully. With his eyes off me, I stole one peek at those muscled shoulders. Sheesh. When he looked at me again, I was carefully inspecting my wrinkled fingertips. "You've stopped wearing your ring," he said abruptly.

Caught. I plunged my hands back beneath the water, thankful I was already pink from the hot water. Not even Joanie or Phyl had noticed that, a day or two ago, I finally wriggled my wedding ring off and, with a kiss, put it in my bedside drawer. "Yes," I managed. "It was time."

He ran his hand through his hair, standing it up. After a pause he returned to his conversational tone: "I have a former law school classmate in Seattle who became an adoption attorney," he said. "She could help, if Nadina considers that option."

"Really, Daniel?" I exclaimed, forgetting my embarrassment and clapping my hands. It would be nice to have that in reserve when I talked about it with Nadina. Then my face fell. "I suppose you slept with her though, in law school, and she probably wouldn't agree to any *pro bono* work."

"She wouldn't have to," he replied in a voice half-exasperated, half-amused. "The adoptive parents usually pay legal costs."

"Oh, that's good news," I breathed. "What a handy person you are to know, Daniel. A regular fund of knowledge and helpful connections."

"Glad you think so," he responded lightly. "And I'll have you know, Cass—not that it's any of your business—I didn't sleep with her."

"Seriously? What was it?" I teased. "Spoon-chested? Harelip? A third eye?" He grimaced, shaking his head. "No, I forgot, you're pickier than that," I continued. "Varicose veins. Split ends. Bad grammar."

"If I recall," he finally broke in, "it was her shrewish tongue and her fingertips that were shriveled up from staying too long in public pools and hot tubs." When I burst out laughing, Daniel asked, "Didn't you say you were going back up?"

"I did and I am. I just don't want to get out with you looking at me."

Obligingly he shielded his eyes, and I hastily splashed over to the shelves of clean towels and wrapped up. "All clear," I said. "See you at breakfast?"

"With bells on." A shirt would do.

. . .

Spending the day in Daniel's and Joanie's childhood stomping grounds proved highly entertaining, not least because Joanie kept darting paranoid glances in all directions, sure she saw her mother behind every spreading tree. We saw the house they grew up in, the summer pool where Joanie lifeguarded—I could just imagine how many teenage boys thought they needed rescuing when Joanie was in the chair—the church where Joanie snuck off to youth group, their schools. "Which bleachers did you used to smoke behind?" I couldn't resist asking Daniel.

Perry joined us for lunch downtown, looking a little haggard but happy. "Full house last night," he announced when we put our menus down. "Granted, the theater only holds two hundred and at least a hundred had free tickets and five more were reviewers, but that meant 95 genuine audience members."

"And? And?" I pressed. "Did the 95 applaud or storm out? Did they laugh and cry in the right places?"

"How did that last-minute understudy work out?" asked Daniel, to my amazement. What did he know about last-minute understudies, especially last-minute understudies I didn't know about?

"Like I said, the kid was dying for a break," said Perry, "and he made up for lack of stage experience by going all out. The *Oregonian* said he was a little too hammy, so he might rein it in for you guys tonight."

"What are you two talking about?" I demanded, looking from one to the other suspiciously and then accosting Daniel with, "How do you know more about what's going on with *Waiters* than I do?"

He merely shrugged, but Perry said, "The wonders of email, Cass. That, and whenever I mention it to you, you usually have some caustic remark. Anyhow, the *Oregonian* also said…"

That lunch gave me plenty of food for thought. For one thing, it was a good reminder of how self-absorbed I'd been over the holidays, not even to notice a budding friendship between my own brother and my housemate. There had been those references to card games in the Lean-To and such, but I thought of Daniel as so arms-length with most people that I couldn't quite get my mind around Perry and him emailing each other.

As if that weren't astonishing enough, someone else's growing affection for my brother had also escaped my notice until today; but maybe it had escaped hers as well: Joanie was unusually quiet at lunch. *Joanie*? Joanie and Perry? His divorce wasn't even final yet! Concerned, I set myself to observe their behavior. Perry clearly admired Joanie—he looked at her a lot, joked with her, made references to things they'd talked about at Christmas—but it might have been no more than his general, open personality, that engaging nature that always made him easier to get to know than I was. It was Joanie's reticence that disturbed me. For once, she wasn't shooting off her mouth or even joining in when I ribbed Perry, and it made me re-think her grumpy comments about the dating hiatus. Much as I loved Joanie, and we already fought like sisters, the thought of her and Perry ever getting involved worried me. He'd already had one wife give up on him, and Joanie was a born expert at giving up on men. Disaster. It could only spell disaster.

By the end of the meal, only Phyl and Daniel and Perry were making any conversation, and I wasn't sorry when Perry had to excuse himself to get back to the theater. Joanie continued quiet that whole afternoon—quiet at Powell's, quiet at the Japanese Garden. That and she stuck close to Phyl, as if anxious to avoid any questions from me. Not good.

· · ·

Waiters wasn't wretched. It wasn't great, either, but it did rise above the Painful stratum of regional theater and would have gone still higher if not for the hammy understudy. There was a decent-sized audience as well, of whom not more than a third were cast friends and relatives. At several points during the show I felt inappropriate snickers rising, but Joanie refused to look at me, and my enjoyment would have been halved, had I not felt Daniel's own repressed laughter jiggling the shared armrest.

When the crowd cleared afterward, we let Phyl speak first. She was an indiscriminate musical nut, at least—even owning the *Starlight Express* soundtrack, for Pete's sake—and had sincerity in her favor.

"Well?" Perry demanded of me, when he'd heard Phyl's effusions.

I bit my lip. "Not bad, Perry. And parts of it were genuinely inspired and entertaining." He must have prepared himself for the worst because when Perry heard my lukewarm praise, he let out a whoop and lifted me off the ground. "Don't get me wrong, though," I laughed. "It's no *Cats.*" Seeing *Cats* together as teenagers had been one of our original bonding moments. Fifteen minutes in, we had caught each other's eye and been unable to stop laughing, to the annoyance of those seated nearby. To this day, if I wanted to make Perry laugh, I had only to say, "The Rum Tum Tugger is a curious cat!"

"Ouch!" said Perry, rumpling my hair. "C'mon—do you all have time for a drink before you hit the road?"

"One," said Daniel, who had volunteered to drive home. "As it is we'll be back at 2:00 in the morning."

The quick drink reassured me of two things: firstly, Perry had no thoughts of Joanie beyond finding her generally attractive; and, secondly, Joanie was aware of this and it ticked her off.

I wasn't the only one busy observing others. When Perry walked us to our car, he whispered to me, "Still with that James?"

"Yes," I murmured. "Why?"

"I'm thinking Daniel looks at you a certain way."

This was neither a new idea nor a welcome one. I had no clue what was going through Daniel's head, but if it was starting to be noticeable to Phyl and Perry, it was going to be a problem. All I knew was that I did not have the emotional bandwidth to deal with it. Denial is our friend.

"Whatever, Perry," I scoffed. "That's the way he looks at every woman who isn't wall-eyed with a pronounced limp."

My brother shrugged elaborately. "Suit yourself, Cass. That was just an FYI."

I sniffed. "Thank you very much, Sherlock Holmes, but I think you'd better stick to dramaturgy."

CHAPTER 34:

The Thing

The second I held out the little box to her my worst fears were confirmed.

"You don't need to buy the name brand," said Nadina irrelevantly, glancing at the pregnancy test box but not taking it from me. "The generic works just fine—they're trying to get to your emotions. Like the thing is even gonna care that you shelled out five extra bucks to know it's there. That's where all that crap starts—designer jeans, where you live, what kind of car you drive—"

"Nadina," I interrupted. My stomach was clenching up. "Stop already. Why do you think I bought this for you?"

"How the hell would I know?" she shot back. "I'm surprised you don't do friggin' random drug tests on me."

"Are you pregnant?" I whispered. No answer and an averted head. "Did you already take one of these tests?" Nothing. "Does Mike know, or Mark Henneman?" I bit my lip in frustration, wishing I could just grab her by the shoulders and shake some answers out of her.

We were sitting in the Palace kitchen because a bitterly cold rain was falling. I hadn't even waited for Tuesday, but rather parked outside Camden School and, like a child predator, lured her into the car with promises of cookies and a visit with Benny. No sooner was she done running him around the house like a madman, than I sat her down for cocoa and oatmeal hermits and sprung the box on her.

Present tactics proving ineffective, I changed course slightly. "How have you been feeling? Still pretty tired? When I was pregnant with Min I slept a lot too, but when I wasn't sleeping, I was eating. I guess that's why I didn't recognize what was going on with you. Every… pregnancy is different."

She unbent slightly, as she usually did when I stopped going for the jugular. "Still tired, but the food is getting better. If I'm not around chicken or broccoli or vinegar or fish it's okay."

"The first trimester is usually the worst for all that—you know, the first twelve or so weeks," I continued cautiously. "By the second trimester I had more energy and my appetite got more normal. How far along do you think you are?"

She shrugged. "My period's all over the map, so I don't have a clue. All I know is that I gotta get rid of this puppy fast because the longer you go, the more expensive it is."

"How—how far along were you the other time this happened?"

"I dunno. Maybe a little over three months." She gave a nervous laugh. "It took me way longer to figure out that time because I wasn't tired or nothing, and that was when Mike and I were trashed a lot. I—I haven't told him this time because everything's going so well for him. I know he'll freak out and get all pissed off. I made an appointment for next week, and I'm gonna ask my mom to lend me some money because if I don't have my half of the rent, Mike is gonna figure it out."

I noticed I was gripping the edges of the table, white-knuckled, and made a conscious effort to relax my hands. "Money for what?"

Her eyes narrowed. "What do you think? I gotta get rid of this thing. I'm not having any friggin' baby! And you can't tell anyone, Cass, because this is my business. I mean it! I'm gonna take care of it, and you can't go telling Henneman. Promise me."

"What will you tell your mom?"

"Who the hell cares?" she snapped. "I'll tell her that Mike's dad has started charging rent and wants a deposit or something. I might even tell her the truth because Mom would be all for getting rid of the thing." Did she really feel this indifferent, or was she bluffing to shield herself from my concern? I heard myself breathing shallowly, needing to speak, but afraid of enraging her or shutting her down. *God, what do I do? What do I say? How can I even get through to her on this? Please let her hear me. Open her heart.*

Nadina knew me too well by now. Watching me fret, her brows drew together, and then she went after me. "What? What the hell are you thinking, Cass? I can tell you've got some kind of friggin' sermon to preach, so preach it. Why do you think I didn't even want to tell you? 'Cause you're gonna go all friggin' religious and judgmental on me, like you could even know what it's like. Mike's okay now! I'm okay now! I don't want this fucking everything up!"

"Would you quit cussing at me?" I asked in a tired voice. "If you haven't noticed by now, you stupid girl, I love you. I don't do and say things that you don't like because I like to piss you off. I do and say things that sometimes you don't like because I care about what happens to you."

"But what?" Nadina demanded. She crossed her arms over her chest defensively, but I detected a slight softening in her expression.

"What do you mean?"

"But what's the catch? Spit it out. I know you friggin' religious types are all against abortion, and don't I know the thing's heart is beating and crap like that. You want to say it, say it."

"I have five things I want to say to you," I said shakily, holding up my hand. Why I put up my hand I couldn't say—maybe to stop the flow of her hostility. And what were the five things I had to say to her? I couldn't even think of one, much less four more. But there were my five fingers raised like a stop sign.

"Your life matters."

I put my thumb down. She waited. I waited. What next?

"Your life … matters."

Down went the index finger.

"Your life matters, Nadina."

Middle finger.

"Your life matters."

Ring finger.

"Your life *matters*."

My hand was closed now. I felt the heat of tears behind my eyes and reached across the table, laying my hand on her shoulder.

Her breathing was as shallow as mine, and I saw her blink rapidly. It was so silent in the kitchen I could hear Benny on his bed, snuffling to himself. Oblivious to any crisis, to lives hanging in the balance. A sudden memory presented itself to me: that time months ago in church when I thought of God as a dog, an unpredictable dog who had turned on me to tear my life apart. It was all wrong. That should go without saying, of course, but it had taken me all this time to believe it. Nadina's life mattered, and so did mine.

Your life matters.

Nor was God like Benny, oblivious, doing His own thing, letting us all go to hell in a handbasket. In that moment, in my passionate desire for Nadina to know that she was loved, that she mattered, I had a glimpse of God's heart. This was how He felt for her. This was how He felt for that little child growing, unwanted, inside her. This was how He felt for me.

Nadina had to clear her throat several times before she could speak. "How—how can you say my life matters," she began unsteadily, "when you know having this baby would wreck it?"

This baby. I felt my heart constrict painfully with joy. It had already begun to change in her mind.

"You matter so much," I said slowly, "to me and—and to the God who made you, that He wants you to live. He wants you to be whole. He wants you to know your life is precious and sacred. To have this baby wouldn't be about wrecking your life—it would be about healing it. It would come from an understanding of how much you matter, how much each one of us matters. When we…deny life…we deny our own."

She sighed deeply, burying her hands in her spiky blonde hair. "I don't know if I believe that. And I can't believe you do. You, with the dead husband and the dead baby. Didn't their life matter?"

"They're okay. Troy and Min are okay. I wasn't ready to let them go, but I know they're all right." I shook my head slowly. "Really, I was more concerned with me, the one who got left behind. I used to wonder, Nadina, why we weren't all in that car that day. Wouldn't that have been easier? If we all three died and went on together? I wondered why I wasn't done on earth yet. I guess one reason must be that I was supposed to talk to you today. To tell you how much you matter."

She stirred the dregs of her cocoa, thinking. "If I did this—and I'm not saying I will—Mike would friggin' flip out."

"He probably would be pretty upset at first," I conceded, "but you're not expecting him to raise the baby or support the baby. It would just be dealing with a few months of you being pregnant."

"He'll freak," she said despondently. Then, "I don't think I could give the baby to some randoms out there."

"It wouldn't have to be random. You could use a selective agency or interview couples yourself, pick and choose."

"They wouldn't give a shit about me," she uttered in a low voice. "Not like you do. They would just want the baby, the second they could rip it away. Be all nice to me and kiss my ass until they got what they wanted."

"That's not true," I protested, "they would care about you because they would be so grateful to you. You don't know—people who can't have babies go a little berserk. They'd probably want to hear from you every day of the pregnancy, get all the gory details."

Her voice dropped even lower, but I think I recognized the expletive. "No way. No friggin' randoms."

"That's what I'm saying," I repeated. "They wouldn't have to be random. You could know them as well or as little as you like, I imagine. It could be a family here in Bellevue or across the country. People you get to know, or people whose names you don't even want to learn. This would be your choice. All yours."

"If—if I got to choose," said Nadina hesitantly. "I—I— " She trailed off.

"You what?" I prompted.

Her pale blue eyes looked straight into mine. "If the choice was all mine, I would choose you, Cass."

There was a sudden silence in the kitchen. Nadina and I were perfectly still—even Benny seemed to be holding his breath. I could hear the clock ticking, Phyl's clock with the orange blossoms on it. Outside, a car whizzed by on the wet pavement. Nadina's words seemed to hang in the air, as if they were painted on a banner unfurling behind a plane, and I looked at them, detached. I-would-choose-you-Cass. Shocking words that, for some inexplicable reason, failed to shock. The banner may as well have read Shop-at-Pendergast-Furniture or Did-you-take-your-vitamins-today?

Twenty months ago, when I came home from that Hot Yoga class, I threw my gym bag in the hallway and called for Min, wondering why she didn't come running to greet me. "Troy?" I called again. "Did you already put Min down for her nap?" No Troy either, as you well know. Just that blinking light on the answering machine and the hospital asking me to call back immediately. *Oh God, no.* I've never been a morbid person, never spent my time imagining worst-case scenarios. Nor was there any reason to suppose the hospital had news of my husband and daughter—it could as easily have been news of my own parents or Max or Raquel while Troy obliviously pushed Min on the swing at the park. But that day when my shaking hand reached for the phone, I already knew what someone dreaded having to tell me. Denial would come later; disbelief would come later; in that moment I knew.

Steadily I gazed at Nadina, the memory of that strange certainty tugging at me. If she had her way, she would choose me. Although I shouldn't have been able to understand her, although I ought to have been on the floor hyperventilating at the thought, I felt instead an eerie calm. Something clicked into place. Hard to describe, but most like the Troy-and-Min experience. It was as if she were telling me something that found an immediate echo inside me and evoked no surprise.

"You would choose me to take the baby," I said, quiet as you please.

"I would choose you to take the baby," she said again, her eyes never wavering.

"You wouldn't want the baby to have a father? Brothers or sisters? A mother with a reliable income?" My questions sounded strangely *pro forma*, as if I were reading down a checklist and this had nothing to do with me.

"You're old, but you're not dead," said Nadina with equal calm. "The baby might one day have a father or brothers or sisters. You might one day get a real job."

Some detached part of my brain was shaking itself awake. You, Cass? Take a baby? You swore off babies, after Min. You wouldn't even consider babies, when James asked you. *James*! What would James say? Where would you live, since you'd have to move out of the Palace? What would everyone say? Remember the last time you felt as certain of something—it led to the worst year of your life!

But it remained a detached part of my brain, squeaking and rattling in the face of what felt unaccountably like a certainty. That strange calm. Knowing.

"This isn't a decision to be made in a day," I said finally. Bemused, I realized I was referring only to her decision, and not to my own. "Sleep on it. Think about it."

"You're not saying no, are you?" Nadina remarked. I wondered if she felt that strange rightness in the air. "Didn't you say no more babies?"

"I did," I replied, giving a short laugh. "More than once. And I meant it."

$$\bullet \quad \bullet \quad \bullet$$

We were quiet when I dropped her at the school bus stop. She got out, waving at me, and I drove away. Without conscious thought, I found myself heading for the church, rather than back home. The sanctuary was empty—no school choirs rehearsing or people setting up for an evening activity. Sitting in one of the back pews, shadowed by the balcony, I sat down, resting my chin on my arms along the back of the pew in front of me.

Peace that passed understanding. That little part of my brain kept trying to speak up, but the rest of me refused to get agitated. It was going to happen. Nadina would have that baby, come what may, and I would take it from there, come what may. Why this should be so—

why I should be so receptive and unruffled at the idea of adopting the baby of a messed-up teenager who had subsisted on coffee and sweets since the moment she got pregnant—was a mystery. I, who fought the very idea of even having another baby by the traditional route. I suspected it had everything to do with my revelation of that afternoon: that, contrary to my fears these past few months, my life mattered utterly to God. I was not a cosmic, unresolved plotline in the Story of Life; the Storyteller was skilled; every character had a role. He could be trusted.

I had fought that trust every way I could, putting up barriers and shields. If I never had a husband again, if I never had a child again, I would never again be so vulnerable. If God were going to give me things, just to take them away, I would just make sure I didn't have anything I couldn't live without. Slowly, slowly—imperceptibly—He had, over the past months, pried my hands open. Not so He could take something out of them, but so that He could put something back in them.

Opening my hands, I stared at them.

Your life matters.

CHAPTER 35:

Breaking News

Who knew that confronting a hostile, secretly distraught teenager over her unwanted pregnancy and agreeing to adopt her child was actually the easy part? As I guessed, additional days of sleeping on it didn't change Nadina's mind, and I ended up needing every ounce and shred of the supernatural peace I experienced to survive that week's emotional, Bataan Death March of Telling Other People.

"Have you lost your mind?" shrilled Joanie, pacing feverishly back and forth in front of Phyl and me. "Are you completely nuts?"

"Maybe," I responded, having prepared myself for this. "I didn't expect it either. It feels right." Phyl reached for my hand and clutched it, wordless and shocked.

"It 'feels right'?" Joanie echoed incredulously. "Adopting the baby of some thieving little toilet-cleaning drug addict and his fifteen-year-old girlfriend? Nadina's a mess! The baby's probably got that fetal alcohol syndrome, if it even has all its arms and legs. How can you do this to yourself? Tell me you're not going to do this, Cass... It took months and months before I could say 'date' around you without you biting my head off, and then when you finally do start dating a great guy, you wig out because he wants to marry you and have kids with you, and now, instead of doing something logical, you decide you want to become some single, welfare mom?"

"Joanie…" Phyl remonstrated.

I winced when she mentioned James. There was the rub. "It isn't logical, I know, Joanie. Do you…do you think James won't want to marry me anymore?"

Joanie stopped short and wedged her behind between mine and Phyl's on the couch, her vivid blue eyes locking with mine. "Cass—if you do this, it's over. Can you blame him? You tell him a week ago you can't even think about marriage or having children and then— oh, scratch that—what you really meant is that you can't stand the thought of him and his children, but you've got no problem with someone else's *crack baby*." Phyl gasped and climbed over Joanie to sit on my other side.

"That's not it," I objected. "I told you on the way to Portland that I was warming to the idea of marrying him—"

"Well go ahead and unwarm," Joanie interrupted curtly. "Forget that idea. Crap almighty! How can this be happening? You don't have a job, you don't have a husband—and you'll never get one if you're saddled with this kid—and you won't be able to afford to live any- where except California with your parents."

"Does she have the gift of encouragement, or what?" I asked Phyl wryly.

Joanie wasn't in a humorous mood. "Speak to her, Phyl. She won't listen to me—clearly."

Phyl fidgeted uncomfortably, being the least confrontational of the three of us. "Cass, we will love you and be your friends no matter what you do, and if it were up to us, that baby could just move into the Palace and be part of our— "

"Never mind, Phyl!" groaned Joanie, "This isn't time to be supportive—it's time to slap her around." She turned on me again. "I can see by your face it's no use. All I can hope for is that Nadina has a miscarriage or changes her mind and gives the kid to someone else."

"She won't," I said. "Do either. Don't ask me how I know, but I know. Come on, Joanie. If my doom is inevitable, won't you love me anyway? You don't want me to move to California, do you?"

"No, you idiot," she cried passionately, "I want to keep on living here just like we're living here, forever and ever. I'd even put up with the crack baby if I thought Daniel would ever go for it. Why do you have to go and ruin everything?"

"And you call me an idiot," I reproached her. "It couldn't last forever, crack baby or no. At the very least, Phyl would say yes to Wayne eventually, and you would pick someone—anyone—and get married too."

"I'm not going to get married," said Joanie unexpectedly in a low voice.

I stared at her, sidetracked. "What, are you joining a convent or something?"

Avoiding my eyes she picked at an unraveling thread on the sofa arm. "No, I just—I've decided I'll never get married. I don't like the guys who like me, and the guy I like isn't interested, so that's that."

"You're not talking about Roy, are you?" I said uneasily. Joanie's scoffing sound answered my question. "Joanie, look at me. You're talking about Perry."

"Oh my God!" exclaimed Joanie, "I knew you guessed. I didn't even know myself until we saw him last weekend for that stupid musical. He's not even my type and his divorce isn't final and—worst of all—he doesn't think of me that way."

"Joanie," I said bracingly, "you know I love you like a sister, but you and *Perry*? He's never had a real job in his life—that would drive you crazy. Even if he fell for you, you'd get sick of him just like Betsy did, and I don't want his heart broken again. He needs to marry some independently wealthy, older woman who wants to keep him as a boy toy."

"You think he could fall for me?" she asked, perking up.

I rolled my eyes. "Oh, probably. Isn't that how it works with you and Daniel? Either one of you could most likely get anyone you really wanted. I'm asking you—don't break Perry's heart."

"Oh, yeah? Well, I'm asking you not to adopt Nadina's baby, but are you going to listen to me? No, you'll move to California to sponge off your parents, and I'll never see Perry or you again. Life sucks."

It wasn't the end of the conversation. No, *that* went on for another hour or two of that day and continued every time thereafter that Joanie found me alone. Phyl, thank heavens, decided to leave Joanie and me to go at it in single combat, but Joanie was enough. She seemed convinced that the only way she could persuade me would be through unrelenting, no-holds-barred badgering and second-guessing. Many things were said in those days—very many—but you get the idea.

. . .

My parents greeted my news with stunned silence. I forced them both to get on the line so I wouldn't have to do this twice. What could they say? I was an adult—a deluded and deranged one, perhaps, but an adult nonetheless. Mom made soft, bubbly choking sounds, as if someone were holding her under tapioca pudding.

Dad recovered first. "Tell me about this certainty you had when you talked to her." Joanie absolutely refused to credit this part of the story, but my father always had a quiet streak of deep feeling. He could hear Spirit talking to spirit.

There was another silence when I finished my account—even

Mom must have crawled ashore out of the tapioca because I couldn't hear her anymore—and then Dad said, "Cassandra, this will be tough. But your mother and I love you and support your choices 100%. You have to do what you have to do."

"Larry," chided Mom, finding her voice at last, "Larry, that's all very well, but someone's got to connect the dots here. Cass, where are you going to live? That Daniel is very nice, but he doesn't seem the type of man interested in running a day care."

"I wouldn't ask him to," I answered hastily. "I'll have to move, but I've got a while yet. I'm getting Nadina in to the doctor this week, but we figure she's only about two or three months along. I think I'll have until around mid-September to get my ducks in a row."

"How will you live in the same town as Nadina?" she pressed. "You can't show up to mentor her every week with her own baby in tow."

"I don't know how everything will work," I said again, aware of spirals and loops of panic in my gut.

"You could always come here," Mom pursued. "Dad and I will want to help you and our—our grandchild."

My throat closed suddenly. I hadn't thought of that—that whatever child I adopted would have a claim on my family. It would have grandparents and an uncle, besides a mother. Children made it with less.

"Mom, Dad," I murmured. "You two are the best. Thank you thank you thank you. I'll keep you in the loop. Just give me a little time to figure things out, Mom, okay?"

• • •

After telling Joanie and my parents, the next person I wanted to talk to was Mark Henneman, but Nadina wouldn't hear of it yet. "I don't want everyone friggin' looking at my stomach, and since I'm having the kid, why do they need to know?"

But it ate at me: would it strike people as shady—the mentor who adopted the student's baby? As if I had exploited her, wanted to get close to her for that purpose. And it seemed to me the longer we waited to speak to Mark Henneman, the shadier I would appear.

Nor would Nadina consent to telling her mother. "You're still on her medical insurance," I pointed out. "She's going to wonder when she gets the statement from the Ob/Gyn."

"Mike first," Nadina insisted. But if I asked when she would break it to Mike, she waffled and put me off. Not that I blamed her—I hadn't yet worked up the courage to tell James.

• • •

These days I was spending a lot of time in my closet, praying. In normal size houses, a bedroom felt intimate enough for prayer, but not in the Palace. In order not to feel adrift in the universe, I preferred to sit on the floor of my closet, leaning against the wall under my folded and stacked sweaters, lights out. By Saturday, after a week of Joanie's hounding and chasing my tail with Nadina and getting increasingly anxious about James' reaction, I went straight into the closet after breakfast and sat there for at least an hour. Psalm 61 came to mind and stuck: "When my heart is overwhelmed, lead me to the rock that is higher than I." *My heart is overwhelmed. Remind me that you're with me. Remind me that you love me and Nadina and the baby, and our lives are in your hand.*

By this point I was no longer sitting up; I was flat on my back on the floor, looking up unseeingly to where the ceiling would be, if I had the light on. I might have dozed a little, having not slept well for the last few nights. In any case I began to think that any positive effects of prayer would soon be counteracted by oxygen depletion if I didn't come out soon, so reluctantly I rose and emerged into the glare of late winter sunshine filling my room.

It took a moment for my eyes to adjust, but when they did I blinked to see Daniel standing by my desk, turned in surprise toward me, something in his hand. It was the picture of Troy holding Min: they were both grinning, and little one-year-old Min had one plump little hand clutching her father's shirt and the other reaching out to me, as I held the camera. That picture had spent months in my desk drawer, face down, but recently I had pulled it out again and set it next to my computer monitor.

"Excuse me," Daniel said quickly, half-dropping the picture so that it hit the desk with a rattling sound. I wasn't used to seeing him clumsy or ill-at-ease and only looked at him questioningly. "I was... going to write you a note," he continued, pointing vaguely at a pen and paper lying on the desk. "I thought you weren't home. Didn't expect you to spring out of the closet."

His discomfiture made me wonder how long he'd been in my room. For all that the Palace was his, he never ventured upstairs, as far as I knew. "Sorry to startle you," I answered. "I was... praying. Did you want to talk to me?"

He nodded, running his hands through his hair. When I gestured toward the window seat, he sat down, and I sat on the cushion across from him. Daniel cleared his throat. "I just didn't get a chance to talk to you alone this week, and I was wondering what was going on with Nadina."

"She's pregnant," I said shortly.

"Did you—have you asked her what she's going to do?"

"She's going to have the baby and give it up for adoption," I replied. My voice was steady and calm. Maybe this was good practice for telling James.

His face lit up, and he reached in his shirt pocket. "That's great news, Cass. The best you could have hoped for. I got the business card for my spoon-chested, harelipped, law-school friend with the three eyes." He grinned at me, holding out the card.

Ordinarily I would have laughed, but his joke reminded me that adoptive parents usually paid all the legal fees. "Thank you," I said automatically, "but I don't know if I could afford her."

"What do you mean 'you'? It would be the adoptive parents who paid."

Unable to find words, I merely looked at him, and after a second, his hand dropped. "You're going to adopt the baby." It was a statement, not a question.

I nodded.

Daniel inhaled sharply and ran his hand through his hair again. He put the business card back in his pocket and stared out the bay window.

The silence made me uncomfortable—why should he be upset? "You must think I'm crazy," I ventured. "Joanie does. She hasn't made a secret of it."

"Will you and James get married before the baby comes, then?" was his abrupt question.

"What?" I yelped. I felt my cheeks warm.

"You're going to get married, aren't you?" Daniel asked. "He's not going to let you do this alone."

Somehow, whenever Daniel spoke of James, there was always that implied criticism, and I felt myself rallying defensively. "He doesn't know yet. I haven't told him. This was my decision."

The blue eyes met mine. "It won't matter, will it? If he wanted to marry you before this, this won't change his mind. Because he loves you." How did he know James wanted to marry me?

I shook my head, flustered. "I don't know. It hardly seems fair to expect him to honor an offer that was made under completely different circumstances—an offer I didn't even agree to at the time."

"Would you agree to it now?"

Would I? The reasons I gave James for not marrying him when he asked a couple weeks ago now seemed moot. How could I balk at marriage and children and say it was too soon, when I had since agreed to an equally lifelong, binding relationship? If anything, Joanie was right, and James would feel hurt that I jumped at one opportunity after refusing the other.

"I would," I said slowly. "If James will still have me."

Daniel made an impatient sound. "If he loves you, he will."

"Honestly, Daniel," I reproved, "who are you to lecture James on love?"

Anger flashed across his face, and I sat back, startled, but an instant later it was gone, wiped clean. "Of course not, Cass," he said coolly. "You've always been very up-front with your opinion of me, and I know you think me incapable of love, as you define it."

It was the day at the Café all over again, when I hurt him by calling him my landlord. Fumblingly, I tried to smooth things over. "Forgive me. How would I know what you're capable of? You've been so kind to me lately." Rather than appearing mollified, Daniel grimaced when I called him kind, and I hastened on. "I'm just a little anxious about how James will respond. It is a lot to spring on a person, and I wouldn't blame him if he thought I changed my mind so suddenly because I was scared and thought the baby should have a father."

"Are you scared? Do you think the baby should have a father?"

"Scared to death!" I admitted. "And I'd love for the baby to have a father—I'd love for all babies to have two parents—but that wouldn't be why I would marry him."

There was another pause, and then Daniel stood up. "Well, if you…love him… I'm sure he's not such a fool—he'll believe you." He was almost to the door when he stopped and added, "Let me know if there's anything you need from me."

For a moment it was on my lips to beg to be allowed to stay at the Palace if James rejected me. Hearing my intake of breath, he waited, but then I shook my head. How could I? He might even say yes because he liked me and wanted to help, but I shouldn't ask it of him. Why would a confirmed bachelor want a tenant encumbered by a squalling infant? What would he tell his girlfriends then?

"Thank you, Daniel," I murmured at last. "I'll remember that."

CHAPTER 36:

To Hell in a Handbasket

Sometimes people let you down. Sometimes you let others down. My conversation with James was some of both.

Nadina and I finally agreed that Sunday would be D-Day. I told her that I would be seeing James and didn't think I could keep my secret any longer, and if James was going to be enlightened, Mike would have to follow. Not to mention Mark Henneman and Nadina's mother.

"This is totally gonna suck," she complained. "Mike is gonna freak, and he's been so cool lately."

"What's it to him?" I said for the hundredth time. "So you'll get a little fat for a few months. He doesn't have to deliver the baby, and then it'll all be over." Yeah, Mike was going to have it easy, compared to James. "Call me tomorrow, and we'll compare notes. Don't chicken out on me."

The weather was warming slightly as we headed into March, and James had it in his head that he wanted to go snowshoeing up at Snoqualmie while it was still possible. After the morning service, where I came within a breath of revealing all to Louella, I waited out front for him to swing by and pick me up.

"Good morning to my favorite girl," he said, leaning across to give me a kiss on the cheek. "How was church? Did the roof open and angels ascend and descend?"

"For a while." I had been debating whether to spill my guts on the drive up or to dump the news on him while we were snowshoeing, but his expression this morning was so sunny that I hated to spoil things. "You're cheerful today."

"Of course I am," he teased, "I didn't have to get up to attend an 8:00 service." He reached for my hand and held it while he drove. "Not to mention it's been a great week at work. I was hoping you'd come in so I could brag some because I didn't want to tell you the news over the phone."

"It's been a crazy week," I answered vaguely. "How did that dinner with the new game publisher go Thursday? We missed you at open house." A white lie—with Nadina's gag rule still in effect, I'd been relieved not to see him.

"That's just it!" James exclaimed. "I think they're really close to picking up *Antarctiquest!* and maybe one other game from Vil's team. They were impressed how we managed to get *Tolt* out at the eleventh hour before Christmas. You wouldn't believe Riley—he's redone his cube in a polar theme to celebrate. You've got to come in next week to give him the pleasure of bragging."

"And to relieve Jeri," I laughed. "I'm sure she's had enough."

James chuckled. "No joke. I think a couple more days of it, and she might quit. Then you'd have to come on full-time, which wouldn't be all bad…I could see your gorgeous face whenever I wanted." I gulped, and he gave my hand a squeeze. "But what's been going on with you? I feel like I haven't seen or heard from you in forever. Did you get that chance to corner Nadina and lay a pregnancy test on her?"

I took a deep breath. "Didn't need to. Pete guessed right—she's pregnant, and she already knew it. But she hasn't told anyone."

"What's she going to do about it?"

I paused. "I think I've convinced her to have the baby and give it up for adoption."

Like Daniel, James was excited, knowing how much I wished for such an outcome. "That's great! And you didn't even call me to tell me? In between working my tail off this week and meeting with those publishers I've been worried for you."

"I know," I said. "I'm sorry. I thought I'd...tell you in person."

He whistled appreciatively. "Yeah, that's good news. I bet Mark Henneman will be relieved. Was she hard to convince? I know it's tough for anyone to say no to you, but if anyone could, I would bet on Nadina."

"She was pretty wary and hostile at first," I remembered. "I think she'd already guessed where I was coming from and what I might say. But there was a turning point in the conversation. It felt like God really wanted me to tell her how much he loved her. When I did, she was more open."

James shook his head, smiling. "I love you, Cass. You are one in a million. Make that one in a billion."

"Shouldn't you make that 'one of a kind'?" I asked. "Otherwise that means there's still at least a few other women out there exactly like me."

"I'm glad to know that, actually," he countered, "in case I can't get you to marry me after all." We laughed, but I had a sinking sensation in my gut for not sharing the whole truth. This couldn't work. Not with James. But could it? He said he loved me and still wanted to marry me. Maybe Daniel was right, and that would be enough.

At the I-90 East on-ramp we noticed some highway patrol cars whizzing past underneath, headed the opposite direction into down-town Seattle. "Someone's trying to make it onto the evening news,"

James joked, raising his eyebrows at me. Although I wouldn't know it for several hours more, the attempt would be successful.

. . .

The snow at the top of the Pass had icy patches and the occasional tip of a rock showed through, but the ranger promised it got better as you went along the loop trail. Because the guided hike scheduled for 10:00 had left some time ago, with the next one not till 11:30, James and I decided to strike out on our own and possibly catch up with the others.

"It's more fun this way, anyhow," he declared, "because now we don't have to behave ourselves." Meaning, he could tackle me when we got around the first bend, sending us crashing into the snow bank. Punching him, I scrambled back to my feet, laughing while I brushed myself clean, only to look up and get a snowball full in the face.

"You jerk!" I shrieked. The fight was on. Snoqualmie snow is never ideal for building snowmen and makes for terrible snowballs that disintegrate mid-flight, but we gave it our best. Ten minutes later we were flushed and disheveled, our hair dripping with melting snow. "You missed some," I said, pretending to reach for his shoulder to brush it off but then dropping a last icy hunk down the back of his neck.

"That's it!" James roared, floundering after me as I tried to take off running in the dumb snowshoes. If a mountain lion or a Sasquatch decided to make a meal of me, there wouldn't be much I could do about it with those things on. And sure enough, James caught me after a few yards. "Kiss me," he ordered. "Kiss me, or I'll bury you in the snow and leave only your head sticking out."

Clearly we weren't going to catch up with the 10:00 guided snowshoe hike, and the 11:30 might even have come upon us not a quarter-mile up the trail, had James not broken off and muttered in my ear,

"Let it be today, Cass. Tell me today that you'll marry me." I gasped and pulled away from him, and he frowned at me. "What?"

Taking an unsteady step back, I tried to screw up my courage. "James...there's something I haven't told you." The air was cold and thin up here, and when I tried to take deep lungfuls of it, it burned on the way down.

When I didn't continue right away, he tried to tease me out of my seriousness. "This looks bad. Let me guess: Troy is still alive. You could marry me, but we'd have to move to a bigamist compound. Fine by me—I'm still in."

"Nadina's going to give up her baby for adoption," I said, not able to bear his happy unawareness anymore, "and I'm the one adopting it."

James grew very still, only his eyes moving over my face, trying to read the truth. I bit my lip, my heart going a mile a minute. Everything depended on this.

"Say that again?" he asked.

I complied.

"I thought you didn't want children," he said at last.

"I didn't," I breathed.

"You mean, you didn't want to have children with me."

"No, no!" I objected. "I didn't want to have children with anyone," I tried to explain. "It's not that I want this child, even—it's that I feel I'm supposed to take it."

"Supposed to take it?" he echoed incredulously. "What does that mean? You're her mentor, Cass, not her mother, not her social worker. You're supposed to pray for her and encourage her, not bail her out when she gets pregnant by taking the baby!"

"I don't mean 'supposed to take it' as an obligation, James," I pleaded. "I mean that, when Nadina and I were talking about it, I felt in my gut that this was what was supposed to happen with this baby. This was God's plan to take care of all three of us: Nadina and the baby and me."

"God? God? How exactly does this take care of *you*, Cass?"

"Because I didn't trust God anymore. I didn't want to invest. But when I was trying to tell Nadina how much God cared what happened to her, I realized that God cares what happens to me, too. That He loves me. That it was okay to invest."

"Hell, yes, it was okay for you to invest," said James, his voice hardened with anger and hurt. "What have I been saying to you? I've been asking you to invest in us—every step of our relationship. And you've been pushing back and pushing back and saying you're not ready, and I've been giving you space and time, and now you go and tell Nadina you're ready to invest? Why the hell couldn't this revelation be that you're ready to invest in us, and you come and tell me?"

I felt the tears coming. It wasn't just that he had never before spoken angrily to me; it was that Joanie was right. I had hurt James beyond imagining. "Listen to me, James," I urged in a choked voice, "this is totally separate from what's going on with us. It wasn't that I chose Nadina's baby and didn't choose you. I did choose you! I have chosen you! Even before I knew for sure she was pregnant, I was already thinking that, yes, I did want to marry you, if you would still have me, fearful and broken and all."

He was breathing hard, his gray eyes like metal. "Is this true? You want to marry me?" I managed to nod, and he exhaled slowly. "Then, can you wait on the decision to take Nadina's baby? Can you tell her you'll help her get it adopted, but it may not be you?"

"James, I can't," I said, my anxiety rising again. "Even if I didn't feel absolutely certain that this is what I'm supposed to do, Nadina won't even consider having the baby and giving it to strangers. She's already said so—she'd rather abort it."

"That's emotional blackmail, Cass," he snapped. "Listen to me: you are not responsible for her actions. You can't let her manipulate you like this. If you don't take the baby, and she decides to get an abortion, that's her choice and nothing to do with you."

Putting my hand on his arm I said gently, "I know that James. I said 'even if I didn't feel absolutely certain that this is what I'm supposed to do.' I'm supposed to adopt that baby, and I'm going to."

We looked at each other for a long time, each one of us searching for something in the other's face that we didn't find. James was looking for wavering on my part; I was looking for acceptance on his.

He turned away at last, a sob choking in his throat, dragging his clenched fists through his curling hair. Feeling my own tears running down my face, I stumbled after him, tripping in those idiotic snowshoes and having to heave myself back upright.

"James, I'm sorry," I cried, everything spilling out at last. "I didn't mean to hurt you. I love you. If you could get your mind around it— it's kind of an unorthodox beginning to a life together, but it could still be a life together." In my clumsiness I ran against him, and for a second he clutched me to him, squeezing the breath out of me. Then he gently pushed me away from him.

"Cass, forgive me. I don't think I can." His voice was soft, the anger gone. "It's—it's not what I pictured for my life."

"Not what you pictured?" My voice strangled against the words. "*Not what you pictured?* Not one minute of the last twenty-one months has been what I pictured for my life, but that doesn't mean it wasn't good—that it wasn't worthwhile—that there wasn't joy. You don't think God might have more for you than what you can picture? That He can't work with this? That we can't work with this because we love each other?"

I could see from his face that it was no use.

He couldn't go there. Or he wouldn't. It was that gap in our experience that I felt from the first.

Without speaking, we headed back to the trailhead. Who knows what the ranger thought of us, shambling out of the woods a mere half-hour after heading in, not looking at each other or talking. Maybe he'd even been able to catch some of our fight in that clear mountain air because he didn't ask any questions or pester us with joviality.

It was all I could do, the entire forty-five minute drive home, to swallow repeatedly, blinking back the tears. Without so many months of practice, I'm sure I couldn't have pulled it off. When we reached the Palace, my hand hesitated on the car door handle. "James. I'm sorry about all this, and I wish you the very best. I think you're wonderful."

He nodded, and his gray eyes met mine sadly. "I'm sorry, too. That I can't—that I'm letting you down. You'll still go through with it—?"

"Yes. But it's okay," I said again. "It's my choice." Quickly I got out and tried to maintain some semblance of dignity until I got inside and heard him pull away. Then I didn't bother anymore, leaning my head against the back of the closed door and bursting into tears.

There was a scrambling sound in the kitchen, and Phyl came running into the hallway. "Cass?" I transferred my wailing from the door to her shoulder, flinging my arms around her neck. Loyal Phyl rocked me back and forth, making comforting sounds and rubbing my hair. "I'm sorry. So sorry, sweetheart."

"Joanie was right," I hiccupped after a few minutes, raising my head and trying to wipe my streaming eyes. "I'm glad she's not here to say she told me so."

Joanie wasn't there, but while I'd been bawling all over Phyl, Daniel had entered the kitchen unnoticed. I saw him now, watching us through the doorway. But, as I well knew, when your life is going to hell in a handbasket, it's hard to drum up lesser, workaday emotions. Embarrassment was too far down the list to trouble me.

Giving him a shaky smile, I said again, loud enough for him to hear, "Joanie was right. And you were wrong."

• • •

It was only hours later, when I was curled up on the couch under the afghan, comforting myself with Phyl's madeleines and taking a break from thinking about the latest shipwreck in my life, that I spared a thought for how Nadina's day might have gone. Even then nothing might have been able to penetrate my self-absorption, had not Daniel decided to watch the news. He had the good sense not to try to talk to me, leaving me to dip my cookie moodily in my tea, while he sank into his favorite armchair and flipped on the television.

The footage ran for at least ten seconds before it got my attention, and I looked up to see an overhead shot of the highway patrol officers zooming down I-90, the ones whose path had crossed James' and mine that morning. "The suspect led officers on a high speed chase across the I-90 bridge into downtown Seattle this morning," read the anchor gravely, "nearly running down several pedestrians and causing at least two other vehicle collisions, before finally crashing his car into one of the barriers police had erected at Aurora and 85th. The police then chased him on foot for several more blocks before finally catching up with him in front of the Sunset Motor Inn. The suspect appears to have been under the influence of narcotics at the time and was currently on probation from an earlier arrest for drug possession. He is now in custody at the King County Jail and will face arraignment tomorrow."

Oh, I thought, watching the police officers yank on the slight, tow-headed figure to get him off the ground and push on his head to force him inside the patrol car. Nadina's had a crappy day too. Looks like Mike didn't take the news any better than James. Maybe even a little worse.

Hearing my stifled gasp, Daniel glanced over at me. "Another of your friends, Cass?"

Unbelievably, I felt a giggle escape me. "No, not a friend. Just the father of my baby."

CHAPTER 37

Disaster Recovery

"Did you drink the whole thing? Show me the bottle."

Nadina groaned dramatically. "I can't drink anymore, Cass. I'm about to friggin' pee my pants! Where the flip is that nurse? Let me just go pee a little of it off, okay?"

"No," I insisted. "They need your bladder full, or they can't get a good look. It doesn't take too long, and then you can go pee to your heart's content."

"I don't see why we have to do this," she grumbled. "Especially on my birthday. The doctor already smeared me in that cold-ass goo and took a look. Flipper's got a friggin' head and heartbeat."

"Well, now they want to do a more thorough job and measure Flipper's growth, Birthday Girl," I reassured her, not for the first time. "Since you can't even say when your last period was, it'll help them nail down how far along you are. Think about something else as a distraction. Tell me what your Aunt Sylvia found out about that school."

"St. Helen's Institute for Girls," droned Nadina obediently, "an all-girls school for 9th to 12th grade in the heart of Cleveland. I've totally memorized their hokey brochure: 'Is the public school system not working for your child? Has your child struggled with substance abuse, promiscuity, or negative peer influences?' Then, have we got the friggin' school for you! You need nuns with rulers to keep your kid's sorry ass in line! Cass, did I tell you I figured out why St. Helen's isn't co-ed?"

"To keep girls like you out of trouble, I imagine," I answered dryly. "Mike was substance abuse, promiscuity, and negative peer influences all rolled into one."

"Wrong!" she sang. "It's because if they took boys too, then they'd be St. Helen's Institute for Teens. Get it? They'd be S.H.I.T.! God, I bet their sweatshirt sales would go through the roof! I should suggest it to them as a friggin' fundraiser. It makes me want to go out for cheerleading: S-H-I-T, Helen's is the place to be! S-H-I-T, watch us go for victory! SHIT! SHIT! Go-o-o-o, SHIT!"

The ultrasound doctor chose this moment to come in, naturally. He merely smiled, however, and said, "I see you're feeling energetic today, Ms. Stern."

"You're a guy!" she said accusingly.

"I am," he replied evenly.

Nadina muttered something under her breath that sounded like "friggin' pervert," which I tried to cover with loud chitchat, but, whether from embarrassment or resignation or both, she settled down after that and submitted to the examination.

We already knew, from the cursory ultrasounds in the Ob/Gyn's office, that the baby had all its limbs, a head and a heart, but Nadina still had some questions for Dr. Keenan. "Can you tell if it's a dwarf?"

"Does dwarfism run in your family?" he asked in the same imperturbable voice. I suppose if you had a job like his, you learned to filter out reactions of horror, wonder, or even surprise, lest you freak out the patients.

On the other hand, we could cross "radiologist" and "ultrasound technician" off the list of Nadina's possible future careers. The mysterious show of lights and shapes on the screen played out to the soundtrack of her questions and exclamations: "Aaah! What the hell was that? Ohmygod, why is the head so friggin' huge? That is not coming out of me—no way. Does it already have friggin' scoliosis—why is it all hunched over like that? I hope this is how it's supposed to look—I swear to you, Cass, I haven't hardly drank anything or smoked anything for months, so if it's all effed up you can blame Mike and his retard felon sperm."

This last comment must have been beyond what even Dr. Keenan dealt with in his day-to-day experience because the ultrasound probe paused, and he glanced at me. I smiled noncommitally, it not being my story to tell, but Nadina looked rather triumphant to have finally penetrated his professional reserve. "Yeah, this is a sad and sorry case, Doctor. My boyfriend, Flipper's dad, is a convicted felon doing 2-5 at Coyote Ridge for vehicular assault and driving while stoned and eluding capture. So he really is a felon, but I added that bit about him being retarded. I'm still kind of mad at him."

Dr. Keenan's eyes had bugged out somewhat, but he cleared his throat a few times and continued with his examination. "That is quite the story, Ms. Stern. I hope he gets his life straightened out. It may help you both to hear that everything is looking good. I would say the measurements and developments are in line with a fetus roughly 19-20 weeks along. Heartbeat is strong; everything checks out."

"Yeah," sighed Nadina, "sounds good to me, but I don't think Mike would be so cool with it. He wanted me to get rid of it—that's why he wigged out that day and got into so much trouble. Even though I told him I was going to give the baby away and it wasn't like he was going to have to change any friggin' diapers or anything."

"Yes, well," said Dr. Keenan placatingly, "people feel ready for parenthood at different times. It sounds like…Mike…wasn't quite ready."

"You can say that again," Nadina agreed. "Cass's boyfriend wasn't ready either," she volunteered, pointing at me. "This is Cass—she's adopting the baby, and when her boyfriend heard about it, he freaked out too."

Turning red, I ground my teeth together. "Certainly, he was upset, but you'll notice James isn't currently incarcerated."

"I meant he dumped you, just like Mike dumped me."

"Yes," I answered briefly. "So he did."

The doctor laid down the probe and passed his hand over his eyes, probably wondering if he'd accidently wandered onto a day-time drama set. After this brief indulgence, he pinned his professional neutrality back on and asked, "Would either of you like to know the sex of the child?"

We looked at each other. "It's up to you, Cass," she said after a pause. "Your baby."

Taking a deep breath, I nodded at Dr. Keenan, and he began running the probe over Nadina's belly more quickly, so that the shapes on the screen came and went, morphing like time-lapse footage of a lava lamp. When he found what he was looking for, he nodded at the image. "There you go."

Nadina and I stared at the twitching, Rorschach blob.

"Help us out here," said Nadina, when the image failed to conjure up any gender we recognized.

"Boy," said Dr. Keenan, as if it should have been obvious. "I'd bet my practice on it."

• • •

Believe me, Nadina was not this chipper in the immediate aftermath of Mike's second arrest. After a couple days of her usual post-apocalyptic pattern where I tried in vain to contact her, I went in to the school determined to lay it all before Mark Henneman and find out what was going on. Nadina's mother was one step ahead of me, however, and I found she had already given him a complete run-down: the pregnancy, the adoption plans, how Mike flipped out, her own opinion, everything. The only thing I could add to his knowledge, and it was significant from my point of view, was why I had agreed to adopt the baby. This I attempted—I was at least getting more used to describing the revolution in my feelings and Nadina's change of heart—but I still hadn't figured out how to make it sound rational, since it wasn't.

"My first instinct was to come and let you know what was going on, Mark," I explained when I finished, "but Nadina was determined to tell Mike first, and she was leery of how everyone would respond. I didn't mean to be underhand or secretive or do things behind your back."

"Cass, I've gotten to know you well enough that I didn't ascribe any of those motives to you," he said, to my relief, "and don't imagine we don't appreciate the role you've played in this situation, getting Nadina to agree to carry the baby, but you'll understand if we worry that other mentors and volunteers might get the wrong idea…"

"Of course, of course," I assured him. "I would think the same thing. Me adopting the baby doesn't fit the mold, to say the least. It's hard to explain, weird, inappropriate."

Mark Henneman and I agreed that, given the sensitivity and complexity of the situation, it would be better if I stepped down as Nadina's mentor. It was hard enough for them to recruit mentors without having one around whose over-the-line adoption scenario blurred boundaries. Imagine me standing up to give my testimony in church: "I never imagined that a simple call to mentor a Camden

School student would lead to total upheaval in my life. When she unexpectedly became pregnant, I felt led to adopt her child. This decision forced me to find a new living situation and robbed me of my opportunity to marry the man I loved." Compelling.

"How's Nadina doing?" I asked. "She won't call me, of course."

"She's struggling right now with all the sudden changes, especially with the Mike situation," Mark explained, sighing. "Mrs. Stern says she's refusing to get out of bed." That was a behavior I understood.

"Since I'm not her mentor anymore, would you object if I went and saw her at home?" I asked.

"Since you're not her mentor anymore, Cass, you can do whatever you please." He grinned at me. "Not that being her mentor ever stopped you."

. . .

Mrs. Stern was a weary-looking, faded blonde, tall as Nadina, but much more gaunt. She opened the door of the apartment and peered out at me suspiciously. "Yes?"

"Hello, Mrs. Stern," I said timidly. "I'm Cassandra Ewan, Nadina's mentor—or, I was her mentor, rather. I wondered if I could speak with her." It would've been more polite to call ahead, but I was afraid to risk a refusal, Mark Henneman having warned me that Mrs. Stern was not gung-ho on the adoption idea.

"Nadina's not up to having visitors," she grunted.

The door-opening narrowed, but, feeling like a vacuum-cleaner salesman of old, I thrust my foot preemptively across the threshold. "Please, may I just see her quickly? I've been trying to call her. I won't stay long unless she likes."

Another grunt. Then, "Nadina?" Mrs. Stern hollered. "That Cass is here. You wanna talk to her?"

"Fuck!" came Nadina's exclamation. Faint, from the top of the stairs.

"You've got to talk to me sometime," I insisted, raising my voice. "Can I come in?"

A pause. "Crap. Let her in, Mom."

Nadina was flopped on her bed facedown, and she buried her face in the pillow when I came in.

"Can I open the window?" I asked. "It's stuffy in here, and it's actually nice out." A muffled sound, which I interpreted as a yes. Sliding the window open as far as it would go, I took a deep breath of the fresh spring air and then perched on the end of her bed. "So I'm sorry about Mike. You were right that he would wig out, and I was wrong. I guess I just don't understand why he went off the deep end."

She sniffed, rolling onto her side. At least it didn't look like she'd been crying this morning, but I'd seen that look too many times in my own mirror not to recognize it. Numbness. "Yeah, I told you," she said slowly. "I knew the shit would hit the fan, and it did. Mike said he was too friggin' young to become a dad, and that, just when he'd gotten his life how he liked it, I had to go and fuck everything up, and didn't he have rights too, and he didn't want this kid, and didn't that count for anything."

"Mike wasn't becoming a dad," I pointed out. "Not in anything but the biological sense. I don't get it."

"I don't totally get it, either," Nadina admitted. "But he was taking it totally seriously. Like, 'I'm not giving any baby of mine to the friggin' church lady. She can go find her own friggin' baby. She thinks 'cause she helps me get some sorry-ass job she can take my kid?'"

The exasperated sigh escaped me this time. For crying out loud, I was sick of being blamed for everything Mike didn't like about his life, and I hadn't heard any complaints about the music studio job up till now. No thanks, of course, but at least no complaints.

"So then he stormed out, and the rest is history?" I prompted.

"More or less. He did say one last thing. He said, 'No way in hell is she getting my baby. I've got rights.'"

Sounds like I was going to need that adoption attorney after all. Daniel told me he'd finagled a free consultation with his law-school friend Lori Lincoln, but if Mike refused to sign the adoption consent, a consultation or two probably wouldn't cut it. Maybe I could ask Daniel to sleep with her after all.

Putting this out of my head for later consideration, I tapped Nadina on the ankle. "So what is this about you refusing to get out of bed? Is it about Mike being in jail again?"

She stuffed her face back in the pillow, and I could barely understand her response. "No. I mean, it sucks, and he's a total friggin' idiot, but—"

"But what?"

"But—but—" Nadina rolled over onto her other side, facing away from me, and burst into tears. "I almost don't even friggin' care that he fucked up so badly, and I won't even see him again for years, if ever. Mike's a stupid loser. But I don't want to do this by myself! I don't want to be by myself! I hate being by myself!"

Patting the coverlet helplessly, I debated what to say. Something as cliché as "you've got me" would probably get my head bitten off. And didn't I know how horrible it was to be alone? To feel like, no matter how much other people liked or loved you, you finally had to live your own life, do it alone. No one else could do it for you.

"I hate being by myself, too," I said, after a moment. "I had Troy from the time I was a senior in high school until he died thirteen years later, and when he died, one of the worst parts wasn't just missing him and missing Min, it was being alone." Nadina was silent, but that was more promising than lashing out at me. Hesitantly, I continued. "And people from church would tell me that God was with me, but frankly I didn't feel it. It really sucked. I believe it now, that God is with me all the time, but only because of the people in my life. My friends and my family and…you. You've been one of the biggest signs to me, Nadina, that I'm not alone."

She groaned. "Oh, shut up, Cass. I don't want to hear your God talk now."

"I'm sorry," I said, biting back a smile. "I just wanted to let you know I wasn't as alone as I thought I was, and you aren't either. By the way, if you'd been returning my phone calls, you'd know already that James dumped me."

This got her attention. Bolting upright, her spiky hair smashed flat on one side, she demanded, "What? That asshole? What was his problem?"

I held up my hands in surrender. "Go easy on the poor guy. He wasn't ready to date a single mom. He's only 27 after all."

"27 is ancient!" retorted Nadina tactlessly. "Why do guys always cut and run when there's something hard to do?"

"That isn't true," I objected. "I know lots of quality guys who can be depended on, like my dad and my husband Troy and my brother Perry." *And Daniel*, a corner of my mind spoke up, but his name didn't make it to my lips.

Reaching for her hand, I grasped it, and miraculously, she didn't rip it away. "Look, Nadina. Not to be irritating, but take it from a girl with no man in her life—the best way not to feel alone is not to be alone. Don't hide out from the people you do have in your life. I may not be Mike, but I'm your friend, and I love you. Love you like your mom does and Aunt Sylvia and Sonya and Ellie and your teachers at school. You've got to get your butt out of bed and back out in the world. Plus, you're bathing my baby in stress hormones, and I don't want it to come out a freak."

• • •

That was a couple months ago. Nadina returned to school, pregnant, Mike-less and mentor-less, but really that last was a mere academic distinction because she and I saw each other and communicated more than ever. I took her to her doctor's appointments and to the initial meeting with Daniel's adoption attorney friend; I made sure she picked up her prenatal vitamin prescription and badgered her to eat well and exercise; I encouraged her to consider what she would do after the baby came, and to explore Aunt Sylvia's offers for a fresh start. Over time, Mrs. Stern and I developed a tentative, polite relationship. It wasn't that she wanted Nadina to keep the child, but she mistrusted my motives and suspected that I must be behind Nadina's ultimate decision to move to Cleveland after the baby came.

"Mom'll come too, eventually," Nadina said dismissively, when I brought it up to her. "She's just grouchy because it means she'll have to try to get along with Aunt Sylvia."

• • •

After Nadina's ultrasound, I treated her to lunch. I claimed it was for her birthday, but it was also so I could stuff some healthy food into her. Especially since, that evening, a whole group of us would be meeting at Red Robin for the official celebration. If it was going to be a cheeseburger and fries for dinner, it was going to be soup and salad for lunch. Nor did I object to eating well myself, since I knew James would be there tonight, and I'd be hard-pressed to choke anything down. Nothing like an ex around to make you lose your appetite.

"A boy, huh?" said Nadina, inspecting her salad for offensive material. She picked out the almonds and broccoli bits but seemed to find the rest tolerable. "Guess you can't name it Nadina Jr."

"Mike's still an option, luckily," I said.

She laughed and flicked a crouton at me. "Really, Cass, what are you going to name him? Don't pick anything dumb, okay? Or too fancy. Look at you and your brother."

"Give me a little credit," I protested. "I didn't pick my name or Perry's. I didn't even get to pick Min's. Family obligations. But I don't have to consult anyone this time."

"But I get veto power, right?" she asked. "On everything else I'll butt out, but I don't want you to pick anything really trendy."

"That's a terrible idea," I said. "You'll burn through every name I like."

She rolled her eyes. "You're the tight-ass, not me. Just give me a couple names."

"Mildred Ewan."

"That sounds like some kind of fungus."

"See?"

"Whatever, Cass. Give me a real name. A real *boy* name."

"Eustace."

"*Cass!*"

"Okay, okay. How about Philip?"

"Uh uh. Then his initials are P-E. Like Pee. No way."

"Max?"

"Max E. Think about it, Cass."

"How about Troy, after my husband?"

"No dead people. You already named Min after dead people—you'd think you'd figure out by now."

Pushing away my empty soup bowl, I looked square in her pale blue eyes. "All right, girlie. Here's the real deal: I want to name the baby Edward. It's my father's real first name, even though everyone calls him Larry."

Seeing that I was serious, she tried to be diplomatic. "But—did you think about—then he'd be called Eddie. Do you really like the name Eddie? Or Ed when he's old, with a beer gut?"

"No," I said carefully, "Edward would be called Ned for short. And I like 'Ned' because it sounds a little like Nadina. I want to name the baby after two people I really love and respect."

Maybe it was all the extra hormones coursing through her pregnant system, but she blinked rapidly several times and began tearing her hunk of buttered bread to bits. Then, to my complete astonishment, she sprang up from her chair, knocking it back with a clatter, and leaned across all our half-empty dishes to hug me around the neck. It was brief but fervent, and before I could react she had released me and regained her seat.

"Dude," she said in a thick voice, "Edward's got my vote."

CHAPTER 38:

Round Robin

I had only seen James once in the past two months.

After he broke up with me, I was at a loss what to do about Free Universe. All along, except when I was doing voice work with Murray, there was never any real need for me to go into the office. I just liked it there, liked the people and the atmosphere and the interaction. It broke up my quiet, solitary days at the Palace. So when going in proved awkward, I stayed away, communicating with Riley via email and making semi-truthful excuses for myself: I had to go to doctor's appointments, lawyer appointments; I was looking into additional job possibilities.

And I waited for James to give me some indication of what he would like me to do.

It came after a month: an email.

> Cass:
>
> We've scheduled a party to celebrate *Antarctiquest's* launch and would like you to come. Nothing big. Maybe a cake outside of Riley's cube. Thursday at 3:00.

Riley has been bugging me about why you haven't
come in lately. I think he's kind of pissed at me, actually.
Let me just say, please don't stay away on my account.
James

Feet and heart dragging, I went to the party. James was cheery,
polite, distant, and he took some personal call right during the cake-
cutting and had to excuse himself. Seeing my eyes follow him, Riley gave me a sympathetic thump on the back and said a shade too
loudly, "C'mon, Cass. That's why everyone knows you don't do office
romances. Take Jeri and me—we've had to throttle back so we can
get some work done." Jeri certainly looked like she'd like to throttle
something, but I appreciated Riley's attempt to comfort me and gave
him a wan smile.

That's right, Cass. Buck up. Lord knows you've been through
worse.

"The emails are fine," Riley continued, "but my working style
thrives on face-to-face interaction, Cass. I need people to bounce
ideas off of. When I'm looking at your stuff, I need to have you right
in front of me—like I'm the guru, and you're taking dictation, right
as the spirit moves me, you know?"

"Yeah, Cass, have mercy," Jeri spoke up. Her reedy voice had a
softer note in it—even Jeri missed me? "I got used to having you
show up and dilute the Riley effect. Without you he's got nobody
else to listen to his ramblings or his frakkin' *Jeopardy!* obsession. If I
hear Riley make one more Alex Trebek crack, I'm gonna stone him
with his own frakkin' petrified candy collection."

Had Murray then proceeded to bemoan my loss, I imagine I
would have caved then and there and started coming in a couple
times a week again, but Murray had always been stony in his disap-
proval of office flirtation, and he continued to eat his cake now, making no show of mourning.

I scraped the frosting off my cake to give me a moment to think. "Just a little more time, okay?" I asked. "I'll start coming in again, but just give me a little more time."

So that was all I saw of James in two months. But now, for Nadina's birthday, a large group of us, including her friends and their mentors, would be meeting at Red Robin for dinner. It wasn't an official Camden School mentor activity, mind you, because I was no longer an official Camden School mentor, but it was close enough. Who knew what Mark Henneman had told the rest of the mentors—he had to say something to them, what with Nadina's and my disappearance from the group and her increasingly obvious pregnancy—but exactly what he said was a mystery to me, since I was now out of the loop.

The restaurant was unusually crowded for a Tuesday night, it seemed to me. Being on pins and needles waiting for James to show up with Kyle, I barely managed to converse with Louella. At least I cleverly arranged to be at one end of the table so there wouldn't be any open seats next to me, but when James and Kyle and Ray and Tan showed up, all the girls shrieked and rearranged themselves, abandoning me at the end so that James had to take the empty chair beside me, after all. It was so noisy, moreover, that he and I were effectively isolated. We managed to make dogged conversation about work, Kyle's progress on his community service and fines, the weather, for Pete's sake.

When the food came we could eat, at least, and Ray across the table occupied James' attention for some time with a mini-tirade against people nowadays spending more of their time living the lives of their video-game avatars than they did living the real thing, a rant James heard out with his usual patience and focused attention.

It was a relief when the food and ice cream and singing waiters were dispensed with, and we turned our attention to roasting Nadina and watching her open a few gifts. Plenty of jokey, cold-weather clothes for Cleveland; a picture frame from Sonya saying "Love" that held a picture of a guy in a Hamburglar-style convict outfit; a stethoscope for her to use on dogs.

The party broke up soon after. Taking leave generally of everyone and avoiding James' eyes, I helped Nadina stuff the gifts in her backpack, walked her out to the bus stop and waited with her until the bus came. When she was safely on, I stood watching it driving away, resting my forehead against the cool pole.

"Cass?"

Glancing around quickly, I couldn't make out where the voice came from until a figure emerged from the shadows. I recognized the precise movements before anything else. "Hello, James."

"Walking home? Can I give you a ride?"

"I was going to cross the street and catch the bus the other direction," I began.

"Please."

Not knowing what else to do, I followed him to his car. It was hard not to hope just a little bit on the ride home that he missed me and maybe wanted to get back together, but he didn't speak. When we pulled up in the driveway, I ventured, "Would you like to come in for a minute?"

He shook his head. "Thank you, no. I just wanted to say that I hope we can get over this awkward stage. No hard feelings, you know."

"No, no," I agreed hastily. "No hard feelings."

"I was glad you came into the office for the cake last month, but I hope you'll feel free to come in as frequently as you used to. Riley's been pretty clear that he works better with you that way."

"Yes," I replied vaguely. "I've been busy with things, but I told Riley and Jeri I would be getting back into the routine when life settled down some." As in, when my awkwardness and lingering feelings for James settled down some.

A pause. "Cass, I'm seeing someone else now." My stomach sank.

Crud. Not missing me, then. "I wanted to tell you before you heard from anyone else."

"Thank you," I answered, unclenching my hands and sitting on them so my disappointment wouldn't be so obvious. "What's—what's her name?"

"Mira. She's great. Maybe one day you could meet her." Oh, yeah, that sounded like fun. "How are things going with Nadina and the adoption?" he went on.

"Okay, so far. She's healthy, the baby's healthy. There might be a hitch getting Mike to sign the adoption consent form, but we'll deal with that later. Thank you for asking."

"How about your living situation?"

"Oh, I've got a couple months yet," I replied. "I'll probably move in the summer. She's not due until September, but I'll need some time to get set up and to find someone to replace me at the Palace."

"Will you live on your own?"

His questions were starting to stress me out because I had put off thinking about them. "I don't know yet. I was even thinking I might ask Louella if she would mind having us underfoot. If I could find a housemate who wouldn't mind a baby, it'd be nice to have adult company." As soon as I said it I blushed, thinking he might misconstrue that comment as a hint or a reproach.

He fiddled with the cuff of his sweater. "Why not just stay with Joanie and Phyl and…Daniel?"

I smiled ruefully. "If it were just Joanie and Phyl I would in a heartbeat, even though they'll probably get married eventually. I wish I could…I love it here. But can you imagine Daniel? I wouldn't even have the nerve to ask."

"Because you think he'd say no?"

I thought about this. "Because I think he'd say yes," I said slowly. "And I like him too well to do that to him."

"You like him too well to ask him," James repeated. "And, if I'm not mistaken, he likes you too well to say no."

What was he getting at, for crying out loud? Did James suspect Daniel had a thing for me, too? I was not going to deal with this. I could not deal with this. "We're friends," I said firmly. "We've become friends."

"Does he know that?"

"Where exactly are we going with this discussion?" I demanded. When he didn't answer, I reached for the door handle. "Thank you for the ride home, James. I'll see you around."

Before I could get out, his hand was on my arm, detaining me. "Don't be annoyed, Cass. I know it's none of my business anymore, but I can't help caring what happens to you." His gray eyes were apologetic. "I couldn't—be who you wanted me to be, but I want you to be happy."

Feeling an ominous lump in my throat, I nodded and got out.

• • •

The Palace was streaming with light, and the sound of voices and laughter greeted me at the door. Joanie had told me after Easter that, in the spirit of new beginnings, she was giving up her dating hiatus, so this must be the result. Or maybe Daniel had given up his, too. Not feeling super social after seeing James, I made to slide past the kitchen doorway and head upstairs, but Joanie called me, her voice warm and thrilled. "Cass! Look who just got here."

Before I turned I knew who it was—why else would she sound so excited? Perry. He jumped up from his barstool to give me one of his bear hugs.

"We're celebrating and mourning!" he crowed, pointing at the wine bottle Daniel was opening. "Come join us."

"What are we mourning and what are we celebrating?" I asked, my voice still unsteady, letting him lead me to the table. It was only my housemates and Perry after all. I didn't look at Daniel.

"Such an optimist," teased Perry. "If you want to get the mourning over with, we're mourning the fact that my divorce is final, and Betsy and I are truly history— " My eyes met Joanie's over my wineglass as she filled it—it looked like she at least was moving on to the celebrating. "And also that my dear sister Cassandra has been soundly dumped by Sweet Baby James—"

"Unless he repented tonight..?" prompted Joanie.

"A hardened sinner," I answered lightly. "He's already dating someone new." To forestall their reactions I added, "And what are we celebrating?"

"Well, for one thing, we are celebrating my new niece or nephew—"

"Nephew," I said, eliciting cheers. "And one who looks perfectly healthy and almost five months along."

"And for another," continued Perry when we quieted down, "I've been offered a part in a new regional production of the much-acclaimed *Waiters: the Musical,* that of Gaspar of the High-End Restaurant."

"Was Gaspar the one played by that hammy understudy who got trashed by the *Oregonian*?" I asked dubiously.

"The very same, so I hope to improve on his performance."

"In Portland?" asked Joanie.

"No, no—a new regional production up in Bellingham," said Perry, "which brings me to my third cause for celebration: Cass and I are moving in together!"

"We're *what*?" I gasped into the sudden silence. "Where?"

"In Bellingham, of course," replied Perry matter-of-factly, oblivious to the reactions around us. "You and my nephew need a new home; I'm tired of living with randoms off of Craig's List; all we have is each other—it's perfect."

"You—you can't steal Cass!" sputtered Joanie.

"I'm not stealing her," objected Perry. "Bellingham isn't that far, and wouldn't you rather have her live with me than that old lady from church she was going to hit up?"

"At least Louella Murphy lives in Bellevue," Joanie insisted. "And Cass's friends are here, and her church is here, and her job—"

"Are you honestly going to keep working for Free Universe, if you've got to see that James hanging around all the time?" Perry turned on me. "That must be awkward as all get out."

"It will only get less awkward, as time goes on," argued Joanie. "If she even continues with it, but what's she going to do in Bellingham? There are more jobs here than in Bellingham, and her adoption lawyer's in Seattle."

"Why do you have to move out?" asked Daniel, right next to me. This was too much! When did my life become something decided in committee? Everyone had a plan for me and an opinion on how best to run my life: James, Perry, Joanie. God, for that matter.

"Stop it!" I cried, pushing my untouched wineglass away. "All of you!"

It was unjust to Phyl, who had said nothing, and to Daniel, who did address me directly, but I included them in my general hand wave. "Stop planning my life and making decisions for me as if I weren't here—I have to make them myself! This isn't a group decision. I love you all, but I have to do it myself. Please."

To my chagrin, I felt the tears that had been so near the surface all evening threatening at the back of my eyes. Before they could spill out, I tried to get out of the kitchen as fast as I could, shoving Daniel out of the way and running for the stairs. The last thing I heard before slamming my bedroom door behind me was the emptiness of their stunned silence.

CHAPTER 39:

Plan C

Everyone gave me some space after that.

My brother returned to Portland after a few days; Joanie worked hard to swallow all the things she wanted to say (seeming to find it easier now that she knew Perry was moving closer); I continued to avoid Free Universe visits and James.

In the meantime, spring had truly arrived. The plants recognized its advent long before the weather, which continued gray and cool and rainy even as May drew to a close. Acting on some unseen cue in March, everything began growing like mad. The ornamental cherries and plums lining the streets burst into snowy blossoms followed by new leaves, the grass grew an inch every night, it seemed, and Phyl's painstakingly-planted bulbs exploded in blocks of vivid tulips and waving daffodils. When the sun finally did emerge one Sunday near Memorial Day, beaming down upon us from a cloudless blue sky, the world felt new-made, fresh from the hand of the Creator.

I walked home from service slowly, drinking it in. It was so warm that I pulled off my cotton cardigan, letting the sun play on my bare arms. If only it could stay like this forever, or at least till October. On such a day, it seemed a shame to spend even a moment indoors, so when I reached the Palace I let myself through the side gate into the backyard, there to lean on the deck railing with my eyes shut. Vitamin D. I am making Vitamin D.

Perhaps five minutes later I heard the sound of the Lean-To door opening, but I didn't open my eyes. The railing flexed as Daniel leaned against it.

Time to face facts, I guessed.

"You could, of course, stay here." He spoke slowly, choosing his words carefully, but without preface, as if he were just continuing the kitchen conversation from a couple weeks ago. "There's plenty of room in the house."

Reluctantly I opened my eyes. Hard to say which was more blinding, the sudden glare of the sunshine or him, closer than I thought. Although his voice was light, I could see his hands gripping the deck railing as he stood with his back against it.

It was what I had not even allowed myself to hope for, loving the Palace and Joanie and Phyl and even him, as I did. But it troubled me that he would offer. "Daniel—"

"If you move out, Cass, it wouldn't be the same here anymore," he interrupted.

"Daniel," I began again. "If I stay here, with the baby, it wouldn't be the same anymore. I've—I've had a baby before. Min turned my life upside down—she turned the house upside down, for Pete's sake. You don't know what you're saying, not that I don't appreciate the offer and the mark of friendship." He exhaled sharply, but I pressed on, anxious to lay all the objections before him so he could withdraw his offer gracefully. "I know Joanie and Phyl wouldn't mind—they've told me so—but who knows how long Phyl can hold out before she says yes to Wayne, and the same could be true for Joanie, if she would only just pick someone. If I stayed with the baby, how could you ever get new people to rent? And what would you tell your girlfriends? It's too bizarre. And if you decided it wasn't working, you'd feel bad kicking a lady and a baby out. It's too much to ask of you—I mean, you've never even wanted to be married, much less have kids."

"I have wanted to be married," he broke in suddenly. Before I could do more than blink at him in surprise, he had my bare arms in a hard grip. "I have wanted to be married, Cass."

"What—what are you talking about?" I stammered.

His blue eyes were blazing at me, and though I felt answering heat in my cheeks, I couldn't think what on earth to say. My incredulous look angered him for some reason, and he gave me a little shake. "God, what an opinion you have of me! I've wanted to say something to you a million times these last few months, but you would never give me an opening. If I ever tried to let you know that I cared about you, you would shut me down, change the subject. Well, you're going to listen to me now. No way am I letting you walk out of my life—you can adopt one baby or ten babies, I don't care, as long as you'll stay."

Then Phyl and Perry and even James had guessed right? Daniel was laboring under the delusion that he was interested in me?

He must be out of his mind to be talking like this. I opened my mouth to tell him so, but he seemed to read my expression because his grasp on my arms tightened almost painfully, and he jerked me against his chest, crushing my lips to his. Frozen with shock, it took me an instant to respond. I put up my hands to push him away but instead found them clutching his shirt. Waves of warmth began to wash over me, starting somewhere in my center and radiating outward, until I found I was kissing him back. With enthusiasm. He tasted wonderful. Crazily, I had the urge to laugh—no wonder women loved him!

Daniel heard or felt the gurgle in my throat, and he pulled back abruptly to look at me. Blushing again, I realized we were both panting a little and my arms were around his neck. His voice came low. "That wasn't so bad, was it? You could love me, Cass, if you let yourself."

Gently I untangled myself, and pushing away from his chest I tried to speak lightly. "Of course I could, Daniel. You could have pretty much any woman on earth—"

He brushed this off and stepped closer to me to close the gap. "Don't. I tell you—I tell you I love you. Do you think you could love me?"

Backing away again, I felt the deck railing behind me. He had me cornered, so clearly I would have to go on the offensive. "Daniel, be serious. I think you just can't stand to have any woman around who isn't dying of love for you, although you weren't very nice to Phyl about it. For the longest time you couldn't manage to talk to me without flirting, and it used to make me so angry. And here I'd thought you'd gotten better."

"You think I'm flirting with you?" he growled. "You think I could have stayed single this long if I flirted with women by telling them I loved them and asking them to marry me?" When I merely raised a skeptical eyebrow, he said slowly, "It's true that I was flirting with you in the very beginning. I didn't mean to—Joanie told me what you'd gone through—but you always seemed so self-contained, so unrattled by me. It was a challenge, at first, irresistible. I liked trying to make you blush, or getting your goat because your eyes would fire up, and you would rap out some comeback. It was unforgivable, I know. I could tell from your expression that you couldn't understand why I acted the way I did and that you resented it, but you were like that damned Snow Goddess you voiced: frozen asleep, suspended, waiting for the challenger to bring you back to life." He shook his head grimly. "It wasn't until that idiot James came around that I realized what had happened, that I was in love with you—and not just starting to fall for you—I was pretty far gone already. It had been so gradual I couldn't even figure out the starting point."

Just like Troy and the yearbook, then, I thought, fighting that urge to laugh. Or James, for that matter. Apparently all it took to turn me into a *femme fatale* was to have me underfoot, unnoticed, for a given amount of time. Daniel seemed sincere in his way, but my imagination wasn't up to the task of picturing marriage with him. Not that it would take too much imagination—any marriage to Daniel would at least be guaranteed to be brief.

"Daniel," I said more steadily, "do you know what I think?"

"I'm sure you're going to tell me."

"I think you've never had a woman friend before, and we've become friends. There's always some…sexual…tension at first, until it gets resolved. I think that's what's happening here."

"Friendship," he repeated flatly. "That would explain why it's so hard to be around you without wanting to touch you. And why I had fantasies about breaking James' legs whenever I saw him. And why I've wondered a thousand times what would happen if I just stuffed you in the trunk of the car, drove to Las Vegas, and refused to let you out until you agreed to marry me."

Okay, so he wasn't buying the friendship theory.

"Daniel," I tried again. "I'm…flattered…that you feel this way, but if you first liked me because I seemed—I don't know—inaccessible, don't you think once you had me you'd get over it pretty quickly?"

His eyes got their customary wicked gleam. "Good point. I don't think so, but we'd better make sure." Taking my face in his hands, he made to kiss me again, so I shoved him away, starting to feel angry. I couldn't tell, though, if I was angry with him for his sheer nerve or with myself for half-wanting to give in.

"It seemed pretty effective in helping you get over every other woman you've been involved with," I pointed out.

"I didn't feel this way about any other woman I've been involved with," he said curtly. "And I haven't been involved with any other woman from the moment I realized I wanted you, or didn't you notice?"

"I did notice," I answered in a small voice. "And I wondered why. But don't you think you might have felt this way about Missy or Michelle or Fiona or Kelly or whoever else, if any one of them had put up the least little bit of fight?"

"You misunderstand me. I said it began with you seeming like a challenge, but I'm afraid it's gone way beyond that now." He dropped his voice again, without coming any closer, and I felt my heart speed up. "You don't know how aggravating it was to discover I loved you just when James the Good came on the scene. To see how much you had in common and how little you actually shared with me. To have to hear him compliment you and see how differently you took it, when he said things that you probably would have hit me for. And thinking that you let him kiss you—that he was going to be the one who woke you from your sleep. But worst of all was knowing that you admired him, respected him—you always made it clear that you didn't feel that way about me. I made up my mind that I was going to earn your respect. Maybe if you could respect me, you could love me."

I thought back over the last few months, things suddenly coming into focus: our Scrabble games; the New Year's party; his willingness to advocate for Mike; his friendship with Perry; my urge to tell him about Nadina's pregnancy; his listening ear and offers of help. He was now a trusted friend, one whose judgment and help I sought.

Hesitantly, I laid a hand on his arm. "Daniel, I do respect you now. You've been so kind and thoughtful and such a friend to me. And for all James' goodness, he couldn't bring himself to stick it out with me after I decided to adopt Nadina's baby. But here you are willing to let me still live here. I can't tell you how much that means to me…"

His face flushed with pleasure, and a heartfelt smile spread across it that I had never seen before, only to fade moments later when I trailed off. "But what, Cass? You respect me now, and you care about me, but you can't marry me?"

"In my defense, most girls do get asked on a first date before they get proposed to," I protested.

He was not to be sidetracked. "Don't change the subject. The only point of going on dates would be to figure out if we wanted to get married. I've lived with you for nine months, and I think we know each other better by now than most people. Why can't you marry me?"

Sheesh. This must be why Joanie said Daniel always got what he wanted. He was unstoppable.

"Is it because of James?" he pressed. "You're not over him yet?"

"Partly," I replied. Though I wasn't positive that ten more minutes of kissing Daniel wouldn't drive James entirely from my mind.

"Then why?"

Reluctantly I said, "Daniel, when you first met me, I was in kind of a bad place in my faith. I was mad at God and not sure what to do with my life or even if I shouldn't throw God out with the trash. And now it couldn't be more different. I have friends and family and purpose—He didn't abandon me after all. I even thought for a while there that maybe I could do marriage again, and now I'm certainly doing a child again. It may be all out of order, but I know for certain that if I do marry again, it'll have to be to someone who sees life from the same perspective."

Unbelievably, Daniel was grinning by the end of my speech. "Let me get this straight: I love you, and you have some positive feelings for me; you respect me; and I'm not only willing to shelter you after you adopt this crack baby but also marry you. Despite all this, are you trying to tell me, Cass, that you won't marry me because I'm not religious like you?"

He had never been slow on the uptake. I nodded. "Um, in so many words, I guess that's what I'm trying to say diplomatically. Why are you grinning like the Cheshire Cat?"

Not just grinning, but actually laughing softly now. "Because I'm not the same godless dog I was when you met me. Close, but not quite. Lately I've been thinking there might be some method to your madness, yours and Joanie's. I wasn't going to say anything until I made up my mind for sure, but in such a desperate situation I obviously have to reveal the ace up my sleeve."

Of all the crazy, not-to-be-believed things that Daniel had said to me in this conversation, this was the hands-down winner. "Are you making fun of me?" I gasped. "You're an atheist!"

"*Was* an atheist," he corrected, enjoying my astonishment. "Now I think I'd be classified as a fence-sitter. Maybe even a fence-sitter losing his balance in your direction. You're not the only one who has seen God at work in your life this year."

"Do you mean you think you've seen Him at work in my life or in yours?" I demanded.

"Either. Both. And. Do you remember that one time you and I were talking books early on, and you said something about love being sacrificial—that you think of the other before yourself?"

"It was about *David Copperfield*," I murmured.

"Yes, and then Joanie said almost the same thing, when she was wrangling with Michelle over that 'transcendent' stained glass Michelle was designing, or whatever the hell it was. I figured I love you and Joanie best in the world, and if this was what you two thought love was, I wanted to know more about it. I wanted to know more about this God who made you think about love that way. Besides, I suspected that, even if James weren't in the picture, no atheist was going to win you over. I've never been an active, proselytizing atheist like Mom; I was more of your lazy, I-don't-need-Him-so-He-must-not-exist atheist. So I started going to the Men's Bible study. It was mostly me and a bunch of old guys, but they were great. They let me ask questions and argue with them."

"Is that where you started taking off to, early Saturday mornings?" I asked wonderingly. "We never guessed."

"That's it. I went with mixed motives—I wanted you and your respect, and I figured this would help—but I heard things that weren't good news at first. They were studying the Gospel of John," he laughed shortly. "In fact, the theme was, 'Greater love has no man than this, that a man lay down his life for his friends—'"

"John 15:13," I said, more to myself, but Daniel heard me.

"That's my girl. So apparently, if I loved you, I wasn't going to try to seduce you and break up your perfectly good relationship, as if I could have. If I loved you, I was going to want what was best for you, even if that didn't involve me, even if it meant letting you marry James. I fought that for a long time. What was the point of getting religion, unless it meant I could have you as a reward? It's not like I didn't have to admit to myself that James was a good guy, good husband material, from your perspective."

"You talk about religion like it's another way to pick up girls," I said accusingly. "Haven't you done any thinking about who God is, or what your relationship might be to Him?"

"Wouldn't you say God meets us where we're at?" he countered. "And where I'm at is wanting to become the kind of man you could love. Learning some humility, some patience. Realizing everything isn't in my control. It's been rough, Cass. Give me a little more time. If I hadn't been thinking about who God is and my relationship to Him, I would've gone with the Las Vegas kidnapping plan months ago. I did just want to tell you how I felt, in case you wanted to wait and see how I turned out. And I wished you would ask me to do something hard for you, so I could show you that I can love the way you understand love."

"And now you are doing something hard for me, by offering to let me and the baby live here," I broke in. "It's not…contingent…on me marrying you, is it?"

"What do you take me for?" He grinned. "Don't answer that yet. I've got to tell you that when James did end up dumping you, I was sorry you were hurt but pretty damned thrilled at the same time. I think in the time it took you to run up to your room I was coming up with my game plan."

"No game plans," I insisted. "Joanie says you always get what you want, and you're such a pushy guy I believe it. If you say I can live here, it's got to be with no strings attached."

"I've already said so."

"Well, all this love and marriage talk is premature," I said. "You're still figuring out who you are and what you want. And you don't know what's going to hit the Palace in a few months when that baby comes. "

"You think I'll change my mind."

"Don't be stubborn, Daniel. Don't *not* change your mind just to prove a point," I urged. "I'm going to hold you harmless for all you've said this morning and ask you not to talk about it again for now. If you still want to bring it up again, six months or so from now, that's your choice, but if you've changed your mind I won't hold it against you."

His blue eyes searched mine. "You mean you'll stay, but you won't date me yet."

Deep breath. "I'll stay, but I won't date you. Can we start over a third time, as friends?"

"Does that mean you'll be dating other people?"

I laughed. "I don't know where you get this idea—nobody's beating down the door to go out with me. One thing at a time. I just got dumped, remember? I have no plans to date anyone right now. But… but I wouldn't mind if you date around. In fact, it might make me feel better—reassure me that you're not sitting there, scheming, but you're actually exploring…thinking about who you're becoming and what you really want."

"What about being Friends with Benefits?" he persisted. I got the feeling he wasn't listening to me. "Not sleeping together, of course, but with the occasional make-out session to look forward to." He took another step toward me, but I evaded his hands.

"That won't help me make rational decisions," I objected. "Not everyone can maintain their detachment like you do."

He cornered me again, brushing his face against my hair. "You might get better with practice, Cass."

My heartbeat accelerated wildly, but I elbowed him in the ribs. "No. No, Daniel. We're not going to do this now—*you're* not going to do this now. I can't stay here unless you agree."

An exasperated sigh. "Tiresome woman." Obediently, he backed a decent distance from me. "Fine. If I keep my hands off you for six months and don't harass you constantly to marry me, you'll stay?"

"And date another person or two," I put in doggedly.

"Define 'date.'"

"You know—you ask someone out or someone asks you out, and you go out a few times and make a sincere effort to determine whether or not that would be a better match."

"But what if I become a good Christian boy? I'm not going to go around playing with people's hearts. Not when I'm in love with someone else." Seeing my brows draw together, he added piously, "And I wouldn't want to go out with a godless heathen anyway. My standards are at least as high as yours."

"I'm sure the Christian girls will be after you now, too," I said dryly. "Do we have a deal?"

"Six months?"

"At least. I'll only have had the baby a little while in six months."

"Can I just kiss you one more time before I swear off?" That would be one time too many for my resolve, so I shook my head. Daniel, reading my mind, bit back a smile, and who knows what would have happened if we hadn't been interrupted by a banging on the window.

Joanie popped her head out. I didn't know how much she'd seen, but from the look she gave the both of us I knew I was in for explanations later. "Good morning, you two. Happy Almost-Memorial Day! Phyl's made mimosas—want some?"

When we were gathered in the sunshine on the deck a minute later, champagne flutes in hand, Daniel announced, "Forget Almost-Memorial Day. This is the real celebration. Cass has agreed to stay."

Joanie and Phyl nearly cost me my mimosa, with their screaming and jumping up and down and hugging me, but I managed to hang on.

"A toast!" demanded Joanie, with Phyl echoing her. "This calls for a toast, Cass."

Laughing and raising my glass I looked at each one of them in turn: lovely, peacemaking, loyal Phyl; blunt, passionate Joanie, who threw me the rope last summer to climb out of my abyss; and now Daniel, the unexpected friend, solid as bedrock, who might yet become much, much dearer.

Clearing my throat, I said, "To happily-ever-after at the Palace."

Three glasses clinked against mine. "The Palace."

Reading Group Guide

1. If you were producing a film version of *Mourning Becomes Cassandra*, whom would you cast in the various roles?

2. Christina has been known to refer to this novel as a "Christian beach read." Do you agree with this classification? In what ways does it conform to "Christian fiction" conventions? "Beach read" conventions? In what ways does it depart from them?

3. Cass and her friends christen their new home "the Palace" and Daniel's in-law "the Lean-To." How are these names appropriate to their role in the story? Does *Mourning* bear similarities to any fairy tales?

4. At the outset of the novel, Cass reflects on how her life experiences have estranged her from God. She compares His treatment of her to "having the faithful family guard dog, who rescued you from house fires in the past, turn on you and maul you." Do you think this is a fair assessment? How does her understanding of God change over the course of the book?

5. What range of beliefs is represented in the book? Which characters move around on the spectrum as the story unfolds? Do the religious types behave as you would expect? Do the non-religious types?

6. Nadina struggles with substance abuse and a toxic boyfriend, two things with which Cass has no experience. How effective do you find Cass as a mentor, over the course of the story? In what ways do she and Nadina change each other?

7. In Chapter 12, Cass starts research for the *Antarctiquest!* video game and says of herself, "I wondered if I was always drawn to whatever I knew least about." Do you find this an accurate description of her? What do the various video games, books, and other entertainment in the novel reveal about the characters?

8. When Nadina accuses Cass of using church and good deeds as a crutch in Chapter 13, Cass responds that, "Everyone's got a crutch, but some of the things we use for crutches are God-given gifts, and other things are just going to break off in our hands and make us hurt worse than ever." Do you agree with her? What are some of Cass's crutches? Nadina's? Daniel's?

9. How would you characterize Cass's views of love and marriage? How do they compare to Joanie's and Phyl's views? Did you initially think James or Daniel the better fit for her? Why?

10. In Chapter 22, Cass explains to Daniel how meeting Kyle propelled her into becoming a mentor. "You might call it coincidence," she says, "but I chose to see it as an answer to prayer." How does this attitude toward the events in her life inform her later decision to adopt Nadina's baby? Do you tend to view life as a series of random events, or do you look for underlying trajectory?

11. Why was Cass so "bristly" toward Daniel for much of the book? How convincing was his transformation to you, the reader? Do you consider her decision at the end to put Daniel off reasonable or frustrating? Which other choices does Cass make, and did you agree or disagree with them?